What she left for me

WHAT SHE LEFT FOR ME

Tracie Peterson

BETHANY HOUSE PUBLISHERS
Minneapolis, Minnesota

To all who bear their secret shame,
who carry the pain of the past,
who long to be set free.

Books by Tracie Peterson

www.traciepeterson.com

The Long-Awaited Child • Silent Star
A Slender Thread • Tidings of Peace
What She Left for Me

BELLS OF LOWELL*
Daughter of the Loom • A Fragile Design
These Tangled Threads

LIGHTS OF LOWELL*
A Tapestry of Hope • A Love Woven True
The Pattern of Her Heart

DESERT ROSES
Shadows of the Canyon • Across the Years
Beneath a Harvest Sky

HEIRS OF MONTANA
Land of My Heart • The Coming Storm
To Dream Anew • The Hope Within

WESTWARD CHRONICLES
A Shelter of Hope • Hidden in a Whisper
A Veiled Reflection

RIBBONS OF STEEL†
Distant Dreams • A Promise for Tomorrow

RIBBONS WEST†
Westward the Dream • Ties That Bind

SHANNON SAGA‡
City of Angels • Angels Flight
Angel of Mercy

YUKON QUEST
Treasures of the North • Ashes and Ice
Rivers of Gold

*with Judith Miller   †with Judith Pella   ‡with James Scott Bell

TRACIE PETERSON is a popular speaker and bestselling author who has written more than seventy books, both historical and contemporary fiction. Tracie and her family make their home in Montana.

Visit Tracie's Web site at: *www.traciepeterson.com.*

Dear Reader,

This story deals with the difficult topics of infidelity and child abuse. I chose to include these issues because of the large numbers of women and girls who are victims in these circumstances. One in four girls will be molested in some manner by the time she reaches age eighteen. This is a crisis that is reaching epidemic proportions, affecting families everywhere—even in the church. My desire is to help readers to better understand the broken and wounded hearts of these women, young and old. Our eyes and hearts need to be opened and prepared to support those who suffer from these emotional and physical traumas. Adultery and child molestation are betrayals of the worst kind, but we Christians need not add to the problem by turning away in fear or revulsion.

While I have carefully developed the story without any graphic references, the implications are there within these pages, and I want readers to be alerted to this prior to reading. Mothers and other caregivers will need to decide if the story is appropriate for their teenage girls.

My hope and prayer with *What She Left for Me* is that readers will learn and grow along with my characters and that all of us will learn to reach out with healing and love to friends and family who may be on a similar journey.

Tracie Peterson

One

THERE ARE worse things than death.

Jana McGuire had heard this phrase so often in her life. Her mother had chanted it like a mantra whenever something unpleasant happened to upset Jana. And now it was all Jana could think of. That voice. That tone, which wavered somewhere between accusation and disgust. Her mother had never shown any sympathy for Jana's fears or hurts. For as long as she could remember, her mother had offered commands and regulations, but never love.

She again scanned the short letter her husband had left her. Rob had offered no love either, at least not in this letter. In fact, he had taken what precious little love Jana thought to possess.

Jana,

I know you'll find this letter difficult to understand, but I made some decisions while you were in Africa. Hard decisions. I've fallen in love with Kerry and very much want a life with her. When you find this letter, we'll already be gone. In time, I hope you'll understand. I've taken care of everything, including the divorce proceedings. You should be getting some papers soon. I know I haven't left you with much, but feel free to sell the remaining household stuff. I don't want any of it and won't ask for it in the divorce.

Rob

There was nothing else. No explanation of why he'd forsaken his marriage vows to run away with his secretary. No explanation of how long he'd been miserable enough with their marriage to look elsewhere. She had a million unanswered questions, and just as soon as Jana felt she could explain even one of those, another dozen followed on its heels.

She placed the letter on the table and stared at it, as if willing an explanation to appear. Rob had said that in time he hoped she'd understand. But Jana had been looking at the same letter for nearly two hours, and so far it was all still a blur.

She'd thought they were happy. She'd thought they had the ideal life. There'd been no warning to suggest that her husband, pastor of Hope Bible Church in Spokane, Washington, was anything but faithful to his marriage vows.

Jana shook her head. *I've watched talk shows and read hundreds of articles about marriage. All so I could counsel women in the church when they were having problems. The signs weren't there. They simply weren't there.*

Rob had been loving and attentive right up until the moment Jana left, with two other church workers, for a mission trip to Africa. She had been gone three weeks, during which time she'd gotten the surprise of her life. A surprise she had very much anticipated sharing with Rob upon her return home.

But last night when Jana arrived at the airport, she was stunned to find that no one was there to welcome her home. No one. Not church members, not Rob. It was all very strange. She had thought at the time that some emergency must have come up to keep Rob away. But when she'd finally arrived home, Jana knew the truth. Rob's letter was waiting for her—but not Rob. He'd left her.

Visions of his secretary, Kerry Broadbent, forced their way into Jana's thoughts. The woman was pretty, there was no doubt about that. Her Italian and Native American ancestry played itself out in an exotic manner. She was smart too. Jana had felt rather intimidated by the woman, who held a master's degree in Native American studies. Jana could only boast a bachelor's degree in art. Not really something she could hold up against an education that enabled Kerry to speak four different Native American dialects. Of course, this was added to her already fluent ability in Italian.

"But she's so much older," Jana whispered. Kerry was at least thirty-five. Maybe thirty-six. "Just like Rob," she murmured.

Maybe the attraction went beyond appearance. Maybe Rob was tired of being married to a woman who was so much younger; a woman who couldn't remember half of the things Rob remembered.

Jana got up from the table and stepped back, still looking at the letter. It was almost as if the extra distance could somehow bring clarity to the simple script. Shaking her head, she went to the cupboard and took down a coffee mug. She turned the cup in her hand for a moment. It was Rob's favorite mug. He was a Seattle Seahawks fan, and their logo was emblazoned on the piece.

She put it aside almost reverently. Then she hurriedly picked up another mug, one with the Olympic rings and dates to show it had come from the Salt Lake City games. Pouring her coffee, Jana felt her hand shake violently. Her stomach lurched as it had every morning for the past two weeks. She quickly put the coffee aside and ran for the bathroom.

Jana was pregnant. She carried a much-wanted child that she and Rob had talked of having—had actually planned for. Of course, she'd gotten pregnant much sooner than either one of them had expected. If she'd known prior to leaving for Africa that she was expecting, she'd never have gone, never have risked the possibility of losing the baby. It wasn't until she was nearly ready to return that it dawned on her the nausea she was facing each day wasn't some dreaded African disease but rather pregnancy.

When her stomach settled, Jana rinsed her mouth and caught sight of her face in the mirror. She looked like one of those victims from a war-torn country. The stunned empty expression matched the feeling in her soul.

She then began to wash her face, feeling the cold water numb her hands. Rivulets ran up her arm, dampening her blouse at the elbow. She'd always hated that feeling, but she couldn't muster the energy to even be irritated now. Jana looked at the water faucet for several moments. It was as if she couldn't quite figure out what to do next. She touched the cold metallic curve of the handle.

"He can't be gone."

Shutting off the water without another thought, Jana turned and dried her face. It had to be some kind of mistake. Some kind of sick joke or misunderstanding. Kerry Broadbent was married. She'd been married for eighteen years—only eight years less than Jana had been alive. Kerry surely wouldn't throw out a commitment of nearly twenty years to run away with the man she'd worked with for less than two.

Jana's thoughts, stifled since finding the letter on the breakfast bar, began to flood her mind at a frightening speed. She should call the church. No! She would just get dressed and go next door and see for herself what this was all about. Rob wouldn't dream of deserting the church, even if in some warped justification he could leave Jana.

She went to the bedroom closet and threw open the doors, reality smacking her in the face. Rob's side of the closet had been cleaned out. There was nothing left behind. Not even the old neckties he no longer liked—and he had plenty of those, as she recalled. Jana stared at the empty space, her momentum halted by the obvious truth.

He's gone.

She went quickly to the dresser where he kept his things. Drawer by drawer revealed the same thing: emptiness. Jana turned and went to the hall closet and nearly wrenched the door off its hinges as she pulled it open. All of their suitcases were missing.

Sinking to the hardwood floor, Jana felt her chest tighten. She could scarcely draw a breath. From somewhere deep inside, she felt a primal scream rise to her lips, but she covered her mouth, forced it back down. How would it look if the Senior Women's candy-making day was interrupted by the pastor's wife screaming her head off in the parsonage next door? She could just imagine Roberta Winsome and Margie Neighbors, self-appointed matriarchs of the church, leaving their special dark chocolate fudge to investigate.

Curling up on the hall floor, Jana tried to reason what should be done. What would happen now? Where would she go? Would Rob change his mind if he knew about the baby? Should she even tell him?

And God . . . how could God have allowed this to happen? Wasn't He supposed to take care of His children? Watch over them? Hadn't she heard Roberta Winsome say, "God never gives a person more than she can handle," during one of their women's luncheons?

Well, this is certainly more than I can handle. This is more than I can even think about—much less actually handle and deal with.

Jana lost track of the time as she lay in the hall. She heard the air-conditioner click on and off several times. It had been an unseasonably warm spring, and Rob had insisted on running the air-conditioner. Jana hated the extra expense. She supposed she wouldn't have to worry about it anymore.

The sound of the trash truck coming through the neighborhood—and the frenzy of barking dogs that always accompanied this event—permeated her thoughts. Had Rob thought to put the trash out before deserting her for another woman? At one point she fell asleep, waking with a start when she heard tires squealing on the street outside her house.

Somewhere in the furthest recesses of her mind, a thought came to Jana that caused her to sit straight up. The bank. She had to get to the bank and find out if Rob had taken their savings. At least with their savings she could afford to live comfortably until she found a job. Surely Rob wouldn't leave her without anything—without any hope of getting by. But in her heart, she already knew with a sinking dread the news that the teller confirmed for her an hour later.

"I'm sorry, Mrs. McGuire, but that account has been closed," the woman told her as she asked about the joint savings account.

"What about the checking account?" Jana asked, shoving her checkbook across the counter.

The teller looked at the numbers, then typed on the computer keyboard and studied her screen. "That account is still open, but there's less than ten dollars in it." She looked at Jana and smiled. "Did you want to make a deposit?"

"No. Is there a manager or someone I can talk to?"

The woman frowned as though Jana were somehow dissatisfied with her work. "Mr. VanCamp is in his office. I'll see if he can meet with you."

Jana picked up her checkbook. "Thank you."

The woman came around from her secured booth and opened a door. Pulling it closed behind her, she walked in determined fashion across the bank lobby. Jana didn't know whether *r* her or not, so she took a few steps in the direction the woman had taken, then paused.

"Mr. VanCamp will see you. His office is down the hall and to the right," the teller announced as she reappeared.

Jana took a deep breath, hoping the bank manager would have some good news for her.

"I'm sorry, Mrs. McGuire," the man said as he studied her account information. "It seems your husband came in two weeks ago and withdrew the entire amount of your savings. Because it's a joint account, there's nothing I can do. He was completely entitled to take his own money."

"It was our money," she said. "Mostly mine, in fact." It was money she had brought into the marriage. Money she had earned and saved prior to her marriage to Rob. Money that had come from her great-aunt Taffy for birthdays and Christmas.

"Be that as it may," the balding VanCamp said as he looked at her over his reading glasses, "the account was in both names, and he was entitled to remove it."

Jana swallowed hard and tried to gather her thoughts. It wasn't really a surprise, so she didn't know why she was taking it so hard; she'd already figured this was the news she'd receive. Somehow, though, it signaled the finality of her circumstance.

She drove home in silence, not even turning on the radio to hear the news. For three weeks in the African bush she'd wondered what was going on in America. She had told herself that when she got home she was going to be more astute in keeping up on current affairs. She had learned, while in some of the poorest regions of the world, that she had it better than she could have ever imagined—that she lived a life of privilege. And while she'd already known that to a certain extent, Africa had proven it in ways she'd never imagined.

"At least I *used* to have a privileged life. How could Rob have done this to me? To us?" Memories of better days were such a fierce contradiction to the circumstances she now had to face.

"Where did we go wrong? What did I do wrong?"

The questions pushed their way through her mind like soldiers taking enemy ground. So, too, did the accusations.

If I'd been a better hostess, things might have been different. If I'd stayed home from Africa, then maybe he wouldn't have had a chance to leave. If I'd called from the airport in London to tell Rob I was pregnant, then maybe he would have called off this nightmare. But Rob was probably already gone by the time she was headed home from Africa.

Her car practically drove itself. Jana didn't even remember the trip, and it wasn't until she sat in her driveway, car still running, that she realized she needed to shut off the engine.

"What am I supposed to do now?" It wasn't exactly a prayer, but it was God to whom she spoke. She looked at the little white ranch-style parsonage. "How long will I even have a home?"

She didn't have long to wonder at this. That evening her doorbell rang, and Jana was suddenly confronted with a team of men who wanted to talk: the elders of the church, men who were often in her home for meetings and other gatherings. She looked at Gary Rhoades and forced what she hoped was a smile.

"Come in, Gary."

She could tell by the looks they were giving her that they already knew what was going on. She pointed to the table and the letter that still lay there from the morning. "You can read that if you want."

The men filed over as a group and passed the note down a line, each giving it a solemn glance before handing it to the next man. It was Gary who finally spoke. "How long has this been in the works?" Gary's tone was almost accusing and instantly set Jana's defenses in motion.

"I didn't know until last night." The men exchanged a puzzled look as Jana continued. "Rob said nothing before I went to Africa. You can read that for yourself in the letter. I thought everything was fine." Her voice held an edge that bordered on hysteria, but she was determined to remain in control.

"Why don't we sit down? We need to talk about this," Gary suggested.

Jana motioned to the living room and put on her hostess face again. "We'll be most comfortable in here." She walked across the room and took a seat on the brick ledge that edged the fireplace. Her calm was an unnatural emotion in the face of such monstrous adversity.

The men took their places and waited for their leader to begin the discussion. Jana could see that some of the men couldn't even look her in the eye.

"As you probably know," Gary began, "Rob gave his notice three weeks ago."

"No, I didn't know," Jana replied as evenly as she could. The last thing she wanted to do was break down in front of these men.

Gary frowned. "Rob told us that he'd talked to you."

"Rob said nothing. I didn't even have an inkling there was a problem until last night, when I landed at the airport and no one was there to greet me."

"Well . . . I . . . that is," Gary stammered, as if looking for an explanation. "He told us that you two were getting a divorce. That it was a mutual decision. That you'd gone to Africa so that he could break it to the congregation and resign his job without a big scene."

"All lies. Read his letter—it's right there. He decided to do this while I was gone. At least that's what he says, but obviously this has been in the works for some time." Jana could barely hold her anger in check. "So while he was telling you how this was my plan, did he also tell you that he was carrying on an affair with his secretary? That he planned to clean out our bank account and leave me penniless before running off with her?" Jana asked bitterly.

"No," Gary admitted. "We didn't know about the situation with Kerry until last Sunday. Rob and Kerry left us a letter in the office. Jason Broadbent called us first thing to ask if we knew what was going on. Apparently his wife left no more details in her letter than Rob left in his."

Jana hadn't even considered Jason . . . how this might affect him. The man was fifty-something and had been talking of an early retirement so he and Kerry could do more traveling. She shuddered. So many would bear the consequences of two people and their sin.

"Of course, when Rob gave his resignation, we tried to talk him out of it," Gary continued, looking most uncomfortable in the silence. "But he told us that . . . well, he said you were determined to end the marriage and that he didn't feel it Scriptural to head up a church while going through a divorce."

"I didn't even know we were having problems," Jana said in a clipped tone. "I thought we were very happy. In fact . . ." She let the words fade. She had been about to tell the men of her pregnancy, then thought better of it. She didn't want them to be the first people with whom she shared her news.

"I'm truly sorry, Jana," Gary said.

"Me too. I'm sorry for a lot of reasons, but I'm really sorry that Rob's actions had to be such a public affair."

"I . . . well . . . I don't know how to tell you this, but—"

She couldn't stand the game any longer. "Just say it."

Her interruption seemed to bolster Gary's strength. "When Rob resigned, we immediately went to work finding another pastor. We have an interim who agreed to move here immediately and take on the church. We signed him on for a six-month trial."

"I don't understand what that has to do with me."

"Well, he's slated to begin next week. That was part of the agreement. Rob said he needed the house until you were back because he couldn't just throw your stuff out on the lawn, and he didn't want to put it in storage. Besides, until last week, Rob was still preaching, so it was only right that we let him stay."

Jana hadn't thought the day could get any worse, but this news made it clear she'd underestimated the situation. "I have to move out by next week?"

"Actually . . . by Saturday."

"I have four days, then?"

Gary and the others nodded in unison. "We will help in any way we can."

"You don't understand," she said, getting to her feet in protest. "I have no money. I have *nothing*. Rob took it all. How do you expect me to hire movers to load up my possessions—what few Rob actually left me with—and vacate this house by Saturday?"

Gary's apologetic tone only served to further her irritation. "Like I said, we'll help in whatever way we can. We can get the church as a body to come and help pack you up. Most of the men in this room have pickups, so we can probably move you as well."

"Sure we can, Jana," Bill Usher said with a smile. "We'll see you through this."

"I have no place to go," she declared. "You don't understand. Rob has cleaned out our bank account. I had nearly six thousand dollars in savings. It was my money, and he took it. There's no money for deposits on rentals or utilities or anything else. I couldn't even go out and buy groceries today because there's no more than ten dollars in my checking account."

The men seemed genuinely stunned as Jana continued ranting. She stalked across the room and picked up her purse. "I have only the money left from the trip. I think maybe there's a total of thirty dollars in here." She tossed her purse onto the coffee table. "That's it. Rob has taken the computer and printer, the tools, the TV and DVD player. He's even taken my jewelry." This last discovery had been one of the hardest of all. Her only pieces of real value had come from either Rob or her great-aunt Taffy. Her afternoon taking inventory had left Jana depleted of hope and energy.

"He took everything?" Gary questioned.

It seemed as though the elders, men who had long worked with her husband, were trying to take in this information and decide if it were true. She hated the looks on their faces—almost as if they were accusing her of lying.

"Go look for yourselves," she said, her voice rising an octave. She felt her throat tighten and tears well in her eyes. Running from the room, she locked herself in the bathroom and remained there until she regained control of her emotions. She despised Rob for what he'd done. But she also questioned God for allowing such a nightmare to be her life, especially when she'd given up so much to be a pastor's wife and missions liaison.

"Couldn't you at least have left me what was mine?" she muttered, not knowing whether she said the words with God or Rob in mind.

Finally she emerged and rejoined the elders. On the coffee table beside her purse Jana noted a check. She looked to Gary for an explanation.

"We had no idea, Jana. Rob made it sound like all of this was your idea. Then when we found out about him and Kerry . . . well, we were still confused as to how it had all come to be. Now it's kind of easy to see that you knew nothing about this—that you're the wronged party here."

Jana eased into the closest chair. "I'm sorry for getting so upset. I simply don't know how to deal with any of this. I thought God was supposed to look after His own. I thought He was supposed to keep evil from overtaking His children." She looked to each man as though to force him to contradict or support this, but no one said a thing.

"I don't think I understand God at all." She crossed her arms and leaned back in the chair. "Maybe I never have."

"God didn't do this, Jana," Bill said. "God doesn't want this for you, any more than we do."

"Bill's right," another man chimed in. "God is just as saddened by this as we are—as you are. It wasn't His desire that something like this happen."

"Guess He wasn't on top of it then, is that it?" Her voice dripped sarcasm. "What sweet Christian platitude will you throw at me to make this one all right? My mother used to say, 'Jana, there are worse things than death.' Guess I know now exactly what she meant."

ON TUESDAY MORNING, Jana made stacks of breakable dishes
and coffee mugs on the kitchen table. She needed to figure out
what to take with her and what to sell. She'd already decided to
have a huge yard sale and get rid of almost everything. There was
very little she'd need to take with her. Just clothes . . . and soon,
even those weren't going to fit.

"I don't even know where I'm going," she said aloud. But
deep inside she knew the time had come to make the most
dreaded phone call of her life. She knew there was only one place
she could turn, and while it wasn't ideal, it would put a roof over
her head. Her head and the head of her baby.

Jana reached for the phone and punched in the number. She
waited for the ring and held her breath. *Am I doing the right
thing? Is there another answer?*

"Hello?" The clipped tone of the woman on the other end of
the line sent a chill through Jana.

"Hello, Mom." Jana hated calling her that. Eleanor Templeton had never desired to be a mother. She had borne Jana in the
hopes of having a son and made no attempt to hide the fact.

"Jana? Why are you calling?"

It was a typical response from her mother. Jana seldom tele-
phoned, usually only making the expected call on Christmas,
Mother's Day, and birthdays. "I'm afraid something has happened and . . . well . . . I need a place to live." She blurted the

words, feeling like a twelve-year-old about to confess some horrible wrongdoing.

"To live? What about that husband of yours? Does he need a place to live as well?"

Jana bit her lip. How much should she tell her mother? It was obvious that she needed the woman's sympathy—not that she'd ever had it before. Jana sighed. She wasn't going to play these games anymore. She didn't have the energy for it.

"Rob left me," she finally managed to say. "He ran off with his secretary and took all of our savings." There. She'd said it all. Well, almost.

"What? Your goody-goody preacher husband . . . committing sin?" Eleanor's voice was edged with contempt.

"Mom, I need a place to stay. Can I come live with you and Taffy?"

"Of course you can!" the enthusiastic voice of her great-aunt sounded on another extension. "We'd love to have you, wouldn't we, Eleanor. Oh my, but it will be great fun with you here."

Thomasina Anderson, or Taffy, as everyone called her, bubbled with energy. Jana hadn't even known Taffy existed until her mother dropped a note several years earlier to say that she was moving to Lomara, Montana, to care for an aging aunt.

"Aunt Taffy, are you sure it will be all right?" Jana asked, completely sidestepping her mother's input on the matter.

"Of course. We have tons of unused space. Why, I'd considered taking up boarders, but your mother wouldn't hear of it. She worries about strangers, you know."

"Taffy, Jana couldn't care less about what I think," Eleanor stated curtly.

Jana smarted at the comment. She and her mother had never been close, never even attempted a real relationship. From Jana's earliest memory, her mother had put her in someone else's care.

To hear her mother tell it, the entire purpose had been to broaden Jana's horizons and make her less dependent upon people. But to the lonely little girl who waited anxiously to see her mother at the end of the day, only to be rebuffed, Jana didn't think the plan had worked out so well.

"It doesn't matter what anyone thinks," Taffy said firmly. "Jana, you come. Come today."

"I can't come today," Jana told her. "I have some things to take care of. I'm selling off most of my stuff in a yard sale."

"Good. You won't need a thing here," Taffy assured. "Why, I have furniture stuck upstairs in the third floor. It's all just storage up there, and what we can't find we can surely buy."

"Taffy, you don't need to throw your money away on this," Eleanor interjected. "Jana will see to herself. Isn't that right, Jana?"

"Haven't I always taken care of myself?" Jana questioned, almost hoping her mother would contradict her. She didn't.

"Wonderful. Then it's settled," Taffy declared. "Why, I'm so excited, I can hardly stand it. We'll have wonderful tea parties and talk about the old days. We can even plant flowers." With a loud click, the receiver fell into place.

Jana smiled in spite of her misery. Taffy was like an eternal light of hope. As far as Taffy was concerned, the world was a beautiful place, with beautiful people in it. Too bad Taffy was a bit eccentric and, as Eleanor put it, "touched in the head." Her mother had commented in the past that Taffy wasn't in charge of her faculties, which was one of the reasons Eleanor had felt it necessary to go live with the old woman when Taffy had asked her to come.

"I should be there on Saturday," Jana concluded.

"If you don't mind my asking, what's the rush?"

Jana cringed at the accusation in her mother's tone. "Well, if you must know, Rob apparently arranged to leave three weeks ago when I went to Africa."

"Why in the world would you go to Africa?"

Again, her mother's tone made Jana want to slam down the phone and find another way to make her way in the world. "I went to Africa on a missions trip. We have a group of missionaries over there, and some of us went over to help. But that's really immaterial right now. When I left, Rob resigned his position with the church."

"What does that have to do with you?"

Jana clenched her teeth and drew a deep breath. Exhaling slowly, trying desperately to keep her temper under control, she replied, "We live in the parsonage. The place is provided for the acting pastor. Rob is no longer that person, so I have to move out."

"But why now? Why so quickly?"

"Because," Jana's voice took on a harsh tone as she snapped, "the new pastor wants to move in on Saturday."

"That hardly seems Christian. If those people care so much—are so holy—then why would they throw you out on the street like that?"

Jana knew her mother couldn't possibly hope to understand. "They aren't throwing me out. They thought I'd known about this for three weeks."

"I would still think they could wait."

Her mother, with her logical and well-ordered mind, had always run things the way she saw fit. No doubt she would even be able to teach Roberta Winsome a thing or two about organization. Unfortunately, the move had nothing to do with order or organization. Jana wished they could delay her departure as well, but she wasn't about to agree with her mother on something.

"Like I said, I should see you on Saturday."

"Well, if that's the way it has to be, I suppose we'll make do."
Jana knew she shouldn't take her mother's indifference personally. Eleanor treated everyone the same way; her lack of sympathy wasn't reserved for Jana alone. It just seemed Jana got the lion's share.

Jana hung up the phone and sat in the stillness of her kitchen for several minutes. She'd always liked the cozy little room. There was hardly space to turn around—the parsonage wasn't that big—but it suited Jana just right.

She looked at the pictures and knickknacks she'd used to decorate the room. It had a country-French feel with its porcelain rooster and hen, butter yellow walls, and antiqued wainscoting. She'd picked this look because it fit the older home and sparse furnishings.

A feeling of resentment rose up inside her. "Why should this be someone else's kitchen? I worked hard on this." She knew realistically, even when she and Rob had painted the walls, that it wasn't hers to keep, but at the time it felt like it would be theirs forever.

Forever.

What a silly word. She and Rob had promised to love each other "forever." Forever meant nothing to Rob and everything to Jana. Forever was the curse of time Jana would bear—raising a child without a father, sleeping alone each night. Forever was how long she'd waited for her mother's love.

Having grown up without a father, Jana felt immediate sympathy and heartache for her unborn child. Eleanor had often told Jana that fathers were unpredictable and incapable of endurance and consistency. Yet Jana had known friends whose fathers were quite constant. And oh, how she'd envied them.

Her childhood friend Danielle had known a father's love in such a vivid way. Every other Saturday, rain or shine, Danielle

28

and her father spent the day together. They did all sorts of things, and Danielle would always come back excitedly chattering about the trips they'd taken, things they'd seen, food they'd tried. Even after Danielle's twin brothers had been born, the father and daughter still made their Saturday pilgrimage.

It sounded heavenly to the fatherless Jana. Saturdays in her life had not been much different from any other day. Especially when she was living at the boarding school. There was no one to talk to about dreams and fears. No one with whom Jana could discuss school or boys or life.

During the week, Jana's mother was up by six and off to work in the bookstore she owned. On weekends, Eleanor slept in until eight, then took herself off to chores and appointments. The bookstore, which specialized in used and rare books, was her mother's life, and Jana had even accused her mother of loving the shop more than her daughter. It was an accusation Eleanor never bothered to deny.

Then later, when Jana was old enough to be helpful, her mother had bemoaned the difficulty of finding trustworthy staff for the bookstore. Jana had volunteered to work there, feeling that this would be a way she could connect with her mother. But Eleanor's answer had been an emphatic no.

"That is my respite and domain," Eleanor had told Jana. "I won't have you there stealing away that bit of solace."

Jana sighed, looking at the stack of dishes. She didn't have a lot to show for two years of marriage. Frankly, she didn't have a lot to show for a lifetime of living. There remained very few mementos from high school or college, and nothing, she believed, from her childhood. Eleanor had repeatedly told her that such trinkets were nothing more than baggage from the past to be carried around and dusted or stored. But Jana's sense was that her mother had systematically erased her daughter's existence. Jana was much like a blank slate, just waiting for someone to write on her—to tell her who she was, who she should be.

Rob had insisted that he knew who she should be. He constantly told her that he had seen the untapped potential in her, potential that he alone could utilize and bring to life. He'd shared the plan of salvation with her as if presenting an investment portfolio.

"This is what you need to make your life worth living," he'd said as they sipped coffee together one night after church.

Jana hadn't wanted to attend the college church gathering, but she'd allowed Rob to talk her into going. He'd met her on the college campus while scouting around for souls to save. Jana had thought him the most handsome man she'd ever seen. He was tall and lean with a mischievous smile that gave his face a boyish quality. His eyes captivated her the most. They were a lovely chocolate brown with thick black lashes. She'd teased him about having lashes that any woman would kill for. He'd laughed it off as being the only way he could keep the dust out of his eyes.

Rob was the first man Jana felt she could really talk to. He was also ten years her senior and, in ways, almost fatherly in his advice. Jana had shared her lonely childhood and miserable trek into adult life. She'd shared her mother's indifference and critical nature.

"Usually," Rob had said, "I find that critical people are the ones who are hurting the most. They use their attitude to cover up the pain so that no one can get too close."

"But why wouldn't they want people to be close?" Jana had asked.

Rob had looked at her as if she were missing some big mystery of the universe. "Because being close to people makes you vulnerable. And being vulnerable means you can get hurt."

Jana looked around the kitchen again and nodded. "At least you spoke the truth on that one, Rob."

It was late that night before Jana finished dragging the yard sale stuff to the front room. She had spared no feelings for nostalgia as she parted with framed replicas of artwork she and Rob had loved. She tried not to think about where she'd gotten the knickknacks she would sell for pennies on the dollar. It was all so unimportant anyway. With Rob gone, living his dream life, none of it mattered anymore.

If only there were time to sort through the situation and approach Rob about reconciliation. Jana had witnessed such breakups in marriages, only to find that in a week or two the lust and enthusiasm for the moment had worn off and the repentant spouse had returned home for a second chance.

"But would I give him a second chance?" It was a question Jana hadn't explored. Mainly because deep in her heart, she had concluded that Rob would never ask for a second chance.

She sank to the couch, her hand falling naturally against her stomach. There was no external sign of the child that grew inside, but just touching that area made her think of the baby to come. Would Rob want to come home if he knew about the baby? Or like he'd done with his marriage, would Rob determine the baby didn't matter to him?

"You'll matter to me," she whispered. "I won't treat you as my mother treated me. I'll want you no matter whether you're a boy or a girl. I'll love you whether you please me or fail me. I promise you: I won't be my mother. I won't leave you alone and frightened. I won't tell you to get over it when you're sad. And I won't ever tell you that you had a horrible father who betrayed me and left me to raise a child all alone."

She wiped a tear from her cheek and added, "Even though it's the truth."

Three

JANA HAD NEARLY finished putting price tags on the items crammed into her living room when the doorbell sounded. She startled, wondering who in the world could be calling. Her heart began to race. Maybe Rob had come home to apologize and tell her it was all just a horrible mistake.

She looked in the mirror that leaned against a stack of boxes and checked her appearance. Her eyes were red and puffy from crying. Her hair lacked any kind of luster or sheen because she hadn't washed it since coming home from Africa. And her blue-and-white-striped shirt was hopelessly dirty from long hours of work. Jana shrugged and muttered, "It can't be helped."

She went to the door and opened it without looking out the peephole. If by some chance it happened to be Rob, she didn't want to see him through a peephole. She wanted to face him— to make him face her.

Instead, Kelly Campanili stood on her doorstep, a small cooler in hand. Kelly was the wife of one of the elders. She smiled. "I knew you'd be swamped and probably not have time for cooking. I've brought you some small meals that you can just pop in the microwave."

"I don't have a microwave anymore," Jana said with a shrug. "Rob took it."

Kelly frowned. "Figures," she said sympathetically. "Well, it doesn't matter. We have an extra one at home. I'll have Joey run it over when he gets home from work."

"Thanks. I appreciate it. I've only got two more days here, however. You might not want to bother."

Kelly shifted her cooler. "No problem. You need to eat." She glanced past Jana. "May I come in?"

Jana sighed. She hadn't wanted company, but what could she do? If she said no, it would sound incredibly rude. "I suppose for a minute. I'm in the middle of getting things ready for the sale and don't have a lot of time for talk."

"What sale?" Kelly asked as she followed Jana into the house.

Jana turned and offered to take the cooler. "I can put this away if you like."

"Just lead the way to the kitchen and we can do it together."

Jana nodded. She wondered what Kelly would say when she saw how stark everything appeared.

"So what's this about a sale?" Kelly asked as she put the cooler on the table. She opened it and began stacking several pieces of disposable plastic containers on top of one another.

"I have to be out by Saturday," Jana explained. "But I assume you know that. I'm selling everything because I'm moving in with my mom and great-aunt. They have a fully furnished house, and since I needed the . . ." Jana stopped. She didn't want Kelly worrying about her lack of financial means.

But Kelly already understood. "You need the money." She met Jana's eyes and smiled sympathetically. "Joey told me Rob left you without any financial support. I'm really sorry. If it helps at all, none of us saw this coming."

"It doesn't help, but thanks anyway," Jana said, slouching against the wall.

Kelly closed the refrigerator. "I see you've already got the kitchen cleaned out. You always were one of the best house-keepers I've ever met. Especially for someone so young." She looked back at Jana and shook her head. "I hope I didn't offend you. I meant it as a compliment. Goodness, but I don't think I could even keep a decent house until I turned forty."

"No offense taken. My mother was such a stickler for order, I had no choice but to learn how to keep a perfect house. If I had so much as a sock out of place, my mother knew about it. I think she had some kind of special sense about those things."

"A kind of ESP?" Kelly asked, laughing.

"Something like that."

Kelly motioned to the chairs. "Could we sit for a moment? I promise I won't stay long."

Jana dreaded talking with anyone at this point. "Well, I have to finish tagging everything for the sale. I advertised it to start at seven tomorrow morning."

"I'll only keep you a minute. I promise." The pleading in Kelly's voice caused Jana to give in.

"Sure. Do you want something to drink? I have water and . . ." She tried to remember if there was any soda left in the pantry.

"No. I don't need a thing. Please . . . just sit a moment with me."

Jana did as the woman requested. She glanced at the ceiling, a bad habit she'd picked up whenever she wished she could be somewhere else.

"Jana, I want you to know that I care about you. I know we aren't all that close. I never felt like Rob ever wanted you to be close to anyone in the church."

"He said it was better that way. In case problems broke out and disciplinary actions were needed," Jana muttered by rote.

"Too bad he never understood that you have to have a genuine relationship with people in order to have them respect your discipline. Sure, you can have the authoritative official who stands to represent law and order, but it isn't the same as, say, a parent who loves her child. If Rob had thought it through, he might have understood that the congregation would have come to respect his direction more if he had shown them more love."

"Well, apparently one person in the congregation was getting that kind of attention," Jana said without thinking. She felt her cheeks grow hot. "Sorry."

"Don't apologize. You have a right to be angry, to be hurt. I've been there before and I completely understand."

Jana looked up at her. "Joey?"

"No. I was married before. My husband left me for his secretary. He was a lawyer. I noticed he had an awful lot of late-night work sessions. Big cases, he told me." She sighed. "It's not easy, even now after fifteen years of a good marriage to a solid Christian man. My first husband and I weren't saved. We didn't care about anything but ourselves. We were selfish, and it cost us our marriage."

"I didn't know." Jana suddenly realized she didn't know much of anything about the women in her church.

"I don't tell just anyone," Kelly said. "It serves no good purpose and seems to stir up discord. The Bible says that God hates divorce; well, so do I, but that didn't mean people understood my situation any better. I was probably more condemned by people who called themselves Christians than by anyone else. I thank God there were no children involved. Otherwise, they would have suffered too." Jana cringed inwardly and looked at the table.

Kelly continued. "When he left me, I turned to God for strength to endure. The first church I went to was rather large and pompous. When they found out I was a divorcée, they wanted no part of me. They told me I needed to reconcile my marriage or I'd go to hell for all eternity."

Jana's stomach twisted at the comment. No doubt some

people would say such things to her.

"I couldn't bear the judgment, so I tried a smaller church right in my own neighborhood. They welcomed me with open arms—gave me love and encouragement. They also showed me what God was all about. I felt I finally understood what was missing in my life."

"But I already had God in my life," Jana said without emotion. "And it didn't do me a whole lot of good." She waited for Kelly to react in shock, but instead the blonde nodded.

"I can understand your feeling that way."

"You can?"

"Jana, everyone feels confused by things from time to time. Everyone even has moments where they feel confused by God. It doesn't make you a bad person, and you aren't going to knock me off my feet by saying so. Let me tell you, when my boy David was dying from leukemia, I had plenty of times when I questioned God. Ranted and raved at Him, too, I'm sorry to say."

"I didn't know you'd lost a child." Jana felt a wave of sadness wash over her. How many people had she seen Sunday after Sunday and not really known?

"It happened about five years before you came. It was a true test of our marriage, and it was hard on the other kids too," Kelly said, her eyes filling with tears. "I didn't think God cared anymore. I couldn't understand why He would allow such a bad thing to happen when we were trying so hard to put Him first. David was just a little boy . . . how was that fair? How could I possibly make sense of it, except to say God had somehow turned against me?"

Jana wanted to deny she felt that way, but she was sure one look into her eyes would tell Kelly everything she needed to know. And so Jana said nothing.

Kelly reached out and covered Jana's hand with her own.

"Don't let this separate you from God. He truly does care and He's there for you, even though this is hard. We're here for you too. The ladies of the church love you, Jana. They really do. They've only wanted an opportunity to get close to you."

Jana didn't know what to say. It was all too much. She would leave Saturday—there was no sense in getting close to anyone now. "It seems a lot of time was wasted," she finally murmured.

"Just don't waste the days to come," Kelly said firmly. "You'll be tempted to, but don't."

"I don't know what I'll be doing. Right now I don't want to think about any of it."

"I understand; you don't want to think about it, you don't want to deal with it. It's okay to give yourself a little time away from it. But you *will* have to come back to it. It will make all the difference in the world if you actually deal with the problems and hurts rather than simply pretend they don't exist. I speak from experience on that one as well."

Jana didn't want to listen anymore. She was already overwhelmed with emotion and frustration. She kept remembering the joy of learning she was pregnant and of all the plans she had for the future. Now those plans would never be. "I really need to get back to work." She pulled her hand away from Kelly's and got to her feet. "I hope you understand. I appreciate the food you brought, and if I'm not here when Joey brings the microwave, tell him the back door will be unlocked."

Kelly stood. "I'll tell him. Will you let me know if you need anything?"

Jana gave a sort of laugh, but it sounded more like a cough. "I need everything to sell at the yard sale tomorrow. If you can make that happen . . . well . . ." She shook her head. "Never mind. Either the stuff will sell or it won't. It isn't your problem."

Kelly reached out to touch Jana's shoulder. "We want to help bear your burden, Jana. Don't forget that we care."

Jana nodded. "Thank you, but I wouldn't wish this on my worst enemy."

———————

Thursday morning dawned clear and beautiful. It was one of those early summer mornings that might have sent Jana and Rob to the mountains for a hike or to the lake to just enjoy a leisurely rest. But instead, Jana was hauling box after box of stuff onto her front lawn.

She arranged things the best she could and then went to put up a sign on the front porch post. It advertised larger pieces of furniture in the house. If people wanted to buy them, and hopefully they would, they would need to make arrangements for getting them moved. If they didn't sell, Jana would simply leave them behind—she had no other choice. She could only take with her what would fit in her car.

By eight o'clock the sale was already proving to be a success. More than twenty people had stopped by, and all of them had purchased something. One man had even made her a generous offer on most of the furniture in the house, promising that he would come Saturday morning to clear it out. At least this way she would have a bed in which to sleep and a place to sit.

To Jana's surprise, a dozen or more women from the church arrived at around eight-thirty. Kelly led the way, with Roberta Winsome running a close second.

"We're here to help," Kelly announced. "We've brought some baked goods for you to sell. We figure once word gets out that Roberta's coffeecake is for sale, you'll have an even bigger draw."

"I don't know what to say."

"Say nothing at all," Roberta declared. "We take care of our own."

The words warmed Jana, but she found herself putting up a wall nevertheless. She didn't want to feel to obligated to these women. And she certainly didn't want to care for them—and then feel another loss.

Throughout the day, however, the love of her church family was clear. People she had hardly gotten to know showed up at her sale and purchased nearly every item she offered. By the time Jana boxed the final items remaining, she had netted herself over fifteen hundred dollars.

"I'll take that to Goodwill if you like," Kelly said, pointing to the box Jana held.

"I suppose that would be a good idea." Jana wanted to say something more but struggled to know how to express her gratitude.

Kelly stepped forward to take the box, but Jana held it tight for a moment. "I don't know what happened here today, but thank you."

Kelly met Jana's eyes. "One of our members was in need. We wanted to come and help as much as we possibly could. That's what true Christianity is all about. Jesus loved us, and we're to love one another."

Jana nodded, but she wasn't sure she'd ever really understand. All her life love had been such an obscure thing. It had never been offered as freely to her as it had been on this day—by these people who had nothing to gain in the giving.

Jana let go of the box and Kelly smiled. "We won't stop caring about you, Jana. Please keep in touch with us. We want to know what's happening in your life."

Jana thought of her unborn child and nearly opened her mouth to tell Kelly, then thought better of it. She didn't know how the church might react if they knew about the baby. They might want to go find Rob and tell him—demand he return to his wife. Frankly, Jana wasn't sure she'd take him back even if he did show up. The trust was completely broken, just like her heart, and Jana wasn't sure that could ever be regained.

Four

THE NEXT MORNING, as Jana was packing up the final remains of her life in the parsonage, a knock sounded. Again she found herself flustered in anticipation that it might be Rob returning. How would she react if it turned out to be him? She smoothed her newly washed hair and went to answer the door. A man she didn't know stood on the other side.

"Are you Jana McGuire?"

She swallowed hard. "Yes."

"This is for you." The man thrust a large envelope into her hands and turned to go.

Jana looked down at the packet. She was certain she knew the contents, for the return address held the name of a well-known law firm in Spokane.

Divorce papers.

She knew without opening the envelope that it had to be this. Rob had said he had the entire matter taken care of. She turned in defeat and closed the door.

"So this is it." She carried the packet almost ceremonially to the kitchen and placed it on the counter.

The thing that bothered Jana most was that Rob had had months to plan, to get used to the idea of leaving her. He had gone through each detail in his mind—had imagined how it would be. Rob had spent time developing his choices. This was all new and fresh to her, yet so many other people seemed to have

41

already dealt with the problem and resolved it in their own way. The elders had a new pastor to run the church. Rob had his mistress, and a divorce was in the works. But the whole situation was only a few days old to Jana. It made no more sense now than it had made that first morning.

"Why is this happening?" she questioned. She looked up toward the ceiling. "God, are you there? Are you listening?" Her anger mounted. "Why would you do this to me?"

Jana swept her hand across the counter, sending the divorce papers to the floor. "What good does it do to trust you if you aren't going to be there to protect us from the bad things in life? I was faithful. I was doing your work. I was sitting in the middle of the African bush teaching children about Jesus. Why would you let my marriage fall apart?"

She stormed from the kitchen, down the hall, and into the living room. Here she had begun packing the last remnants of her married life: her photographs. Picking up her wedding album, Jana began ripping the pictures out of the expensive leather binder. She'd paid top dollar for the best pictures she could get. She'd thought this marriage would last forever.

Forever.

There was that word again. Jana picked up a picture of the bride and groom and tore it in half. "There! That's forever too."

She lost track of time as she destroyed one picture after another, her good sense and reasoning temporarily leaving her. Jana gave no thought to whether her unborn child would one day want to see the photos of his or her parents.

It was only at the sound of another knock at the front door that Jana halted her tirade. She looked at the mess around her and knew she could never allow anyone to see what she'd done.

"Oh no," she muttered, gathering the ragged pieces together. She shoved them all back into the box and threw the album on top before hurrying to answer the door.

Jason Broadbent wasn't a handsome man. His rather homely appearance and quiet demeanor often put people off—or so it seemed to Jana. But one look in his eyes and Jana knew that he was possibly the only other person in the world who felt as awful as she did.

"Jason." She murmured his name with an emotion she couldn't even begin to describe.

"Jana, I know this probably is uncomfortable for you, but I heard you were leaving tomorrow and I . . . well . . . given the situation . . ."

She stepped back. "Come in." In a heartbeat, she felt the only genuine connection to another human being that she'd known in days. Jason had been hurt by the same thing. He knew exactly what she was going through . . . with the exception of being pregnant, of course.

She pointed to the sofa. "Have a seat. I can't offer anything in the way of refreshments. I've gotten rid of most everything."

"I didn't come for that." The stocky man lumbered over to the couch and waited until Jana took a seat opposite him before seating himself. "I just figured to talk about what's happened."

"Did you know this was coming?" she blurted out.

He shrugged. "I knew Kerry wasn't happy. I even thought she was having an affair, but I figured once she got it out of her system, she'd settle back down. I guess I never thought she'd up and do something like this."

"Why was she unhappy?" Jana knew it was a personal question, but she felt desperate to understand the situation.

Again he shrugged as though it were some great mystery. "I don't really understand. She tried to tell me, but it never made sense."

"What did she say, Jason? Maybe I can help you sort through

this and you can do the same for me."

He fidgeted a bit. "Well, she told me I was never there. But, Jana, I swear I was. I never went anywhere."

She nodded. "Maybe she meant emotionally you were never there."

"What's that supposed to mean? I provided the woman with everything she needed—house, food, all the clothes she wanted. She could spend a lot of money on clothes and things, but I never complained."

"But maybe she was lonely. Maybe she wanted you to just talk with her . . . for companionship. Did you take her places? Do things with her?"

"Sometimes. It never seemed to be enough, though. She'd get all mad and argue with me about how we never went anywhere, so I'd tell her to plan us an evening and I'd go. I even went to Seattle to see some ballet performance."

Jana lowered her head and fought a smile. No doubt Jason thought that was the supreme sacrifice. "Jason, you probably did everything you had in you to do. Some people are just never happy."

"I think a lot of it was because I was so much older."

Jana looked up and nodded. "Rob was ten years older than me. I wondered if my youth and inexperience was part of the problem for him. I remember one time he tried to tell me something about Ronald Reagan. I was only a little girl during the Reagan administration and didn't remember anything about it. He was really upset with me. He said even if I was a child, I should have known about whatever it was he was talking about." She eased back into the chair and gave her own sigh. "I guess there were a lot of things I should have known."

"Don't blame yourself," Jason replied. "I can't see any of this being your fault. Rob knew the age difference when he married you. The same as I knew when I married Kerry. I didn't figure the years would matter much if we loved each other."

"Do you know where they went?"

His expression betrayed the fact that he did. "I went looking for her. I wanted to talk to her face-to-face about this. I found them in Seattle, but I couldn't go to her. I just didn't have the words. So I turned around and came back home."

Rob had always loved Seattle. He'd been hoping for a church there when the call had come that he had the church in Spokane. "That figures. Rob talked of moving to Seattle. Of course, he talked about a lot of things . . . most of them lies."

"Jana, I'm so sorry about all of this. Like I said, I figure if I'd been a better husband—if I'd showed Kerry more of the attention she needed—none of this would be happening now."

Her chest tightened and her breathing felt strained. "But it has happened and there's obviously nothing we can do about it. My divorce papers came just a short time ago. Rob means for this to be a done deal."

"Are you going to be okay?" the older man asked.

Something in Jana broke. "Okay? Am I going to be okay with the fact that my husband ran off with his secretary?" Her voice raised in volume. "Okay? What a stupid word."

"I'm sorry, Jana. I didn't mean it like that." He shook his head. "This is all my fault."

She waved him off. "No, Jason. It's not your fault, no matter how much you blame yourself. But I have no energy to try to convince you of that. This is Rob and Kerry's fault. They're the ones who have to answer for this. They're the ones who planned this out.

"I'm not okay with any part of it. I'm not okay with the fact that Rob took all of my savings and cleared the house of everything of value. I'm not okay that he planned this all behind my back while I thought we had a strong enough marriage to plan a family."

"A family?" he asked, his voice breaking slightly. "Does that mean . . ."

"Yes. I'm pregnant." Jana looked at him as though challenging him on the matter. "I didn't even find out until I was in Africa. They thought I had food poisoning or had ingested some bad water. But instead, I found out I was going to have a baby."

"And Rob left anyway?" Jason sounded as though the very idea was completely unreasonable to him.

She got up and began pacing. "Rob never knew about the baby. I never had a chance to tell him. I wanted to share the news in person, but as you already know, he was long gone by the time I got home."

Jason buried his face in his hands and shook his head for several moments. Jana was unable to control her outrage. "I had no idea Rob was having an affair. Kerry was always kind to me— she gave me presents. I sold them all in the yard sale yesterday." She wasn't sure why she'd added the latter. It could only hurt Jason, and he wasn't the one she wanted to hurt.

"I have nothing, Jason. Nothing at all." He looked up, and Jana could see there were tears in his eyes. She stopped in mid-step. "I have my car, probably only because Rob couldn't drive two of them at the same time. I have my clothes and what money I made at the sale yesterday, but that's all there is. Rob took *everything*. He took my trust and my dreams. He took my savings and my property. He even stole my great-aunt's jewelry—a gift to me." She collapsed on the chair, her rage nearly spent. "I would have been better off if Rob had died. At least then I'd have my savings and his life insurance."

Jason got to his feet. He pulled out his wallet and dumped the contents on the coffee table. "There's not much here. Maybe a couple hundred. I want you to have it."

"No, I'm not your responsibility," Jana said, leaning forward. She pushed the money back toward him.

"I want you to have it. Business has been bad lately, but I'll sell some equipment and get you some more money."

"No, Jason!" She stood and looked him in the eye. "You don't need to take care of me. You didn't cause this to happen. You've been just as wronged."

"It doesn't matter for me. I've got my business and my house. You don't have either one. I've raised my kids; you're just starting a family. It may not be my responsibility, but I intend to see to it that you get some of the money you need. Give me the address of the place you're heading."

Jana forced herself to calm down. "I'm going to live with my mom and great-aunt in Montana, but I won't give you the address. Jason, you can't worry about me. I'm sorry for my out-burst. But when you asked if I'd be okay, something snapped." She was quiet a moment. "I don't feel like I'll ever be okay again, but I cannot make that your burden."

He put his wallet back in his pocket and headed for the door. "I'll be in touch."

She scooped up the money and went after the man. "Please take your money back."

He turned and shook his head. "I won't do that. Do with it what you will, but I won't take it back." With that he left, shoul-ders slumped forward, steps almost uncertain. He got to the door of his truck and looked back at her. He didn't wave or say another word—he just looked at her as though trying to figure it all out for himself.

Jana suddenly felt very self-conscious. She couldn't under-stand how she could have lost control. Jason didn't deserve her tirade, and she certainly hadn't expected his money.

She waited until he drove away before going back into the house, then wandered into the kitchen, the money still in her hands. She threw the wad down on top of the counter, spotting the envelope that she'd sent to the floor earlier.

Jana stepped across the room and picked up the packet. Drawing a deep breath, she forced herself to open it. She pulled out the papers and read the cover letter title.

Divorce: McGuire vs. McGuire

"But I don't want to be a part of this," she said sadly. "I've never wanted this . . . never asked for this." She stuffed the papers back into the envelope and put them on top of the money. Nothing made sense anymore. All she wanted to do was crawl into bed and pull the covers up over her head and hope that it would all go away. But Jana knew it wouldn't. The only thing that had gone away was Rob. And with each passing day, it was clear he wasn't coming back.

Five

JANA SPENT HER last night in the parsonage amidst furniture that would soon belong to someone else. She wandered from room to room, gazing at the cold, sterile spaces with a surprising rush of emotion. She had come to this house with such high hopes, such plans for the future. How could that all be gone now?

"I trusted Rob and God," she said, fingering the living room drapes. She'd pored over catalogs, then gone to church to show Rob the pictures of what she'd selected to make sure he liked the color. He'd told her that she had excellent taste. She wondered if the new pastor would feel the same way.

Jana looked back at the living room. She'd piled her things against the wall by the door. Six boxes of clothes and other items she couldn't bring herself to part with. That was all. That was her entire life.

Her childhood dreams and adolescent plans were overwhelmed by the reality of adult sorrows. Why had this happened? It was the question that refused to leave her. Had her love for Rob been false? Was it not the thing she thought it to be?

"No, I loved him. I loved him with my whole heart," she muttered. "I saw him as saving me from a life where no one loved me. Not my mother, not my father." She sighed. "Especially not my father."

Jana had never even known her father. He had divorced her

mother when Jana had been an infant. "He wanted a son—we both wanted a son" was the only explanation her mother ever offered.

Jana couldn't understand why the man had been so heartless when a daughter had been born instead. She could understand disappointment, but not desertion. And to make matters worse, her mother would never talk about him. Jana had often longed to hear a story about how her mother had fallen in love. She had begged for tales about the engagement and wedding. Was it love at first sight? Had they known each other long? But her mother would share nothing.

"The past can only hurt you," her mother declared, "if you dwell on it."

But those words hadn't prepared Jana to deal with the present. The past hadn't been dwelt on or even discussed, but it still hurt. All of her life, Jana had wondered why she hadn't been worthy of her father's love. She never knew his name—her mother had kept her maiden name as was so popular with the women of the time—and for some reason beyond Jana's understanding, the hospital had allowed her mother to leave the father's name off of the birth certificate.

Jana remembered drilling her mother about that issue when she'd obtained a copy of her birth certificate for her driver's license.

"Why isn't my father's name on this?" she'd asked.

"He didn't want to be a part of your life, so I saw no reason to list him."

"But he *is* a part of my life," Jana protested. "He helped to create me. He can't just *not* be a part of who I am."

"Your father had nothing to do with any part of your life," her mother replied bitterly. "His money may have seen you placed in good schools, may have bought me a decent business to run—but he had nothing to do with you. He didn't want you, and if I'd been sensible, I would have gotten an abortion."

Her mother's words—in their cold, no-nonsense manner—crushed Jana. She felt haunted by them, and it wasn't until she met Rob that Jana felt she could begin to heal. Rob helped her see that the past couldn't be changed, but the future could be completely altered. Jana saw hope in that.

"A lot of good it did me," she said, going to her bedroom.

Like the other rooms, this one had been reduced to nothing more than a generic setting. A bed and dresser were all that suggested its purpose; tomorrow morning even those things would be taken away. The room would be stripped of the last remnants of the McGuires.

Jana slipped out of her clothes and then pulled on an old T-shirt and crawled into bed. She reached across to where Rob used to be, an old habit she hadn't yet found a way to break. She stroked the pillow, thinking of the times they'd stay up late talking. Rob had always fascinated her with the things he knew. It had been part of the reason she'd been attracted to him in the first place. That and his loving nature, his sympathetic heart, his devotion. When he'd asked Jana to marry him, she had jumped at the chance.

"But it was all lies. His love was a lie. He didn't love me. He couldn't have loved me and walked away with another woman."

And if Rob's love was a lie, then maybe God's love was a lie as well.

Jana stared blankly in the darkness. A sliver of light slipped in through the side of the blinds, making eerie shadows on the ceiling and walls. She wanted to pray, but the words wouldn't come. Instead, the fear that maybe God wasn't at all who she thought Him to be haunted her every thought.

Surely if God was really the loving Father Jana believed, He would have protected her from this horror that had become her life. And if God loved her, as Rob had always assured her, why would He allow her to be hurt like this? Jana thought of the baby in her womb.

"I'd never let my child hurt like this. If I had the power that God has, I would never allow anything bad to happen to my children."

So that made God indifferent, at least in Jana's mind. It made Him no different than her mother.

It was a terrifying conclusion for Jana. How could she have been so duped? How could both Rob and God have so completely fooled her?

"I used to think I was fairly smart," she said with a sigh. "I thought because of my upbringing that I would be cautious . . . I thought I understood so much more than I do." She pounded her fists into Rob's pillow as though the action could somehow relieve her misery.

"I don't understand any of this! Why is this happening?"

Those questions were still on Jana's mind as she loaded her car the next day. Keith Ribley, the man who'd bought her furniture, had come with a large truck and the help of three other men. To Jana's surprise, she learned that the man was the father of one of the church members. It became increasingly clear that her church family had come to the sale and bought up most everything solely to help Jana on her way.

For some reason it made her feel guilty instead of loved. Maybe that was because Jana wanted no attachment to these people or to God . . . yet both seemed to continue imposing themselves on her.

Even this morning, Jana's first instinct had been to pray, but in anger she had refused. *God doesn't care about me,* she had determined. *If He cared, He would have kept all of this from happening.*

She saw several cars pull into the church parking lot and wondered what was happening. She couldn't remember anything being on the schedule; then it dawned on her that the new pastor was probably coming.

Jana tried to ignore the additional vehicles that arrived. Maybe the church members were coming to help the new pastor move in. Maybe there would be a potluck dinner afterward. She pushed the notion aside. It hurt to imagine life going on for Hope Bible Church of Spokane. Months, years from now, no one would even remember that Rob and Jana McGuire had pastored the church.

For reasons beyond her understanding, that thought hurt almost as much as Rob's desertion. It was here at this church that Jana had felt a sense of family for the first time. And even though Rob had discouraged her from getting close to people, Jana had known their respect and consideration.

"Jana!"

She closed the trunk and turned to see a large group of people crossing the lawn between the church and parsonage. Kelly and Joey were leading the way.

"We wanted to come and say good-bye and to bring you a few things," Kelly called.

Gary Rhoades and his wife, Mary, came alongside Kelly and Joey. "We wanted to send you off properly," Gary said. His tone was serious, but he offered Jana a smile that bespoke compassion and genuine concern.

Jana stiffened. *I won't let myself get hurt again. I can't care about these people.* She wanted to send them all away. To chastise them for something that wasn't even their fault.

Bill had finished unloading the furniture from the house and came to join the group, as did his helpers. Gary looked to Kelly and nodded. Kelly in turn looked to Roberta Winsome.

The older woman motioned to a younger man, whom Jana knew was her grandson, to come forward with a large sack. "I've made you some goodies for the trip," Roberta announced. "There's also some extra to take to your mom and great-aunt. Thought it might help you feel better not to go to them empty-handed."

Jana felt dumbfounded and for a moment had no idea what to do or say. Were these people for real? Did they honestly think to comfort her with baked goods? She immediately regretted her sarcastic thoughts. They were trying their best—it wasn't their fault. She had to get a grip on her emotions, but it was as if her hands were too slick to hold on to them.

"We also pitched in to get you a few things to remember us by," Kelly said, coming forward with yet another sack. "There are a few books we picked up for you and some other things we thought might bring you comfort."

Jana continued to stare at them. She wanted to say something, but she knew if she opened her mouth her words would be harsh—sarcastic. *Why can't they just go away and leave me be? I don't want to hurt them.*

"And the elders voted," Gary announced, "and decided you deserved this." He extended a card. "We've given you a sort of severance pay. You worked as hard here as Rob did, and we want to reward you for it."

Roberta nudged her grandson. "Go put those things in the car. Take Kelly's bag too." The young man did as he was told, but still Jana could only watch. She couldn't even will herself to reach out and take the card that Gary offered.

Kelly seemed to understand and came to put her arm around Jana. "It's not much, but we wanted you to know how special you were to us. We want you to know that you're always welcome to come back. We know it can't be comfortable for you right now, but maybe in time you'll want to return."

Jana finally forced out her thanks. "It was kind of you to come." She took the card, seeing that Gary was growing rather uncomfortable. "I'm sorry . . . I don't know what else to say."

"You don't have to say anything," Kelly replied. "We didn't come here for a speech. We came to give you these things and to pray with you. We don't want to send you off without prayer." Some of the group nodded, while others verbalized their agreement.

Jana bit her lip. *Prayer? They want to pray with me? Isn't it a little late for that?*

But even as she was thinking this, the people gathered around her. Several of them reached out to touch her, while Kelly looped her arm through Jana's. Gary suggested they all bow their heads, but Jana could only stare wide-eyed at the group.

I don't want to hear their prayers or their sympathy. She was glad now that she'd never mentioned the baby. Gary was already thanking God for having the chance to know Jana. Her heart hardened a little bit more. Was Gary also thankful for knowing Rob? Would he have wanted the young pastor and his wife— wanted to know them and care about them—if he'd known this moment would come?

Kelly was praying now. "Watch over her, Lord. Keep her from harm."

Keep me from harm? Where were your prayers weeks ago, when my husband was planning all of this? Where was God's protection from "harm" then?

Even at this time, Jana knew that little by little she was building a wall that would help her survive the pain. If she quartered herself away from people—kept her heart hidden behind a protective shell—she wouldn't be hurt anymore. And after all, wasn't this exactly what her mother had tried to teach her?

"Don't care too much about people, Jana." Her mother's words echoed as clearly as if she were standing at Jana's side. "You'll only end up hurt. Focus on something that can't be taken away from you—something you have power over."

But what was that thing? It wasn't friendship, because soon enough these people would forget about her and leave her behind. It wasn't the child she carried, because Jana knew from her own experience that mothers and daughters could be as distant as the east was from the west. What one thing could Jana cling to and know that she could trust?

"Let Jana hold on to you, Lord," Kelly was saying. It almost seemed prophetic, but Jana refused to yield to that idea.

God can't possibly care about me. He just can't. I wouldn't be standing here now if He was truly concerned with my well-being, Jana thought. *If these people only knew what a farce it all is—that we aren't safe or cared for.* She wanted to scream at them all. Yet looking around the circle of peaceful expressions, Jana knew it would do little good. These people were convinced that God did care—that His love could conquer all problems.

I'd like to believe that is true, but it hurts so much right now. Maybe I can think about all of this later. But for now, I'd just as soon be left alone.

The prayers concluded and everyone came up to hug Jana and wish her the best. She found herself offering a weak smile. There was nothing left to do. It was time to go.

"I left the keys to the parsonage on the counter. I . . . well . . . I don't know if Rob left his set with you. I only had my own."

"I have Rob's keys," Gary said.

Jana drew a deep breath. She should have figured that Rob would have planned for every detail. She moved to the car and opened her door. Kelly remained at her side, although she had released her hold.

"Call me and let me know you've arrived safely, okay?" she requested. "Here's my number and a calling card."

Jana took the items and stared at them for a moment. "I'm not going that far. Only five hours or so."

"That's a long ways for a woman by herself," Kelly chided. "I'd just like to know that you're safe and sound. Please?"

Jana looked into her pleading expression. "All right." She supposed it could do no harm to allow this one bit of comfort.

Fighting her emotions, Jana got into the car and started the engine. She tucked the phone card into her purse and looked at the house one last time. *I thought I was happy here,* she reflected with a sadness that threatened to swallow her whole. "I guess I didn't know I wasn't happy."

AT FORTY-EIGHT, Eleanor Templeton was a refined woman who liked peace and order in her life. She dressed in nice clothing ranging between selections from the department store discount racks and name-brand designers. She went to the beauty shop once every two weeks and had her short, dark blond hair trimmed and occasionally recolored. And she continued to manage her New York business, a large independent bookstore, from this remote location in Montana.

"I'm so excited about Jana coming!" Taffy gushed, fairly dancing around the room. For a woman who was approaching eighty, she certainly had more than her fair share of energy.

"I think it's a mistake," Eleanor said, speaking over her cup of tea. "I've considered this ever since she called, and I think it's wrong. What if her husband comes back to make amends?"

"I'm sure the people at the church will give him the address." Taffy began rummaging through the kitchen drawers. "Where did you put the aprons?"

"They're in the laundry room cupboard. Why?"

Taffy straightened and smoothed her sweater. The lavender-and-yellow creation trimmed around the neck with wisps of dyed purple rabbit fur was better suited to a teenager, as far as Eleanor was concerned, but Taffy was known for her extravagant sense of fashion. Her long black skirt and ankle boots completed the look, but for the life of her, Eleanor couldn't figure out why the old woman thought this a sensible outfit for a senior citizen.

"We need to clean the Rose Room," Taffy told her niece. "Jana said she'd arrive today. I've put it off too long now as it is. If only I hadn't promised time to the senior meals delivery, I could have spent it cleaning. But you know Elmira Rogers couldn't be expected to continue her duties with a broken arm."

"That room is perfectly acceptable. Let Jana clean it if it needs additional attention."

"I'll do no such thing," Taffy said indignantly. "This is my house. I wouldn't ask a guest to come in and clean such a mess."

"It sounded to me like Jana was asking to be much more than a guest," Eleanor replied, unable to keep the disapproving tone from her voice.

"She *is* more than a guest. She's family, and we'll treat her as such. I've never understood the way you handle her. She's your daughter and you'd think you two would be very close."

"My relationship with Jana is no one's concern but mine. But I can tell that her coming here will disrupt everything."

Taffy laughed. "Good. I hope so. We've grown too quiet and boring."

"I like it quiet. You should too. You're nearly eighty years old, Taffy. You need to slow down and take better care of yourself."

The old woman frowned and looked down at her body and back to Eleanor. "I'm in better shape than you are. I exercise for thirty minutes every morning and walk five miles a day. I have yet to see you walk around the block. Honestly, Eleanor, you should consider the specks in your own eye before worrying about mine. I read just the other day that olive oil is good for you. Why don't you buy us some when you go to the store? We'll eat French bread and olive oil every day and see if that doesn't help your disposition."

Eleanor stiffened. She had never fit anyone's image of what

she should be, and now her aunt figured that olive oil would make life better. If only Taffy could understand that the hurts of days gone by could in no way be benefited by olive oil.

"I'm sure moderation is the key to life," Eleanor finally replied, getting to her feet. She put her cup and saucer in the dishwasher, then turned to find Taffy had already left the room. She could hear her aunt opening cupboard doors in the laundry room. Apparently they would clean the Rose Room whether Eleanor wanted to or not. It was a good thing she'd dressed casually, though she wasn't sure her suede pants were exactly appropriate for housekeeping.

"I found them!" Taffy announced, coming back into the kitchen with two aprons. "Here's one for you." She tossed the apron at Eleanor.

"I'll gather the cleaning supplies." Her tone still bore disapproval, but Eleanor tied the apron on nevertheless and went to work. She knew better than to refuse. If she walked away from the job, Taffy would simply do it by herself.

"You know, the Rose Room has always been one of my favorites," Taffy said as they climbed the stairs to the second floor. "I still think it's a marvelous room. The southern exposure is good for one's health, you know. Perhaps we should move you into that room."

"Taffy, my health is fine. I had a physical not two months past," Eleanor protested.

"Still, a little extra sun never hurt anyone. I read the other day that the sun provides valuable vitamins. Can you imagine that?" She stopped on the stairs, waiting for Eleanor's response.

"Yes, I've heard about the value of the sun. But I've also heard about the dangers. Which is why I've told you over and over to use sunscreen when you go for your walks."

"I don't like smearing lotion all over my body. My pores can't breathe," Taffy countered. "That's not good for you either. I read it in one of my ladies' magazines. I told you they were worth having."

Eleanor stifled the urge to roll her eyes. Taffy had subscriptions to at least thirty magazines. Eleanor had tried to get the old woman to cancel the orders and save her money, but Taffy only chided her for interfering with her quest for knowledge.

Taffy was again headed for the last bedroom on the west wing. Turning to the left, Taffy opened the door and pushed it back with great flourish. "Ah, the Rose Room."

It was aptly named for the rose-printed wallpaper. Eleanor thought it a ghastly room, reminiscent of the Victorian age. Large cabbage roses and twining greenery were offset with green trim around the baseboards and windows. Overhead, the walls were topped with white crown molding and a white ceiling. Below, the hardwood floor was accented with a rose-and-green rug that had been created uniquely to match the wallpaper.

The room smelled musty and old. The furnishings had been stylish when first purchased in the 1950s, but Eleanor seriously doubted anyone but an antique collector would have interest now. And perhaps even they would shun the heavy oak monstrosities Taffy loved.

"My, but it is dusty in here. We should have started sooner," Taffy said, pulling on her pinafore-styled apron. "Sometimes I don't know how the time gets away from me."

"We should consider taking on a housekeeper," Eleanor commented, putting the cleaning supplies on the floor.

"Nonsense. Especially now that Jana is with us. Why, we will positively run right over each other in cleaning. A housekeeper would have nothing to do."

Eleanor watched her aunt, silently wishing she could feel the same enthusiasm. Nothing ever seemed to discourage Taffy or get her down for long. For as long as Eleanor had known the woman, Taffy had always been a light of hope and encouragement. People used to come from all over the globe to spend time with her aunt, it seemed. Most were likely now dead or no doubt they'd still come.

"Oh my. Can you believe this old thing?" Taffy asked as she pulled a dated satin gown from the closet. "I had this for the presidential inauguration in 1953. We were good friends with the Eisenhowers, although Adlai Stevenson was also a dear. In fact, I have a recipe for pork chops that his cook gave me shortly after the election."

She held up the faded blue gown and posed with it against her. "My, but I felt like dancing all night in this wondrous creation." Then without warning, she tossed the gown to the bed and began to take off her apron. "I wonder if it still fits." She pulled her sweater off, and before Eleanor could even comment, Taffy was working herself into the strapless dress.

"The most important thing about a gown like this," Taffy said as she pulled up the side zipper, "is having the right accessories." She leaned back into the closet.

"We're wasting time," Eleanor said, trying not to sound too impatient. Taffy was always chiding her for her lack of patience.

"Here they are!" Taffy's muffled voice declared. She straightened and pulled out two long white gloves. "These were absolute necessities for this style. Look," she said, pulling them on over her elbows. "Don't they just make it perfection?"

Taffy took herself to the cheval mirror and admired her appearance. "Oh, I feel twenty again. Of course, I was a bit older than that at the inaugural ball, but not by much. I had the most marvelous time."

Eleanor wanted to say something about those days being long gone but held her tongue. It was bad enough that the woman was twirling around like an eight-year-old. "Taffy, we really need to get this work done."

"I don't know why women don't wear gloves more often. They feel delicious." She suddenly stopped. "I didn't think you cared about this room. You said we should let Jana clean it."

"Well, now that we're here, we might as well get it done. I'm just not looking forward to any of this. I can't understand your joy over having someone who has made such a mess of her life coming here to disrupt our peace."

Taffy cocked her head, as if pondering the truth of Eleanor's comment. "Well, she may have a messy life, but messes are made all the time. The important point is to clean them up." Taffy began pulling off the gloves. "Like this room. It's a lovely room but hardly serviceable at this point. It just needs the mess cleared away."

"Jana's life isn't a bedroom that can be cleaned, Taffy. She has some very big problems to confront—issues that won't simply go away."

Taffy placed the gloves on the bed, then unzipped the gown. "And this room could be as messy as the attic. Bigger messes just require more time to clean—more patience."

"It's not that simple and you know it," Eleanor replied in her most serious tone. Sometimes she thought Taffy might be losing touch with reality.

"Human beings are never simple," Taffy replied softly. "That's why they need God. Only the Creator could understand His creation and what they need. Why, the Bible says that God can cleanse away all unrighteousness. So why would He have any trouble cleaning up a little girl's life?"

"Jana's no little girl. She's a grown woman whose husband has run off with his secretary. She's going to have to face a divorce and the problems that come with being betrayed in this manner."

"But she doesn't have to face them alone. She's a Christian, and she knows that God will help her through these bad times. You used to think the same thing. You used to believe that God cared. Why, I remember when you found Jesus."

"I found Him, all right," Eleanor said in anger as she picked up a bucket. "And like everyone else in my life, He didn't want me."

"Eleanor! You know that isn't true. How can you speak such a lie?" Taffy actually sounded angry. It surprised Eleanor.

"I say it because that's the way I feel. My life has proven to me that God has no real concern for my well-being." Eleanor headed for the door. "I'm going for some water."

Taffy stared at the place where Eleanor had stood and shook her head. How could her niece be so hard-hearted? Sure, she'd endured more than her share of misery, but pain and sorrow haunted every life. Not just Eleanor's.

Taffy finished dressing and began to fold the satin dress. How she longed to share some encouragement with Eleanor. Some glimpse of light that would give her strength for the journey. The light, of course, was Jesus, but Eleanor wanted no part of Him. She would often comment about Taffy's upbeat personality and positive spirit, but she refused to believe it was as simple as abandoning her life to a higher power—to the only power worthy of her love.

And soon there would be two of them. Two bitter, angry, betrayed souls who were sure that love could never again come to them—never be faithful—never be worth the pain.

Taffy looked upward. "Well, you've got your hands full this time, Lord. Let me know if I can help." She put the gown aside. "I wish I were younger; maybe then they'd take me more seriously when I suggest the way to find real peace."

"Who are you talking to?" Eleanor asked as she reappeared with the water.

Taffy smiled. "You know me. Sometimes I talk to God, sometimes I talk to myself."

Eleanor put the bucket on the floor and straightened. She gave Taffy a look that suggested she didn't see the value of either option. "I'll get the vacuum and then mop the floor. If you'll strip the bed, I'll wash the linens while the floor dries."

"We must dust first," Taffy said, glancing around the room. "I learned that from the housekeeper who cared for one of the former governors in New York. We were talking one day about housekeeping, and she, being a paid servant, felt no hesitation in expressing her opinion. She was of Irish decent, so she gave her opinion with great enthusiasm. I simply love the Irish—don't you?" she asked, then continued without waiting for an answer. "She told me it was important to open the windows, dust the room, then let it settle for exactly ten minutes before sweeping the floors. I would imagine we should leave the linens in place while dusting—that way the dust will collect on the bedding and it can then be laundered."

Eleanor considered the suggestion for a moment. "Very well." She went to open the windows while Taffy smiled to herself. Eleanor didn't always like her advice, but when she saw the logic of it, she generally acquiesced.

"You remember that woman, don't you? The Irish maid. What was her name?"

"Mrs. Lindquist," Eleanor said flatly.

"Oh, that's right, she married a Swede. He worked in the garage. Big man, with thick blond hair and a drooping mustache. I wouldn't have wanted to kiss that mug."

Eleanor looked at her in shock. Taffy merely laughed.

Sometimes it was fun to shock the sour look off her niece's face. "Well, would you?"

"I never really considered it, nor do I desire to do so now."

"Well, you do remember them, don't you?"

"Of course. I was fifteen when I first accompanied you to their house."

Taffy nodded. "You were indeed."

Seven

THE MENTION OF being fifteen caused Eleanor a moment of serious panic. Sometimes she could stave off the past—almost forgetting the life she'd known before coming to live with Aunt Taffy and Uncle Cal. But other times she couldn't.

Often the past came drifting in like a slow-moving cold front, chilling everything in its wake. But once in a while it roared down on her like a powerful tornado, devastating—destroying—leaving her in complete despair.

Eleanor had repeatedly told herself that the past couldn't hurt her if she didn't let it. Unfortunately, she hadn't figured out a way to keep it from creeping in on occasion. Like now. Eleanor felt her thoughts drift back in time as she began to dust the framed pictures. She felt herself slip away, powerless to ignore the memories.

———

"Mom, are the police going to come back and take some people away again?" Eleanor questioned her mother. The night before, she'd seen two of her parents' friends dragged away in handcuffs for drug possession.

"Eleanor, you're such a little worrywart," her mother proclaimed as she helped her daughter hang clothes on the line outside their house.

At twelve, Eleanor had no idea if this was true or not, but

her mother certainly had never proven herself to be a liar. "Mom, why aren't you worried? You have drugs too."

Melody Templeton, scarcely sixteen years her daughter's senior, had embraced the '60s lifestyle with great flourish . . . and never walked away, even as the decade came to a close. "We aren't meant to worry. That's something the establishment wants from the people. If the government can keep the people in fear, then they'll be less likely to break free and revolutionize life for themselves—for everyone."

"But if drugs are illegal," Eleanor tried to reason, leaning over the basket of wet laundry, "shouldn't we get rid of them?"

Her mother sighed in exasperation. "But who says they're illegal—and why do they say that? It's the establishment again. They want to keep the masses as unhappy as possible. They don't want us to free our minds and be creative."

Eleanor picked up one of her mother's long skirts and shook it out. Hanging it over the line, she pushed two clothespins down to hold it in place. Her mother and father were always talking about the woes and harms caused them by the establishment. Eleanor had never understood who they were speaking of until the night before, and the whole event had frightened her greatly.

"But will they come again?" Eleanor couldn't help but ask.

"I suppose it's possible. They hate us, so they'll try to destroy us."

Eleanor frowned. In her secluded world of free love and harmonious feelings, hate was something she didn't understand. "Why do they hate us?"

Melody picked up the last skirt in the basket and flung it over the line in a haphazard manner. "Because we're free and they aren't."

"But why can't they be free too? Then they wouldn't hate us."

"They can never be free until they get rid of their rules and laws," her mother explained before walking back toward the run-down shack they called home.

Eleanor followed a pace behind, contemplating her mother's words. Melody continued in a way that suggested the entire conversation was futile. "They won't get rid of their laws because they don't know how."

"How did we figure it out, then?"

"We had smart people, people who weren't afraid to expand their minds and look beyond the reality of what we'd become. We were all living in fear—living in chains. Everybody was worried about wars and when the bomb might be dropped on us." Melody stopped and looked at her daughter. "Do you know that when I went to school we actually practiced trying to protect ourselves from the bomb? Duck and cover, they called it. We would drop down and cover our heads. As if that was going to keep us safe if a bomb fell on us. The whole notion of the bomb was just used to keep the people in line; I don't think it has ever been a real threat. Keeping people scared is like, well, it's an opiate for the government. Duck and cover has been the mentality of the establishment ever since. They don't want to see the truth because the truth is too frightening. Better to stay with what they know—even if they're miserable."

Her mother's words simply didn't make any sense to Eleanor. She wanted to ask her more questions, but there were chores to do.

"Eleanor, go find your brothers. I think they're fishing. Tell them it's time to help in the garden."

Eleanor pushed back her stringy blond hair and ambled off toward the creek, visions of flashing police car lights in her mind. Those people had frightened her so much she'd been unable to sleep until well into the night. She hoped they never came back with their rules and regulations.

The oldest of five, Eleanor took her responsibilities in stride. There weren't many demands placed upon her. Their communal life was one that allowed for many freedoms. Her days were spent helping raise herbs and do household chores, and then she had a few hours of schooling. Eleanor loved to read and would read anything she could get her hands on. Unfortunately, the commune didn't have many books; her parents didn't allow for any with "decadent worldly views." It was also the reason they had no television, although Eleanor had heard about the device from one of her friends.

"Ellie! Ellie!" Sapphira called as she approached at a dead run. Sapphira Newton was a good friend, and Eleanor always had the best times with her.

"I have to get my brothers from the creek," she told Sapphira.

"I'll come with you. I want to tell you about Marty." The dark-haired girl gasped the words as she halted just short of Eleanor's lanky frame, struggling to regain her breath. "I ran all the way," she said, as if to explain.

"What's going on with Marty?"

"Well, you know it was her dad they took last night—along with his friend Joe?"

Eleanor nodded. "I know."

"Well, Marty said her mother went to town to talk to the pigs who took him. They ended up calling Marty's grandfather, and now Marty may be leaving."

"Why would she leave?"

Sapphira shrugged. "I don't know. Marty's all upset. Said her mom came home crying and talking about how unfair life was."

Eleanor listened as she continued toward the creek. She could hear her brothers Allan and Tommie even from this distance, and it didn't sound like they were fishing. Their mom was going to be mad at them if they came home empty-handed.

There was some sort of herbal remedy their mother planned to make, and she needed fish oil or some part of the fish.

"I hope Marty doesn't go away," Eleanor said, still thinking about the night before. "I thought it was scary when the police came."

"Call them pigs. That's what my dad calls them. He says they're no better than a bunch of stinking animals."

"But why? I thought we were supposed to love everybody. My mom said that the world would be a perfect place if everyone would just love one another and let each person do their own thing." To Eleanor the contrast of responses was confusing. How could they treat some people—like those in the government—poorly but respect others and supposedly love everyone?

"But the pigs don't want us to do our own thing," Sapphira countered, as if Eleanor should already know this. "My dad says we're a threat to them, so they have to try to put us in our place before we try and overtake them."

"But if we're loving everybody, why would we be overtaking anybody?"

"Beats me."

Eleanor came to the shallow creek banks. "Allan! Tommie! You're supposed to come home now."

Moans from the four- and six-year-old followed, but Eleanor was not moved. "Right now!"

"I don't wanna," the older Allan protested.

"Momma said to come right now. There's work to be done."

Eleanor knew other people in the community who barely did anything, but because her father was a doctor, he insisted on two things: one was that the family keep clean; the other was that they grow herbs for his healing practice. Both required a fair amount of work. Sometimes Eleanor resented the additional responsibility. It seemed Sapphira never had to do much of anything. She didn't even have to bathe, which was evidenced by her matted hair.

Rounding up her brothers, Eleanor turned to Sapphira. "Can you come over later?"

"Oh, for sure. I think my folks are going somewhere tonight. I'll come over when they leave."

Eleanor nodded. "My mom said something about a party, so maybe they're all going to the same place."

With her brothers trotting off toward home, Eleanor considered the things she had heard and seen in the last twenty-four hours. She couldn't understand why people were so cruel to each other. She didn't understand why the police—or "the pigs"—should care if people smoked pot and used LSD. It wasn't like they were going anywhere or hurting anybody. It didn't make sense.

By late afternoon Eleanor had worried herself half crazy with the issues at hand. She was relieved when her mother suggested she take a bag of herbs to her father's clinic. The worn-down trailer was on the opposite side of the small hippie community, and it provided Eleanor a bit of time to put together in her mind exactly what it was she would ask her father.

She opened the trailer door without knocking. That's the way it was for most every place in the commune, be it houses or businesses, although in truth there weren't many of the latter. Freed people didn't seem too inclined to spend their days in long labor. Eleanor often wondered how people got their money, but she figured part of it had to do with drugs. She knew several people raised pot; still, it hardly seemed enough to support the community.

"Dad?" she called out from the front office area. Her father had always given her strict instructions to never come into the back rooms, as this was where he examined patients.

"Hey there, Ellie girl," her father said, emerging from the back room with a guy Eleanor knew only as Coon. "Now keep that cut clean, and it should heal just fine."

"You still want me to work on your carburetor, man? You know, like to pay for this?"

Eleanor's father seemed to contemplate the situation. "Give your hand a rest for at least two days, then you can look at my van. It's not like we're planning a trip anywhere long distance."

Coon laughed in a snorting kind of way and nudged his elbow at Eleanor. "You plannin' any trips, little sister? Gonna run off with your boyfriend?"

Eleanor shook her head. "I don't have a boyfriend."

"You should," he said, letting his eyes travel the full length of her body.

"What're you doin' here, Eleanor?"

Her father's tone told her he wasn't pleased. Eleanor wasn't sure what she'd done wrong, but she shrugged it off. "Mom sent this stuff," Eleanor replied, placing the bag on the counter.

Her father, hair just below his collar and his face bearing a beard and mustache, was Eleanor's favorite person in the entire world. She adored the man. He picked up the bag, undid the twist tie, and sorted through several small clusters of dried herbs.

"Is that pot, Doc?" Coon's eyes widened.

"No, it's medicinal herbs. I'll see you later, Coon. Go take care of your hand."

The man frowned, definitely disappointed in the dismissal. "Okay. I'll see you later."

Eleanor's father waited until Coon was gone before he closed the bag. "This is exactly what I needed." He put it aside and offered his daughter a smile. "So how's your day, Ellie?"

"Rotten." She jumped up on a bar stool and frowned. "I'm afraid. I don't like what happened last night."

Her father crossed his arms against his chest. "I didn't either. Those were good men who didn't deserve to be hassled."

"Well, I heard now that Marty might have to leave because of it."

Her father seemed to consider her words a moment. "Seems gossip gets around fast, but the truth of it is, she might. The fuzz wasn't at all happy with her father or her mother. When her mother went to see about the arrest, she was threatened with jail too."

"Why?"

Her father sighed. "They're worried that Marty's at risk by living like we do."

"But what's wrong with how we live?"

"There's nothing wrong with the way we live. But the way we live tends to annoy those who aren't living that way."

"Mom said they were living in chains." Eleanor shifted, thinking back over the things she had wanted to ask her father. "But why can't they live the way they want and we live the way we want?"

"A good question. We keep asking that too." He sat down on a stool opposite her. "You don't remember when we came here or why, do you?"

"I only know what you have told me."

"Well, we lived in a big city and it was horrible. There was so much pollution in the air and war talk all the time. People were afraid of everything. Crime was really getting bad. People were killing each other over the stupidest thi—"

"Nobody has ever killed anybody here," Eleanor interrupted. "A lot of people got born, though." She was thinking of her brothers and the many other children in the community. Her father had boasted of delivering more than forty kids over the last eight years.

"That's right. We have no reason to kill. We're at peace with nature and one another. We aren't harming our bodies, we eat good food, and we use the remedies offered by mother earth for our medicines. That's not at all the way the world is outside of our commune."

"But why? If we have a good life, why don't they want to have a good life too?" To Eleanor's logical mind, it didn't make sense that a person wouldn't want to have the best—to be happy.

"Ellie, the world is full of unhappy people. They aren't necessarily bad people, although they do bad things. But their unhappiness makes them do it. People rob one another because they're sure that what somebody else has will make them happy. People kill because they believe if that other person is gone, things will be better and they'll be happy. Every bad thing done is because someone is desperate to be happy. Yet day after day, they continue in their sorrow and bitterness. They judge one another's motives, positions, and hearts as if they were God and could see the truth about each person all at once."

"But the rest of the world thinks we're bad. I heard them call us 'stinkin' Commie hippies.' Why'd they say that?"

Her dad shook his head. "Because they don't understand. It's true enough we don't dress like the rest of the world. I used to wear a suit. I had to when I was training to become a doctor. When your mom was in boarding school, she had to wear a uniform. Did those things make us better people? I don't think so."

Eleanor knew her parents had grown up in structured environments. So structured, in fact, that her father had described it to be like a noose around his neck. They had both come from moneyed families, but the money couldn't make them happy—or so her father had said on more than one occasion.

"So what's a Commie?" Eleanor asked.

"Well, that's a person who believes in Communism."

She frowned, her brows knitting together. "Is that a bad thing?"

"I don't think so. People are terrified of it, however, because it's different. Communism focuses on everyone sharing everything they have with one another. It encourages people not to be rich or poor, but to be equal. It's just another way of living—one that even the Bible promotes."

"So if God wants us to live like this, why does the world hate us for doing that? I thought the Bible was a good thing."

"It is. But the world hated Jesus too. He even said so. There's a verse that talks about how the world hates me, so they'll hate you too. It's the sad truth of how things are."

Eleanor tried to comprehend it all. It seemed so silly that people should strive so hard and yet be so miserable. She worked up her courage and asked her father the same question she'd asked her mother earlier. "Will the police come back again?"

Her father leaned back on his stool and shrugged. "Probably. They really didn't know about us before, but now that they do, they'll probably hassle us until we choose to move or they haul us all out of here. They've already judged us to be lawbreakers; they'll probably come up with a few more laws and come back to tell us how bad we are."

"But we aren't bad," she protested. "We're good people. We were happy. Now I hate them and want them to stay away." She hadn't realized the anger that she held inside.

"No, Ellie. You don't hate them. It isn't right to hate. You need to love them. Love them because it's the right thing to do. They won't understand it, but it will make you feel better."

Eight

ELEANOR WENT HOME in time to find her mother topless, taking in the laundry they'd hung together earlier. Nudity was common in the commune. Children were taught not to be ashamed of their bodies, and Melody had often told her daughter that this was how God had made people, and that was how they should stay whenever it was comfortable to do so.

Eleanor had begun to grow very uncomfortable with the matter, however. She felt shy around other people and didn't like the way they stared. Especially as her body began to change and develop. The entire matter distressed her mother, who said that despite her efforts to give Eleanor an idyllic world, her daughter just didn't appreciate the effort.

"God never intended for Adam and Eve to leave the garden," her mother had once taught during homeschool. "And He certainly hadn't planned for them to wear clothing."

Eleanor supposed her mother was right. She had read the Bible for herself and saw that Genesis indeed revealed this truth. But still, now that things had changed—since Adam and Eve had left the garden—perhaps wearing clothes was a better idea than going around naked.

"Don't forget," Melody called from the line. "We're going over to Star and Ringo's tonight. I need you to watch the boys."

Eleanor nodded. Allan and Tommie were a handful, but three-year-old Deliverance and two-year-old Spirit were even more difficult to deal with. At least she could reason somewhat with the older two, but because of her mother's rejection of discipline in any form, Deliverance and Spirit were completely out of control at times. If Eleanor so much as threatened to spank one of them as she'd seen Sapphira's parents do with her younger siblings, Eleanor's mother would demand she "cool it."

Eleanor hated being told that. She felt it was a complete dismissal of her feelings. It was as if her mother were saying that her frustration was unimportant—that her feelings weren't valid. "Cool it" was her mother's response to every single protest Eleanor had ever made.

"Sapphira's coming over," Eleanor offered. "But we can watch the boys. No big deal."

Her mother turned and smiled. Her long silky hair blew gently in the breeze. *She really is a beautiful woman,* Eleanor thought. *I hope I'm pretty like her when I grow up.* Right now Eleanor felt totally out of sorts with her body. It seemed she was all legs and not very coordinated.

"Okay, but like, feed the boys before you get all caught up in playing with Sapphira—is that cool?"

Eleanor nodded and went into the house. All four boys were playing in the front room. Deliverance and Spirit were devoid of clothing, but Allan and Tommie still had on their pants. The boys were filthy from their day of play, but even then, they were never as dirty as some of the kids in the neighborhood. Most of the people weren't keen on baths—mainly because no one had running water. If you didn't go to the creek and carry water back, you didn't have it.

The smell sometimes bothered Eleanor. That was the one thing she found less than perfect about her world. It always seemed to stink. Whether it was pot smoke or dirty bodies, none of it appealed to her. Her father kept their household in better order than most, but only marginally. Melody often told her husband that he might be wrong about the medical value of cleanliness, and sometimes Eleanor thought her father was convinced that his very young wife might be right.

Eleanor rounded up a bowl for each boy and went to the stove, where a vegetable stew was simmering. She spooned it up, mashed the vegetables for the younger two, then put it on the table with thick slices of bread. Her mother was a decent cook, but it was never anything too elaborate or exciting. Eleanor could remember one time when someone brought in a case of chocolate bars for the commune. The flavor had been unlike anything she'd ever known or had experienced since. She asked her mother when they might have some more chocolate, but Melody Templeton wasn't at all supportive of the notion.

"It's not natural," her mother had declared, and that was the end of the candy bar conversation.

To Eleanor's relief, supper went smoothly. Her mother and father slipped in, changed clothes, and left before the boys finished their food and began to fight. Eleanor shooed Allan and Tommie outside to play, while doing her best to clean up Deliverance and Spirit. She'd just finished when Sapphira popped her head in the open door.

"Are your folks gone?"

"Yes," Eleanor replied in exasperation as Spirit refused to open his hand in order for her to wash it. Prying his little fingers apart, Eleanor gave a quick swipe with the washcloth and then let him down. "I'm going to put the babies in their beds."

Deliverance and Spirit howled at the injustice of being taken to their bedroom, but at least here Eleanor knew they would be safe and eventually fall asleep. The five kids shared a small bedroom where three rather beat-up mattresses were placed on the floor. There was nothing else in the room—there wasn't space for anything else.

"It's nighty-night time," she told the boys as she tucked them into their places on the mattress. No doubt they'd get up and play or fight with each other, but at least they were out of her hair.

The boys cried and screeched from behind the closed door while Eleanor began clearing away the dinner mess. Sapphira wasn't inclined to help but instead struck up a conversation.

"They're leaving."

Eleanor precariously balanced a stack of dishes. "Who's leaving?"

"Marty and her mom. They're packing their car."

"Where will they go?"

"Out there somewhere," Sapphira replied. "I guess they'll go live with Marty's grandma and grandpa. My mom said that Marty's mom hasn't been happy in a long time and she always figured they'd leave."

Eleanor had heard the same thing from her parents. There were several people in the community, folks who hadn't been there all that long, who never seemed happy. They didn't cause trouble, at least; that was what Eleanor's father always said. He figured that as long as they didn't cause trouble, it was okay for them to stay around.

"Sometimes, Ellie," he had explained, "it takes a lot of effort and time to wash the world out of your system. Some people try and are never able to do it."

"I don't think they'll like it any better out there," Eleanor said as she finished putting the last of the dishes in the sink. She would let her mother worry over washing them. As Eleanor glanced around the kitchen, she could see there were already plenty of other dishes that needed attention. She hoped her mother wouldn't ask Eleanor to go for the water this time. Allan was getting big enough to help with that chore. In fact, Eleanor would send her brother down to the creek to get the water before her mother could ask.

"I'm going to have the boys get some water," she told Sapphira. "I'll be right back."

"Allan! Tommie!" she called as she exited the house. Both boys were lying face down on the ground, running toy cars over mounds of dirt. It was nearly dark.

"Allan, I need some water. Take the bucket and go down to the creek."

"I don't wanna."

"You never wanna do anything," Eleanor protested. "Just do it or I'll make you go to bed right now."

She knew the last thing her brothers wanted was the dreaded threat of bedtime. Reluctant and grumbling all the way, the boys moved off to do the chore.

"I can't stand boys," Sapphira announced from the doorway.

"I can't either," Eleanor agreed. "They're lazy and they always complain." She sat down on the step outside the back door, and Sapphira did likewise.

"Do you ever wonder what it's like out there?" Eleanor finally asked, then added, "In the world."

Sapphira seemed pleased with the topic of conversation. "Oh sure. Don't you?"

"Well, I hadn't so much until last night. I wondered what it would be like to be taken away to another place. To live somewhere else. My dad says the cities are full of unhappy people who do bad things because they think that will make them happy."

"I think I'd like to move away. I think my parents are crazy," Sapphira stated boldly.

Eleanor looked at her friend aghast. "How can you say that?"

"Well, because it's true. Do you know that the houses in the city have bathrooms and water that runs through pipes? They have electricity and air-conditioners in the summer."

"I've heard about the bathrooms and kitchens, but so what? They aren't free. They have to pay for all that stuff."

"Maybe, but there's television too. I saw a television once. It was the grooviest thing. I want a TV so bad."

"My dad says TV is a bad influence. It ruins our happiness. They show things there that make people unhappy with what they have."

"What do you mean?" Sapphira asked, her tanned face wrinkling slightly as she pondered the matter.

"Well, they show people with all sorts of things. Sometimes it's things you didn't even know you didn't have or need. Dad says it makes people who are otherwise happy suddenly believe they aren't happy, and all because they don't have something they saw on the TV."

"Well, I saw this cool show called *The Beverly Hillbillies*. It was so funny. It had some people sort of like us. They didn't dress like fancy people, and they did a lot of stuff by hand like we do."

"That doesn't sound that cool," Eleanor countered.

"Well, they weren't exactly like us. They were funny. They were always doing things that other people didn't understand. Oh, and they were living in this fancy house, because they found oil on their property and all of a sudden were rich. The house was so beautiful." There was a hint of desire in Sapphira's voice. "They had a swimming pool in the backyard. I wish we had a swimming pool."

"We've got the creek," Eleanor said in disgust. "We've got a good life here. We don't have to answer to anybody else. I don't know why Marty and her mom would want to leave."

"Well, I heard that Katie's mom was thinking of running off too. Katie told me in secret right before I came here."

"But why would they want to go?" Eleanor wondered aloud. "I can't imagine ever leaving here. I love it."

"Well, Katie said her mom wanted to get out before it got ugly."

"What does she mean by that?" Eleanor could see her brothers trudging back toward the house with the bucket sloshing water between them.

"I don't know, but apparently Katie's mom thinks there's going to be more trouble like last night."

Eleanor shuddered at the thought. "I hope she's wrong."

Later that night, Eleanor waited for her parents to come home. As usual, her mother was high on something. She stumbled into the house, laughing her head off and mumbling something about being hungry. She patted Eleanor on the head, then went to the kitchen and began rustling through the cupboards.

"Dad?"

Her father looked at her oddly for a moment. His gaze appeared distant even as he spoke. "Ellie girl, what are you doing up so late?"

"Sapphira said that Marty and her mom were going to leave here. She said Katie and her mom were going to leave too. Why are they leaving, Dad?"

"Why shouldn't they?" he asked, his words a bit slurred.

"I don't understand."

"It's a free world, Ellie girl. People can come and go as they like. That's the beauty of it. That's what makes our way so much better." He swayed a bit, then stabilized himself by grabbing hold of the table. "They shouldn't stay if they aren't happy. Life is all about harmony. They need to find the harmony."

Eleanor thought about what he'd said well into the night. She tossed and turned on her mattress, wishing she could make sense of everything. Sometimes she felt like she didn't belong. She loved her folks and her brothers, but sometimes things just didn't seem to fit.

Nine

THE NEXT DAY Eleanor tried to push aside her discomfort and fears for the future. Sapphira was too busy to come over, but that was okay too. Eleanor had more than enough work to keep her busy. Her mother had told her to wash the dishes after Eleanor's father had demanded the place be cleaned up.

By evening Eleanor had pretty much forgotten her worries. The boys had been particularly rowdy and had been sent to bed early. It was a relief to have the house quiet and more or less to herself. Her mother was doing something in the back room, but it didn't involve Eleanor, so she sought her own amusements.

"Now, how does this work?" She positioned some yarn around a crochet hook. Sapphira's mother had been trying to teach her to crochet, but it wasn't going well. Saphhira's mom had promised she'd be good at it in no time, so Eleanor kept practicing.

Winding yarn around her finger, Eleanor focused hard on the stitches. She thought at one point she heard someone yelling, but she ignored it. There were often fights and screaming matches between couples throughout the commune. It never amounted to much, and as her father always said, it was best not to crowd someone else's space.

But just as she thought things were calming down, there were additional voices. Loud, obnoxious voices. Name-calling and loud comments edged with hysteria caused Eleanor to forget her craft. She ran to the window and pressed her nose to the smudged and dirty glass.

They were back.

She could see the police cars from here; this time there were four of them. "Dad!" she called, then realized her father was still at his makeshift office.

"Mom, you'd better get in here!" Eleanor yelled.

Her mother came in from the back room and wiped her wet hands on her long patchwork skirt. She wore a halter top that was more revealing than concealing and a headband to hold her hair in place.

"What's the buzz?"

"Cops are back," Eleanor said, then watched her mother's face in order to gauge how critical this turn of events might be.

Her mother cursed softly. "I'd better hide my stash in case they want to search the place." She turned to go, but Eleanor couldn't help reaching out for her.

"Mom, will they try to . . . will they . . . take us? Will they take more people?" Her mother frowned and pulled away.

"I don't know, Eleanor. Now keep it down. Your brothers are sleeping, and you don't want to get them all stirred up. Stay here and keep the lights off." She leaned over and blew out the lamp Eleanor had been using. "I mean it. Keep it off."

Her mother's orders did nothing to put Eleanor's mind at ease. In fact, they had the opposite effect. Her mother sounded frightened.

Eleanor eased back against the glass and stared into the darkness. She couldn't be sure, but it looked like Ringo, Dwight, and Moody were all arguing with the cops. The three men were good friends of her parents, and Moody was even Sapphira's uncle.

Eleanor knew she shouldn't leave the house, but she couldn't resist. She pulled on her shoes and crept out the front door. The commune was nothing more than a few shacks, tents, and trailers all congregated on a piece of land owned by one of the members' parents. Eleanor knew this because her father had once revealed their circumstances when Eleanor had asked about land ownership. Her father was completely against owning property, as he felt that no one could really "own" a piece of land. He told Eleanor he felt that way because years ago, their ancestors had been Native Americans who roamed the land at will.

Eleanor wrinkled her nose at the smell of rotting garbage and trash. There was no trash pickup here in the middle of nowhere. Most of the time it accumulated until Eleanor's father talked some of the men into burning it for the sake of community health. Eleanor had seen big rats running through the mess, and now as she crept along beside the piles, she feared each step, knowing that if she stepped on a mouse or other animal she'd scream for sure.

Using the debris as a shield from prying eyes, Eleanor eased in close enough to hear the conversation.

"You hippies think you can just do whatever you want. Dodge the draft, use your drugs," one man was saying.

"Not to mention avoiding income tax," another authoritative voice declared. "Half the vehicles here aren't even properly tagged," the same man added.

"We don't have no hassles with you, man," Moody piped up. "You got no right to be out here giving us a hard time."

Eleanor moved in closer to better view the situation. A crowd was beginning to gather, and the tension of the confrontation was building. The sheriff and his men had big flashlights they were using as well as the headlights of their cars. It gave everything a distorted appearance. People's faces looked harsher— more brutal. Even Moody looked like a shadowy monster. Eleanor pulled back.

"You have to pay taxes if you're going to be a citizen of the United States of America. That's the law." This came from the only outsider who wasn't in uniform.

"That's your law, man. We don't recognize it." This came from Ringo.

"That's right, dude, we don't need your laws and your war machines. We've got a better way," Moody added.

"You potheads. What would you know about war or the law?" another man questioned. "I don't suppose I care what happens to you, but you've got kids here as well."

"Our kids are cool, man. There ain't nothing wrong with them," Ringo protested. "They know how to love. Your kids only know how to make war and more rules, but your way is dying. Your time is over."

"We'll see about that." The man in the suit stepped forward. "You're all in violation of the tax codes. Investigations are going to commence. I will return here in the morning. Meanwhile, the sheriff and his men will see to it that you have no chance to run off and hide."

"All we want is to live in peace," Star announced as she joined her husband. "We just want to live in peace."

"Yeah, you pigs need to go back to your mess in the city."

"Yeah, get out of here," several yelled in unison.

Eleanor trembled at the sound of the next voice.

"We all need to calm down."

Daddy! Would they take him? She moved toward the group, terrified that someone would see her and take her away, yet equally fearful that the officers might leave with her father and she'd never see him again.

"We'll give the orders here," the man in charge said as he came to stand directly in front of her father. "Who are you anyway?"

"I'm Dr. Allan Templeton."

"A doctor? Sure you are, and I'm the mayor of Los Angeles." The men around him chuckled.

"I am a doctor, and that fact doesn't change just because you choose not to believe me. I did my residency in New York City; you'll have little trouble tracking that down."

The sheriff seemed to reconsider. "Then what are you doing out here with these drug freaks? Why have you let your hair grow down to your shoulders? Doctors make good money, but I can't imagine that's the case out here—unless you're making your money illegally."

"There's more to life than making money," Dad countered.

"But you need money to stay alive."

"There are worse things than death."

Eleanor shivered at her father's words. What could possibly be worse than death?

"Look, mister, if you are practicing as a doctor out here, you owe taxes on every cent you make." The man in the suit stepped closer to Eleanor's father, as if to emphasize his words.

"I don't take pay for my practice."

"Then how do you exist? Goodwill doesn't put food on the table or gas in your car."

"Doesn't it?"

Eleanor watched her father. His calm demeanor seemed to cut through the malice the strangers obviously felt for the commune people. She was proud of him. Proud of the way he stood up for what he believed.

"Doc, you don't make a whole lot of sense. But I guess I shouldn't expect you to—after all, you're living out here. Probably fried your brain on that LSD and speed."

Eleanor's father kept his voice low and unexcited. "I simply mean that we work the land together, we share things, we offer

89

help where it is needed. I don't have much use for money."

"Even if you work for barter, you have to pay taxes," the man reiterated.

"I don't believe you're out here without funds. You have to have clothes and bedding," the sheriff countered. "I don't suppose medicine comes free either."

"It does if you grow it yourself."

"You need money for seed."

Eleanor's father shrugged. "We have what we need, when we need it. Look around. Do we look like we're starving or sick?"

"You look sick all right. I can hardly stomach the stench. Don't you people believe in taking a bath? You smell like yesterday's garbage. And speaking of which, look at the piles around here. It's worse than the dump. This place will be condemned as soon as the health department gets word of it. If you're such an intelligent and educated man, why'd you allow this kind of thing?" The man didn't wait for an answer. "Guess he's dumber than he looks. Probably practicing some sort of voodoo hippie medicine."

Eleanor wanted to rush forward and defend her father. He was a very smart man. Why, he'd saved several people when they'd gotten sick. Sapphira said it was from drug overdoses, but Eleanor didn't care. Her father had been the one to save them, and that was what mattered. She started to step forward but felt someone take hold of her and pull her back. She looked up. It was Daniel, Sapphira's father. He put his finger to his lips and Eleanor nodded.

"Sheriff, I want this entire area quartered off. Round up the people you think you must, but otherwise, just secure them and keep them from leaving. I want to bring in additional people to help us. Maybe even get some national guardsmen."

"So they can shoot us?" someone cried out. "Like at Kent State?"

"Guess they hear the news occasionally. Probably never keep up with it though. Probably know nothing about the moon landing or that Bobby Kennedy got shot down."

Eleanor wondered about the comments. Who was Bobby Kennedy? And had there really been some kind of moon landing? She looked up to the full moon overhead. It was too far away to fly to. Why would the man say such a thing?

"My concern is that this is another Manson family," the sheriff said in a serious tone. "That Charles Manson and his hippies were no different than this bunch. Said they wanted to make things right in the world—so they murdered innocent people."

Eleanor had no idea who Charles Manson was. She looked to Daniel in hopes that he might offer answers, but he merely pushed her back behind him and knelt. "Go home, Ellie. This is like really heavy stuff, and the pigs are probably gonna start something."

"But my daddy—" Ellie tried to protest, but Daniel again put his hand to her mouth. His dark brown eyes were pleading with her.

"Go home before they see you. Hide out. Go now." He turned her toward home.

"We aren't the killers, man. You are," someone challenged. "You with your guns and your big important titles."

Eleanor reluctantly headed toward the house, but her confusion was only mounting at the accusations hurled back and forth by the adults. At the sound of her father's voice, she stopped and turned. She couldn't see him, but there was comfort just in hearing his voice.

"We need to go back to our houses and deal with this in the

morning. The daylight will show these men that we're doing nothing wrong."

"You'd best listen to the doc. I'm staking my men at the opening of this field. You're not to leave the premises."

"Stupid pigs." Eleanor turned back to find her mother had joined her. "They won't be happy until they make us like them."

"Are they going to hurt Daddy?" Eleanor asked.

Her mother never even looked at her. "If they get the chance—they'll hurt us all."

Eleanor paced through the small house until well after midnight. Her mother and father were still talking with the others about the situation. The cops had pulled back to barricade the long road that led into the grassy field where the commune had been living. Eleanor felt her heart pounding rapidly and wished with all her might that she could turn back the hands of time to the days before the first drug raid.

Why did they have to come now? Why did they have to bother innocent people?

"Ellie girl, what are you doing up?" her father asked, coming into the kitchen.

Eleanor hadn't even heard her folks come home. She ran to her father and jumped into his arms, wrapping her arms and legs around him. "Daddy, I've been so scared."

"Stupid pigs," her mother spewed, then turned to light a joint she'd taken from her halter top.

"Daddy, are they going to take us away? Are they going to hurt us?"

"No, sweetie. We're safe enough. We might have to move, but so what? It's a beautiful country and we'll be all right." Her father's soothing voice and gentle touch reassured Eleanor. She clung to him nevertheless. "Where are your brothers?" he asked.

"Sleeping. I tried to sleep, but I kept hearing things. I figured they were comin' after me." Her voice broke despite her desire to be strong. She buried her face against her father's neck and cried.

"It's all right, Ellie. They aren't going to hurt you."

"Promise?" she asked, pulling away to look in his eyes.

He smiled. "Of course I promise."

She relaxed her hold a bit. "Can I sleep with you and Momma tonight?"

"Sure you can." He gave her light frame a bit of a toss in the air and then hugged her close.

That night, sandwiched between her mother and father, Eleanor finally found herself able to relax. She scooted close to her father and pulled his arm around her as if it were a blanket. They weren't going to hurt her. Her daddy had promised, and he had never lied to her.

Ten

"ARE YOU GOING to just keep dusting that dresser?" Taffy asked in a way that suggested more amusement than concern.

Eleanor pulled herself from the memories of the past and looked at the dresser. She didn't remember even going to work on it, much less how long she'd been there. "Sorry. I guess I was a bit lost in my thoughts."

"It happens to me all the time. Only they call it old age," Taffy said with a laugh. "I think it's just that when you're my age, you have far more memories and experiences to consider."

Eleanor said nothing. She'd lived through a lifetime of things she'd rather not have to remember. "Well, I believe we're ready to vacuum," she said, looking around the room.

Taffy began stripping the bed. "I'm so excited. Just think of the fun we'll have with Jana in the house."

Eleanor stared at her aunt for a moment. "I don't know why you think this will be so much fun. Jana will be depressed and angry."

"So you won't have the corner on that market anymore," Taffy teased.

Eleanor stiffened. "I beg your pardon?"

Taffy moved to Eleanor and took the duster from her hands. "You walk around here in a mope half the time. Maybe together the two of you can find a way to be happy."

"Taffy, I do not go around moping. I may not be as lighthearted as you are, but that doesn't mean I'm not happy. If you'd had to bear the sorrows and betrayals I've had to bear, you might very well think better of me."

Taffy's wrinkled expression sobered. "Child, I have never thought poorly of you. The things you've had to endure were heaped upon you. My sister, God rest her soul, was never able to face the responsibilities of being an adult. It was much easier to use drugs and a rebellious lifestyle to ease her misery. Your father—"

"Taffy, stop." Eleanor shook her head. "It does no good to go over and over the details of the past. Some things are better left alone."

"Sometimes that's true, but I can't help but think Jana will need to talk about what's happened to her, and we'll need to listen. There is a difference, you know, between dealing with a problem and simply pretending it never happened."

Eleanor felt a sense of annoyance. "Of course I know there's a difference. I also know it does little good to sit around talking and rambling on and on about the same old troubles."

"Do you?" Taffy asked, eyeing her with a raised brow. "I seriously doubt that. You haven't talked or rambled on since you first came to live with me. If I hadn't pried information out of you, I'd still be in the dark."

Eleanor opened her mouth to reply, but the doorbell sounded and drew Taffy's attention away from the conversation. "Oh, she's already here! And we haven't even vacuumed."

"I'll manage it. Let's go let her in and then you can entertain her while I finish," Eleanor said, grateful for the distraction.

Taffy was already out the door and halfway down the hall before Eleanor could follow. Eleanor always marveled at how well the old woman got around. She suffered a bit from arthritis but otherwise was, as she often pointed out, probably in better shape than Eleanor.

But Eleanor was grateful for her aunt's health. When Taffy had pleaded for her to come live with her, Eleanor had been certain the woman knew something devastating about her health. But as the years passed, Eleanor could see that Taffy had simply been lonely and was happy for the companionship.

The real adjustment had come on Eleanor's part. As usual. Eleanor had been alone for most of her life. Even when raising Jana, Eleanor had allowed Jana's father to pay for expensive boarding schools to keep the child out of her hair. Eleanor was adept at handling the solitude; it was interactions with others that stressed her out. She had never learned to find comfort in relationships. To her they were tedious and dangerous. In fact, every person she'd ever cared about had let her down in a big way—with exception to Taffy.

Taffy threw open the huge oak door, ready to receive Jana, and found Stanley Jacobs instead. Eleanor would have preferred the old man remain next door in his own home, but the eighty-two-year-old had an affection for her aunt that kept him a constant in their life.

"Taffy, darling. I thought you might want to come with me to Summerfest. It's been going on all day, and tonight there's even a dance."

"Oh, Stanley, come in, come in. I can't go to any dance tonight—my niece Jana is coming."

"Great-niece," Eleanor muttered.

"Yes, yes. She's my great-niece. The only one I have and she's due here today," Taffy said, reaching out to take hold of Stanley. "You will have to come later and meet her. We should probably plan a party to welcome her."

"Taffy, the circumstances hardly warrant a party. I'm sure that would only make Jana feel more conspicuous, and she can hardly want that." Eleanor cringed inwardly at the thought of someone imposing a party in the midst of such tragedy. *I would have absolutely died on the spot had someone tried to force that upon me.*

"I suppose we should give the girl time to adjust," Taffy replied, nodding. She patted Stanley's arm. "But you'll see. She's a sweet girl and she'll fit right in. She'll probably even go to church with us." She turned to Eleanor and smiled. "You're always welcome too."

Eleanor refused to take the bait. Taffy had been after her for years to piece back together the relationship she had once had with God. "I need to get back to cleaning that room." Eleanor headed for the stairs, determined not to give the matter another thought.

Taffy shook her head once Eleanor had disappeared from sight. "That girl has never allowed her hurts to heal."

"Some folks can't. They pick at it like a wound until it's all festering and infected," Stanley said. "So who is this great-niece you've got coming? Is she as pretty as you?"

Taffy laughed and pushed Stanley ever so playfully. "She's twice as pretty and much smarter. She'd never be swayed by your sweet talk."

Stanley grinned impishly. He had a boyish charm about him that Taffy found very endearing. Her husband, Cal, had been charming too, but his charm had won him political seats and throngs of admirers, whereas Stanley's charm was much more down to earth. If Cal's charm had been a gourmet meal, then Stanley's was home-cooked fried chicken and mashed potatoes and gravy. Simple but filling.

Taffy leaned closer and lowered her voice. "Jana's husband left her. He was a pastor and he ran off with his secretary while Jana was in Africa on a missions trip. I don't know much else, but the poor girl is devastated. Apparently this was in the works for some time, and while she was abroad, her husband resigned from the church. The church hired a new pastor and *voila*! Jana has to be out of her house almost before she had time to realize what happened."

"That's a pity. Some fellas don't know a good thing when they have it in their hand."

"I'm amazed that a man of God could make such a choice. Of course, many people hide in pretenses of being saved. Perhaps he really didn't understand what it was to accept Jesus as his Savior."

"And maybe he did. We're all sinners and none of us is perfect," Stanley countered. "Just forgiven."

Taffy knew he was right, but already she was deeply concerned about her great-niece. And about Eleanor. The prospect of her only child coming to live under the same roof had set Eleanor on her ear.

"You will keep us in your prayers, won't you?" Taffy questioned.

"Of course," he replied. "And we'll continue our devotions each morning, right?"

"I wouldn't miss it for the world. What a wonderful way to start the day—reading the Word with a friend. I have no greater joy."

Eleanor stacked the dusty bedding outside the bedroom door and went back into the room. Unwinding the cord on the vacuum, Eleanor realized she felt almost panicked inside. Her nerves were stretched tight, and a heated, choking sensation had laid hold of her neck and head.

She grabbed for the end of the bed and managed to sink onto

the bare mattress instead of falling to the floor. She eased onto her back and closed her eyes. When she opened them again, the light fixture fairly danced in a side-to-side motion, while the rest of the ceiling seemed to swirl in a pulsating rotation.

"I don't have time for this," she moaned. Panic attacks were not unknown to her, but she had to admit she hadn't had one since coming to live with Taffy.

What's wrong with me? I should be able to handle this situation. But even those thoughts caused her heart to beat a little harder and her breathing to accelerate. Having spent numerous years in the company of panic attacks, Eleanor knew she needed to slow her breathing and take in deeper breaths. As she did this, the tingling sensations that ran up and down her arms ceased and she started to relax.

This is all about Jana. If Jana weren't coming here, I wouldn't be feeling like this. The thought made Eleanor angry. *My life has been spent in relative peace these last years. Why does she have to change all of that now? Why can't she run to a friend?* But even as she asked herself the question, Eleanor knew the answer. She'd never taught Jana to have friends. In fact, she'd warned her daughter that whenever the moment presented itself, she should trust no one.

"You've done this to yourself, Eleanor. You have no one else to blame. If you hadn't been so convinced that friendships and relationships were dangerous, then maybe you wouldn't have insisted that Jana feel the same way." Eleanor spoke as if there were another person in the room. It was the way she often addressed herself, scolding and rebuking as though speaking to a rebellious child.

The spell passed but left her feeling weak, spent. She sat up and pressed her fingers against her temples. "I won't let this happen. I won't allow Jana's problems to completely upset my life. I need peace and order, and I will have it. Or . . . I'll move back to New York and Jana can be Taffy's companion."

Eleanor forced herself to get to her feet. She put her toe to the lever on the vacuum and went to work. She felt better just knowing there was a way out. After all, she'd been happy in New York. She still went back to check on the shop four times a year. It wouldn't be hard at all to move back. She had rented out her house there and the lease was up in two months. Perhaps she could even pay the tenants something to move early.

Her mind clicked into high speed, and with it, all feelings of helplessness passed. She had the room vacuumed and mopped in less than twenty minutes, then hauled the supplies and bedding downstairs without giving her daughter another thought.

I have a contingency plan, she told herself. *I'll set it in motion, and if I need it, I'll use it. I won't be a victim. I don't have to be a victim anymore.*

Eleven

JANA'S FIRST GLIMPSE of Aunt Taffy's house brought back a surge of painful memories from the previous Christmas. She'd talked Rob into making her first and only trip to Lomara in hopes of creating a tie to the only living relatives she had. Her mother had immediately thought it a suspicious attempt to spy. Jana could hear the accusations even now.

"I suppose you've come to see what might be in this for you," had been one of her mother's first statements, followed by, "We don't need you here, and there isn't any chance of you and your husband getting your hands on Taffy's wealth. Perhaps it would be best if you just gave her the gifts you've brought and left."

Jana shut the engine off and stared at the house. No doubt there would be new accusations, new hurtful comments. *If there had been any other way,* she told herself, *I never would have come. No one is foolish enough to put themselves through that kind of pain for no good reason.*

But of course, she had a good reason. The child she carried needed to be cared for properly, and Jana had no chance of doing that on her own. She wasn't one who could easily admit defeat, but in this moment, Jana was certain she had lost not only the battle, but also the war to come.

Stepping from the car, Jana looked at the three-story house. She recalled that Taffy referred to it as being two-and-a-half stories because, as she said, "The attic is hardly worthy of being called a 'story' unto itself."

The thought made Jana smile. Taffy was the only thing that made coming here bearable. Jana had long wanted to know the woman better. Now maybe she'd have that chance.

Jana looked again to the house with its dark blue shutters and glossy white porch. The porch itself was quite inviting. It wrapped around a good portion of the house and had several nice pieces of lawn furniture that beckoned her. It was an appropriate porch for such a large place. Jana remembered that within were massive rooms with high ceilings reminiscent of the Victorian age, rather than the 1950s, when it was built. It certainly had far more room than two older women could possibly have use for. It had a nice big yard too. That would be nice for the baby.

What am I thinking? I don't plan to be here long enough for the baby to enjoy being outdoors. Jana shook the thoughts from her mind. *I have to find a way to become self-sufficient in a very short time. I can't stay here and endure my mother's insults.*

"Jana!" Taffy called from the porch.

Jana hadn't even seen her aunt come out the front door. She forced a smile and waved, then froze in place as her mother stepped out behind Taffy.

"Jana, I thought you would never get here," Taffy announced. She swept down the porch steps wearing some kind of mauve and green creation. Jana thought perhaps it was lounging pajamas, but as her aunt approached she could see it was more of a dinner party-type outfit. Far more dressy than Jana's casual "after-six" arrival deserved.

"We expected you much earlier."

"I know. I'm sorry. I stopped for lunch and it took longer than I thought it would," Jana explained as Taffy embraced her. There was no sense in telling the older woman that the lunch stop had been extended due to Jana's nausea.

"Don't worry about your things just yet. Let's first get you into the house and feed you. You must be famished," Taffy said, pulling Jana along. "I've been cooking all afternoon and have a wonderful chicken pie made. I remembered that you liked that from last Christmas."

"I did," Jana replied. The thought of the sumptuous meal actually met with her stomach's approval. "It sounds delicious."

"Then come with me and eat. It will be light long into the evening, so there's plenty of time to retrieve your things afterward."

Jana did as she was told and allowed Taffy to take her to the house.

"Doesn't our girl look great, Eleanor?" Taffy questioned as they mounted the stairs.

"She looks exhausted," Eleanor said in a not quite insulting tone. The disapproval, however, was carried in her expression.

"I am tired," Jana said, deciding to ignore her mother's questionable look.

Taffy patted Jana's arm. "Of course you are. We'll make supper as easy on you as possible, then get you settled in your room. I've chosen to give you the Rose Room. It's next to mine and one of my favorites."

"Then I'm sure it will be my favorite too." She was grateful that her mother remained silent.

Over supper Taffy chatted about Lomara and all the things that were going on. She mentioned her church on three different occasions but didn't ask Jana about attending until the meal was nearly concluded.

"If you don't mind," Jana said with a quick glance in her mother's direction, "I would like to stay home. I'm particularly worn from this week's events, and I'd just like to have some quiet rest."

"Of course." Taffy offered Jana another helping of peach

cobbler. "I'm entirely insensitive to have even suggested such a thing. Your mother will be here if you need anything at all, and I should be back by twelve-thirty. We can have a nice lunch in the backyard garden. Well, it's not exactly a garden yet. The roses are just starting to bloom and the grass only greened up last week. We do things slowly here in Montana."

Any other time Jana might have relished the idea, but right now she needed rapid results and instantaneous answers. Slow simply wasn't in her vocabulary.

Eleanor dabbed her mouth with a napkin. "It's supposed to rain tomorrow."

Taffy considered this a moment. "I forgot. I did hear that on the weather this afternoon. Well, no matter. There will be plenty of time for outdoor dining."

Jana was unable to suppress a yawn. She knew her mother would consider it unacceptably rude, but she couldn't help herself. Taffy immediately got to her feet. "We can clear this away later. Come, let's help Jana get her things into the house." She was nearly halfway across the dining room before Jana could even push back her chair.

"I wish I had half your energy," she mumbled, not sure what else to say. She got to her feet to follow Taffy.

"I don't suppose I need to tell you how awkward this is for me," her mother suddenly said.

Jana stopped in midstep and turned. "I don't suppose I need to tell you how awkward this is for *me*. At least you haven't had your entire world turned upside down by someone you trusted to be there for the rest of your life."

Eleanor lifted her chin in an almost defiant pose. "I hope you don't plan to dump your baggage on us and cause grief to this household. We were enjoying a rather peaceful existence until you called."

"So was I, Mother," Jana said, turning to walk away. "So was I."

She fumed over her mother's words all the way out to the car. Why couldn't the woman ever put Jana first, instead of always playing things out as to how they related to her needs—her feelings? Jana was convinced that her mother had never made a selfless move in her entire life.

Taffy had already taken it upon herself to pull one of Jana's boxes from the back seat. "Is this all you have?" She glanced back over her shoulder at the car.

"Taffy, you shouldn't be lifting such heavy things," Jana said, taking the box from her great-aunt. "I have some things in the trunk as well, but if you want to help, there's a sack of baked goods on the front seat. One of the women in my church made them for you and Mom."

"Oh, how wonderful! I find church women to be the best cooks in the world." Taffy's enthusiasm helped to soften the blow of Eleanor's words.

"All I really need tonight is this box," Jana said, replacing the one Taffy had pulled out with another. "This has some of my clothes and overnight things. I can get the rest tomorrow."

"Oh, that sounds like a perfect plan," Taffy said, taking up the sack. She peered into it like a child unable to keep from sneaking a peak at her Christmas gifts. "I can smell wonderful things inside."

Jana grinned. "I had some of my own on the way. And you're right; they are wonderful." She was amazed at how much lighter her heart felt in Taffy's company.

"Well, come along and we'll indulge later. I want to make sure the Rose Room is to your liking."

Jana followed Taffy back into the house, having no idea where her mother had gone. She climbed the stairs, admiring the oak banisters and intricately carved newels at the base and landing. As if reading her mind, Taffy began to discuss the merits of the house.

"Cal spared no expense in building this place in the fifties. Then, of course, we had a large holding of land and the neighbors weren't so close. Those houses were mostly built in the seventies and eighties. But in its day, this old house was a showpiece."

"It still is. I think it's beautiful." And Jana meant every word. She had loved the house at first glance. Last winter, with snow trimming the porch and pine trees, the scene was suited for a postcard.

"Here we are," Taffy said, opening the door. "The Rose Room."

Jana stepped back in time as she crossed the threshold. She immediately had thoughts of Victorian sitting rooms. "It's . . . well . . . it's lovely." It took her by surprise.

"You can change it any way you like. I think it's rather perfect, but I know younger tastes often prefer a different way of decorating. You won't hurt my feelings—even if you'd prefer to find another room altogether. We have three others that aren't being used."

Jana put the box on the floor. "I think this will do very nicely. It's huge." She thought immediately of the baby. She would want room for a crib and dressing table. Then just as the thought came, Jana chided herself once again for imposing herself into the future of this household. *I'll have my own place by then,* she reminded herself.

"This room has served as refuge and respite for many people," Taffy told her. She went about the room, adjusting the drapes and making sure the pictures were hanging straight. She looked toward the door and then glanced over her shoulder before leaning into Jana conspiratorially. "In fact, several high government officials have shared this room. Including the governor of New York and his wife, who, I believe, and quite scandalously so, conceived their third child in this very bed."

Jana couldn't help but giggle at the look on Taffy's face. She was serious, but she had a devilish twinkle in her eyes.

"Taffy! That is an inappropriate thing to discuss," Eleanor declared from the open doorway.

Taffy rolled her eyes. "It isn't inappropriate. It's true. The governor's wife told me she suspected it herself."

"Well, it's a lovely room, and I'm certain it will suit me just fine," Jana said, watching as Taffy turned down the covers.

"The bathroom is down the hall. I couldn't remember if you'd ever made it upstairs for your brief visit at Christmas."

"No, there just didn't seem to be time."

Taffy nodded, as if suddenly remembering. "Eleanor, you did put fresh towels in the linen closet, didn't you?"

"Of course I did. Everything Jana could possibly need is easily accessible."

Jana looked at her mother and back to Taffy. "I'm sure I'll be fine."

"Wonderful." Taffy moved to the door where Eleanor remained. "We'll leave you to see to your needs and get some sleep. I promise to be as quiet as a church mouse in the morning, and when I return, we shall have a wonderful lunch. Agreed?"

Jana couldn't help but nod. "That sounds perfect."

When Jana slipped between the crisp sheets of the queen-sized bed an hour later, she sighed. The comfort was immediate, and before she even realized it, sleep came upon her and eased her pain.

———

Eleanor set the table for lunch and then went back to the kitchen to finish preparing the salad. Taffy hadn't instructed her to create a meal, but since she'd promised one to Jana, Eleanor figured the responsibility fell to her shoulders. After all, if they waited for Taffy to put it together, it would be two o'clock before they could sit down to eat.

Eleanor glanced upward and thought of Jana's arrival. Her daughter hadn't even bothered to come downstairs for breakfast. In fact, there'd not been so much as a single bit of noise coming from the Rose Room. Had Eleanor not been worried about how Jana might take the intrusion, she would have checked on her daughter. Something didn't seem quite right with Jana, but Eleanor had yet to put her finger on it. She knew of course that Jana was distraught over the breakup of her marriage, but there was something more. Of this Eleanor was certain.

It was strange to have Jana in the same house—living there as though all the years behind them had never taken place. They were both used to living in uncomfortable silences when it came to the past. Jana understood that this was Eleanor's wish, and while she had never had any real degree of sympathy for her mother's needs, Jana at least respected this one desire.

But how long could it last? How long could Jana be there with them and not cause the past to rear its ugly head—steal the only years of peace and contentment Eleanor had known?

"Hello, Mother," Jana announced from the archway into the dining room.

Eleanor looked up and noted her daughter's appearance. She was dressed in a casual zip-up maroon sweater, sleeves pushed up and neckline opened a bit. Her black jeans revealed a slender frame. "Did you sleep well?"

"Like the dead. I just woke up about fifteen minutes ago. I

think it's the first real sleep I've had since . . ." The words trailed off.

"So what are your plans, Jana? Are you getting a divorce?" Eleanor didn't mean for the questions to sound so interrogative, but years of no-nonsense business deals had left her with a certain standard and approach.

She heard Jana sigh, then watched as her only child walked to the back door and looked out on the yard. "Rob had papers served to me prior to my leaving Spokane. I brought them with me, and I suppose I'll have to get in touch with the lawyer at some point." She turned around. "As for my plans . . . well, I really don't have any."

The sound of a car door slamming let Eleanor know that Taffy was home. Stanley, ever sweet on Taffy, had shown up faithfully to drive her to church. She wished Taffy wouldn't ride with the man; he was ancient and no doubt negligent behind the wheel. But Taffy wouldn't hear any of Eleanor's concerns.

"That will be Taffy," Eleanor stated. She picked up the salad bowl and motioned to a basket of bread. "Bring that, would you?"

Jana nodded. "Something smells good."

"It's lasagna. I made it this morning."

Jana followed her into the dining room, the uneasy truce between them threatening to break at any moment. Eleanor could feel her daughter's contempt, but she refused to acknowledge it. Not now. Not with Taffy due to bound through the door at any moment.

And bound she did. The elderly woman swept into the room like a grand dame of regal background. She wore a bold purple suit and a huge hat that was trimmed in all manner of decoration. Eleanor cringed inwardly and forced condemning comments from her lips.

"Taffy! You look wonderful! And what a great hat." Jana's

enthusiasm only served to frustrate Eleanor further. Jana had said nothing about Eleanor's cream-colored sweater and camel-colored slacks. The outfit was far more distinguished than her aunt's brazen attempt to thumb her nose at sensible fashion.

"Why, I simply love to wear hats. I think everyone should wear them. Back in my day, a lady never went out without a hat; it simply wasn't appropriate. Gloves too. Why, I was just telling Eleanor the other day that women should wear gloves more often. They give you a feeling that nothing else can. A sort of elegance in tiny white packages." Taffy turned to the dining room buffet mirror and pulled a large hatpin from the oversized creation. She pulled the hat from her head and replaced the pin before placing the hat atop the buffet.

"I believe that must be Eleanor's marvelous lasagna I smell. I've been hoping to convince your mother to make it. You'll absolutely love her recipe." She turned to Eleanor. "Thank you, dearie, for your hard work." She surprised Eleanor with a quick peck on the cheek before moving to where Jana stood. "And are you feeling better today?"

"Yes, thank you. The bed was so very comfortable."

"Goose down!"

The declaration left Jana staring wide-eyed, but Taffy wasn't in the least bit concerned. "The top mattress is goose down. I think it always adds a special touch for sleeping."

"Well, it definitely did the trick for me. I told Mother it was the first decent sleep I've had in some time."

Eleanor put the salad on the table. "Dinner is ready if you are."

"I'm very ready. Come, Jana. Let's sit down and Eleanor can serve us. She hates it when there are too many people in the kitchen."

Eleanor wanted to comment but didn't. Instead, she went

after the lasagna and brought it to the table. "I hope you don't mind, but I've poured iced tea for each of us."

"That's perfect," Taffy said. "I once had red wine with lasagna and thought it a beastly combination. I've never taken to spirits like some. Of course, in Washington, D.C., spirits accompanied every meal and conversation." She pulled out her napkin from under the silver and gave it a firm shake. "Shall we pray?"

Eleanor watched as her aunt bowed her head and began to thank God for the food. The woman appeared genuinely refreshed and joy-filled from her time spent in church. Prayers poured naturally from her lips, and the gratitude Taffy felt came from a heart of sincerity that Eleanor could not understand. Looking across the table, Eleanor realized Jana was staring directly at her. Neither woman had bowed her head to pray. It seemed as if Jana were declaring her feud with God and wanted Eleanor to know where she stood.

"Amen," Taffy said, then looked up. "Now, where was I? Oh yes. Washington. My, but you saw a lot of well-dressed women in that town. The colors were very dull and dark until Jackie Kennedy arrived. Oh, but that woman possessed a sense of fashion that put us all to disgrace. It was as if we'd never truly known how to dress until she came along."

"You knew Jackie Kennedy?" Jana asked in surprise.

"Oh, mercy yes. We were still in Washington, and Cal, my late husband, was quite good at riding a fence. He played it safe in politics but also got exactly what he wanted. He was such a supreme diplomat that President Kennedy used him in foreign positions. We were actually in Greece for a time, and later we journeyed to Italy."

"I had no idea," Jana said as she took a roll from the basket and passed it to her aunt.

"I shall simply have to get you caught up." Taffy took the

salad Eleanor offered and smiled. "I see you've chosen to impress Jana with your feta and black olive salad."

"I'm not trying to impress anyone," Eleanor replied in a clipped tone. "It's simply what I serve with lasagna. I find the flavors are very complementary."

"Indeed they are," Taffy agreed, passing the bowl to Jana. "You do like feta, don't you?"

"I love it."

Eleanor wasn't sure why, but her daughter's answer pleased her. Perhaps it was because it seemed a tiny connection to the child she'd never allowed herself to know.

"I feel I know so little about you, Aunt Taffy. Did you have any children?" Jana asked as she began to poke at the romaine leaves.

"We were never blessed with children of our own. It was probably for the best because for so many years we were always on the run. Politics is such a consuming game to play, and my Cal played it very well. Perhaps too well. He was quite widely liked by both the men and the ladies." Taffy took a sip of her iced tea. "No, God never gave us our own babies, but He gave us Ellie, and that filled the void in my heart."

Eleanor wanted to crawl under the table. She saw the confusion on Jana's face and knew she would ask the question.

"Who's Ellie?"

It was innocent enough. Eleanor had never explained her childhood to Jana, nor even told her about Taffy until the day she'd decided to come and live with the aging woman.

Taffy laughed as if Jana's question were silly. "Why, your mother, of course."

Eleanor met Jana's eyes. They had a definite look of questioning, but also of something else. It almost looked like regret. "I didn't know you had raised my mother."

"Oh, she was mostly raised when she came to live with us at fourteen, but it was a blessing to me nevertheless. She was such a sweet girl—pretty too. I loved spoiling her. Why, I remember—"

"Would anyone care for butter?" Eleanor interrupted. She extended the butter dish in Taffy's direction but couldn't help but look back to Jana.

Her expression was accusing now. Almost as if she had nearly come to understand something of great importance only to have her mother snatch it away.

Well, let her think what she will. I won't have the past bandied around at the dinner table. There's no need for it. Not now. Not ever.

Twelve

AFTER A WEEK in the great rambling house, Jana decided it was time to call a family meeting. She needed to explain a few things, not the least of which was her pregnancy.

"I hope you don't mind," she told her mother and great-aunt, "but I felt it important to share a few things with you. That's why I've asked you to join me for a few minutes." They took their seats around the large dining room table. It seemed the most appropriate place to gather.

"I hope you are going to announce your desire to have a party," Taffy said with a broad smile. "I wanted to host one for your arrival, but your mother thought it might be best to wait."

Jana nodded. "Mother was right." It was hard to concede even those few words of approval toward her mother. All week the woman had gone out of her way to avoid Jana. She seemed very unhappy with the entire arrangement, and rather than start a fight over the issues at hand, Eleanor had chosen instead to make herself scarce.

"Well, if we're not to host a party for you, then what's on your mind?" Taffy smoothed out the crocheted lace of the dining room tablecloth but looked directly at Jana.

"I feel I owe you a bit of explanation," Jana began. "I've told you very little about the things that happened to me in Spokane, but in truth, I don't know much more than you do." She looked down at the cup of tea her mother had given her a moment before. It had been a thoughtful gesture, almost one that suggested the offering of comfort, but Jana was convinced her mother had no such notion.

"I thought things were wonderful between Rob and me. We had a good life in Spokane." She cleared her throat uncomfortably. "The first part of the year, the church started talking about having several of us go over to Africa, where we had an established mission group. We were to go and assist their ministries, experience how things were done, and then return and share with the church. The purpose was to stir up support and understanding for what our missionaries are up against.

"Rob said it would be impossible for him to go because the timing for the trip coincided with another event that we had previously scheduled at the church. Rob felt it was important for him to remain there and fulfill the duties related to this event." Jana paused and looked up. Her mother's expression was stoic, neither showing interest nor concern. Taffy, on the other hand, looked very caught up.

"Go on, sweetheart. What happened then? Did you go to Africa?"

"Yes. I went for three weeks. It was a marvelous experience, something I'll never forget . . . for so many reasons. The people were incredible."

Taffy nodded knowingly. "Cal and I once spent time in Zambia. I know exactly what you mean."

"Well—" Jana took a deep breath—"while I was there, I got sick. I figured I had food poisoning or had failed to use bottled water at some point. I kept throwing up and finally went to the refugee camp doctor, a wonderful man from Great Britain. He examined me and told me the truth about my condition."

"Which was what?" her mother asked, as if the conversation finally interested her.

115

"I'm pregnant," Jana replied flatly.

"How marvelous!" Taffy exclaimed. "We're going to have a baby! Jana, this pleases me to no end."

But Jana was watching her mother's face. Her expression changed from indifferent to hostile. "Get an abortion," she said without emotion.

Jana had no time to reply. Her shock was so great that she stared openmouthed at her mother. Taffy picked up an apple from the fruit bowl and actually threw it at Eleanor. It smacked her in the arm before landing on the floor with a thump. Eleanor looked at Taffy in stunned silence.

"You mind your manners, missy. You have no right to say such a hideous thing. If you can't behave yourself, you might as well take yourself to your room." Taffy was more serious than Jana had ever seen her.

"She's in the middle of a divorce," Eleanor said frankly. She looked at her aunt and then back to Jana. "You can't possibly know how awful it is to raise a child on your own, but I do."

"You scarcely raised me. I was at boarding schools and with nannies more than I was with you. Why, I wouldn't have even known I had a mother if you'd had your way about it."

Eleanor folded her arms across her chest. "And that probably would have been best for both of us."

"Stop it, you two. I won't have this. I want to hear the rest of Jana's story." Taffy's disgust was evident.

"Very well," Jana's mother said but offered nothing more.

Jana tried to gather her thoughts. "Well, I decided not to call Rob from the airport on the way home in London. I wanted to tell him face-to-face. By the time I got home, I was close to three months along. I stepped off the plane expecting to find my husband waiting, maybe even some people from the church—but there was no one. At least no one waiting for me."

She paused long enough to sip at the tea. She wasn't sure how much to say or not say about Rob and Kerry. Her aunt deserved to know everything, but Jana resented sharing anything with her mother.

She put the teacup down and drew a deep breath. "I got a cab home, thinking there must have been some sort of emergency that had kept Rob away. You know—someone in the hospital or a death in the church. When I got home, however, I found a note from Rob on the coffee table."

Jana felt a lump rise in her throat. "It said nothing more than the fact that Rob had left me for his secretary, Kerry Broadbent, and that he'd already arranged for a divorce. Needless to say, I was stunned. Here I thought everything was fine."

"That's usually the way it goes," her mother muttered.

"Go on, dear," Taffy encouraged.

"Well, that wasn't the end of it. I went to the bank and found that Rob had taken all of our savings. My savings, really. I'd put in all my birthday and Christmas money from you, Aunt Taffy, and I'd saved good portions of my salary from when I was working. Rob took all of it, plus anything of salable value in the house." She paused, not wanting to confess about the jewelry. "He even took the jewelry you gave me."

"The scoundrel! How very thoughtless."

"He ran off with his bimbo secretary," Eleanor declared. "What else did you expect?"

"I don't know, Mother, but I didn't expect this." Jana knew there was no logic or reasoning in her situation, and those were the two things her mother demanded at all times.

"And you didn't see this coming? Be reasonable, Jana. There are always signs," her mother said in disbelief.

Jana shook her head. "I honestly thought we were happy. We planned this baby. Rob talked about how he hoped we would have a son—someone to carry on his family name. And Rob wasn't gone long hours. He didn't show up with lipstick on his collar or someone else's perfume on his clothes. He was affectionate . . . supported me. I honestly found no reason to harbor any doubts about our marriage."

"What about the other woman?" her mother asked. "You said she was the secretary at the church. Surely you had dealings with her as well."

Jana nodded. "I did. She was openly friendly with me. It wasn't like she snuck around when I'd show up at the church or that she tried to avoid me. She was sort of sad to be around, but I'd heard that she was unhappy in her marriage."

"Well, that should have been a warning."

"I don't know why it should have been a warning for me any more than when another church member left her husband and filed for divorce. It didn't seem to have anything to do with me or with Rob directly, except that she was a part of our church family and we cared that she was hurting."

"Apparently Rob cared a little more than he should have," her mother said snidely.

"Well, be that as it may," Jana said, unable to keep the annoyance from her voice, "no one at the church knew it was coming either. Neither did Kerry's husband, although he admits knowing she was unhappy."

"So what's your plan now?"

Jana looked to her mother. "I plan to get a job as soon as possible and get out on my own."

"There's no need for that," Taffy protested. "There's plenty of room here, and I have more than enough money to see you and the baby well cared for. Your mother won't take any help from me, so the least you could do is let me assist you in this way."

Eleanor voiced her exasperation and disapproval. "Taffy, you may well need your money in the years to come."

Taffy laughed and shook her head. "I'm almost eighty years old. I have stock dividends that are paying me well, despite the economy going up and down. I have money in the bank that I don't know what to do with, especially now that I've sold all my other properties."

"I don't want to be a burden to anyone. I get the impression that Mom thinks I came here to use the two of you, but it isn't true. I'll work around the house and care for myself. Or I can stay in my room all day if that will please her." Jana looked to Eleanor, feeling more contempt for her mother than she had in some time.

"There's no need for any of that. This is my house," Taffy said with a tone of authority. "I've invited you to live here the rest of your days, if you so choose, just as I did your mother. It's a free gift, one that I gladly offer. I'm blessed with plenty, and it does me much good to bless you in return. Besides, before your mother came here, I was lonely. It will be good to have you and a new baby in the house. We're getting much too old and frumpy without young people around us. Don't you agree, Eleanor?" She looked at Eleanor as if daring her to contradict her statement.

"I don't think being reserved and living quietly is the same as being old and frumpy," Eleanor said, taking the challenge. "And frankly, I think a baby will disrupt the lives of everyone around it."

"Like I did?" Jana asked bitterly. "This isn't about the baby, is it? It's about me. You might as well say it. You don't want me here."

"Ladies, I refuse to have combat at my dining room table," Taffy interjected. "The matter isn't open to discussion. Jana, you are welcome to stay here as long as you like. You needn't worry about money. We'll go tomorrow, just you and me if need be,

119

and set up a checking account for you. You think about how much money you need monthly, and remember you won't have rent or utilities or food to pay for. You will, however, need new clothes and personal articles, things for the baby. Do you have health insurance? Probably not, eh? We will work out the details of your medical expenses as well. You are not to worry—simply have a wonderful time anticipating your baby. Oh, what fun! You can plan an entire nursery."

"You don't have to do that. I'm perfectly capable of working."

"I won't have it. You need time to recover from this tragedy in your life. I'll help you in whatever way I can—pay for the lawyer or anything else that needs to be done."

Jana could see that none of this boded well with her mother, and in that moment a spirit of defiance rose up in Jana's heart. Her mother didn't want her to take Taffy's money. Her mother didn't want her here. This would be a definite sore spot—a thorn in her side—but Jana didn't care. "Thank you, Aunt Taffy. I'm blessed that someone cares. I know my baby will be blessed because of it too." She refused to look at her mother, but Jana knew she was seething.

———

Jana finished arranging her things in the Rose Room and collapsed into a nearby chair. For the little that she'd brought with her, it certainly had taken a lot of work. A knock sounded on her door, but rather than get up, Jana simply called out a welcome.

The door opened and her mother stepped in. "We need to talk."

Jana straightened in the chair, as if caught doing something wrong. Her mother closed the door behind her and crossed the room to where Jana sat.

"I know you think I'm being unduly harsh with you, but I

want you to seriously consider the situation you're in and think about what you can and cannot offer this child."

"Well, I know one thing," she said, getting to her feet to face her mother. "I can offer this child a mother who loves her or him. That's more than you gave."

"Love doesn't put food on the table or a roof over your head."

"Aunt Taffy has already offered all of that."

Eleanor shook her head. "That old woman is growing more confused as the weeks go by. She's probably got the onset of Alzheimer's."

"You don't know that," Jana countered. "Taffy is a wonderful woman who has a remarkable sense of joy and humor. I have never in my life been around anyone who emits such happiness from just existing. I certainly never saw that kind of happiness growing up. Which reminds me . . . why didn't you ever tell me about Aunt Taffy raising you?"

Eleanor's face seemed to pale. "It wasn't important. There was absolutely nothing that could have benefited you by knowing."

"I might have benefited by knowing *her*! At least then I could have known what it was like to be loved and cared about." Jana stepped closer to her mother. "I've never understood what the problem was between us. I know that somehow I offended you merely by being born and being female, but how in the world you justified keeping me—but never loving me—I'll never know."

Her mother looked genuinely stunned by Jana's words. She opened her mouth to say something, but Jana waved her off. "Don't even start. I don't want your excuses or your condemnation."

"I wasn't going to offer either."

"That would be a first."

Her mother shook her head and turned to walk away, then

stopped at the door. "You don't know anything about my life. You have no idea why I made the choices I made, yet you condemn me for every one of them."

"I have no idea what the truth is," Jana countered, "because you won't share it. You won't talk to me—you never have. When I've asked questions about the past and about my father, you simply clam up and tell me the past needs to remain in the past where it can't hurt us. Well, in case you didn't realize it, the past has hurt me plenty. And the present is doing an equally good job."

Jana didn't want to break down and cry in front of her mother, but hot tears were welling in her eyes. "I'll never understand why you hate me so much."

Her mother's mouth dropped open, as if the statement actually took her by surprise. "I don't hate you. How could you even suggest such a thing? Everything I've ever done has been done out of love. I should have aborted you, but I didn't. I should have given you up for adoption, but I didn't. What I did do was protect you from the things in the past that could hurt you most. Unfortunately, the truth—and the details of what took place— was among those things I kept hidden. Now you want me to parade them around like some kind of novelty?"

"No," Jana said, moving back to her chair in defeat. "I don't want a parade. I don't want lectures or advice from a woman whom I clearly believe did it all wrong." She paused. "I only wanted your love. And I never got that. Because in order to love someone, you actually have to have a relationship with them, and you flatly refuse to open yourself up enough to do that."

Her mother said nothing for several moments, and Jana hoped she would just leave. It hurt to know that Taffy, a woman who scarcely knew Jana, could open her heart so freely, while Eleanor could offer her nothing but anger.

"Everyone always says they want the truth," Eleanor said softly. "They tell you how opening yourself up and being honest will make healthier relationships, closer bonds. But I can tell you from experience that no one is honest—not when the truth is ugly and deformed. No one wants to hear the truth when it's not rosy and full of sweet platitudes." She moved to the door and opened it.

"I can't give you the fairy-tale relationship you want. I can't give you the truth you claim to be in need of . . . because you won't want to hear it. But there is one truth I can say, and you may deny it all you like. But I do love you. I loved you enough to protect you from the cruelty of what happened to me—to us. I still do."

With that she left. Her words rang in Jana's ears. Nothing of her life and relationship with Eleanor Templeton could in any way relate to love. Nothing.

Thirteen

THE NEXT DAY Taffy was true to her word. She arranged a checking account for Jana much to Eleanor's protest.

"She needs to be self-sufficient," Eleanor told Taffy later on as the two drove home from running errands.

"She needs to be loved and cared for," Taffy countered. "I don't see that being self-sufficient has given you any great joy or advantage in life."

Eleanor looked at Taffy oddly, then quickly focused back on the road. "It's kept me sane."

Taffy felt an instant sorrow for the woman she'd helped to raise. "I suppose it's my fault," she began. "I always stressed being a strong woman—being capable. I just didn't figure it would cause you to put up walls around your heart."

"Being cautious where emotions are concerned is always wise." Eleanor turned onto their street and slowed the vehicle. "I know you think me cruel, but Jana cannot allow herself to sink into despair over this. She'll be eaten alive by depression and hopelessness if we allow it. I've been through enough psycho-analysis to know this. I've studied it too; not in depth, but I do understand how this works."

"But she's entitled to grieve. She's suffered a loss—the same as if it were a death. You are always saying there are worse things than death; well, this is one of those things. Jana needs to let go of those feelings of loss. You should have learned to do that yourself. Instead of bottling up all the sorrow and hurt, you could have purged those emotions and been done with it."

"You're never done with it," Eleanor protested. "Just because you have a good cry doesn't mean the problems are solved or that they go away." She pulled the car into the driveway and turned to Taffy as she shut off the engine. "I don't want to cripple Jana with pity. Pity doesn't help anyone. I want her to be strong so she can deal with the blows of life. If she doesn't need anyone, she won't fall apart when people leave her."

"Did that honestly work for you?" Taffy questioned.

Eleanor stiffened. "Like I said, it kept me sane. If I'd chosen another path I would've been dead by now because I wouldn't have been able to bear the sorrow, the misery. You don't understand. You've lived a life of wealth and comfort. You had a husband you loved—who loved you. You never had to worry about the things I have. You never had to face being taken from the only comfort you knew, the only people you loved. And you certainly weren't responsible for killing your mother."

———

Jana enjoyed the warmth of the day. June in Montana was a wonder. There was the strong suggestion that summer had arrived, while at the same time the nights were chilly and the mountains still bore snow. Taffy had even told her that the previous year they had awakened to four inches of snow in the middle of June. The stuff didn't last long, but Jana found it amazing nevertheless. She almost hoped it would snow this June.

The town of Lomara wasn't all that big. It took less than five minutes to run the full length of Main Street. There were a few bars and cafés, a couple of banks—one of which held Jana's new checking account—a clinic that boasted four doctors, a dental office, and the police station. A convenience store and gas station marked the edge of town, along with a grocery store and pizza place. The town had the requisite casino that every Montana town seemed to have. What was it with gambling and this state? Offshoots from Main Street led to a variety of other businesses: a taxidermist, a couple of car repair services, a post office, and the fire department, as well as those ever-famous golden arches.

Jana, against her better judgment, had indulged in a fast-food lunch, simply because there was comfort in the familiar. Was there any place in the world that didn't have a McDonald's?

She thought back to her days in college and all the times she'd popped into a similar McDonald's. It hadn't been that long ago, but it seemed like an eternity had passed. She'd studied art and in particular interior design, but looking around her now, Jana was pretty confident those skills wouldn't help her here.

In a way, she knew she was stuck. Stuck accepting her aunt's help if she remained in Lomara. Stuck in Lomara unless by some miracle she won the lottery. "Which is hard to do since I don't believe in risking my money that way," she muttered.

She drove back through town, noting a florist she'd missed on her previous examination. Pulling into a parking place, Jana thought it might be nice to take some flowers to Taffy. Why couldn't she have had a mother like Taffy?

The window held a display of baskets and greenery with a large fifty-percent-off sign overhead. Jana opened the door, hearing a little bell ring somewhere in the shop. An older woman appeared at the counter, soon followed by another. They smiled sweetly and welcomed her in unison.

"Good morning!"

"Hi. I'd like to pick up a bouquet for my aunt, but I'm not sure what to get," Jana said, looking around the tiny room. Stuffed animals and potted plants were positioned next to crockery, candles, and ceramic vases. Several signs advertised that

Mother's Day has come and gone, but fathers like flowers too. Father's Day had never meant much to Jana except to serve as a reminder that she had no father.

"You're not from here, are you?" the woman with white hair asked.

"No, but my great-aunt is. You might know her . . . Taffy Anderson?"

"Oh, of course we know Taffy. Why, we're dear friends. We go to the same church," declared the woman with brown hair. "I'm Myrna and this is Trudy."

Jana smiled. "I'm Jana McGuire, her great-niece."

"Well, it's a pleasure. We're so glad to meet you," Trudy said as Myrna nodded.

"Likewise." Jana gazed at the cut flowers in the refrigerated display case. "Do you know what Aunt Taffy likes?"

"But of course. She loves the wild flower look," Myrna replied. She turned, assessed the displays, and shook her head. "I'll put something together. What price range did you have in mind?"

Money wasn't such an issue anymore, but even so, Jana didn't want to be too frivolous. "I hadn't really thought about that."

"We can do up a nice bouquet for fifteen—just don't tell anyone. It's our Taffy special," Trudy said with a grin. Myrna nodded and disappeared around the corner as if it were already settled.

Jana couldn't imagine that fifteen dollars would make much of a bouquet, but surely it would be adequate. "That would be perfect." She reached into her purse and shuffled the things there in order to take out her billfold. Pulling out a five and a ten, she looked at Trudy. "What's the total?"

"Just fifteen. There's no sales tax in Montana. It's a source of contention among the residents, and every so often we think they'll surely change it, but so far they haven't."

Jana handed over the money. "Well, it's nice not to have to worry about it."

"How does this look?" Myrna asked, coming out with a nice-sized bouquet of daisies, lilies, and other flowers Jana couldn't identify.

"Oh, put in a few orange dahlias," Trudy instructed. "Those are some of her favorites."

The two women fussed over the arrangement until they had it exactly the way they wanted. Jana was certain it was worth more than fifteen dollars but figured the women were throwing in what they wanted without thought to price in order to please their friend.

"There. It's perfect," the ladies said in unison.

"Thank you. I know Aunt Taffy will love it."

Trudy topped the vase off with water and handed the arrangement to Jana. "Are you sure you can get this home okay? Is someone riding with you?"

She hadn't thought about that. "I don't have anyone with me, but I'm sure I'll be fine. I don't have far to go."

"We have a kind of holder," Trudy said, turning to Myrna. "Run and get one of those boxes."

Jana started to protest, but Myrna was already on her way. She quickly returned with a little fitted box that they popped the vase into. It would help stabilize it, Jana realized. "Thanks again."

"You come back soon," Myrna said.

"Yes. Any niece of Taffy's is always welcome here," Trudy added.

Jana thought them two of the sweetest women she'd ever met. Their generosity and love for Taffy was most sincere. Smiling to herself, Jana pushed out the door, paying no attention to the man who happened to be entering at the same time.

"Oh, I'm so sorry!" she said as they collided outside the door. Water splashed from the vase and trickled down the front of his shirt.

Jana looked up to meet the stranger's startled expression. "It's not a problem," he said, wiping the water away.

"I feel awful. I wasn't paying any attention." Jana gauged the man to be somewhere in his early thirties, perhaps even his late twenties.

He laughed and shook his head. "It's really no big deal. Here, let me help you. Is your car nearby?"

"It's over there," Jana said, pointing as he took the flowers in hand.

"Ah, the Washington tags. So are you here visiting someone?" He followed her to the car.

"I've moved in with my great-aunt." Jana had fully intended to stop with that but for some reason added, "I'm going through a divorce."

"I'm sorry to hear that. Is there no chance of working things out?"

His question surprised Jana. She couldn't keep the sarcasm from her tone. "Not unless he gives up his secretary. I doubt she'd want to lose what she has with him."

The man frowned. "That does make it kind of bad."

"Tell me about it," Jana said, opening the door for him to put the flowers on the seat. "You can put those there."

He quickly complied, then straightened. He held on to the open car door and smiled. "Life doesn't always work out the way we think it should. I'm sorry you're going through such a bad time. Look, I'm the pastor of a small church here. We'd love to have you come. In fact, if you aren't busy tonight, my family and I would love to have you over for dinner." He let go of the door and reached into his back pocket. Pulling out his wallet, he handed her a business card. "My address is listed under the one for the church."

Jana refused to look at the card in her hand. She'd taken it while still in a stunned state of mind. Another pastor! What was she, some sort of magnet for them?

"I'm not interested in church right now," she said, staring at the man hard. "My husband was the pastor of our church in Spokane. Pastors aren't high on my list right now. Neither is God."

He seemed unshaken. "I can understand why. You probably feel that when your husband deserted you, he took God with him."

His answer took her by surprise. "Yes . . . well . . . I need to be going." She turned to walk to the driver's side. "Please close that door."

He did as she asked, then came around to her side of the car. "Could I at least pray for you?"

Jana stopped and turned. "No."

"But why? It can't hurt."

Jana felt her throat tighten. "Neither can it help. So why bother?"

───────

Eleanor glanced out her bedroom window as Jana pulled into the drive. Having spent the last thirty minutes on a call to New York, Eleanor was relieved to finally be free of the phone and conversation. She longed for a peaceful afternoon, but Jana's arrival was a sure sign against such a thing.

Watching her daughter struggle to take flowers from the car, Eleanor wondered who in the world they were for.

"Surely she isn't bringing them to apologize to me," Eleanor murmured, though she was unable to deny she would have liked that very much. Jana had been nothing but rude and angry with her since her arrival.

Eleanor straightened and walked to the mirror. She assessed the red blouse and black slacks. Running the brush through her short blond hair, Eleanor steadied her nerves. *If the flowers are for me,* she told herself, *I'll be gracious and apologize for the comment I made about getting an abortion. It was wrong to suggest such a thing and I didn't actually mean it, but I was upset. I don't want her to endure the things I've had to go through.*

But you could make it better for her, her heart protested. *You could offer her all the emotional support you never had.*

Eleanor considered the thought for a moment. No, it would cost too much. Not in money, because she had plenty of that. But rather in what she would have to risk. If she helped Jana and made her feel safe and protected, then Jana was taken from her or somehow betrayed her, what then? And how much better off would Jana be if she came to depend on Eleanor and then Eleanor could suddenly no longer help?

"I can't make this easy on her," Eleanor told herself. "She'll grow weak, and then the world will destroy her. The only reason she's still standing today is because of the strength I gave her."

Eleanor squared her shoulders and moved to the door. "If the flowers are for me, I'll be kind and gracious, but nothing more. I won't give her a false sense of hope."

Descending the stairs, Eleanor could hear Jana and Taffy in animated discussion. Jana was laughing about something and Taffy responded.

"Oh, but we've been friends for a long time. You'll like getting to know Trudy and Myrna a little better. They are wonderful cooks and make some of the nicest crafts. They sell things every year at the different festivals."

"Well, they certainly love you."

Eleanor stood in the hall, not knowing whether to intrude on the conversation or not.

"They are such dears. And they make a beautiful arrangement. I'm going to enjoy these by putting them right on the dining room buffet. That way we can see them at every meal."

Eleanor turned and headed back to the stairs. The flowers were for Taffy. She should have known. No one in her life had ever brought her flowers; why should that tradition be broken now? Especially by a daughter she scarcely knew. She pushed aside the disappointment and strengthened her resolve. She had almost let her guard down too much, and look at what it had done to her. She was upset that a simple bouquet of flowers wasn't for her, and there was no reason to be.

"That girl will mean nothing but grief to me. Her coming here was a big mistake."

Fourteen

SEVERAL DAYS LATER, Jana drove home from the doctor's office. The small clinic was completely up-to-date, but they informed her that their patients generally gave birth in Missoula at the nearest full-service hospital. Jana didn't find that at all convenient. No doubt when the baby's due date drew near, she'd have to figure out the details of getting to the hospital, but for now she wasn't going to worry about it.

She had also learned by checking the phonebook and talking to Taffy that there were a couple of good lawyers in town. Jana thought about the divorce papers that now sat on her dresser at home. She'd finally forced herself to read through them the night before. The words were so cold and indifferent. Two years of marriage were summed up to no more than a few pages of legal mumbo jumbo.

Rob had been true to his word. He hadn't wanted anything more than what he'd taken, which he classified as "personal items." How the microwave and video camcorder fit into that category was beyond Jana, but she decided she didn't care. She would divorce him without protest. That way it would be fast, and hopefully no one would ever even know about the baby.

Her mother had told Jana that legally she would have to declare the baby to the court—that she wouldn't be able to let that issue remain untold. But Jana had other plans. She had no desire for Rob to play any role in her baby's life. In her heart, however, she knew that would be unfair, especially given her own past. She had longed so many times for a father in her life.

"And now you want to do that to your baby?" she asked herself. "You know how hard it was, how sad it was . . . and still you're willing to keep Rob out of the child's life?"

A million emotions swirled around her. None of this was fair. If she did the right thing and told Rob and the court about the baby, things could change. Rob could wake up to the realization of what he was about to lose. But did Jana want a husband who would leave his mistress and return to his wife because of a child on the way? Furthermore, why should Jana even believe that he wanted a child? What if she told him about the baby and then he rejected it—told her to get an abortion, just as her mother had suggested?

Jana didn't know what the right answer was. She was steeped in these thoughts when she pulled into the driveway, but her confusion was instantly pushed aside at the sight before her.

Taffy and Stanley were working frantically and laughing themselves silly, all in the midst of a birdbath fountain gone mad. Water was spraying everywhere, and just as either Taffy or Stanley managed to grab hold of the hose and reposition it, a new direction of spray would assault one or the other or both.

Jana sat behind the wheel for a moment, smiling to herself. Taffy was always having such fun. Much more fun than Jana had ever had. In fact, Jana knew if the same thing were happening to her, she'd be furious. She'd be angry that nothing was working out right, and she'd probably give up and let someone else figure it out.

But not Taffy. The woman simply wouldn't be defeated. She chose to enjoy herself, even in the middle of adversity. No doubt such an attitude kept her young.

"I want what she's got," Jana murmured to herself. "If only I could figure out her secret."

Jana stepped out of the car and called, "Is it safe to approach or should I put on armor and take up a weapon?"

"A raincoat would serve you better," Stanley answered.

"Mercy, yes. A raincoat would have been divine." Water dripped from Taffy's face and outfit. Her hair, usually styled in soft curls, was drooping sadly in white-gray rings.

"What's going on out here?" It was Eleanor and she looked none too pleased at the ruckus. Standing at the front door, she bore the expression of an irritated mother about to scold her children. "It sounds like you have a circus going on out here."

"We were putting in a birdbath fountain," Taffy offered soberly. Then she smiled. "But it turned into a birdbath hurricane instead." Jana laughed at this. It was the first time she'd felt like laughing—really laughing—in some time.

"It's more like a people bath," Stanley said with an impish grin.

Taffy began laughing all over again at Stanley's wit, which only served to make Stanley chuckle. Jana couldn't help but be amused with the older couple, but her mother was clearly unhappy.

"This is ridiculous." Eleanor came down the steps, careful to stay to the far side and avoid even a hint of mist from the malfunctioning fountain. She went to the faucet and turned off the water without a word. Straightening, she eyed Taffy and Stanley in complete disgust.

"Taffy, you must get inside and change out of those clothes. You're drenched, and if you aren't careful, you'll come down with pneumonia."

"Now, now, Eleanor, pneumonia isn't caused by cold water," Taffy said with a shake of her head. "I read in my ladies' magazine that it's either bacterial or viral, and that—"

"I don't want to hear it!" Eleanor interrupted. "Stanley, go home. Go home and get dried off. Taffy needs to change too, but I'm sure she won't do that so long as you are here. I honestly don't know what's wrong with either of you. You're much too old to be messing around with putting together a birdbath. What if you'd gotten seriously injured?"

Stanley looked much like a forlorn child at the suggestion that their fun should end. Jana hated the way her mother was treating the two grown adults. It wasn't right for her to belittle them and treat them with such a lack of dignity.

"Mother, they have a right to do what they choose. You act as though they have one foot in the grave already, when both of them show more spirit and enthusiasm for living than either you or me."

"They may not have one foot in the grave," Eleanor countered, "but neither are they children. Yet they insist on acting like children. Always giggling and teasing each other. You'd think we were witnessing some sort of junior high school crush rather than two octogenarian neighbors busy with a yard task."

"You're just jealous. No one has ever giggled and teased with you, so you don't want anyone else to have fun. Honestly, Mother, you need to cool it."

Eleanor's expression hardened at this. Without another word she went into the house, surprising the trio in the yard.

"Well, I suppose I should get on home. I'll be back tomorrow, and we can try to figure out what's wrong," Stanley said. "And while I think you look pretty good in wet clothes or dry, you'd best go change and warm up."

"Oh, pshaw," Taffy protested. "Eleanor worries about the silliest things. I'll have a talk with her and calm her."

Jana seriously doubted that a simple talk would take care of the matter. She'd seen the expression on her mother's face; she had been truly offended by Jana's comment.

"I'm the one who'd better talk with her," Jana said, coming up the walkway. "It's obvious she didn't appreciate my taking your side in the matter."

"I didn't know sides needed to be chosen," Taffy said, smiling. "We're family. We're all on the same side."

"I seriously doubt that, Taffy," Jana said, her heart suddenly feeling very heavy.

"Well, it probably is best that we wait to finish this. Maybe tomorrow you can help us, Jana."

"I'd love to. I think it's a very cute birdbath." She gazed at the faux marble creation. "If I recall, Mother will be tied up most of the morning in one of her business meetings. That might be the perfect time."

"Great," Stanley said, finally having retrieved all of his tools. "I'll be over after breakfast."

Taffy blotted some of the water from her blouse and nodded. "Wonderful. I'm so excited about this. With Jana's help, we're sure to master the thing."

Later that evening, Jana's conscience would not let her be. Maybe it was the fact that she'd learned from the doctor that morning that her baby was due in mid-December that caused her nurturing emotions to run high. But whatever it was, she knew she had to try to make things right with her mother. Jana simply had too much anger in her life. Anger at Rob. Anger at Kerry. Anger at herself . . . and worse still, at God.

Jana sat on the porch and contemplated what she could do. *I can continue to be angry,* she thought. *It's simple enough. I have justification to be angry.* Surely no one would say she had no right to be upset, given everything that had happened. But did having a right to something necessarily mean that it was a good thing to do?

She rocked back and forth, wishing for an easy answer. *I wish I could figure out why Mother is the way she is. I don't understand why she lived with Aunt Taffy. I don't understand what happened to my father and why I've never had any contact with him. And I especially don't understand why she's always put me at arm's length.*

"You appear to be quite reflective," Taffy said as she stepped up from the walkway.

"I am, I suppose." Jana wondered if Taffy might give her answers.

"Is your mother still making marmalade?"

"Last time I looked in on her. She hasn't said a word to me, however. I wish I knew what I could do to make things better." Jana shook her head. "Why did Mother come to live with you?"

Taffy considered the question for a moment. "That's really Eleanor's story to tell. I feel it would betray a trust to share it with you. However, I will say this much. Her life was far from ideal and many things went wrong. She was a deeply wounded person when she came to me."

"So that's her excuse for the attitude she puts off?"

"Mercy, child, isn't that enough? We're all dealing with the wounds we've been given. Some folks just don't know how to let the wounds heal."

"My psych prof in college would say it's all about the baggage we're carrying around."

Taffy nodded. "I believe that's true. Remember Dickens's *A Christmas Carol* and old Mr. Scrooge? His friend Marley showed him the chains and weights he was dragging around—the burdens he'd made for himself in life. He warned Scrooge that he had an equally long and heavy chain when he passed away."

"But Scrooge didn't believe him."

"No. He had to learn for himself in another way. Just as your mother must learn."

"I wish I understood. I feel that if I knew the truth about the past, I wouldn't be so . . . well . . . so lost."

"You needn't be lost anyway. What's happened to your faith in God?" Taffy questioned.

It was Jana's turn to stiffen, just as she'd often watched her mother do. "God allowed my husband to run off with another woman. I don't think God much cares about me and what's happening in my life. I'm beginning to seriously wonder if God isn't more like some universal overseer—He doesn't actually care, but He knows He has the job and can't get out of it."

"So you don't believe God is invested in His creation?"

"Look around you. There are wars and murders, kidnappings, drug abuse, and families being torn apart. People are dying for want of love and someone to care. Children are abused and neglected and murdered. Do you realize how many abortions are performed yearly? People are throwing away their children, and then we wonder why the ones they choose to keep rise up and murder them in their sleep. No one respects life."

"And you think God can't possibly care because He's not stopping the slaughter."

"Well, do you think He cares? Can you prove to me that He cares?"

"Certainly. It's all there in the Bible. But equally importantly, it's here with me—with you. God may allow for many things, Jana, but it doesn't mean He's stopped caring. If your child grows up to ignore the things you teach him or her—if she becomes rebellious and hideous in nature—will you love her any less? Will you walk away and cease to be interested in her well-being?"

Jana knew in her heart that she could never turn away from

her baby, no matter what that child grew up to do. "I suppose not."

"Don't throw God out simply because you're hurting. Don't discredit His care . . . that He's still there for you to turn to. He told us we'd have trouble in this world, but He also promised us a Comforter—the Holy Spirit. You don't have to bear this misery alone, and you don't have to let it ruin your life and that of your child."

Jana said nothing but allowed the words to sink in. She wanted desperately to believe there was hope.

Taffy went inside without another word. She seemed to understand Jana's need to contemplate the matter more thoroughly. Taffy always knew things like that. Perhaps it was her many years on earth or her multifaceted experiences that gave her clarity and understanding. Whatever it was, something about the woman and her advice rang true.

After about an hour, Jana got up and went inside. She noted that it was nearly nine o'clock. Summer days, with the long hours of sunlight, always made her lose track of the time. She often found herself well into the evening, not even realizing how late it truly was.

She heard her mother still working in the kitchen and decided to speak to her. Jana knew her mother would probably reject any kindness, but Jana wanted her to understand that she hadn't intentionally hurt her that afternoon.

"Smells good in here," Jana said, breathing in the heady scent of oranges.

"Orange marmalade is one of Taffy's favorites."

Jana smiled. The conversation had opened in a peaceable fashion. "Where did you learn to cook? Marmalade seems like a complicated thing."

"I took a few classes, but mostly I'm self-taught."

There, Jana thought. *That wasn't so hard, was it? You've actu-ally shared a piece of your life with me that I never knew.* "I'm not much of a cook," Jana admitted. "I need to learn. Maybe you . . . could . . . well . . . show me sometime?" It came out more of a question than a statement.

But at least I asked. She can reject me, but at least I asked. That alone made Jana feel better.

Eleanor looked at her for a moment, as if surprised. "I sup-pose I could."

Jana decided to leave well enough alone on that particular matter. "Look, Mom, I'm sorry I upset you earlier today. I didn't intend to. I know you thought I was ganging up against you, but it really wasn't that way."

Eleanor went back to work. "What way was it, then?"

Jana took a deep breath. "I just felt bad for Aunt Taffy and Stanley. They were having a good time, and you came out and treated them like children. Would you like it if I treated you that way?"

"You'd have no call to treat me that way. I don't catch myself up in such stupidity. If I did, I would hope that you would stop me."

"But whether or not it was stupid was only your opinion. I'm an adult, and I didn't see it as the fiasco you did. I saw two elderly people having fun."

"I saw an accident waiting to happen. The sidewalk and stairs were slick with water. Either Taffy or Stanley could have fallen. Did you think about that?"

Jana bit her lip to keep from blurting out a snide comment. *I have to try to reach her. I have to try.* "Mom, you're always so negative. I wish I could understand it, but it seems to me if there's a positive way or a negative way to look at things, you choose—and I do mean choose—to go with the negative."

"It's not that way at all. It's a matter of seeing a smart and sensible way or an irresponsible way to deal with things. In that case, I always choose the sensible way," she said very matter-of-factly.

"But you hurt Aunt Taffy's feelings. Stanley's too."

"And you hurt mine. So let's call it even and be done with it."

Jana looked hard at her mother. She wanted so much to use Taffy's words and tell her it hadn't been a contest. Instead, she changed the subject. "But don't you want to be happy?"

Eleanor finished pouring the last of the marmalade into a jar and turned. "Being happy isn't all it's cracked up to be. Being on a constant emotional roller coaster is exhausting."

"So you'd prefer to be miserable."

"I'd rather be even keeled. I'd rather there not be any highs or lows."

"But to never enjoy the highs—the positives."

"Not if doing so means you have to experience the lows and negatives. You think me negative—you think me a sour old woman even though I'm only forty-eight. But what I am is a realist. I know what the world is all about. I know what is required of me, and I do it."

"But that's not living. That's just existing . . . just getting through."

"Which is better than not getting through."

Jana supposed there was some logic in what her mother said, but she pressed on. "But happiness—true contentment—is so much better. They've proven that happy people live longer, that learning to be content lowers blood pressure. What about quality of life?"

Eleanor folded her arms. "What about quality of life? By whose standards shall we judge 'quality'? Jana, honestly, being happy isn't all it's cracked up to be. People think they're happy all the time until someone comes along to show them that they aren't. I was happy as a child and then someone told me the life I had was wrong. That I shouldn't be happy with what I had. Do you see what I'm saying here?"

Unfortunately Jana did see. She remembered the moment just before she left the parsonage. *I thought I was happy here,* she recalled thinking.

"I think I do understand, Mother. Maybe for the first time."

Eleanor looked at her and opened her mouth as if to say something more, then closed it and turned back to her canning. Jana knew it was a clear signal that the conversation was over, but she longed for so much more. That simple taste—that brief glimpse into her mother's past—had stirred Jana's imagination.

She said she was happy as a child, but then someone told her the life she had was wrong. Jana shook her head. What did it mean?

Fifteen

AS THE DAYS went by, Jana knew she needed to take action in regard to her divorce. She made a phone call to one of the two lawyers in town and was advised that he could see her at two o'clock that afternoon. Taking up the papers from her dresser, Jana shoved them into her large purse and went downstairs.

The house was pleasantly quiet. Jana tossed her purse on the slate-tiled table by the door and went into the kitchen to scout out some breakfast. She made toast and slathered it with her mother's marmalade, then poured a cup of coffee that someone had thoughtfully made.

It was probably Mom. She was always very efficient in this area. Jana was actually surprised that there wasn't some kind of breakfast platter waiting to be warmed. With toast and coffee in hand, Jana sat down at the dining room table and began to eat. She felt awkward not stopping to pray. She and Rob had always prayed over meals—even small ones.

She pushed the thought aside and reached to her right to pick up the local paper. It was actually the Missoula paper, but at least there was information that was somewhat relevant to their area.

Browsing through the pages, Jana read briefly of fears for the summer's fire dangers. Missoula, it appeared, was quite well known for some sort of firefighting, smoke-jumper's school, and they were already preparing for the worst. Another article mentioned problems with one of the school districts, while another touched on bear control.

It seemed so strange to read of wildlife problems. In Spokane, Jana had been completely focused on city life and the faster pace it brought. Here in Montana, she felt as if she'd stepped back in time. Things moved at a much slower pace, and the focal issues were completely different.

Jana was about to head to the kitchen for a second cup of coffee when the doorbell sounded. She couldn't imagine who would be calling at such an early hour. It was barely past eight. She headed to the door but heard her mother conversing with someone.

"Yes, she lives here. May I ask what this is about?"

"We need to speak with Jana McGuire. That's really all I can say at this point," a man stated.

Jana stepped forward. "I'm Jana McGuire."

Her mother moved back from the door. "This is Detective Tim Cooley from Spokane and Brian Moore, one of our local police officers," her mother explained.

"I don't understand. What's this all about?" Jana questioned.

"We'd like to talk to you about your husband," the older of the two men announced.

"My husband? I'm in the middle of a divorce."

"If we could just sit down together," Brian suggested.

"Of course. Come in." Jana had no reason to suggest otherwise.

Eleanor motioned them to the right and into the living room. Once they were all seated, Jana looked to the detective. "Again, I don't understand what this is about. As much as I hate to talk about it, my husband left me for another woman. If you want to talk to Rob, you'll have to go to Seattle. At least that's where I was told he'd gone."

"Mrs. McGuire, I don't know how else to break this to you but to simply come out and say it. Your husband is dead."

Jana's eyes widened as she emitted a gasp. "What?" She looked to her mother in stunned disbelief. "What is he saying?"

Eleanor immediately took control. "Yes, what are you saying? Is this some kind of a joke? Let me see your identification again." She stood and went to the detective.

The man withdrew his badge and ID card and handed her both. "I'm sorry to shock you in this manner. We thought you might have already heard. It's been on the news."

"When . . . how?" Jana could barely issue the words.

"Your husband was shot by Jason Broadbent. I presume you know whom I'm talking about."

Jana's shock ran deeper. "Jason? Oh no. Oh, I can't believe any of this is happening. Rob can't be dead. He just can't be." Tears flooded her eyes as she buried her face in her hands. Nothing seemed real in that moment. Then Jana remembered her mother's adage: *There are worse things than death.* Oh, it was so true.

The detective waited a moment before continuing. "I need to ask you what you know about this situation."

Jana shot him a look. "What? I don't know anything about this situation."

"Well, let me be the judge of that." The detective took out a pen and small spiral notebook. "Why were you and your husband divorcing?"

"He ran off with Jason's wife, Kerry. Rob filed for divorce while I was in Africa on a missions trip for our church."

"And when were you in Africa?"

Jana gave him the dates and shook her head, but it was Eleanor who spoke. "I don't understand. If you have her husband's killer, why do you need to speak with her about all of this?"

The man ignored Eleanor, something Jana was sure her mother wasn't used to. "Mrs. McGuire, when did you first become aware that your husband wanted a divorce?"

"When I returned from Africa. He didn't show up at the airport, and when I finally got home, I found a note from him. We'd never even discussed the idea of divorce; in fact, we were planning a family. I learned while I was in Africa that I was pregnant." Jana didn't know why she shared this information with the officer, since she'd had no intention of sharing it with the divorce court.

"And how did you learn that your husband was leaving you?" he continued, writing all the while.

Jana frowned. "I just told you he left me a note."

"Do you still have it?"

She nodded. "Yes, it's with my divorce papers. I thought I might need it."

"Would you mind getting it for me?"

Jana got to her feet and went to the front door table, where she'd left her purse and the papers. Bringing the entire envelope, she suddenly realized she wouldn't need them anymore. There would be no divorce.

She handed the envelope to the detective. "You might as well have it all. Those are my divorce papers and the bank statements showing Rob depleted our account when he left, as well as the note and a list of items Rob took with him. Including my personal jewelry." She sat back down and tried to calm her nerves.

The detective reviewed the contents, made a few more notes, then replaced the papers before looking back to Jana.

"Did you hire Jason Broadbent to kill your husband?" he asked very matter-of-factly.

147

Jana was totally unprepared. "What? Is that what Jason said?"

Eleanor reached out and touched Jana's arm. "Maybe you shouldn't say anything more. Perhaps we should call a lawyer."

"I'm not a criminal," Jana declared, getting to her feet. "I was deserted. My husband stole my bank savings, my jewelry . . . even my microwave." She flushed, unsure of why she'd thrown such an absurd comment in there, but it was done now and she couldn't take it back. "I didn't want a divorce. I didn't want Rob dead. I wanted my life back. I wanted to wake up and find out that everything had just been a terrible nightmare. But instead, the nightmare goes on."

"Jana, you need to calm yourself," Eleanor said, coming alongside her daughter. She put her arm around Jana's shoulders.

Jana was surprised at her mother's comforting touch. It was so foreign, yet so needed. She was further strengthened by her mother's obvious support as she turned to the interrogator.

"Are you filing charges against my daughter?"

"No, ma'am. We're merely here to clear up a few things. Jason Broadbent fully admits to what he's done. Two other people witnessed the act, one being his wife. However, as we spoke to Jason, we were curious about something he said."

"And what would that be?" Eleanor asked coolly.

"He said that Jana had expressed that she'd be better off if her husband were dead—that at least she'd have the insurance money."

Jana's heart sank. She felt her knees grow weak. "Oh no." She pushed away from her mother and sank back onto the sofa.

"Did you say that, Mrs. McGuire?"

Jana was sickened by the memory of her words. Had that prompted Jason to go out and kill Rob? Had her flippant remarks caused Jason Broadbent to forfeit his life and the life of her husband? She wanted to close her eyes and make it all go away, but she knew she couldn't. She knew anything she said or did could be used against her. *Used against me in a court of law . . . isn't that what they say when they read someone their rights?*

"Mrs. McGuire?"

Jana looked up and met the detective's watchful gaze. "Yes. Yes, I said something to that extent. But you have to understand." She forced her breathing to steady and refused to look away even though her heart flooded with fear. "I was angry. I had just been taken for everything I had of any value. My husband left me for another woman, even though I thought we had a perfectly good marriage. Jason came to my house asking me if I'd be okay, and I lost it. I told him I'd never be okay again, and I won't be. Especially now." She shook her head and closed her eyes.

"I told him I would have been better off if Rob had died because then at least I'd have the insurance money to see me and the baby through until I could find a job. But as it stood, I had nothing. That's why I left Spokane so quickly. The church had already hired another pastor while I was in Africa and they needed the parsonage for him and his family. I had no means to move out on my own—no job, no money—so I called my mother here in Lomara and asked if I could move in."

She opened her eyes and again met the detective's scrutiny. "I didn't ask Jason to kill my husband, and that's the truth."

The detective nodded. "That's what Jason told us too. He also told us about the baby."

"Then why put her through this torment?" Eleanor snapped. "You come here with distressing news and then treat her like she's played some part in it?"

"We have to explore all the possibilities in a homicide case, ma'am." The man appeared completely unconcerned about Eleanor's outburst—it was almost as if he were simply laying out

149

all his cards and getting their reaction.

But of course, Jana thought. _He's watching me to see how I'll react to the news of Rob's death, to the fact that Jason killed him. To everything. He's watching my every move—every word._ She straightened ever so slightly, almost relieved to finally understand the game he was playing.

"Is there anything else you'd like to ask me?" Jana questioned. "Do I need to come to the police station or back to Spokane?"

"Not at this time," the detective said, closing his notebook. "Will I be able to reach you at this address and telephone?"

"Of course. I'll be here—it's the only place I have. It's all that's left me."

Her heart felt as though it were breaking all over again. How could Rob really be dead? Deep within she'd grasped on to the feeble chance that maybe someday, somehow, they might come back together. That the baby might allow them to put the past behind them. But now that would never happen. Rob was dead.

Sixteen

THE DAYS DRAGGED BY and the nights were impossible. Jana could find no solace in sleep or in wakefulness. She sat alone in her room, thinking of Rob and all that they'd once known together. Rob had been a mainstay in her very unsettled life. And though she'd already battled her anger over his betrayal, she couldn't accept the fact that now he was dead.

For several moments Jana let her thoughts run wild. She tried to imagine Jason coming to Rob. She wondered if he told Rob about the baby. Had Rob died knowing that he was going to be a father?

The baby.

Jana kept thinking of how she would one day have to explain to her unborn child that his or her father had been killed by the heartbroken spouse of the woman he'd run off with.

"No, I could never tell my child the truth about that. I'll simply tell him his father died, and maybe later explain that he was murdered. But I won't reveal why."

Even as she said the words aloud, Jana felt a twinge of discomfort. After all, she felt her life had been built on secrets and lies, and now she was planning to do the same for her child. But what else could she do? How could anyone, much less a child, get his mind around the truth of this situation?

Maybe that's how Mom feels when I ask her to discuss the past.

The thought startled Jana. Was that the truth? Was the past

so hideous that her mother had no way to convey the information? *But surely my situation is much worse.*

It was so hard to come to grips with the reality of what had
happened. Where was Rob killed? How had it all happened? She
had so many questions. Questions that only Jason and Kerry and
some unnamed witness had answers to.

"I could go see Jason," she reasoned. Then just as quickly she
dismissed the idea. Nothing would look more like a conspiracy
than to have the widow of a murdered man show up at the jail
to have a talk with the murderer.

But even if she knew the truth and all its details, Jana seriously doubted it would make things any better. Her husband,
louse that he was, did not deserve to be murdered. Cut down in
the prime of his life. Jana had never wished that for him.

"I might have wished he'd simply disappear," she told the
room, "but I never wished him dead."

She stroked her stomach. "Baby, I'm so sorry for all you have
to face in life. You're not even born yet, but your path is already
being decided for you."

The thought made Jana sad. She tried to imagine her child
growing up without a father. All she or he would have would be
an angry, confused mother, an indifferent grandmother, and a
zany great-great-aunt, who, chances were better than not,
wouldn't be around much longer.

That thought only led Jana to more depressing and discouraging thoughts. Taffy might, if really blessed, live another ten or
twenty years at the most. It wasn't enough time. Jana began to
resent her mother for keeping Taffy from her all these years.
How different might things have been if Taffy had been a part
of them? Maybe Jana would have been happy and secure. Maybe
she would have never met and married Rob. It might have been
possible that she and her mother would have had a wonderful

relationship instead of none at all.

Jana grew bored with her speculation and contemplation. She went to the closet and pulled out a burgundy blouse and jeans. She dressed with no real interest in her appearance, but she did note as she fastened the waistband of her jeans that they were nearly too tight to fit into. Despite the pregnancy, Jana hadn't been eating well and had lost nearly fifteen pounds. Because of this, her own clothes were still fitting, and she'd given maternity clothes very little consideration. She supposed now she'd have to do something about it. Her tops might well take her into another month or so, but her pants and jeans wouldn't last much longer.

She looked in the mirror and saw the hollow, haunted reflection of a stranger stare back. The woman Jana saw bore little resemblance to the person she'd once been. But in spite of having plenty of makeup to help remedy the problem, Jana did nothing more to help her haggard appearance than run a brush through her long, straight brown hair. Rob had always insisted she wear it long. She touched her hair, remembering the way Rob liked to play with it when they were curled up watching television.

A sigh escaped her lips. She would never love again. Her life of romance and companionship with a soul mate was over. The thought left her very sad and almost sent her back to bed.

Forcing herself to go downstairs, Jana went into the living room and glanced around for any sign of her mother or Taffy. There was no one. The silence of the room welcomed her, and Jana accepted the invitation. For several moments she did nothing but stand quietly and gather her thoughts. She couldn't help but wonder about the woman whose home this had been for so many years.

Jana began to study each picture and piece of memorabilia. Who was Taffy Anderson? What had she loved? Where had she traveled? Picking up an ebony carving of a black panther, Jana remembered Africa. She could almost feel the heat on her skin.

"If I hadn't gone . . ." she whispered to the figurine. But she knew her time in Africa had nothing to do with the destruction of her marriage. Apparently that had already been in the works.

She replaced the panther and continued to study the pieces on the fireplace mantel.

"You know what you need, dearie?"

Jana turned to find Taffy watching her. "No, what?" she asked her aunt.

"A drive up into the mountains. Stanley and I already have a trip planned today. Why don't you join us? We'll have great fun. We're going to picnic by a stream."

While the idea sounded inviting, Jana had no desire to be around other people. "Thanks anyway," she replied, shaking her head. "I'd rather not. But please ask me again sometime."

Taffy smiled sympathetically. "I will, but you must promise me something."

Jana cocked her head to the right. "And what would that be?"

"I want you to promise me that you won't dwell too long on 'what ifs.' It won't bring Rob back to you, but it very well might destroy your chance for further happiness."

"I doubt I'll ever be happy again."

"I used to think that way too. But it isn't true."

"But Rob was . . . I thought he was my soul mate, and I thought he felt the same toward me. That's why it hurt so much when he left me for Kerry. I'll never find anyone like that again— nor do I even want to try."

"And for now, thinking this way is perfectly fine," Taffy said, coming to where Jana stood. "You need time to mourn and to let go of the anger and hurt. You will never be the divorced wife of Rob McGuire. You are his widow. That's something no one can take away from you. It's a respectable title."

"You make it sound like an honor. He's dead, and I'd much rather have him back than have a respectable title."

Taffy reached out and touched Jana's cheek. Her hands were cold, but Jana didn't mind. "It's not that I want to make it sound honorable; it's just that I know how much it hurt you to think of being divorced—of bearing that title when you did nothing to deserve it. So many women suffer this fate, and sadly enough, even good Christian people treat them horribly for that title." Taffy patted Jana's face, then squeezed her hand. "It only matters because I'm coming to know you."

Jana had to admit the woman was right. It had bothered her a lot to think she would bear the title of divorcée when she had never done anything to instigate the dissolution of her marriage.

"I guess I see what you're saying," she finally replied. "Yet, being divorced or being widowed . . . I'm still left with nothing."

"Not true. You have the good memories and your baby."

"But the memories must have been false," Jana said. This was something she had concluded only a short time ago. "Just because I remember them as good doesn't mean they were. I thought things were fine. I thought we had a wonderful marriage with a great future. My memories are based on that, but apparently Rob had completely different thoughts on the matter."

"But we'll never know for sure, will we?"

Jana looked hard at Taffy. "We know he didn't feel that way, because he just walked away. He'd been planning it for some time. He couldn't have felt the same way I did about our relationship."

"Possibly," Taffy said softly, "but does that invalidate your feelings?"

Jana shrugged. "I don't know. I honestly don't. To me it seems that I believed an illusion—something not at all real."

"And is that how you feel about God as well?"

Jana turned away. "My relationship with Him seems as false as my marriage. I thought He was good and that He protected us from harm if we loved Him. I never worried about things even once in Africa because I believed God would care for me."

"But you don't believe God will care for you now?"

"I don't know what I believe," Jana answered honestly. She met her great-aunt's face, fearful of finding condemnation in her eyes. Instead, she found only compassion.

Taffy nodded. "It's best not to try and reason it all out overnight. Give yourself time, and maybe instead of focusing on the past, you could focus on the future. Your child will need you now more than ever."

"I'll try," Jana replied. There was something about this coming from Taffy that made her sincerely want to try.

Jana thought about Taffy's words long after her great-aunt had left for her mountain trip with Stanley. Lomara sat in a tiny valley with mountains all around them, so Jana knew the couple wouldn't have far to go on their adventure. She almost wished she'd gone with them—especially when Eleanor joined her in the living room.

Jana acknowledged her mother, then picked up one of Taffy's dozen or so magazines and pretended to be absorbed in an article about basket weaving. Eleanor looked like she was thoroughly captivated by a book on business, but Jana got the feeling her mother wanted to talk. That so surprised Jana that she put down the magazine and asked frankly, "How was it you came to live with Aunt Taffy?"

Eleanor looked over the top of her book as if annoyed. She seemed to contemplate the question for a moment, then closed her book. "There were problems with my parents, and Social Services came and took me away. Eventually I ended up with Taffy and Cal."

"Why didn't you ever tell me about them?"

"It didn't seem important. I mean, what was there to gain?"

Jana felt her anger rise and pushed it back down. "There were relationships to gain. I would have liked knowing them both—growing up with them as grandparents or grandparent substitutes."

Her mother clearly bristled at this suggestion. "Cal died shortly after you were born. There would have been no chance of knowing him."

"What about Aunt Taffy? That must have been a very hard time for her. Why didn't you want to be with her? I mean, surely she would have relished having family around her. Unless, of course, there are other family members you've kept hidden from me, and they were comforting her."

Eleanor quickly looked at her hands. For several moments she said nothing, making Jana confident that she'd hit upon a truth. Could it be possible? Did they have relatives Jana knew nothing about?

"Taffy had no one else," Eleanor finally stated.

"But there is other family, isn't there?" Jana questioned. "You've kept other people—other relatives—from me."

"I did what I had to do to protect you," Eleanor said, looking up. "Someday you'll understand that when you find yourself working to protect your child."

"Rob had no one left in his family. He was an only child, and his mother died last year from cancer. His father died before I even met Rob. So I'll have no need to protect or hide my child away."

"Then you'll be blessed."

Jana felt complete frustration at her mother's flippant answer. "Mom, what family members do I not know about?"

"It isn't important, Jana. They aren't a part of your life and never will be. Why do you always insist on living in the past?"

It was Jana's turn to stiffen. She had spent most of the morning in a world of memories, so her mother's words hit very close to the truth. "I suppose because I'm still trying to understand it. To understand us . . . you and me."

Eleanor shook her head and put the book on the table beside her chair. "That's the trouble with people. They analyze things to death—always looking for answers. Quite honestly, sometimes there are no answers, Jana. Like with Rob and this situation. Do you really suppose you'll find an answer to why he left? Why he was willing to forsake his vows and run away with his secretary?"

"Yes—I need answers. I need to understand why."

"But that may never come. Can you move forward anyway? I never got the answers I needed either, but I learned to get on with my life."

"But you were never happy. Hearing the truth might be painful, but at least I'd know and then I might have some understanding."

"Understand what, Jana? That your father wanted nothing to do with you unless you were a boy? That we had to make our way on our own?"

"But why? Why did my father only want a son? Why did having a daughter cause him to walk away from his marriage vows?"

Eleanor looked away. "There are too many *why*'s in life. It's better to ignore them. Sooner or later you'll understand this."

"But my father didn't want me!"

"Well, mine did want me and it still didn't make life good!" Eleanor declared a little louder than Jana expected.

They fell silent then, each retreating to the safe haven within that they'd created for themselves. Jana had a million questions she wanted to ask. It was strange after all these years that now, here in this place, she should finally have the chance to speak her mind. And yet something held her back.

Maybe it was the way her mother looked so childlike . . . so lost. *She looks like I feel*, Jana thought. *She looks like the world has completely betrayed her and she doesn't know how to go on.* Yet here was a woman who prided herself in her strength and ability to need no one.

Jana knew it probably wasn't the right time, or fair either, but she posed the question that had been on her heart.

"Mom, why did Social Services take you away?"

Eleanor looked at her for a moment, and Jana fully expected a snide comment. But instead her mother closed her eyes. "My mother died."

Jana had often wondered about her grandparents but had never been allowed to ask much about them. "How did she die?"

Eleanor's eyes seemed to glaze over. "Why do you want to know?"

Jana hadn't expected this. "I don't know. I guess to share it with you. You sound so sad. I know it must have been painful. You were just a kid."

"I don't think talking about it will make it any better," she said without emotion.

At least she isn't yelling at me. This conversation was much better than any Jana could remember having with her mother previously on the topic of family members. Still, if she didn't want to talk about her mother's death, Jana suddenly wanted to respect that.

"Well, how about telling me about my grandmother? I don't know anything about her—nothing," Jana said, hoping her mother would open up.

Eleanor's surprise was reflected in her face. "Tell you about her?" She sighed. "I wouldn't know where to begin."

"Start anywhere. Tell me about a good day—a day when things felt right."

Eleanor leaned back in her chair and closed her eyes. "I can't say that anything ever felt exactly right. I was always different. Nothing like my parents. Even then, I wanted nothing more than to have order, and their world brought me mostly chaos."

Jana was intrigued. "So tell me about it."

Seventeen

THE MEMORIES RUSHED over Eleanor and swept her back to a time shortly after the police fiasco. They had moved the commune, which wasn't hard to do considering many people lived in old campers, tents, and trailers. But it had started a sense of insecurity in Eleanor that she was hard-pressed to understand, much less deal with.

"I don't like this place as much," Eleanor told her mom.

Melody was an eternal optimist in most things. "This isn't so bad. We've got a few trees and plenty of good water."

Eleanor looked around her at the scrub ground. "But there isn't any good grass. Most of the yard is just rocks and sand." She hated this desertlike terrain. It seemed so barren, lifeless. Even more, she hated the fact that they had fled in the dead of night like criminals eluding the law. Eleanor could still remember the feeling that they would be stopped and forced to turn back around. She was terrified that her father and mother would go to jail.

Her mother seemed oblivious. She worked on a piece of macramé, sitting cross-legged on the ground outside their trailer. They were now living in her father's former office. It was all they had and, though cramped, it was better than living outside like some of the folks who had followed them to this area. Melody's cutoffs were caked with dirt from washing clothes at the river, and her T-shirt was torn in several places from years of wear.

Still, Eleanor thought her a pretty woman. She didn't worry about makeup or fancy ways to fix her hair, but her beauty was still evident. There weren't even any signs of worry on her face.

This was simply one more change in their life. It wasn't like she desired any kind of permanency. Eleanor knew this full well, for her mother spoke about it all the time.

"We're just a vapor—a mist. Here today and gone tomorrow. Even the Bible says so," her mother would say.

"Why can't we live in a house like other people?"

"What are you talking about? You've lived in a house before."

"But I mean in a real town, with running water and television."

Her mother stopped what she was doing. "Why would you want the hassle? There are all kinds of rules and complications. I've lived like that before. It's all about work and about money. You never have time to enjoy anything."

"But other people like it. I've heard some of the people talk about living like that. I think it would be fun to have all those neat things."

Shaking her head, her mother tried to explain. "People talk about owning things, but the truth is, things end up owning you. The more you have, the more time it takes. You, like, never realize it because it just sort of happens. Little by little. All of a sudden you realize you have to fix this and clean that, and pretty soon you need more money to get more things. It only leads to greed and envy. I know. I saw it all the time when I was a girl."

Eleanor sat down beside her mother. "Tell me about when you were growing up."

Melody shrugged and went back to the piece she was working on. "I grew up in a pretty big town. There were lots of people, to be sure. I had my own bedroom and lots of toys. I was born late in my parents' life—after my mother had lost several babies."

"Lost them?" Eleanor asked.

"You know, she miscarried them. They died before they were born."

"That must have been sad."

"It was hard on her, so when I was born she was extra excited. My sister was sixteen years older than me, so it was like having a new family. Kind of like with me and you—I was sixteen when you were born. My mother spent a lot of time with me. She used to take me shopping and to movies and symphonies. My father used to yell at her for all the time we were together. He said she was shirking her other duties."

"What duties?"

"They were rich, so they had to attend a lot of parties and events. They were always doing something with someone, but my mom sometimes said she was sick so she could stay home with me."

"She lied?"

Melody shrugged. "Something else was more important. Sometimes that's the way it is."

"So it's okay to lie?"

Melody looked at Eleanor and appeared to think about her answer for a moment. "Sometimes it's necessary. If Momma had told the truth, my father would never have allowed her to stay home. She wanted to be home, so she did what she had to do."

"Still, that doesn't seem right."

"That's a matter of opinion."

"Well, if everybody goes around lying so that they can do whatever they want, nothing will ever get done."

Melody seemed unconvinced. "And what needs to be done now that can't be done tomorrow?"

"Well . . ." Eleanor thought about it for a minute. "What about Dad? He's a doctor and people sometimes need him for emergencies. What if he tells that person that he can't help them because he feels sick? But what if he isn't really sick—he just wants to spend time with me?"

"Then someone else will have to help with the emergency."

"But there isn't anybody else. Dad's the only doctor here."

Her mother sighed in exasperation. "Eleanor, you worry too much. Life isn't all that complicated."

"I'd just like it to make sense."

Melody laughed. "Well, I doubt that will ever happen. Not with the way people act and think. Even my own parents were far from understandable. My parents sent me to boarding school when I was about your age. I hated it. They didn't care, though."

"Why did you hate it?" Eleanor pulled up her knees and propped her folded arms atop them.

"First of all, it took me away from my mother, and we were having a lot of fun together. I was scared too, but nobody cared. My dad said it was the way things would be done, and my mom told me to be brave and make her proud. I was depressed for weeks after I arrived at the school. I was a little bit chubby when I left home, but within six weeks they were worrying about the fact I'd dropped thirty pounds. I simply wasn't eating anything. My dad ordered me to start eating and stop being such a big baby, so I did my best." She shook her head sadly. "He never cared how I felt."

Eleanor felt sorry for her mother. She sounded so sad. "Why else did you hate it?"

"There were too many rules. They told us how to dress—we had to wear this awful uniform. White blouse, long blue sweater, and blue skirt. It was so confining. I remember once I forgot to wear a slip under my skirt and got detention for a week." She shuddered as though she were still wearing the thing. "They told us how we could wear our hair, and we weren't allowed any makeup or jewelry. We had to do our homework at a certain time, in a certain way, and we could never question our teachers about anything."

"But what kinds of questions would you have asked?"

Melody didn't answer for a minute. "Well, I would have questioned their negativity toward Communism. They were so terrified of it that they blasted it at every turn. They were always speaking out against the Russians. Always telling us they were our enemies. But Russia wasn't the enemy—they were. They couldn't stand people being such free thinkers."

"But why? Isn't free thinking a good thing?"

"Of course it is. But it's also a scary thing for people who think they have all the answers. The establishment of that school thought they knew the right—and the only—way to do things. They had their rules and they demanded everyone conform."

"Did your mom miss you?"

Her mother stopped working but didn't look at Eleanor. "I think so. I sure missed my mom. She and I were really close until I disappointed her and made my own way in life. She grew hateful, just as my father had always been, when she found out I was pregnant with you. After that, she wanted little to do with me."

"Why would she be mad that you got pregnant? Didn't she like babies?"

"She was mad because I was so young. She said that I'd ruined my life—that I had the chance to become someone special. I thought I already was." Melody looked at Eleanor, and Eleanor thought the expression on her mother's face was one of regret.

"But," her mother continued, "she was right on the issue of age. I was too young. I don't recommend having a baby at sixteen. You have no time to explore the world or do other things, because you have a child and some very heavy responsibilities. It's not cool at all. It's a drag because you're always having to worry about whether they have enough to eat and drink and clothes to wear. And if you don't have money to take care of the baby, that creates a problem."

"Did your mom stop talking to you because of me?" Eleanor suddenly felt consumed with guilt. She had caused her mother great pain and never even knew it.

"She stopped talking to me—stopped associating with me—because I wasn't married. It was a shameful thing in her society. People just didn't do things like that, and she was really upset. I was only fifteen, and she was completely scandalized by the entire situation. Plus, the school kicked me out, and that made it rough for her with my father."

"What do you mean, you weren't married?" Eleanor felt as though her mother had gut-punched her. "You and Dad weren't married when you made me?"

She frowned. "We never married, Ellie. I thought you knew that. We told my parents we'd eloped, mainly so they'd stop hassling your father. He was a new doctor helping at the boarding school and . . . well, I was underage when I, like, started sneaking out to be with him. Of course, this was against all the rules. He was so cool. Such a free thinker. I loved hearing his ideas and thoughts on the world. He hated that school as much as I did."

Eleanor's mind was whirling. "Wait!" She jumped to her feet, little swirls of sand and dirt falling from her as she moved away. "You and Dad aren't married?"

Melody looked genuinely surprised. She pushed her blond hair back and leaned back on her hands. "Of course not. Why should we be? We have a free and open relationship. We can be with anyone we want to be with—we just chose to stay with each other."

"But that's not right," Eleanor declared.

"Says who?"

"Well, that's not the way you're supposed to do it. You're supposed to have a ceremony and make it special. We even have weddings here in the commune."

"They wouldn't be deemed legal by the state," her mother countered. "We do it merely for the fun of doing it. Sometimes it makes people feel more married. But do you realize the stupidity of *legal* marriage? You go pay money and get a license—a piece of paper—that says it's okay for you to live together, pay bills together, raise kids. The state is telling you that this is okay, and not because they think you will be happy with each other or that you are a perfect choice for each other or that you think alike enough to make a good couple. They say it's okay because you've paid your money. That's all."

Eleanor felt sick inside. The idea that her parents weren't married truly bothered her for some reason. She'd never considered it before. She and her friends always talked about falling in love and getting married. How could it be that her parents weren't a part of this?

"Then you go to some church or judge and they say a few words over you, and that makes you married. Just like that. Why should I be a part of that? I love your dad and we've had all you kids because of that love. The rules of the state don't change that."

"But what about promising to stay together?"

"You mean a commitment?" Melody shook her head. "We are committed in our own way. But, Ellie, if your dad decides he wants to be with someone else, why should that bug me? Sure, I'd miss him and I wouldn't stop loving him, but why would you want to force someone to be with you when they didn't want to be there? You can't hold on to people like they're some kind of possession. Your dad isn't some nice piece of furniture I found at the store. He's a human being with his own mind. I don't own him and he sure doesn't own me."

"But you could break up."

"But we could even if we were married. It's called a divorce. Eleanor, I don't see why you're so upset. It doesn't change anything. Your dad and I are married in our minds, our hearts. That's all that matters. We have our own kind of commitment, but we don't hassle each other. That would be a bum trip. It would destroy what we have."

Eleanor couldn't stand any more. She ran off toward the river, heartbroken to know the truth. Her mother called after her, but she ignored her. Why bother? She'd probably tell Eleanor something else that she didn't want to hear.

She didn't realize she was crying until her nose got all stopped up. Sniffing, Eleanor wiped her face on her shirt. She felt terrified of what the future might hold. What if her mother grew tired of her father? What if she decided to pick up and move away, taking the kids with her? Or what if she decided she didn't want to be a mom anymore and left them all behind?

Eleanor wasn't a naïve child. She'd heard enough from other people in the commune—new people from the outside—that there was a whole different way of doing things in the outside world. She'd always known this to be true, but the things she'd been hearing were intriguing to her—maybe even calling to her.

There was, in her soul, a need for something more permanent. Something she could call her own. She dreamed of living in a real house, with floors that didn't creak and walls that had good paint. And a dog. A dog would be so nice to have. A little dog. Her folks never wanted to have pets because of the hassle and cost. Her father said it wasn't good to take food out of the children's mouths and give it to a dog. He hadn't relented on his position, even when Eleanor offered to share her food with the animal.

"I'd get a dog," she said, sobbing the words against her arm. "I'd get a dog and a house and I'd find somebody and marry them with the license and everything." In that moment, Eleanor's heart changed toward her mother. For some reason she felt confident that most of this had been her mother's idea. Her father surely wouldn't have done this on his own accord. He loved Eleanor— he was always there for her in a way no one else had ever been. Eleanor was certain that living in such a haphazard way could never have been his plan.

That night, as Eleanor lay in bed trying to sleep, she grew even more resentful toward her mother. *Just because she didn't like living in a house and having rules, she has to force me to live like this. It isn't fair.*

She fell asleep with a bitterness in her heart that she'd never known. It was still with her the next day when her mother rallied her and her brothers for breakfast. Eleanor sat at the table listening to her brothers' incessant chattering and complaining.

They have no idea what they're missing out on, she thought. *They're too little to understand like I do. I've heard stories and know about things.* She watched her mother slip around the kitchen as if she had the world by the tail.

Our parents aren't even married, she thought, looking down the table at her siblings. What did that mean? What would happen if her parents decided to suddenly give up being parents— just as they had the choice to give up being together? The thought sickened Eleanor. Where would they go? What would she do? Would she have to take care of her brothers? How in the world could she do that? She was only a girl without any money or real education.

"Where's Dad?" she suddenly asked.

Her mother looked up from wiping Spirit's face. "He's seeing people. Since we need this place to live, he's going to them. You know that's how it's done."

"Oh, are those *your* rules?"

Her mother looked at her oddly. "What's with you? You've been sour-faced all morning and you're bringing me down. It's a beautiful day and I was in complete harmony until you woke up."

"Well, I was in complete harmony until you told me you weren't married to Dad," Eleanor snipped.

"Oh, forget it, Eleanor. It's not a big deal. We've been together so long now, the state probably considers us married. They call it common-law marriage."

"I don't care," she said. "I don't consider it anything." She got up and stormed out of the trailer, nearly losing her balance on the rickety metal steps her father had put in place at the front door.

It was one defining moment in her life that Eleanor would carry with her forever. It changed her heart—not only toward her family, but it redefined who she was and wanted to be. She had thought she was happy, or at least satisfied with the world she lived in. Now it was as if a door of discontent had been opened.

"I want something more," she muttered and walked past her hippie neighbors and the clutter of communal living.

Eighteen

FOR THE NEXT COUPLE of days, Eleanor avoided her father. She almost felt ashamed of him, yet she didn't understand why. There were no rules in their world that said her parents had done wrong. She'd even found out that many of the other couples in the commune were unmarried. It never seemed a problem to any other children that their parents were unwed.

Eleanor kept mulling the situation over in her mind. Why did it bother her so much? *It just seems,* she concluded, *that everything I've been taught is a lie.* But how could that be? Her father loved her, and everything he'd ever done for her had proven that.

I shouldn't want to avoid him, but I'm not sure I want to deal with this truth either. Nothing feels right. The whole world—my world—seems so wrong. She knew her father would have answers, but she wasn't convinced they would be helpful ones. Her parents' loose philosophy of open marriage and free love didn't provide what she longed for: confidence and security. Still, it wasn't right to say nothing. Sooner or later her father would realize she was avoiding him, and then he would be hurt. She didn't want that.

With this on her heart, Eleanor decided it was finally time to have a talk with her father. She went in search of him, knowing from her mother that he had gone for a walk along the river. All the way, walking slowly and contemplating her words, Eleanor hoped fervently that he might explain her fears away.

The day was hot and dry, and when the wind did blow, it seemed to be full of grit and sand. Eleanor felt she was always eating sand. It was in the air, in the food.

"I don't like it here," she muttered, wiping her mouth with the back of her hand. "It's ugly, and I wish we could live somewhere else."

Eleanor wandered along for about half an hour before she finally spotted her father sitting beside the river on a rock. She felt nervous about approaching him. If she didn't talk to him now, she might not ever talk to him again. She knew that above all else, she didn't want that.

"Dad?" she called.

"Ellie girl, come on over. What are you doing out here?"

"I came to see you," she said as she approached. *He looks tired,* she thought. *Tired and more dirty than he usually likes to be.* His hair was a bit longer than he usually wore it, but that was because her mother hadn't had time to cut it.

Her father drew her into his arms and positioned her on his lap as he had done for as long as Eleanor had memory. "So what do you want to talk about?"

She looked away. She felt she very well might start to cry. She sucked in her lower lip and waited for the feeling to pass.

"Ellie," he said softly, brushing back the hair from her face, "is this about what your mother told you the other day? About us not being married?"

Eleanor nodded but didn't trust herself to speak. She hadn't realized that her father knew about the discussion she'd had with her mother.

"That really bothers you, doesn't it?"

Again she nodded, but this time she met his eyes. The love he held for her there was more comforting than any words he could have spoken. She felt in that moment that if the world suddenly fell apart, her daddy would find a way to protect her and keep her safe with him. She wrapped her arm around his neck and put her head on his shoulder. He cradled her for several minutes, his hand gently stroking her arm and leg.

"Ellie, it doesn't mean you aren't loved. It doesn't even mean that Mom and I don't love each other. We just don't believe in the same rules that the world wants to put on us. The establishment doesn't understand our hearts."

"But it scares me," Eleanor finally whispered. "I don't know why you never told me the truth before now."

Her father shrugged, causing her to sit back up. "One man's truth is another man's lie. Who defines truth?"

"Well, there's gotta be some things that never change," she declared. "Some things have to be true no matter what."

"Sure, there are some things. Like we have to breathe air. We have to have water to survive. Those things don't change."

"But love does, doesn't it?"

"Love?" he asked. "Why do you worry about love?"

"Because you and Mom could decide you don't love each other and leave. You could decide you don't love me."

"Ellie, that will never happen. I'll always love you."

She found no comfort in his words. "But what about Mom? What about our family? Will we always be together?"

"Well, as far as I'm concerned, we'll be together for a good long while. But, Ellie, you'll grow up and want to move out. You'll want to start a home of your own."

"Do you and Mom love each other?"

"Of course we do." He looked at her thoughtfully. "But it's our definition of love. Not someone else's. See, that's what I mean about truth. The truth is a matter of perspective. I have one truth, and for me it works well. Someone else has another truth and for them, that's the answer."

"But it seems to me there should be only one truth," Eleanor said seriously.

"Why?"

She looked at him for a moment. "Well, one truth would make things more simple. If everybody has their own truth, it seems to me that things will get pretty complicated. Like I told Mom the other day: what if your truth causes someone else to get hurt?"

"You can only be hurt by people if you let yourself be hurt. It's all up to you, Ellie girl. You don't have to let people hurt you."

Ellie shook her head. "Daddy, that doesn't make sense. You and Mom hurt me by not getting married. It wasn't just me *letting* myself get hurt."

"Wasn't it? You weren't hurt until you decided that the way we'd done things was wrong. In fact, as I recall, you were pretty happy. You let the world come in with its regulations and say you were unhappy, and all because we weren't doing things by their rules. You didn't have to let this hurt you, Ellie."

She thought about that for several minutes. Maybe he was right. Maybe she didn't need to be hurt about anything ever again. If it were only a matter of willing the pain to go away or refusing to feel anything in the first place, maybe that really was the way to get by.

"Ellie, the world is full of lies. It tells you that you need certain things in order to be happy, and it sets boundaries for you that you don't need or understand."

"Like what? What kind of boundaries?"

"Like the rules and laws that govern the land. The politicians will tell you that this is to make things better, to help our lives run smoother. But do you have any idea how complicated things have gotten?"

"Complicated, how?"

"Well, for instance, it used to be that anyone could be a doctor who wanted to be. A person only had to learn about medicine and people's ailments and he could be a healer. But now you have to be licensed and go through all sorts of college and training."

"But training is good, isn't it? Isn't learning about stuff helpful?"

"To a degree, but sometimes the best learning comes from actually doing the job. I think I could have been a good doctor even without college. I spent half of my college years learning a lot of other things that had nothing to do with being a doctor. I took art classes and English and history. None of those things helped me learn about medicine. I could already communicate by reading and writing. I didn't need more English to teach me that. I knew history enough to understand how wrong we were in our philosophies and ideologies, but I certainly didn't need more of the same in order to be a good doctor."

"So boundaries are wrong?" Eleanor asked.

"Boundaries are deceptive. People set boundaries because they're important to them. They tell each other, 'These are my boundaries and you can't cross them.'"

Eleanor's confusion grew. "But isn't that what they do with their different truths too? Aren't they saying, 'This is my truth and it doesn't matter what you think or how it hurts you'?"

Her father sighed and tousled her hair. "Ellie, I don't expect you to understand everything right now. You're not even a teenager yet. Almost," he said with a grin, "but not quite." He hugged her close.

"I can't help feeling scared, Daddy. It seems like everything that makes me feel safe is gone. I liked our old house, but then we had to move. I heard some of the girls talking about moving to the city and the places you could go, and it sounds like fun. I think I'd like to go to the city. Does that make me a bad person?"

"No, it doesn't make you bad. I just don't want to see you conform to a world that doesn't care how you feel. Our friends out here care about one another. We share what we have with one another and we don't worry about a lot of rules. We keep things cool."

"But I feel like something's missing. I feel all empty inside. Like I need something, and I don't even know what it is."

Her father nodded. "All you really need is love. And you have that. I'll always love you and so will your mom. You don't need to be afraid."

"But sometimes people stop loving," Eleanor said frankly. "They stop caring." She sat up and looked at her dad. "They leave each other and everything changes. What if Mom decides to leave? What if you decide to leave?"

"I know this won't make things better, but, Ellie, everyone has the right to walk away when the time comes. You can't hold on to people—you can't put a leash around their necks and force them to your side. Would you like it if I said you could never grow up and leave?"

"Well, no, I suppose not."

"Then why do you worry about that with me?"

"Because you're an adult and you can do what you want. I'm just a kid. If you left, it would be bad, and I would be scared. I need you."

"Ellie, you shouldn't need anybody. That's why you're scared. You're putting too much dependency on the people around you. We could all die tomorrow. I have no say over life and death in that way. I don't want you to need me for your existence. If you do, then I've done something wrong in raising you."

Ellie looked at her father quizzically. She pushed up from his lap and stared at him, trying hard to take in all his words. He stood and shoved his hands in his jean pockets. "The less you need in life, Ellie, the happier you'll be. Think about that and you'll find out soon enough for yourself that it's true. If you don't need people or things, then when they go away you won't feel that sense of loss—that hurt. That's one of the ways you control whether or not you get hurt."

She felt a deep sadness wash over her. "So you don't need me?"

Her father's expression grew almost stern. "No, Ellie. I don't need you. I love you, and that will never change. But I don't need you."

"And you don't need Mom or the boys?"

"No. I don't need them either. To need them would be to set up boundaries for myself that would fence me in and kill me."

"So if Mom leaves or I leave, you won't feel anything about it? You won't care?"

"I didn't say I wouldn't care, but, Ellie, I'm a doctor. I see people being born and dying all the time. If I let myself care too much, it would destroy me. It'll destroy you, too, if you don't try to understand it now."

"I'll try to understand, but I don't know if I will."

She walked away and he didn't call to her. She almost wished he would. There was a part of her that felt crushed and broken inside. She hated the feeling. What was wrong with everybody? What was wrong with her?

Eleanor spent the next few weeks longing to understand. She even talked to Sapphira about it, but neither girl could grasp what Eleanor's father had been talking about.

"It seems to me that everybody needs somebody," Sapphira reasoned.

"That's what I think," Eleanor replied. She and her friend were spending the night together in a tent not far from the Templeton trailer.

"I don't think I'd like to go all my life and have nobody need me," Sapphira confided. "I mean, that sounds awful to me."

Eleanor knew exactly how her friend felt. It hurt inside to imagine that her father didn't need her. She used to feel important in his life, and now she didn't.

"Do you suppose we'll get married some day?" Eleanor asked.

"I guess so. I think Tommy Meyers is kind of cute. I wouldn't mind fooling around with him."

"Sapphira!" Eleanor was surprised by her friend's comment.

"Well, why not? That's what people do with each other."

"I know, but I didn't expect you to, like, well, say it that way. It sounds bad when you talk like that."

"Well, Ally and Samantha have been fooling around with some of the boys. Ally told me it feels really good. And if it feels good, it can't be bad."

"I guess that makes sense." But in truth, Eleanor wasn't sure anything made sense.

"The real key," Sapphira explained in her thirteen-year-old wisdom, "is that you love each other. If you love each other, then fooling around is okay. That's what my mom told me."

"But a lot of people around here fool around with each other. Do you suppose they love each other?"

"Sure. Why not? We're supposed to love everybody."

"Then does that mean we can fool around with everybody?" Eleanor's question sounded strange in her own ears. The logic seemed skewed somehow.

"I think it does," she said. "It's all about love."

"My dad said love was all we needed."

"Yeah, I think that's right." Sapphira yawned and rolled over, leaving her back to Eleanor.

For a long time Eleanor stayed awake, thinking. She was supposed to love people, and they in turn would or could love her back. She should never need anybody or let anybody else need her. And physical intimacy was all right as long as you loved the person you were with. And truth? Well, that was what she made it.

Somehow none of it set well with her. It just didn't figure. Eleanor liked things reasonable and logical, and she couldn't understand why it didn't make sense. It was like trying to work a puzzle, but the pieces didn't go together. They just didn't fit.

———

The clock on the wall chimed and Eleanor opened her eyes. Gone was the tent and Sapphira. Gone were her twelve-year-old worries. She looked at Jana, somewhat surprised. She'd never intended to share all of that. What had gotten into her? By the look on Jana's face, Eleanor knew her story would only lead to more questions, more demands for explanation. That was always the way when you shared something.

"I need to start supper," Eleanor said, getting to her feet. She didn't wait to hear any protest or comment from Jana, so she hurried into the kitchen, images of yesteryear still lingering around her.

She leaned against the counter and sighed. *Why did I tell Jana all of that? Why did I open myself up? I can't let it happen again. I can't let her know the truth. Not about my mother and certainly not about my father.*

Nineteen

JANA SAT IN stunned silence as her mother left the room. How could all of that have been in her mother's life and yet the woman had never said anything about it? It wasn't like she'd experienced the difference between rural and city life. Jana's mother had grown up in a heavy drug culture as a hippie, living free and wild. Jana would have been amused by the idea had it not been so extraordinary.

How had her mother journeyed from such loose morals and chaos to absolute order? Jana got up and followed her mother to the kitchen. Determined to get answers, she stood in the arched dining room doorway and watched her mother for a moment. It was clear she was upset, but Jana so desired more answers she selfishly decided to push for them.

"You can't just stop there, Mom. You know that."

"I can stop wherever I want to," Eleanor said in a rather clipped manner. "I never meant to share that information to begin with. It was a mistake."

"No it wasn't. I hardly know anything about you—about my family. The things you told me give me some insight to better understanding why you raised me the way you did. That whole thing about not needing people could have been a page out of the textbook you used to raise me."

"So what?" Eleanor took a package of celery out of the refrigerator and placed it on the counter. "It's not important now."

"But of course it's important now!" Jana declared. She crossed the room and came to stand beside her mother. "Don't you see? We're finally having some real communication."

"Oh, don't be so melodramatic." Eleanor turned away to retrieve a cutting board.

"I'm not being melodramatic, I'm being honest—something I don't think we've done a lot of together. What little 'together' time there has been."

"You make it sound as though you grew up in an orphanage. For pity's sake, Jana, you've had a good life, and yet all I've ever heard from you has been complaints. You never went hungry or had to worry about the clothes on your back. You never had to live in danger or fear that all you enjoyed would suddenly be stripped away from you."

"I also never grew up with a sense of family. You were always gone or else I was at boarding school."

"I had a business to run, Jana," Eleanor said, turning to look at her daughter. "That's something you've never understood. The bookstore didn't succeed on its own steam. I had to put a lot of hours in."

"But you also had a child. I wasn't succeeding on my own steam either, yet that never seemed to bother you."

Eleanor began to cut the celery into chunks. "No one is ever happy with their upbringing, Jana. They can always point to some flaw, some indiscretion or frustration. They do this in order to blame someone else for the problems in their life. You want to blame me for the fact that your husband left you, but it's not my fault that Rob ran off with his secretary."

Her words stunned Jana. Was that what she thought this was all about? Did her mother honestly think Jana was simply look-ing for someone to blame? "I've never thought you were a part of my situation, Mother. I'm not even sure why you would suggest such a thing."

Eleanor paused and looked at Jana. Jana thought her mother seemed to genuinely search her face for the truth of her statement. Then, shaking her head, Eleanor went back to work.

Jana decided a cup of coffee might be in order and went to the cupboard for a cup. "You want some?" she asked, holding out a mug.

"No."

Jana poured her own cup and then went to the fridge for cream. There had to be a way to break through her mother's walls.

"You still didn't tell me much about what your mother was like," Jana said.

"It really doesn't matter. She's dead, and there's no purpose served by dredging up her memory."

"I don't understand you." Jana walked to the back door and stared out at the well-tended lawn. One of Stanley's great-grandsons came and mowed the grass every other week, while Taffy still puttered around planting flowers and trimming bushes. Jana often liked to take her coffee outside to the little picnic area Taffy and Eleanor had put together.

Jana turned away from the sanctuary, however, and decided to ask another question. Perhaps this would be enough of a curve ball that her mother would take the swing without thinking.

"When you said you loved me enough to protect me from the past," Jana began, "was this what you were talking about or was it something else?"

Eleanor said nothing for several minutes, and Jana wasn't even sure she'd heard the question. Finally, however, Eleanor put the cleaver aside and bent down to pull a pan from the bottom cupboard.

"The past is full of pain," her mother stated as she put the celery into the pan. "What mother wouldn't want to protect her child from that?"

"But the past is also full of good things."

"Not according to you."

Jana frowned. "What do you mean?"

Eleanor went to the faucet and turned it on. She let the pan fill halfway before shutting the water off. "Everything you've ever said about your childhood has been negative. Despite my best efforts to give you everything you needed to be healthy and well educated, it wasn't enough. You bemoan the fact that you know nothing about your family ancestry, as though it negates everything else that was done for you."

"Didn't it ever occur to you that all I really needed was a mother and father who loved me—who wanted to be with me? That's all I wanted."

"Well, Jana, we don't always get what we want." Eleanor put the pan on the stove.

"That's not a good enough answer. I'm a grown woman now, and I won't be hushed up by my mother." Jana nearly slammed the coffee mug down. "You owe me an explanation."

"I owe you nothing," Eleanor said indignantly. "I have a right to my own life. I have a right to have done things in the best way I could for me."

"Is that some more of your father's hippie philosophy? 'If it feels good, do it'?"

Jana could see her mother's jaw clench. She'd pushed her too hard.

"You don't know what you're talking about."

"Of course not, because you never tell me anything."

"I just told you quite a bit and it still wasn't enough. This is exactly why I don't talk about the past. Look at the way you're acting. Look at the anger in your heart. Nothing is ever enough for you, Jana. It never has been. Not when you were a child and not now. You'll never be satisfied, so please stop coming to me for the answers."

The words cut deep. Jana leaned back against the counter. Was she right? Did her mother have a better grip on her than she had on herself? It hadn't been enough—that much was true. Her mother had opened Pandora's box, and Jana wanted another peek inside.

"Just answer me this," Jana said, her voice more calm. "Is the past you're protecting me from yours or mine?"

Jana didn't expect her mother to answer, but she did. The simplicity of the reply chilled Jana to the bone—and for reasons she couldn't even put her finger on.

"Both."

Jana picked up her coffee again and drank the entire cup. She poured herself another, this time not even worrying about the cream. She felt very close to understanding something—something crucial. Yet unless her mother was a willing participant in this game, Jana knew the revelation would never come.

She went to the back door again. Taffy and Stanley had come home and were roaming around the grounds together. Taffy was pointing to one thing and then another. Jana knew they would soon come inside and that if she wanted any answers, she would have to ask now.

"Do you know where my father is?"

The question came out in such a low, soft tone that Jana wasn't positive she'd even asked it aloud.

"He's dead." Her mother's flat, matter-of-fact reply only served to make Jana angrier. Ignoring the couple in the garden, Jana turned back to her mother once again. Eleanor crossed the room to the refrigerator and took out a wrapped platter of chicken breasts.

"Dead?" Jana asked. "For how long?"

"A long, long time."

"Why did you never tell me? When I asked where he was, you always told me you didn't know."

Eleanor shrugged. "For a while, I didn't know. It was years before I knew the truth."

"But when you learned it, why didn't you tell me?"

"To what purpose? Why should I have explained or attempted to explain to a little girl that a man who'd never wanted her in the first place was dead?"

"Why was he so against having a daughter?" Jana always felt her heart break a little more each time her mother mentioned this aspect of the past. How could a father be so cruel as to deny a child based solely on her gender?

"Jana, none of these questions serves any purpose."

"They serve the purpose of helping me deal with who I am and why I made the choices I made. Remember what you told me when you found out I was marrying Rob and how much older he was than me?"

She shook her head. "I'm sure you'll tell me."

"You told me I was looking for a father and that marrying Rob was a big mistake."

"And it was."

"Yes, it was," Jana admitted. "But maybe, just maybe, if you would have talked to me about the past—about my own father—maybe I wouldn't have made that mistake."

"See, I told you." Eleanor took a bottle of herbs off the rack and shook some onto the chicken. "You're just looking for some-one to blame."

"No, Mother. I'm looking for a way to understand who I am

and why I made those choices. My choices. They are my mistakes—my problems. I'm not asking you to take credit or blame, and if that's what you're so terrified of, then rest assured it's not my goal."

"I'm not afraid of your questions. I simply see that they serve no purpose. Why should I waste my time? You've ruined an otherwise perfectly quiet day by pushing me for answers."

"If you cherish the silence so much, why are you here? Taffy is hardly a quiet person. She's vivacious and happy. You are neither."

Eleanor stopped what she was doing and took a deep breath. "She's getting too old to be alone. That's the only reason I'm here."

"I don't believe you. I think you need her as much as she needs you. You've blown your first rule of living."

Eleanor looked up, but instead of anger, Jana thought her expression registered hurt. "Think what you will."

"I want to know who my father was and who his family was. I want to know my background—my ancestry. I can't believe you'd be so selfish as to keep it from me just because you're afraid that by sharing the truth with me you'll somehow be changed or wounded further."

"I would be changed. Everything would be changed . . . everything." She sounded shaken—almost scared.

"So that's it? That's all I ever get? No answers. No understanding. I don't get to know my father because it would change things for you?"

"Your father was an irrelevant mistake. Nothing more." Her mother seemed to regain control over her emotions. "The past will only hurt you, Jana. I wonder, will you give the gory details of your husband's adulterous affair and betrayal to your child? Will you spell out all the facts simply because your daughter or son demands that you do so? Will you explain the hurt—the rejection—the lies?"

Jana's chest tightened. She felt completely silenced by those few brief questions. There was no way she wanted her child to know the truth and grow up hating her father. But she also didn't want to lie to the child if she asked questions—if she needed to know the truth. What was the answer? Her mother had chosen one way. Had it been the right one?

———

"Do you suppose they're done arguing?" Stanley asked. "It seems like it's quieted down in there."

Taffy made a face. "I doubt they'll ever be done arguing. That's what happens when you build your relationship on lies."

Stanley joined her at the garden table. "They could be so helpful to each other."

"They could indeed, but they won't let it happen. They are so afraid of the way it might feel—the pain it might cause. They never think about the joy or happiness they might know. I tell you, Stanley, it's like living with two kegs of dynamite. I'm just waiting for one or the other to go off."

"Here you are," Jana said as she came around the corner. "I saw you in the garden earlier."

Taffy smiled. "We had the most glorious drive. You really should have come with us."

"I probably should have. Mother and I had a bad time together." Jana looked away. "Well, it was good and bad." She looked at Stanley and immediately apologized. "Sorry. I shouldn't be airing dirty laundry, as Taffy says."

Stanley laughed. "Well, it's not the most efficient way to clean it, but at least an airing helps to blow off some of the dirt."

Taffy motioned to a chair. "Why don't you sit down and tell

me what you fought about this time."

Jana glanced back at the house, then sat down and looked to Taffy. "Mom told me a little bit about her childhood—growing up in a hippie commune."

"Well, that's something," Taffy said, looking to Stanley. "She's never talked about that with anyone but me, and that was many years ago. I'd say that's a major breakthrough that should be celebrated."

"I thought so too, but Mother uses it to point out that it only served to stir up more questions. When I questioned her about the past and asked for more answers, she got mad. She told me that it wasn't important—that it could only hurt me. I know there's some truth in what she says, but frankly, I feel like if I could just deal with it once and for all, it would hurt me less in the long run."

"We'll have to keep praying that she finds the strength to share it," Taffy said thoughtfully. "I have a feeling, however, that God has brought you two together for this very purpose."

Jana frowned and looked at her hands. "I don't think God has anything to do with this."

"Well, that's the way pagans usually feel," Taffy quipped.

Jana's head shot up. "I'm not a pagan."

Taffy laughed. "No, you're not. So stop acting like one."

Jana seemed to consider this a moment. "I just don't think I understand God any better than I do my mother."

"Are you trying to understand Him?"

"What do you mean?"

Taffy cocked her head to one side. "Are you reading His Word? Are you praying for insight?"

Jana lowered her head again. "Well . . . not exactly."

"Then why get mad that you don't understand? Quite frankly, there's a lot I don't understand, but the Bible has taught me that sometimes it's all about walking in faith. That I don't necessarily get to know the answers."

"So I might never understand why Rob and Mom have done the things they've done. Is that it? If it is, what comfort is there in that?"

"None," Taffy said solidly. "Why should there be comfort in anything of this earth? Comfort is found in the Lord alone—not in earthly understandings or human relationships. Oh, of course we find comfort of sorts in our relationships, but it's not lasting. People die."

"Mom said that her father told her she should never need anyone. That seems to be a philosophy she's taken to heart."

"Excuse me for saying it, but this world is full of all sorts of false theologies and philosophies," Stanley threw in.

"Stanley's right. The world would tell you that there are many ways to happiness—to peace of mind—to eternal life. But the Bible says there is only one. One way."

"Jesus," Jana whispered. "I remember that verse in John that says, 'I am the way and the truth and the life.'"

"Exactly. If you can't find your way through all of this, remember that verse. If you think the truth is obscured and you feel desperate for it, remember that verse. When you feel like your life is over, remember that verse," Taffy said, reaching out to take hold of Jana's hands. "Jana, I really don't think you are looking for earthly understanding as much as you are spiritual . . . heavenly understanding."

Twenty

"WE'RE HEADING OFF now," Taffy called to Jana.

Jana emerged from the kitchen, where she'd been putting away dishes from the dishwasher. "How long will it take for you to get to Missoula?"

"Only a couple of hours," Taffy replied. "Unless your mother drives like a pastor."

Jana looked at her great-aunt oddly. "What in the world do you mean?"

Taffy laughed. "Every pastor I've ever ridden with—anywhere—went well over the speed limit. I figure it's because they're prayed up and feel confident of the situation. Either that or they figure to scare their passengers into salvation."

Jana laughed. "Rob drove fast too." The memory sobered her. She sighed. "Well, I wish I felt more like going," she said, rubbing her abdomen. Up until that morning she'd fully planned to make the trip. "I'm afraid given the way I feel, it would be a mistake. I'm just worn out today and a little bit on the green side. I thought I was past the morning sickness."

"Are you sure you'll be all right by yourself?" Taffy questioned. "We could put this off for a couple of days."

"I'm fine; I'm not disabled—just pregnant." Jana hoped Taffy wouldn't cancel her trip.

"Well, if you're sure." Taffy looked at her as if trying to size up the situation.

"I'll be great. Go on without me."

Taffy nodded. "You rest and enjoy the day. Don't worry about fixing any supper. We'll be back around eight or nine tonight, so I'm sure we'll eat in town. I have your list of things and your sizes. And I have lots of party shopping to do."

The twenty-fourth of July was Taffy's eightieth birthday, and she was throwing herself a party. Eleanor thought it scandalous and chided her aunt for not allowing her and Jana to organize the celebration. But Taffy would not relent.

"Who better to throw me a birthday party than me?" she had said.

"What are you planning for us?" Jana asked, sizing up her great-aunt. Taffy had dressed for the shopping trip in an emerald-green pantsuit with a wild, almost psychedelic, patterned blouse.

"Oh, we'll have such fun. It'll all be outside, of course," Taffy began. "We'll invite all of the neighborhood, and I'm going to have the dinner catered."

"There's going to be a dinner?" Jana asked.

"Oh yes. A dinner, a dance . . . a regular whirling dervish." Her aunt laughed in great amusement. "And a photographer to take pictures so that I might remember it all in the years to come. One does not turn eighty every day, after all."

"It sounds like a lot of fun," Jana admitted.

"It sounds like a lot of work," her mother added as she stepped into the room.

"Oh, pshaw. I'm hiring most of it done," Taffy declared. "You won't have to weary yourself with it."

"I wasn't worried about that," Eleanor replied. "It just seems a bit out of control."

Taffy grinned and winked at Jana. "Sometimes we have to be a bit out of control. But only a bit. We'll still be very sensible. I

191

haven't completely lost my faculties, even though you think I have."

"I have never said any such thing," Eleanor said rather indignantly.

"Well, be that as it may, we need to get started or we might as well spend the night in Missoula. I want time to eat out— especially at the Montana Club. No sense going to Missoula if you can't eat there."

Jana thought Taffy had a wonderful perspective on life. Even Jana's mother never managed to get the best of the older woman. Taffy had a flare for living and a zest for life and mankind that Jana had never known. *Not once in my life,* Jana thought, *have I ever known her kind of enthusiasm.*

She watched them leave, Eleanor chiding Taffy about her shoes, questioning whether they'd be good for walking long distances. Jana thought the silver sandals trimmed in beadwork were charming, but for once she wondered if her mother was right about her concerns.

Taffy waved Eleanor off and got into the car without another word. Jana smiled. "I want to grow up to be just like you, Taffy."

Jana spent the next couple of hours going through magazines and catalogs for nursery furniture. It had been her plan to settle into some serious buying for the nursery. She was wearing her first maternity outfit that day, a white and yellow capri set with delicate flowers embroidered on the blouse. She felt ever so maternal, as the style accentuated her growing stomach. There was something about maternity clothes that made the pregnancy seem all the more real to her.

Jana had planned to go shopping in Missoula; the excitement of picking out baby accessories was something that had kept her in a positive, upbeat spirit. She hated missing out on the trip, but to compensate, Taffy had suggested she shop by catalog for some things and give them a list for the others. Jana had complied, giving Taffy a list of various items that she was certain the older woman would have no difficulty finding.

Jana enjoyed dreaming over the tiny clothes and nursery furniture. For a time, she was able to set aside the serious nature of her situation, but the questions continued to lurk in her mind. What if the state of Washington decided she was an accessory to the crime Jason had committed? What if she actually ended up going to prison? She shuddered.

"I can't think that way."

She forced her attention back to the catalogs and turned page after page in first one and then another. Her mother had surprised them all by suggesting they go online to see what was available there. Jana hadn't even realized there was a computer in the house. Her mother explained that it was in her room and, as if Jana were four years old, told her that if she would refrain from disturbing anything else, she was welcome to use it.

Ever since their talk about her mother's past, Eleanor had been different. Jana wasn't sure why or what it signaled, but her mother honestly hadn't seemed quite so closed up—so harsh. It was a welcome change, but Jana wondered how long she could count on it. Jana had tried on a couple of occasions to instigate another conversation about her mother's childhood, but Eleanor had merely redirected the subject. Rather than being confrontational, she had simply moved to another arena. It seemed more tolerable than fighting.

Jana was getting up to call in an order for a lovely white crib when the doorbell sounded. She thought it might be Stanley coming over to bring some tomatoes he'd promised Taffy. He was very proud of his hothouse efforts and loved to share them with Taffy. To be honest, Jana was sure that Stanley loved Taffy, but nothing was ever mentioned about this.

Jana put the catalog aside and went to let him in. She opened the door with a smile, but instead of finding Stanley there, Jana came face-to-face with Kerry Broadbent—the one woman she'd hoped never to see again.

For several moments Jana couldn't think clearly. Memories rushed to her mind, swirling around her and paralyzing her with something akin to fear. She wanted to say something, but the words wouldn't come. Instead, she stepped back a couple of paces, almost as if to distance herself from her enemy.

"Jana, I know this is awkward, but—" Kerry suddenly gasped and tears came to her eyes. She sobbed out the next phrase. "So you are pregnant." Her gaze was fixed on Jana's midsection.

Jana's defenses went into place as she armed herself with sarcasm. "Yes, I'm pregnant. Did you think I would lie about something like that?"

Kerry pulled a tissue from her purse and wiped her eyes but continued to look at Jana. "Jason told me you'd said that, but I thought maybe it was just your way of getting at Rob. That you were lying in order to get him back."

Jana crossed her arms. "Why would I have wanted him back? After he took everything I had and betrayed me with you, what life could we have had together?"

Kerry shook her head. "Look, I'm doing this all wrong. I know this isn't easy for you. It's not easy for me either, but I'm begging you to hear me out."

Jana wanted to slam the door in her face. She was grateful that her mother and Taffy were gone for the day. "I don't know why I should give you the time of day," she finally replied.

"You certainly don't owe me anything, but I feel like it's the right thing to do, to come here and . . . and answer any questions you might have. No matter how difficult that might be. For both of us."

"Oh, you mean questions like why you thought it acceptable to steal my husband? Or how a woman who calls herself a Christian could violate not only her own marriage vows but seduce a man of God away from his calling? Those kinds of questions?" Jana didn't care how snide she sounded.

Kerry wept and nodded. "You have a right to ask those questions and more. Seriously, Jana, I want to give you answers."

Jana couldn't help but be intrigued by Kerry. After all, no one else wanted to give her answers. "All right. I'll let you in on one condition. When I say you need to leave, you leave. Do you understand?"

"I do, and that's fine, Jana. You have the right to call all of the shots."

Jana wanted to comment but didn't. Instead, she motioned to the living room. "Have a seat."

She followed Kerry into the room, noting that the woman was stylishly dressed in a red blouse and navy slacks. The jewelry she wore nicely matched the colors she'd chosen but didn't appear ostentatious or over the top. The jewelry reminded Jana of how Rob had taken her precious keepsakes. She wondered if he'd given them to Kerry and decided to ask her flat out.

"Do you have my jewelry?"

"No. Rob pawned it," she admitted. "Along with most everything else he took from the house."

Jana was disappointed. She had hoped that at least if he'd given it to Kerry, she might get it back. "And I don't suppose you know where he pawned it?"

"No. I'm sorry, but I don't. He had everything ready when we left."

"Sounds like him. You do realize he took not only the jewelry he gave me, but pieces that my great-aunt had given me as well? Pieces that were family keepsakes."

"I'm sorry, Jana. I didn't know." Kerry seemed to compose herself.

They fell silent, just staring at each other. Jana didn't know how to make the conversation work. She felt like hurling insults and condemnation, but there were so many unanswered questions, and Jana feared if she didn't remain calm, she might never hear what Kerry had to say about any of it.

Kerry broke the silence. "Jana, first I want to say how sorry I am. I know that seems like a lousy offering, but it's an honest one. I never meant for this to happen. It got out of control before I realized it."

Jana bit back a retort. "Why don't you tell me how it did happen, because I have no clue. I never saw it coming. In fact, I thought we were secure enough to start a family."

"You didn't have any reason to think this would happen. I truly believe Rob was very happy with you and the church." She looked at the knotted tissue in her hands. "My marriage has never been all that happy. Jason was so much older than me that at times I felt like I was living with my father. His parents and mine had been good friends, and we were pushed together— expected to marry. I went along with it because I didn't think I had any better prospects. But it wasn't for love, and that made it wrong." She paused and looked at Jana as if expecting some sort of affirmation.

"Go on." Jana had no desire to enter the conversation. She was barely holding on to her restraint as it was.

"Well, things got worse over the years. Jason was never really there for me. He was always tied up with the business or too tired to care. I was always complaining and nagging for him to change, and it always turned ugly, or else I came away from the situation feeling more alone than when I'd gone into it. I remember once forcing Jason to dress up and take me to a new restaurant. He was miserable the whole evening, but he sat there and went through the motions. When we got home that night, I realized we'd spent nearly a hundred dollars to be more unhappy than if we'd stayed at home. It was awful."

Kerry stared off to the wall behind Jana. "I told Jason that if things didn't change, I would leave. He told me I could do or have anything I wanted—whatever would make me happy. He let me spend outrageous amounts of money, remodel the house, take trips. He didn't care. His only provision was that I not divorce him.

"When I started working for Rob, I asked him to counsel me one day. I told him about the situation and Rob advised me to sit down and set some goals with my husband. He suggested marital counseling with a therapist he knew, and that was that. It was all perfectly innocent."

"At that point maybe."

This brought Kerry's gaze back to focus on her. *You called me friend,* Jana thought, seething at the misery and pain in Kerry's reflection. *I don't want to care about you in this. I don't want to care about how much you're hurting.* But Jana's heart wasn't quite hard enough to ignore the woman's anguish altogether. There was something about the suffering in Jana's own soul that cried out in recognition at this woman's pain.

"Yes, at that point, it was innocent. Rob would ask me how I was doing—how things were going. It seemed he was the only person in the world who cared. I started depending on him more and more for my affirmation. I'd come and tell him what I'd done to try to fix my marriage, and he would assure me I was on the right path."

"That doesn't explain how it turned into an adulterous affair," Jana finally interjected.

"No, it doesn't. I suppose because I started turning to Rob

more often than I did Jason, things just developed. One day we decided to go for a drive. Rob had to deliver some papers to one of the elders and then to the bank. I went along as his secretary, and then afterward we drove to a park and sat and talked. Rob told me that you were unhappy and he figured you were probably going to leave him."

"When was this?"

"Oh, last year, I think it was shortly after Christmas. He said you were upset because the two of you had gone to see your mother and she didn't like Rob and things kind of blew up. He said you were angry with him for making your mom mad."

"Well, part of that's true," Jana had to admit. "We did visit my mom here at the house. And he did make her mad, and she made him mad. I was fed up with both of them, but I calmed down on the way home and told Rob we didn't ever have to see her again if that would make him happy."

"He didn't tell me that part. From that point on he was the one talking about marital problems. We talked to each other because we thought no one else would understand. Rob said you couldn't get into the things he loved because you were so much younger. I would tell him how Jason wasn't interested in the things I loved because he was so much older. We were spending more and more time together, and one day, when I was crying, Rob took me in his arms. Things just got out of hand."

"I don't want to know any of those details," Jana said flatly. She already had visions of Kerry in Rob's arms, and it was unbearable.

"Jana, I came here today because I want you to know how sorry I am," Kerry said, her eyes filling again with tears. "If I could redo everything, I would. I would do it completely different, and Rob would still be with you. I honestly didn't set out to take Rob away from you. I didn't want to hurt you. I always liked you—thought you were a breath of fresh air for our church."

"I don't care how sorry you are," Jana said, getting to her feet. "Do you suppose sorry makes it all right? I have a child on the way—a child who will grow up without a father. Do you suppose sorry will help him when he longs for a father's embrace?" Jana began to pace in front of Kerry. "I grew up without a father. I know how that feels. The emptiness cannot be filled. You sentenced my child to that same punishment."

"I know." Kerry barely breathed the words.

"I went to Africa thinking everything was fine. I was doing a mission for the Lord. I was happy and enthusiastic to come back and share what I'd learned and seen. I never had a chance, however. I never saw my husband again. Instead, I learned that Rob had stripped me of everything—money, possessions, dignity." She stopped and looked hard at Kerry. "I had to get out of the parsonage in less than a week. I had to sell everything in order to have money to move. I had to humble myself and deal with my mother—who doesn't want anything to do with me—to beg for a place to stay."

"I thought Rob and you had already talked it all out," Kerry said, sobbing. "I thought it was your idea to walk away."

"I learned in Africa," Jana said, ignoring the woman's comments, "that I was pregnant. I couldn't wait to return home to tell Rob about the baby. A baby we both had agreed to create. This baby was very much planned. Did you know that?"

She shook her head. "Rob didn't even know about the baby until Jason told him."

"I know. I didn't have a chance to tell him. But you know what? I don't think it would have mattered to him."

"It would have mattered to me."

"Why?" Jana questioned. "Why is it all right to steal a man from his wife—but not his unborn child?"

199

"I didn't mean it like that. If I'd known you were against separating and divorcing, I wouldn't have gone with Rob. He convinced me that it was all your idea—that he was the injured party. That he was all alone. I felt sorry for him, Jana. I loved him, but I would have stopped the affair and never have left with him had I known the truth."

"Oh, give me a break, Kerry. Adultery is wrong no matter who agrees to it. You chose your way out." Jana had taken her fill. "I want you to go. I don't want to listen to anything more. I don't know how you found me, but I'd appreciate it if you didn't bother me again. Otherwise I'll be forced to get a restraining order."

Kerry got to her feet. "Jana, please. I don't want to leave things like this between us. I know I did wrong. I want to make peace. I want you to forgive me."

Jana looked at the woman in disbelief. "Well, we don't always get what we want, Kerry." Jana startled at how much she sounded like her mother with those words. Still, she wasn't about to forgive Kerry Broadbent for what she'd done . . . and the woman was insane to think she should.

Twenty-one

"OH, WE'RE GOING to have such fun!" Taffy declared for the fourth or fifth time that morning. She was sitting at the dining room table filling out invitations to her party and acted as though she had the world by the tail.

Jana had been in a bad mood since three days earlier, when Kerry had come for her visit. Jana had told no one of Kerry's appearance but knew her mother and Taffy were puzzled by Jana's change of attitude.

The visit had left Jana with more anger inside than she had ever known possible. Why Kerry had thought it acceptable to come and try to cleanse herself at Jana's expense was beyond any rational thought.

"You didn't even hear me. What's going on with you, child?" Taffy asked.

Jana looked up from the task Taffy had given her. "I'm sorry. What did you say?"

"I said you're going to have to tie those bags shut with ribbon, and I left it in the pantry."

Jana noted the small party favor bags in front of her. She'd been filling them with candy, a gift for the children and anyone else who wanted one. "All right. I'll take care of it."

"Well, I'm going to take this stack of invitations down to the post office." Taffy got to her feet and pulled together a large stack of sealed envelopes. "It's time for my walk anyway."

"I could drive you down," Eleanor offered as she came into the room with a load of laundry.

"Nonsense. It's a beautiful day, and I need my exercise. You should come walk with me—both of you."

"No thanks," Jana said. "I'm not good company today. I'll get the ribbon and finish these favors."

"I've got three loads of bedding to do," Eleanor replied. "I think I'll get enough exercise."

Taffy shrugged. "Suit yourself. I'll be back in a little while. I'll probably see if Stanley wants to walk with me since neither of you have any ambition to join me."

Eleanor was already going into the kitchen and said nothing. "Have fun," Jana called. She got up from the table to retrieve the ribbon, yawning as she did. She'd been exhausted for the past few days—weeks. She supposed it was depression, but she didn't like to admit it.

If anyone has a right to be depressed, I do, she reasoned. *Maybe I'll just stay in bed tomorrow.* She yawned again but this time didn't try to suppress it.

"Didn't you sleep last night?" her mother asked as Jana came into the kitchen. Her mother was folding clean clothes at the breakfast table.

"Oh, I slept—just not that well," Jana admitted. She went into the pantry, a small room situated next to the laundry room. The ribbon was right there on the shelf—a hot pink ribbon that seemed appropriate for Taffy's party.

Jana came out with the ribbon in hand and found her mother standing idle. "What?" Jana asked. She looked down at her clothes as if something were amiss.

"You've been moody ever since Taffy and I went to Missoula. I've been wondering if something happened while we were gone."

Jana heard concern in her mother's words. It sounded odd coming from her, but Jana felt a sense of relief. She'd said nothing about Kerry's visit, but she'd wanted to. She needed to unload the anger and pain it had caused her, but she didn't figure her mother would care enough to listen or have any answers.

"Kerry Broadbent came to the house shortly after you left."

"The wife of the man who killed your husband?" Eleanor looked completely stunned. "What in the world would possess her to do that?"

Jana sighed and leaned back against the kitchen counter. "She wanted to say she was sorry."

"Oh, brother." Jana's mom turned back to the clothes. "Why do people think that as long as they say they're sorry, it will make everything all right? As if their actions had never happened."

"That was my question. She wanted to cleanse her conscience at my expense, and I really resented that."

Her mother turned abruptly. "That's the way it always is. People hurt you and walk all over you. They lie to you and betray you, and then with those two little words, they expect it should all somehow be wiped from the slate. As if *I'm sorry* had some sort of magical powers to take away the pain."

Jana nodded. "She thought I wanted the divorce. Rob told her I was leaving him. She said if she'd known it wasn't true—if she'd known about the baby—she'd never have done what she did."

"Well, that's easy to say now that it's all said and done. There's no way to prove or disprove her on that," her mother replied angrily. "I hope you didn't buy into it. I know your faith says you're supposed to forgive people when they ask for it, but I think that's malarkey. Why give absolution to someone when they're only seeking forgiveness to ease their own conscience? They don't care that what they've done has permanently scarred you. They don't care that they've robbed you of all security."

Jana suddenly felt like her mother was no longer talking about Kerry. There was something else going on in her mother's mind.

"Why do you say that, Mom?"

"Because it's true. When pressed for a reason for their actions or when facing the consequences, people are suddenly ever so sorry and apologetic." She looked at Jana, but Jana was sure she didn't see her. Her mother was a million miles away.

"Consequences don't just go away. They aren't suddenly dissolved just because forgiveness has been desired or given."

Jana studied the expression on her mother's face. She had dropped the façade of strength that always accompanied her. As her voice broke ever so slightly, Jana was compelled to question her mother.

"Who are you talking about?"

Eleanor looked at her oddly and then seemed to snap back to reality. "I'm talking about you, of course."

"I don't think you were. I think you were talking about yourself. About something that happened to you."

Her mother turned back to the clothes on the table. "Don't try to make something out of nothing."

"I'm not," Jana said, putting the ribbon aside. She came to where her mother stood. "This isn't about nothing. This is about something that happened to you. Something that hurt you enough to talk about consequences not just going away."

"Jana, we were talking about that Broadbent woman coming to see you. You've been in a mood ever since, and that's one consequence of her coming here. She needed to feel better about herself, so she put that on your shoulders. She no doubt believes that if you can forgive her, then so can the rest of the world and she can go on."

Jana decided to try a different approach. "You know about abandonment. That's why Rob's leaving me made you so angry."

Her mother shook her head. "Don't try to psychoanalyze me, Jana. I'm not in the mood for it."

"I'm not trying to do that. I'm trying to share whatever it is you've been bearing for so many years—alone. I want to help, if I can."

"You can't even help yourself," her mother said, turning to look at her. "You're already so deep in depression and frustration from what you're going through, you barely function. How do you imagine you can help anyone else with anything?"

Jana felt as though her mother had slapped her. "I can still feel. I know you're hurting. I realize now that your show of anger has always been to cover up the pain. I don't know why I didn't see that sooner. Who hurt you, Mother? Who hurt you so bad that you can't dare trust anyone—for any reason? What happened that left you unable to show love or any other emotion but rage?"

Her mother stiffened. She gathered the clothes and put them into a neat stack in the basket. "I don't want to talk about this anymore."

"Well, good for you! I do want to talk about it," Jana declared. "I'm tired of you shutting me down. Tired of you showing me just a tiny snippet of concern, then pulling back just in case it costs you too much."

"Like having to deal with conversations like this?" her mother asked, turning to face Jana.

"What?"

"You have no idea the toll this takes on me. I doubt you have ever considered the way it causes me to suffer."

What was the woman talking about now? "Why do you say that?"

"Because it's true. I am suffering because you badger me day and night with questions—with the need to dredge up a past that I have worked hard to put behind me."

"You didn't just put the past behind you, Mother. You sought to eradicate it."

"Well, possibly so. If a building is condemned, you tear it down and get rid of it. If your life is condemned, why not do the same?"

"But why do you consider your life condemned?" Jana softened her voice. "Why?"

Eleanor shook her head. "I have my reasons. Reasons that have nothing to do with you."

"But it has everything to do with me. You've passed that anger . . . that condemnation . . . on to me. I think your past has more to do with my present life—and therefore my future—than you want to admit. I know it has more to do with the problems between you and me than you'll say."

Her mother actually seemed to think about this for a moment. Jana wondered if maybe she would begin to open up again. But then without warning, Eleanor turned and picked up the basket and started to walk away.

"Mom, don't do this," Jana said, going after her. She followed her to the staircase before reaching out to stop her. "Please talk to me."

Eleanor turned, and to Jana's surprise, there were tears in her eyes. "I don't want to talk about this anymore, Jana. Every time you do this—every time you try to force something from my life into understanding—I fervently wish you had never come here."

Jana felt a chill run through her. "Like you wish I'd never been born?"

"I never said that."

"You said you wished I'd been a boy. You used to tell me that all the time. How you didn't want a daughter. Well, you got one anyway, and I'm sorry. I don't know why being female is so wrong in your book."

"It wasn't wrong," her mother replied, her words coming out in a broken, dejected manner. "I didn't want them to hurt you like they'd hurt me. Women have very little defense against men. You know that yourself now. I didn't want you to get hurt, and had you been a boy, you could have been the stronger one." She began to sob, the basket of clothes shaking in her hands. "I never had a choice. Do you understand? I just wanted it better for my child." She tucked her head as if embarrassed or ashamed and hurried up the stairs, not even once looking back.

The words were a blow to Jana's senses. *"I never had a choice."* What did she mean? *"I didn't want them to hurt you like they'd hurt me."* But worse than the words were her mother's tears. Jana had never seen her mother break down and cry like that.

Jana followed her mother upstairs. She wavered between wanting to offer her comfort or an apology. Jana didn't understand her own emotions. Her mother always did this to her. Why couldn't they just talk and not fight? Why couldn't they reveal the things that had hurt them or caused them grief without causing more?

"Mother?" Jana knocked on the closed bedroom door. She could hear her mother sobbing in abject sorrow. Jana tried the door handle, but it was locked. "Mother, please let me in." Eleanor refused to respond.

It went on like this for the rest of the day. Taffy came home to Jana's confusion and worry. "She's been crying for hours. It's not right. I've never seen her like this." Jana explained everything that had happened prior to her mother's breakdown.

"We need to give her time," Taffy said calmly. "Eleanor needs this time to come to terms with so many things."

"What things? Why can't we be a part of bearing that burden? The Bible says that's what we're supposed to do for one another," Jana said, her gaze fixed on the stairs.

"I thought you didn't care about the Bible or what it said."

Jana caught her great-aunt's expression. Her brows were raised questioningly. "I . . . well . . . I don't know anymore what I care about. I don't understand an awful lot."

"I think the Lord is working on your heart, Jana. Your mother's too. It's a painful process, but cleansing a wound so it can heal usually is."

"I'm going up there to talk with her," Jana said, grasping the newel post.

Taffy reached out and held fast to her arm. "No. Give her time. If you care about her—if you love her—give her time to work through this."

Jana said nothing, her focus still upward. Finally she turned toward Taffy. "But what if there isn't any time left? What if we run out of it?"

"God is never too late or too early," Taffy said softly. She let go of Jana's arm and reached up to touch her face in a loving manner. "He'll give you time to work through all of this—I'm confident of it. I feel it here, in my heart," she said, putting her other hand to her chest.

Jana wanted to believe that Taffy was right. She wanted to feel something of comfort—comfort that she'd had prior to Rob's leaving. While her faith in God had been weak, she'd at least had something. Now there was nothing, and it left a hollow ache inside.

"But I haven't had much to do with God," Jana said with a deep sigh. "Why should He give me anything—even time?"

Taffy smiled. "Because He loves you, child. Just because you stopped loving Him doesn't mean He stopped loving you."

Jana swallowed hard. Had she stopped loving God? Or was she merely ignoring Him like a pouting child would do with a parent?

"Give Him another chance, Jana. He's waiting for you. He's never left you. Just like He's never left your mother."

Twenty-two

THAT EVENING, Taffy and Jana ate alone in the garden. Climbing roses sent a delicate scent on the breeze, while dahlias, bachelor's buttons, and daisies waved in unison from their places along the fence. The setting was well suited for a summertime meal.

"This is perfect," Taffy said, enjoying the flavor of the lemon-pepper salmon. Jana had surprised her with the dish, and it seemed ideal for a late garden supper. A salad and iced tea rounded out the menu.

Jana picked at her food, pushing it around the large china plate. Taffy knew her mind was on her mother. She wished she could give Jana insight into the past, but that was Eleanor's job. To betray her niece in that way would be devastating. So instead, Taffy decided to share about her own childhood.

"When I was sixteen," she began, "your grandmother, Melody, was born." She watched Jana perk up at this information and continued. "My mother had so wanted another child. She had suffered through eight miscarriages before Melody was brought to term."

"How awful," Jana said in a whisper.

"It was awful—but made more so by my father. He was a strict religious man who believed my mother's failed pregnancies were due to sin in her life. He constantly berated her for not confessing, not repenting. He made her fast for days at a time in

210

hope of gaining favor with God."

"That's terrible. Why did she tolerate that?"

Taffy smiled at the naïve question. "Women in those days had very little choice. Divorce was out of the question. Few women left their marriages, and those who did were ostracized by 'decent' married women."

"Even Christians?"

"Especially Christians. I can remember being taught to have nothing to do with such women. They were sinners." Taffy shook her head. "How very blind we can sometimes be." She took a sip from her iced tea. "My mother longed to give my father a son. He wanted a son to carry on the family name and business. He wanted a son to become an extension of himself. So when Melody was born, he was more than disappointed. He was outraged. He acted as though Mother had done this solely to spite him."

"He sounds completely unreasonable. I'm glad I didn't know him."

"Yes, he was unreasonable. Mother spent her every waking hour trying to serve him, and it was never enough. She kept a perfect house, cooked marvelous meals, and accompanied him to all the parties and affairs that required their presence, and still he was not satisfied. As his business flourished and he began to make his fortune, my father grew even more unbearable. I believe he even hit my mother on occasion."

"And still she didn't leave?"

"Jana, dear, there was nowhere to go. Other family members would simply never have taken her in, and short of living on the street, she would have been without a place to live. There were no shelters. The mentality was that to have such places would only encourage discontentment in wives. The wisdom—and I use that term loosely—of the day was that if you ignored a problem, it would go away."

"But that's not how abuse works."

"No, it isn't. Things did get worse. My sister was born just days before the bombs fell on Pearl Harbor. The world changed quickly after that. My father's industry boomed, and he suddenly found himself wealthy enough to have anything he wanted. Except the one thing he truly desired, which was a son. He cursed my mother for giving him another girl, then walked away from all of us. Oh, he didn't divorce my mother or leave the house, but he might as well have done both. He immersed himself in his business in such a way that we rarely saw him."

"But wasn't that better than dealing with his anger?"

"In some ways it was nice to have things quiet again. But in spite of my father's bullying and fierce temper, he was the only man in the house, and we were a country at war. We lived in fear of what might happen if the Germans or Japanese invaded. I was sixteen years old, and all I wanted was some reassurance that everything would be all right—that the future would be all right."

Taffy stopped and put down her fork. "That's all your mother is seeking right now. She just needs to know that the future will work out in a positive way."

"That will never happen if she doesn't deal with the past."

"And what of you, Jana? Have you dealt with the past? Did it give you the answers you needed in order to make a better future?"

Jana considered the question for a moment. "I've dealt with as much as I could. I went to therapy for a time while I was in college. . . . I tried to figure out why I couldn't seem to move forward. I felt eternally tied to the past."

"Many people are."

Jana smiled. "But not you. You live freely in the present. You don't seem at all concerned with the future."

Taffy laughed. "Well, there probably isn't a whole lot of it left—as far as an earthly future is concerned."

"Don't say that," Jana countered quickly. Taffy could sense her fear.

"Jana, I'm not afraid of dying. I'm not afraid of what this earth holds in store for me, because God holds my future. He has already promised to never leave me nor forsake me. Why should I worry?"

"Things don't always work out. The plans we make fall apart."

"Then maybe they weren't plans we should have made in the first place."

"Maybe, but once they're made, shouldn't we try to see them through to fruition?"

Taffy thought for a moment. "If you are going on a road trip and you take the wrong highway, do you keep right on going on the wrong road—in the wrong direction? Or do you stop, turn around, and head back to take the right path?"

"But sometimes you can't back up or turn around. Sometimes you aren't on wide highways but rather narrow alleyways with no crossroads, just tall buildings to line your way. God hates divorce, so how could dissolving my marriage have been the right change?"

"I never said changing your marriage status was the answer. I was talking about your heart. I don't propose to know all the answers, Jana, but I do know that God sometimes calls us to abandon our plans. God has shown me many times in my life where I chose a false path. Sometimes He's helped me to change my way, but other times, as you've pointed out, the road can't be changed. At least not at that point and time. So God has given me direction, grace, and encouragement to endure the trip. Just as He's doing with you right now. Like He's done all these years with Eleanor."

"But I want to do more than endure. I want more than that for my mother. Anyone can endure, but I want to succeed. I want to be victorious—like you."

Taffy nearly cringed at the compliment. The child had no way of knowing the battles she'd fought in life. Jana only saw Taffy on one side of the mountain—the good side—the side Taffy had reached only after years of struggle and heartache. Jana had the impression that everything Taffy had done or said had resulted in perfection and order. Perhaps it was time to show her that hadn't always been the case.

"I married Calvin Anderson in complete rebellion," Taffy began. "I met him at one of the many parties my parents held. My mother was ill that night, so I acted as hostess at my father's request. Cal had a presence about him that made all the women swoon. He was a cross between Charles Boyer and Gary Cooper. My, but he was gorgeous. He swept into the room that night, dressed in a tuxedo and carrying a bouquet of flowers intended for my mother."

"What happened next?"

Taffy recalled the evening in vivid detail. "I was wearing a gown of dark gold satin. It was one of my mother's dresses that had been made over for me. The style was a bit severe and matronly, but I made the best I could of the situation. My hair was a dark honey color in those days, and I wore it pinned up in rather the same fashion Audrey Hepburn had worn it in *Breakfast at Tiffany's*—do you remember?" Jana nodded and Taffy continued.

"Father introduced us and Cal bowed low and handed me the bouquet, explaining that he'd brought the flowers for my mother. I accepted on her behalf, and my father went off to greet some new arrivals. Cal looked me over, you know, in that way that makes a young girl blush."

Jana giggled at Taffy's description. "I can imagine."

"Well, he was just so bold and so outspoken. He didn't care what anyone thought. He told me then and there that if I were his wife, he would dress me properly in colors and fabrics that would complement my figure and complexion. Well, I didn't know what to say, he had so startled me. So I came back at him with the only bit of wit I could muster."

"Which was what?" Jana actually leaned forward at this point.

"I asked him flat out if that was a marriage proposal."

Jana laughed and it did Taffy's heart good. "That sounds like you. What did he say?"

"He gave as good as I'd given. He said, 'Would you like it to be?' And that began everything. We were seldom out of each other's company after that. He was popular with my father because of his entrepreneurial talents. He was a lawyer originally but found that he was adept at making money in many fashions. I had no idea of his wealth when we first started seeing each other, but as time went on and his gifts became more elaborate, I figured it all out."

"How romantic," Jana said wistfully.

"Well, yes and no. You see, even then, I had a check of sorts in my spirit. Cal cared nothing about God, so at first that was attractive in light of my father's zealous religious nature. Cal didn't flaunt that he wasn't interested in spiritual matters; in fact, quite the opposite. He played the game just enough to convince my father of his virtues."

"But you knew the truth?"

"Yes, and unfortunately, I told myself at the time that it didn't matter. So since God couldn't convince my spirit that marriage to this man was wrong, He came at me in other ways. I saw how Cal treated people. He used them. He manipulated them with the greatest of ease until they were begging for his company and his bidding. I'd never seen anything like it, but again, I let it go. I was falling deeply in love with the man." She shrugged. "Perhaps he had unwittingly manipulated my heart as well."

Taffy ate a mouthful of the salmon and wondered how much more she should say. It was difficult to share all that had transpired. It would take too long, and frankly, she was growing tired.

"Anyway, there were signs that warned me to turn back, but I chose instead to move ahead. When Cal formally presented me with a diamond engagement ring—a ring much too elaborate and expensive for a simple girl of eighteen—I immediately said yes. I knew eventually my father would learn the truth about Cal's lack of spiritual interest, and it seemed to be my perfect revenge. I wanted to hurt my father for the pain he had caused me and my mother—even my sister. I even wanted to hurt my mother for loving Melody more than me. Besides, even though I had my misgivings, I pushed them aside in the belief that everything would work out. I was, after all, marrying my fairy-tale prince. Why should I spoil that with reality?" She smiled.

"Love does tend to blind us. Especially when we're desperate to leave what we have for something else."

"Yes, and when we ignore God's warnings."

"Sometimes we don't know about God's warning. I had barely become a Christian when Rob proposed. Up until then I thought it was just my soul he wanted." She paused for a moment and her expression changed.

"I was so lonely," Jana admitted. "So desperate for love—for someone to get close to. I could never understand why my mother rejected me, yet she wouldn't let me get close to my nannies or even tell me about you. How different my life might have been if I'd had you in it."

"Your mother was afraid you'd be hurt by relationships, just as she had been. We all have that fear to some degree."

"But to cast off her own child?"

"She couldn't risk more damage," Taffy said seriously. "It doesn't make it right, but that was her justification. She couldn't risk getting close to even one more person."

"But why? I don't understand."

Taffy felt sorry for the girl. "Because being close meant being vulnerable. She couldn't allow that in her life. She'd been vulnerable too many times before, and it had resulted in her being used most grievously."

"But everyone gets used sometime. The world is full of players."

"True . . . but sometimes the game gets out of hand."

Twenty-three

TAFFY'S BIRTHDAY affair was one of the biggest events in Lomara. It seemed to Jana that everyone in the small town had turned out to wish the woman well on her eightieth birthday.

In her typical flair for the dramatic, Taffy attended her party dressed in a full-length ball gown. She completed the look with white gloves and a tiny tiara in her white hair. Stanley escorted her dressed in a stylish tuxedo with a tie that matched the color of Taffy's gown. They were truly in contrast to their party attendees, most of whom wore jeans and cowboy shirts or shorts and T-shirts. But that didn't matter to Taffy. Jana wished she could come to the place where people's feelings about her no longer mattered. Jana still found herself fretting over what the members of her former church thought of her. Did they blame her for what had happened to her marriage—to Rob?

Jana watched as Taffy interacted with the crowd. No one seemed to mind at all that her great-aunt had dressed more for a Washington, D.C., social than for a small Montana birthday party. They loved her. They adored Taffy Anderson.

And why not? The woman was a friend to all. She had generously donated to the town's various fundraisers. She was faithful to her church congregation and a true neighbor to anyone in need.

How does she live like this and survive with her feelings intact? Jana questioned. Surely there were those who condemned her silliness and her ostentatious fashion. But even if there were, Taffy probably just laughed it off. Jana could almost hear the kind of reply she might have.

"Why should I deny myself the pleasure of dressing up if I want to? Who cares what other people think, Jana? You have to be true to yourself and to God."

That thought only served to prick Jana's heart. Be true to God. What did that mean? She felt so awkward when even considering her faith and what it meant to her life. Taffy had admonished her to give God another chance, but how exactly was she supposed to do that?

A small country-western band struck up a lively dance number, and soon all of Fourteenth Street was filled with couples doing a Montana two-step. Jana smiled at the excitement generated by the music and pushed her worry about God aside. Most of these people seemed genuinely happy with each other—pairs who fit together, as though made for each other.

An ache built inside Jana's heart. It radiated from within and filled her like no other pain. She was alone. Rob was dead. There was no hope of his coming back to apologize and start again. But even so, Jana was beginning to wonder if what they'd had really had been love, after all.

"Taffy certainly knows how to host a party," a man declared as he came to stand by Jana.

She looked up and noted it was the same pastor she'd run into outside the flower shop. She stiffened but pasted a smile on her face. "Yes. Yes, she does."

"I know I gave you my card, but I didn't properly introduce myself last time we met. I'm Kevin Clifford."

"The preacher," Jana said dryly.

"Yes, but I'm also a friend of your aunt's."

"The entire world is friends with Taffy," Jana replied, glad to

219

turn the focus away from herself.

"That's because she makes herself a friend to everyone around her." He turned and watched the dancers for a moment. The band began a cowboy waltz, and Stanley and Taffy were leading off.

Jana wondered if Taffy missed Cal and if it were Cal she thought of when she allowed Stanley to take her in his arms. It seemed that Cal and Taffy had had a wonderful marriage. At least Taffy talked of her time with Cal as though it had been something truly special.

"When is the baby due?" Kevin asked, pulling her from her reflection.

"December." Jana looked up to find him smiling. "What?"

"My sister is due in December as well. I'm going to be an uncle for the first time."

Jana couldn't help but smile too. "Well, congratulations." But as soon as the words were out of her mouth she felt awkward again. Taffy would tell her to just be honest with the man, while Eleanor would say to give him the cold shoulder and walk away. Given that Taffy was much happier than her mother, Jana decided to give her great-aunt's way a try.

"I'm sorry. I'm not very comfortable with you," she finally admitted. "I guess I'm afraid you'll break into some soul-saving speech or something."

He laughed, and it instantly relaxed Jana. "I'm not known for that, to tell you the truth. I do speak the Word of God and do have a passion for saving souls, but I try to let God lead me in conversations that include those things."

Jana nodded. "I didn't want you to think I hated you or anything just because you're a pastor. It's not that. I'm just uncomfortable."

"I can imagine. You've been through a great deal. Your husband's death must have been a real shock."

"It was worse still when they called me to make funeral arrangements. I had no desire to be a part of that."

"What did you do?"

Jana shrugged. "Delegated it to someone else. I arranged for some friends at the church in Spokane to take charge."

"So you didn't go back for the funeral?"

"No. I figured I'd already buried him, in a sense. When he left me for his secretary, it was the death of what we'd known."

"I can understand that. So what about the murder itself? Your aunt said she was concerned about whether you would be dragged into that."

"Nothing came about. I guess between all the character witnesses and Jason's testimony, they realized there was nothing to charge me with."

"That had to be a relief."

Jana couldn't begin to tell him what a relief it was. Final word had come only two days ago. "It was huge. I didn't realize how much I'd been fretting and worrying over it. But when the call came, I nearly broke down."

"It's still going to take a good long time to put this behind you. The baby will be both a help and a reminder. You should prepare your heart for that."

She looked at him oddly. "I'm not sure I understand."

"Well, the baby could end up reminding you more of what happened. You might even find that you start distancing yourself from your child because he reminds you of your husband."

"I won't do that!" Jana insisted a bit louder than she'd intended. "I won't desert my child. It won't be his fault that his father was a jerk." Her anger poured out. "I'm not my mother."

It was Kevin's turn to look a bit puzzled. "I'm sorry. I didn't mean to upset you."

Jana suddenly felt embarrassed. He hadn't done anything wrong. "I'm sorry," she said, taking a deep breath and letting it out slowly. "Some topics are just difficult. I think I'll head back to the house. Please excuse me."

"Of course. I am really sorry that you have so much to go through. I hope you know that you are welcome to join us at church. Taffy would love to have you there, and so would everyone else. We've been praying for you."

Jana started to quip off a sarcastic remark, then thought better of it. "Thank you," she said instead and hurried toward the house.

Making her way to the backyard gate, Jana slipped inside and sighed. She hadn't meant to lose her temper that way, and the pastor certainly didn't deserve it. *It's just so hard,* she thought. *Hard to make sense of my life and all that is transpiring around me. How do I put the pieces back together? How do I make it all work?*

She walked across the lawn and around the house and found her mother sipping tea in the garden.

"I thought you'd be enjoying the party," Jana said.

"I am. In my own way."

Jana thought her mother looked older—more weary. It bothered Jana, especially when she thought it might have something to do with her own arrival. "Taffy certainly knows how to have a good time," she offered, growing uncomfortable.

"She does. She knows how to be happy and have fun. All the things that have eluded me," Eleanor said honestly. "Sometimes I envy her and other times I despise her."

"Why?" Jana couldn't help but ask. She'd fully intended to head upstairs and soak in a nice hot bath, but something in her mother's tone held her captive. It was so out of character for her.

"I guess because she's so comfortable in her own skin. She's truly happy. I've not ever known anyone as happy as Taffy."

Jana sat down at the table and looked at her mother as if seeing her for the first time. "You've really not been happy, have you, Mother?"

Eleanor considered this for a moment. "I never felt that I could afford to be happy, Jana. I guess it stems from childhood." She paused and Jana feared that would be the end of the conversation.

"I've given a lot of thought to the questions you've asked," her mother began again. "Questions about the past—your father—my childhood. I was always convinced that if I forced the memories to remain in the past and refused to think about anything unpleasant, those things couldn't hurt me. They'd have no power over me."

"I've often thought the same," Jana admitted. "Maybe because that's the way you raised me."

"Maybe," Eleanor said. "This is hard for me to say, but I hope you'll hear me out."

Jana nodded. Wild horses couldn't drag her from this spot. Her mother was actually opening up, and Jana wasn't having to force the words from her. Her mother was actually volunteering information.

"You were a part of the past I put from me. I see that now. I didn't see it at the time. I thought I was helping you to be strong and self-sufficient. I thought I was molding you into a responsible human being who wouldn't be dependent upon anyone— not parents, not a man . . . not even God." Her mother's gaze grew distant. "I wanted you to avoid the pain and misery that I'd known. I wanted you to be safe from the things people might do to you. I figured if you trusted no one—if you stood only on your own two feet—then you would call the shots. You would determine what to allow in your life. But now," her mother said, shaking her head, "now I know it was more than just that." She looked at Jana. Her eyes were piercing, searching. "I didn't understand that I was putting you away as systematically as I was every other thing or person who could hurt me."

Jana started to say something but held her tongue. Her mother was making a confession of sorts, and she didn't want to interfere.

"Jana, you were a hard reminder of the days gone by. You were a reminder of the pain and sorrow I'd endured. You were like a doorway, and by keeping you close at hand, I feared I might actually pass through the threshold into the awful truth of what had been.

"I know it wasn't right—I see that now. You weren't to blame, but you were an intricate part of it. I did what I did to protect my heart, but I didn't think about what it would do to yours."

She looked away again. "I sentenced you to as much misery as I had known—by my own hand. Now that I see it, it's almost more than I can bear. I was selfish. I was terrified."

"Of what?" Jana couldn't help but ask.

"Of you," Eleanor replied, turning back to meet her daughter's eyes. "Don't you see? I'd known all sorts of rejection and lies. Fierce betrayals that I couldn't bear to endure even in memory. I couldn't risk that happening again. I couldn't risk growing close to a child—loving that child—and then being rejected by that child.

"I knew that if I poured my life into you, I would end up being hurt. Sooner or later you would betray me, and Jana, I couldn't let that happen. I knew that if it did, I'd go insane."

"Insane?" Her mother's choice of words surprised Jana.

"Yes. Things had happened that had nearly destroyed me. I knew, unlike most of the people around me, that I wasn't the strong character they thought me to be. I was barely hanging on by a thread. I constantly thought of suicide."

"You?"

She nodded slowly. "I wanted to die—I thought it was the only way to forget the past completely. I truly figured to take my life, but things happened and I found it impossible."

"What happened? What things kept you from killing yourself?"

For several minutes Eleanor said nothing. Then the answer came in a voice that was almost inaudible. "You."

Jana took in her mother's statement and shook her head. "Me?"

"I found out I was pregnant with you. I could reconcile taking my own life, but not yours. You weren't to blame for my unhappiness, although my guess is I made you feel that you were. I just wanted a way out, but there never has been a viable option." She sighed. "There still isn't."

"You still wish you were dead?" Jana dared the question, her heart breaking for her mother. It was the first time in a long while that she'd felt something more than hatred and anger.

"I don't wish myself dead. I just wish the memories would stop . . . the pain would end. You have to understand, Jana, your coming here brought so many things back to me. I don't know how to deal with that, and because of it," she said honestly, "I don't know how to deal with you."

Jana searched her heart for the right words. "I wasn't asking to be dealt with. I just wanted to be loved."

"I know, and in the only way I knew how, I have loved you. But I wasn't strong enough to be a real mother. I don't know that I am strong enough now. I know you hate me because of that, but I can't help it. I'm weak, and frankly, I'm terrified of the future for you and this baby."

Her words caught Jana off guard. "Why?"

"Because I know how hard it is to be a single mother.

Because I know how difficult it is to invest yourself in a situation where so much pain has walked before you." Her voice broke. "I don't want you to end up like me, Jana."

Jana reached out on instinct and covered her mother's hand with her own. She opened her mouth to speak, but no words came out. Nothing she could say would add comfort or well-being to her mother's state of mind. Perhaps this simple gesture would relay her thoughts.

I want to start over, Jana thought. *I want to begin again. It's not too late. I just know it's not too late.*

Twenty-four

AUTUMN IN MONTANA moved in with a subtle change of temperature and lighting. Before Jana even realized it, the trees had turned to gold and orange, the brush a brilliant red and yellow, and the grass a buff brown. Farmers baled hay as though snow might come any day, and in truth, Taffy said it could do just that. Therefore, the entire atmosphere of September and early October was completely different from the summer.

"Winter can be quite hard up here," Taffy told her one day as she trimmed back her rosebushes. "We can be buried in snow or suffer sub-zero temperatures for weeks. A person has to be ready."

Jana believed in preparation as well, but her plans were focused on the child she would deliver in a couple of short months. The baby moved often and reminded Jana that she was not alone. Of course, her mother and Taffy helped her to realize that as well.

Things had changed between her and her mother after Taffy's party. Jana and Eleanor were still not close, but something different was starting. Like a tentative truce. Not a real understanding, but at least it was something. The anger had dissipated—at least for the most part. Jana still had moments of frustration and the feeling that she could do nothing right, but even those passed more easily and did far less damage than before.

Jana felt she understood her mother better, and because of

that, she'd asked very few questions in the months that followed their discussion on Taffy's birthday. She instead began to see her mother's frailty. The woman she'd always believed to be as hard as rock, as strong as steel, wasn't at all what she thought. Her mother had a delicacy about her that Jana had never bothered to notice.

One thing that had changed and truly surprised Jana was that her mother had offered her a job in her book business. Jana was stunned, but Eleanor went on to explain that she was considering getting out of the business altogether. If Jana wanted no part of it she could definitely understand, but on the other hand, if she did want to be involved or even have the business for her own, Eleanor no longer wanted to deny her that. After all, Jana's father had purchased the business for them.

Jana surprised her mother and herself by agreeing to learn enough to be helpful. But, Jana explained, she'd truly rather be involved in interior design, as she'd studied to do at school. She was pleased that her mother didn't get mad. In fact, she was supportive, telling Jana that it was probably wise to stay with her passion.

So there were many things with which to occupy her mind, but still Jana found her thoughts consumed by memories of Rob. She supposed it was because of the baby. She didn't know if it was a boy or girl—she'd specifically told the doctor she didn't want to know. But she kept thinking about it. If she had a son and he looked like his father, would she grow to resent the child?

She wanted to put the past behind her—to deal with the resentment and anger. She wanted all of those things put into neat, orderly packages and stored away before the baby came. But could that even be done? Was it reasonable to want such a thing?

Taffy told her there was a difference between truly dealing with her past and simply pushing the memories aside. Jana knew her mother was an example of someone who just shoved things aside, and she didn't want that for herself.

She had to admit she was a bit fearful she might end up treating her child poorly, all because of who his or her father had been and what he had done. She supposed Kevin's comments at the birthday party had only brought to the surface the thoughts she'd buried inside. If a complete stranger could imagine the potential for her to judge her child by his parentage, Jana knew she had to face the facts herself.

Each person, she reasoned, *deserves to be treated based on his own merits, not his parents'. I've always believed this. But can a person hold something against another without even realizing it?*

Jana continued to contemplate this, which in turn stirred up old questions. Questions about her birth and her father. Questions about her mother's childhood and Grandmother Melody's death. She wanted to brave those questions with her mother, but the uncertain peace the two had between them was probably too fragile to risk. If Jana were to show true compassion and concern for her mother's feelings, she would have to let the matter drop— at least for now.

This was the conclusion Jana came to as she sat on the porch, enjoying the crisp morning air. Rather than deal with issues of her childhood, she tried instead to remember something that would have signaled the demise of her marriage. Some sign that things weren't as they should be. Perhaps it might somehow lend understanding.

She remembered an evening in January when Rob came home from the church. He seemed to avoid her, telling her that he was sweaty and wanted to shower first. She wondered now if he'd been trying to hide the fact that he'd been with Kerry.

Another time came to mind when she had wanted to talk to Rob about having a baby, and he'd suggested maybe it wasn't a good time for them to have a family after all. This had confused Jana, because prior to that moment, Rob had been the one who'd instigated the idea. He'd been talking about their having a baby for nearly a year.

Maybe his growing closeness with Kerry had brought about the change of heart. He'd only mentioned it once, however, and he'd never come back to the topic after that. Jana thought at the time that it was nothing more than momentary cold feet at the idea of such serious responsibility. Even she had her moments when she wondered if getting pregnant was the right thing to do. After all, what did they know about being parents? But now there was certainly no turning back.

"So here you are," Taffy declared, coming around the porch. She had been planting tulip bulbs and still wore her kneepads and gloves.

"Yes, I was enjoying the morning."

"They say it will rain later this afternoon, so I thought I'd better get to work on those flowers."

Jana nodded and patted her belly. "I'd help you if I could get down on my knees. I swear this will be a big baby, but the doctor tells me the size is just right."

Taffy laughed and pulled off her gloves. "I've heard every mother-to-be say the same thing. I wouldn't fret over it one bit."

She sat down on the porch steps and leaned back against the rail. Jana found it hard to believe her great-aunt was eighty years old. The years didn't slow her down at all. It must have been the good life she'd lived. She no doubt had always had plenty of money to take care of herself and plenty of people to support her should she be in need. Jana envied that.

"Stanley thinks we'll get our first snow soon. He says his knee is swollen and hurting him something fierce, and it only does that when it's going to snow."

"I think I'll enjoy the snow." Jana liked cold-weather clothes. The bulky sweater she wore now would work even after the baby was born.

They sat in silence for a time, staring out at the yard, lost in their thoughts. Jana thought Taffy might be the perfect person to discuss her heart with, but at the same time she worried about being too open. A big part of her still wanted no part in being vulnerable to Taffy or Eleanor. She kept hearing the same messages play through her head like a broken record: *Don't get too close. Don't care too much. Don't trust.*

It was all a part of the heartache that haunted her life, and Jana didn't know any way to break the cycle. *Well, how do you break a bad habit?* she thought. *You just stop doing it. And you keep at it—you keep not doing it.* Was that the same way it would be with false thinking—with damaged thinking?

"Aunt Taffy?"

"Yes?"

"Did you ever have to forgive someone for something really big? I mean like me forgiving Rob and Kerry or even my father— for deserting us?"

Taffy gave Jana a look of compassion. "Child, everybody has to forgive someone for something big. It's all a matter of what you deem big. I've had my problems and painful moments. Don't think that just because I am happy now doesn't mean I haven't struggled. I thought I'd explained that before."

Jana leaned forward but her stomach wouldn't allow her to bend too much. "But there's a difference between forgiving someone who accidentally hurts your feelings or does something to you without meaning to and people who do things . . . things they meant to do and knew full well were wrong to do. Have you had to forgive someone like that?"

"Of course. The point isn't whether or not I've suffered

through horrible things—the point is whether or not I forgave them."

"Why do you say that?"

Taffy thought for a moment. "Do you remember a time back when we talked about my childhood?"

Jana nodded.

"Well, if you'll recall, I mentioned that I was sixteen when my little sister was born. Now, I was as excited about a new baby in the house as anyone, but what I didn't expect was the way that baby would dominate our lives. I felt completely forgotten when Melody came. First of all, remember again that the Second World War was going on. My mother was completely absorbed in my sister, and my father was caught up in the war. I was pretty much left to my own devices. I had been in boarding school, but because of the war I came home. A part of me resented that, while at the same time I was relieved to be close to my loved ones.

"But the real problem was the way my mother no longer had time or interest in me. I questioned her about it one day, and she told me that the baby was more important to her. She said it wouldn't be long before I found a man and married and left her behind without another thought. It was her plan, I truly believe, to leave me before I could leave her."

"Oh, how sad." Jana couldn't imagine anyone rejecting Taffy.

"I learned to forgive her, although for years I wanted nothing to do with her or Melody. I was jealous, even after Cal came along. And of course, Cal was an entirely different matter. A whole different reason to forgive."

"What do you mean? I thought you two were very much in love. What happened?"

Taffy closed her eyes. "My Cal was quite the looker, but of course I told you that. He drew attention to him wherever he went. He was worse than the Kennedy boys."

Jana shook her head. "The Kennedy boys—as in President Kennedy?"

"Only he wasn't the president then. His father was an ambassador in England for a time, and they definitely lived the good life. The boys were being groomed for politics even then. But so, too, was my Cal. Cal was grooming himself. He had great plans for his future. He wanted to be in the limelight. He loved attention. He loved female attention especially."

"Did he ever cheat on you?" Jana asked frankly.

Taffy opened her eyes and met Jana's gaze. "Only about a hundred times."

"What?" Jana couldn't keep the surprise from her voice. "You're kidding me."

"I wish I were." Taffy straightened. "Jana, you think I'm happy because you believe I've never had to deal with horrible hurt and betrayal, but you're wrong. I'm happy because I've learned to let God take the injustice of it all and forgive. I've learned that my heavenly Father cares more about me than any human being ever could and that my trust should be firmly placed in Him—no matter my circumstances. When that happens, and only then, you can stand strong against the most brutal attacks."

"But I was trusting God when Rob and Kerry ran off."

"And now you won't trust Him, because Rob and Kerry ran off, is that it?" Taffy's eyes were piercing, and Jana looked away.

"He let me down."

"God did?"

"Yes." Jana knew it sounded silly, but she had no other answer.

"Jana, my guess is that you've tied Rob and God together. You came to know God through Rob and figured the one equaled the other. That's not at all true. You can surely see that now."

"But I thought I understood."

"We are only human, Jana. We make mistakes. Isn't it possible that you allowed your relationship with God to be developed through your relationship with Rob?"

"I suppose so. But our relationship—mine and God's—well, it had been changing. I was reading the Bible more on my own and doing studies. I would talk to Rob about things I'd learned and felt that I was finally seeing for myself all those things Rob had been trying to teach me. When I went to Africa, I really had my eyes opened. I got closer to God than I ever thought possible. I was so excited about that, but now I feel like it wasn't real—that I must have misunderstood what was happening. Otherwise why would Rob have left me?"

"God is faithful, Jana; people aren't. People will fail. Rob failed you in his imperfect state of being. People have their own struggles and burdens to deal with. But God doesn't. God is there for you on a daily basis, and He's calling you to be there for Him—with Him."

The words struck a chord deep in Jana's heart. Dare she believe them? "And you took Uncle Cal back even though he cheated on you?" she asked in amazement.

"Cal never had any intention of leaving me. He just had no regard for our vows. Cal was a looker, as I said. He used his appearance to entice people, to woo them and make them feel as if they were the most important person in the world. People like that. The human ego craves that kind of attention, and Cal had a gift." Taffy shook her head. "I forgave Cal his indiscretions and sinful nature. Not for his sake, but rather for mine."

"For your sake?" Jana couldn't begin to understand. "What are you saying?"

Taffy straightened. "I'm saying that forgiveness is as liberating to the one who forgives as it is for the one being forgiven. Holding someone a grudge keeps us in bondage just as it does them. It ties us to that person and the sin as we stand there guarding the grudge—keeping it in place. You can never be free as long as you hold yourself to that kind of responsibility. That's why I think the Bible speaks to taking every thought captive. If you let yourself be controlled by your thoughts, then you will be in bondage. However, if you take your thoughts captive, you control them. You alone determine what holds merit in your life."

She got to her feet and dusted off her backside. "Jana, I loved my husband, but my love for him wasn't enough. He needed God. And on his deathbed, he found Him. We had been separated for nearly a year when Cal suffered a heart attack. He sent for me, and I couldn't very well deny him."

"Why were you separated?" Jana asked.

Taffy opened her mouth as if to reply, then closed it as she seemed to reconsider. "That isn't important," she finally responded. "The point is I forgave Cal, face-to-face. But more importantly for me, I'd already forgiven him, because that was the example I saw of my Lord in the Bible when people betrayed Him. It didn't mean I approved of what Cal had done—I couldn't. You must never confuse forgiveness for approval; it's not the same thing at all. I simply released my right to hold it against Cal—to seek retribution."

"But that couldn't have been easy."

Taffy smiled. "Good things, worthwhile things, seldom are. But I can say it was the most valuable thing I've ever done."

Eleanor stood to the side of the open window, listening to Taffy tell Jana about forgiveness. She felt a longing to know the freedom and liberty Taffy spoke of, but she couldn't bring herself to step out on the porch and ask her own questions.

People are always speaking of forgiveness, she thought, *as though it were simple.* Just forgive and you'll feel better. People usually gave this advice when someone lied or slandered or even cheated a person. *But what about really ugly, horrible things? What about things that forever change the lives of the people involved?*

"Could you be so forgiving of Cal," she murmured, walking away from the window, "if you knew the truth?" She looked back over her shoulder, shaking her head. "If you knew Jana was Cal's daughter, could you forgive him then? Could you forgive me?"

Suddenly a wash of emotions swept over Eleanor. She felt as if the wind were knocked from her. She grabbed for the stair railing to steady her feet. The ugly truth that she'd fought so long to keep buried had emerged from her subconscious memories. And with it came many other memories—each more ugly, more terrifying than the first.

Eleanor sank to the floor, her vision blurring. *What's happening to me? Am I dying?* She wanted to call out, but no words would come. Instead a cold darkness overtook her like icy fingers, choking out her breath.

Twenty-five

ELEANOR CELEBRATED her fourteenth birthday by watching her father pump her mother's stomach. Melody had overdosed, the second time in less than a month. Eleanor was frantic. This time had been much worse than the last.

"She's going to die, isn't she?" Eleanor questioned, standing at the end of the table where her father worked.

"Ellie, you can't think like that," her father chided. "I'm doing my best to keep that from happening, but you're sending some pretty bad vibes my way."

"Sorry," she murmured and eased back away from the exam table.

She remained quiet as her father continued to work on his wife with the help of a couple of the local women. Melody moaned but remained unconscious as the contents of her stomach were brought up and expelled.

Eleanor could no longer stand the scene. She rushed from the trailer, letting the metal screen door flap in the breeze behind her. Several people were waiting outside to see how things were going. Friends, she supposed, if they could be called that. They were no doubt the same ones who'd given her mom the pills in the first place.

"Is she okay?" Ringo asked.

Eleanor shrugged. "Dad's still working on her."

There were other questions, but Eleanor refused to answer

them. Instead she hurried away to be alone. She was thankful her brothers were with the neighbors. Cleo, a redheaded mother of four boys of her own, seemed to enjoy the Templeton children. She always said it kept her kids occupied. Eleanor didn't care so long as they stayed out of her hair. Today especially.

"Ellie," Sapphira called from the corner of the shack she lived in with her folks, "is your mom okay?"

"Who knows? If she dies, then she'll get what she deserves," Eleanor snapped.

"You don't really mean that. You don't want your mother to die," Sapphira protested.

"Well, she certainly seems to want to die. So why not let her?" Eleanor turned and walked on, mindless of Sapphira.

"My mom says your mom is an addict—that she can't help herself," Sapphira said as she followed Eleanor.

"Well, apparently she's getting to the point where there aren't too many people who can. My dad is working hard to save her, and this time it isn't going well." Eleanor plopped down on a rock and fought back tears. "How could she do this to me on my birthday?"

Sapphira sat down on the ground beside Eleanor. "I don't know. But I'm sure sorry. It's not much of a birthday present for you."

"I just don't understand anymore. Nothing seems real. I want her to be happy like she used to be, but she never is. She's always miserable. She's always talking about how she became a mother too young—how she has too many responsibilities and she wants to be free. I'm afraid one of these days I'll wake up and she'll be gone. Either she will have run off or died."

Sapphira said nothing. Eleanor didn't really expect her to. After all, what could she say that could possibly make sense of this? Eleanor's mother lay near death for the second time. Why would a person do something like that? Her father told her the first time that it was a mistake—that her mother had lost track of how many pills she'd taken—but now Eleanor wondered if that was true. What if her mother had meant to take that many pills? What if she was trying to kill herself on purpose?

The thought made Eleanor sick to her stomach. *I can't even think about that. If she meant to do this—to kill herself—then she meant to do it on my birthday. What kind of mom does that to her kid?*

They must have sat there for hours in silence. Eleanor knew the day was passing, but she didn't care. She couldn't go home. That's where she'd found her mother. She'd been crumpled on the floor, unconscious, when Eleanor awoke that morning. The rest of the day had crashed down around her. Cleo had come to take the boys, and others had arrived to help get Melody to the trailer hospital.

When the commune had moved the year before, they had settled into a collection of rundown buildings that constituted something of a ghost town. The place was owned by some rock star who had great sympathy for the hippie movement and was actually the brother of one of their members. He'd encouraged the collection of homeless pilgrims with the promise they could stay there as long as they wanted—rent free. Of course, this place was only marginally better than some of the other places. It did have electricity and running water, plus there was a single phone booth at the end of the main drag. It provided access to the outside world that they'd never had.

The best part, however, was that Eleanor's father again had the trailer for his work. Eleanor was glad of this fact. If her mother did die, she would die somewhere else—not in their home. Of course, if the commune got kicked off this property, the trailer would again be her family's only shelter, but she couldn't think about that right now.

Eleanor heard someone calling her and realized Ringo was approaching them. She steeled herself against the news. He looked exhausted.

"She's gonna make it," he told Eleanor. "Your dad wanted you to know."

Eleanor let go the breath she'd been holding. "Is he taking her back home?"

"No. He's gonna keep her there at the trailer. Star and some of the others are going to stay with her."

Eleanor got to her feet. "I'd better go let the boys know."

Sapphira joined her. "I'll come with you."

Eleanor informed Cleo and the gang of children that her mother had once again pulled through. "Dad's going to keep Mom at the trailer for the night." The boys stayed just long enough to hear the news before they ran off to play. They seemed so oblivious to the situation, and Eleanor wondered if they knew how serious it was.

"Well, why don't you just let the boys stay here?" Cleo said. "Tell your dad they'll be fine. If I need him, I'll send one of them home. You can stay here, too, if you want."

Eleanor nodded. She was relieved to know she wouldn't have to cook and clean up after the brood of rowdies. "Thanks, Cleo. I think I'll stay at home, though." Eleanor felt overcome with relief. Her words choked in her throat. "I'd . . . better go."

The woman tousled Eleanor's hair. "Don't you worry, baby. She'll be okay."

"Yeah . . . until next time."

And that was Eleanor's biggest fear. When would it happen again? It had already happened twice, and countless other times her mother had been so stoned that she was of no use to anyone. What if no one was around next time? What if her mother took too many drugs and no one found her?

Eleanor left everyone and went to the solitude of her own house. She wanted to be alone, but the memories of what had happened that morning haunted her. She stood in the doorway for several minutes, staring at the spot where her mother had fallen. There was nothing out of place to suggest what had happened, but Eleanor could very nearly see her there—as if it had just happened.

Out of desperation to feel that things were under control, Eleanor began to clean the house. She was ruthless with disposing of things her brothers would probably protest. She washed and scrubbed at the filthy floors until she could no longer picture her mother lying on them half dead.

It was in the middle of scouring the sink that her father came home. He watched her for a moment, not saying a word. Eleanor knew he would be wondering at the clean state of things, but she couldn't begin to explain to him how it was the only thing that had given her any peace all day. Glancing at the clock, she was stunned to realize it was already ten at night.

"Ellie? What are you doing?"

"I'm fixing things up so Mom won't have to worry about them when she gets home." It was true, although it wasn't the complete truth. The fact was, Eleanor couldn't put into words the comfort she found in setting things in order.

She continued working at a particularly stubborn stain on the white porcelain. *Why wouldn't it come clean?*

"Ellie, come here," her father said softly.

She stopped what she was doing and did as he directed. She was afraid to look at him but needed to know the truth of how her mother was doing. "Mom?"

"She's going to make it. She's got some problems, though . . .

the drugs. Well, you know." He reached out and lifted Eleanor's chin.

She met his worried expression and tears immediately flooded her eyes. "She's just going to do this again, isn't she?"

Her father pulled her close. "She's not happy, Ellie. I can't make her happy and neither can you."

"But she's living free. You two always told me that would make people happy." She pulled away to look at her father again. "Was that all a lie?"

He dropped his hold. "No, it wasn't a lie. Sometimes people just put themselves in bondage without even knowing it. Your mom isn't free anymore. She's in bondage to the drugs."

"I hate drugs. I wish we could go someplace where there aren't any drugs."

"I know this has been hard on you." He glanced around the room. "Where are the boys?"

"Staying the night with Cleo. She offered to do it, so I just let them stay there."

"That's probably good. They know their mom is okay?"

"Sure. I told them after Ringo told me." Eleanor tried to hold on to her emotions, but it was no good. "Daddy, I don't want Mom to die."

He took hold of her again. "Shhh. It's going to be all right. I'm here for you. I love you more than you'll ever know."

"But I feel so scared. She was just lying there. I thought she was dead." Eleanor's terrifying memories came rushing back. "It was so awful." She sobbed against her father's chest.

He began to massage her neck and shoulders as she cried against him. His touch was comforting, gentle. She felt soothed by it in a way she couldn't explain and relaxed against him. Then to her surprise, without a word, he lifted her into his arms and carried her into his bedroom.

He placed her on the bed and sat down beside her. His hands began massaging her upper arms and the front of her shoulders. "Sometimes," he whispered, "you just need someone to show you that things will be okay."

Eleanor felt a strange sensation creep over her as her father began unbuttoning her blouse. "I have some oils," he said. "You get undressed, and I'll get them. You'll see how much better you'll feel after I massage you."

Eleanor later remembered that first encounter with her father's touch as something special. She hadn't been afraid, even though the experience was completely foreign to her. She forgot the worries about her mother and relished the tender words her father spoke. Still, something didn't seem quite right. Eleanor couldn't explain it. Free love and open marriage were commonly practiced in the commune, but she'd never considered that such a thing might take place between children and their parents.

As she dressed the next morning, she wondered where her father had gone. It was still very early. She could tell because the light was very soft on the horizon.

"Dad?" she called as she crept from the room. She found him sitting in the living room, meditating. She watched him for a moment. She'd never felt more special—more loved—than by this man.

He opened his eyes and looked up at her. For a moment he just stared at her as though trying to figure something out. Ellie smiled. "Are you okay?"

This seemed to break the spell. "I'm fine, Ellie. What about you?"

She nodded, still not sure she understood this new relationship. She wanted to ask him questions about the things they'd done but didn't know how. She wondered if this would continue after her mother came home.

She sat down beside her father. "I'm okay, Dad. I . . . well . . . I guess . . ." Her voice trailed off.

"You wonder about what happened last night."

"Yeah. I mean, was that all right?" She was so confused.

He drew a deep breath and let it out. "What we did was very special, Ellie. You have to know that. We love each other, and we were just helping each other to feel better. You know what I mean, don't you?"

"Sure," she said, nodding. "And Mom won't care?"

"Your mom and I have always had an open relationship," he said thoughtfully, "but you know, given her problems, we probably shouldn't tell her about it. She might think that I love you more than her, and since she has this drug problem and all, we don't want to make her think that."

"Of course not." The last thing Eleanor wanted was to make her mother feel bad.

"So let's keep it to ourselves," her dad said. "If we say anything to anybody else, it might get back to her. I know you don't want to hurt her or confuse her more than she is."

"No. I don't," she agreed. She didn't want to do anything that would send her mother back to the drugs she already sought too often. "I won't say anything."

He reached out to run his finger along her jawline. "You're a good girl, Ellie. You're a beautiful girl too. Don't ever forget that."

She smiled. "I won't, Daddy."

That night after she and her father again shared this new strange intimacy, Eleanor drifted to sleep, thinking of her mother. Her father said Melody would come home the next day.

Eleanor wondered how she would face her mother now—what with this new secret to keep from her. Eleanor didn't want to make her mother feel bad, yet she was already feeling awkward about seeing her again.

Twenty-six

ELEANOR NEEDN'T HAVE worried. Her mother was so depressed and disinterested upon her arrival home that she barely paid attention to any of her children. Eleanor wanted very much to embrace her mother and tell her how much she loved her—how sorry she was for the stress she'd caused—but her mother would never allow her to get close.

Melody went to her bedroom, closed the door, and left Eleanor and the boys to their own devices. This went on for weeks, and during that time Eleanor hardened her heart more and more against her mother. She felt a sort of fearfulness in caring too much. Eleanor watched her father become more and more distraught as he tried to coax his wife back into life. He never approached Eleanor sexually during this time. In fact, at times he, too, seemed to ignore her existence. It left Eleanor feeling displaced.

Fighting her emotions and the need to feel close to someone, Eleanor finally went to see her father at the trailer. It was the end of the day and there were no patients.

"Dad?" she called out, wondering if he was there after all.

"Yeah?" He came out from the back room. He looked haggard, drained of the vibrant life she'd always known in him.

"Are you okay? I mean, you seem so different. I feel like . . . well . . . like everything has changed. Like I've lost something."

He eyed her curiously. "What do you mean, Ellie?"

"Well, you and I used to talk a lot and we used to be together a lot. Then after mom nearly died . . . well . . . you know . . . we had our special time together." Eleanor didn't know whether to bring it up or not. She felt strange about everything, fearing that somehow what had taken place with her father had forever changed all the other good things they'd had.

"Oh, Ellie," he said, shaking his head. "If you think I'm mad at you, I'm not. I've just been worried about your mom. I've been torn up inside at how unhappy she is. I don't know how to help her."

Eleanor went to her father and wrapped her arms around him. She wanted so much to comfort him. She wished she had the ability to make him forget his pain.

Before she knew it, things were once again taking a strange turn. Her father locked the door to the trailer and led her into one of the back rooms. This became their routine over the next several weeks. Her father had decided to train her to help him in his medical practice. He said Ellie had a gift for healing, and her mother was too disinterested to care. So every day Ellie went to the trailer. Sometimes her father taught her about medicine, and sometimes he just advanced their intimate relationship.

The encounters seemed to empower Eleanor in a way she didn't understand. Her father would often talk to her about his problems—about the way her mother was ignoring him. She began to rekindle her anger toward her mother. After all, her father had saved Melody's life. She could at least have the decency to be grateful.

The more her father talked about his own sorrow and frustration, the more Eleanor felt herself take over the role of his wife. They discussed people in the commune and their problems. Her father would show her how to assist him in routine duties around the office, and before she knew it, Eleanor found herself working nearly full time in the little trailer. These were some of the happiest times she knew. She helped deliver babies and treat sick people, and she learned all sorts of things she had never known. Her father told her she had a real mind for medicine and that she'd make a great doctor. This pleased Eleanor to no end. She felt grown up—important. She felt loved.

It was at home that Eleanor found the nightmare worsening. Her mother was angry all the time. She screamed nonstop at the boys and accused Eleanor of never doing anything to make herself useful.

"Mom, I washed all the dishes," Eleanor declared. "What else do you want?"

"Don't sass me," her mother said, weaving slightly as she crossed the room. She was wearing nothing more than an oversized T-shirt, her once beautiful blond hair matted and filthy. "I want you to clean this place up."

Eleanor looked around the room. It wasn't that dirty. She'd worked on it earlier. "What do you want me to do, Mom? It's already clean."

Her mother smacked her hard across the face, then looked at Eleanor in shock and began to cry. "I'm sorry. I'm sorry." She sank to the floor and began to sob in earnest. "I need a fix."

Eleanor didn't know what to do. She despised her mother's weakness and her state of confusion. She wished that her father would take her away from it all. She wondered if she might even be able to suggest this to him sometime when they were alone.

"I need a drink," her mother said, struggling back to her feet. "Get me some vodka."

"We don't have any, Mom. Remember? Dad took all of the alcohol out of the house so that you could get better."

Her mother looked at her oddly. "You don't know how to

make me better. I need a drink and a fix, and I'm going to go find both."

Mindless of her state of undress, Melody went to the front door but then paused as if to gather her wits. "Where are your brothers?"

"Outside. It's the middle of the day and they're playing," Eleanor said in disgust.

Her mother nodded. "Good. You make sure they're safe— that they don't get hurt." With that she left.

"How am I supposed to do that?" Eleanor questioned, knowing her mom would never hear the words.

It wasn't long before her father came through the front door, dragging her mother behind him.

"You can't be out there drinking yourself into oblivion," he said angrily as he tossed her to the couch. "Sometimes I think you'd rather die than be sober."

"Well, maybe I would. This life is nothing but pain," her mother countered.

They fought like this all the time now, and Eleanor wanted no part of it. She left the house, slipping out the back door, praying all the while that no one would call to her and force her to stay. She couldn't stand watching them fight. They were heartless and ugly toward each other. They called each other names and said the most hideous things.

"Why can't it all stop?" Eleanor said, seeking solace in her favorite hiding spot in a heavy grove of trees. An old abandoned lean-to made it possible to completely disappear inside. Eleanor had never told anyone about the place—not even Sapphira.

She crawled into the corner, where she'd stashed an old blanket and a few other things, and fell asleep. Her last conscious thoughts were of how wonderful it might be to run away to the city—just her and her dad. He could be the doctor and she could be his nurse. They would be happy there—she just knew it.

To Eleanor's surprise, things seemed to get a bit better. Amazingly enough, her parents stopped fighting as much. It was like a tentative peace had settled back over their lives. Her mother, for whatever reason, came to breakfast one morning fully dressed, her hair combed. She wasn't what Eleanor would call happy, but she wasn't miserable and teary either.

For nearly a month Eleanor watched her mother take on more of her old personality. She was more lighthearted and capable. She started paying more attention to the boys and began working in the garden again.

Eleanor relaxed a bit in this new phase. She hoped it meant her mother had the drugs out of her system and was finally able to live her life again. But Eleanor still had fears deep inside. Fears that this was temporary. Fears that everything would fall apart and she'd be crushed as it all tumbled down around her.

"Mary's having her baby," her father announced as he came into the house toward evening. "You need to come help me."

Eleanor was certain he was talking to her; after all, she'd already helped in two deliveries and her father had been training her for weeks. But it was her mother who got up and responded. "Sure. Sounds groovy. I love it when babies are born."

As the couple left, Eleanor's strong feeling of resentment took her by surprise. *She's taking my place. I was the nurse.* She fumed about this all evening—even after her brothers fell asleep in various places all over the house. In her annoyance, she'd forgotten to send them to bed, but she didn't care. Raising children was her mother's job—not hers.

Nothing could console Eleanor as the hours passed. Didn't her father love her anymore? Didn't he know how much she wanted to be with him—helping him? Why had he let her mother go with him? She determined she would talk to him about it tomorrow at the clinic. He needed to know how she felt.

Eleanor dozed off, only to be awakened some time later by her father. At first she thought it was a dream as he lifted her in his arms and carried her to bed. She felt strange—trying hard to reconcile the moment. Was she asleep?

She came fully awake as he began to undress her—to kiss her. "Where's Mom?"

"She's staying with Mary tonight. The baby was born a little while ago. A girl."

"Cool."

He said nothing more about it, but Eleanor's mind wandered as her father found his comfort with her. *He does still love me,* she thought. She didn't understand her feelings and the confusion, however. What was going to happen to them? She supposed as long as her father still loved her, there would be a way to make things right. Eleanor tried to comfort herself in this.

Her mother's shrieks of indignation shattered Eleanor's illusions of comfort.

"What do you think you're doing? You animal! You pervert!"

Eleanor's father jumped up out of the bed. "Melody, you need to calm down."

"I won't calm down, you child molester." She threw the nearest object at him.

Eleanor scooted to the far side of the bed. She was naked and suddenly felt more aware of it than she'd ever been before. She grabbed for her clothes and yanked them on in something akin to fear. What was going on?

"I should call the fuzz. You know, you're the sickest man I've ever known."

Her mother continued to rant and rave, but Eleanor couldn't

understand what was wrong. Why was she so upset? Her father had said she might worry that he loved Eleanor more than her, but this seemed to be something completely different.

"Melody, you don't understand."

"I understand plenty. I understand that fathers aren't supposed to have sex with their daughters. I understand that you're the worst kind of monster there is. How could you do this to her? To us?"

Eleanor stared at the couple in dumbfounded silence. She looked to her mother and then to her father. His face said it all. He had lied. He had betrayed her. What he'd done wasn't right.

How could he have done that to her? He said it was a good thing, a right thing. He'd made her feel special—wanted.

"You said it was all right," Eleanor murmured.

"Of course he said it was all right," her mother countered. "That's so he could have his way—do his thing. Well, you're sick, Allan. Sick!"

Eleanor looked at her father, desperate for answers. Was her mother right? Was this why they couldn't tell her about it—or anyone else? It was all so clear now. Eleanor felt so stupid. But he'd said it was all right, that this was how people learned, this was how they showed love for each other.

"Ellie, I'm sorry," he whispered.

"Don't!" she said, holding up her hands. "Don't say anything more. I hate you. I hate you both! I wish you were dead!"

She ran from the room, stumbling through the house and into the crisp night air. Why had he lied to her? Confusion overwhelmed her—blinded her. Eleanor struggled to find her way to her hiding place in the dark.

"I'm going to leave here forever," she told herself.

She hid herself away, terrified of the night and being alone, but more terrified of the truth she'd just learned. Her mother's face had been so full of rage and hate. Her father, on the other hand, had held a look of regret that absolutely consumed Eleanor.

Why? Why had he done this to her? She loved him and wanted him to be pleased with her—to love her back. Now she had nothing. Nothing.

Eleanor awoke to an eerie silence in the morning. She couldn't remember at first where she was, and then it all came back to her. The ugliness of it all. She tried not to think about what had happened as she gathered her things. She wanted to slip back into the house and get the rest of her stuff, and then she planned to run as far away from this place as was humanly possible.

She slipped through the woods and headed around the other dilapidated buildings, trying hard to remain quiet. She heard sounds coming from somewhere past her house, and Eleanor felt certain it would help to keep her movements unseen. She hurried toward her house, sneaking in the back door as silent as a mouse. She'd nearly made it to her room when someone took hold of her.

"Are you Eleanor?"

It was a police officer. The man was huge, with glaring brown eyes. She wanted to say no, but she feared what might happen if she lied to this bear of a man.

"Yes."

"Hey, Sarge! We found her!"

He pulled Eleanor along with him, causing her to drop the few things she held. Another uniformed officer appeared. "You're going to have to come with us."

"Why? Where's my mom and dad?" She looked around the house and realized her family wasn't there. "Where are my brothers?"

The man called Sarge knelt down. "Look, sweetheart, I don't know how to tell you this. Something bad has happened. Your mom is dead. She called us to tell us about some trouble here with your dad." He looked at her knowingly, and Eleanor wanted to die. "Apparently your mom shot up and—"

"Where's my dad?" Her voice trembled, and she couldn't hide her fear. Somehow she'd always known that her mother would overdose one time too many.

"We don't know. We were hoping you could tell us."

She shook her head. "I ran away last night. I don't know." The truth spilled from her against her will.

"It's all right. We're going to take care of you and your brothers now. No one will ever hurt you again."

"I don't believe you," she cried. "I'll never believe anybody again." Her father had once told her there were worse things than death. At least he was right on that count. Death would have been much simpler in Eleanor's estimation. Maybe her mother had the right idea after all.

———

Eleanor didn't realize she was crying until she pushed the memories aside and opened her eyes. She was sitting on the floor at the bottom of the stairs. Getting up quickly, she hurried to her room. How long had she been there? Had anyone seen her? Surely not, or they would have tried to help her. But there was no help for her.

Eleanor had tried so hard not to remember that awful time in her life. Her father's betrayal had nearly consumed her. Having been raised in the commune, Eleanor had seen no reason to think her father's attentions were out of line. Worse still—and the source of the guilt that she'd been forced to live with—she'd enjoyed the things he'd done to her.

She buried her face in her hands. *Jana wants to know about the past, but how could I ever explain this? How could I ever hope for her to understand that I not only was molested, but I actually sought it out—I enjoyed myself? What kind of horrible perverted person am I?*

Eleanor had lived with this guilt all of her adult life. Of course, she hated the man now—hated him for his lies and manipulation. Hated him even more for the false sense of love he'd given her. But when she was fourteen, she'd thought she was special. Then she'd awakened to find herself a hideous abomination—a perversion of all that was good and holy.

Twenty-seven

"I HAVE AN APPOINTMENT this morning," Eleanor announced as she joined Taffy and Jana at breakfast. She didn't bother to eat but took a cup and poured herself some coffee.

"I'm also heading out," Taffy said. "Stanley and I are going to have devotions, then go for our five-mile walk. After that, we'll probably have lunch at the café in town, so don't plan on seeing me until later."

Jana felt rather deserted but said nothing. She'd been feeling more moody as the pregnancy lengthened. As Thanksgiving approached, Jana knew the time before her baby's arrival was growing short. *But I still haven't worked through everything,* she thought. *I'm not ready to have this baby . . . to be a mother.*

She didn't know what to do with the fears that had crept in over the last few weeks. She'd busied herself with the nursery, but even that hadn't helped. Instead, it only emphasized how time was slipping away from her.

"Do you need me to pick up anything?" Eleanor asked.

Taffy shook her head. "No, but next week we need to head into Missoula. I want to pick up some things for Thanksgiving, and I don't want to wait until the last minute. Besides, Jana is supposed to make a visit to the hospital and check out everything prior to the baby's birth. I think it might be nice if we planned an overnight trip and really enjoyed ourselves."

Jana forced a smile. "Sure. Sounds like fun."

"Well, good," Taffy declared, getting to her feet. "It's settled, then. Eleanor, you figure out what days would suit us best."

"All right." Her mother put her cup aside. "I need to get going. I'm running behind."

Jana watched the house empty, almost feeling like her mom and great-aunt were rats deserting a sinking ship. She wondered if her mood had caused them to flee. Everyone seemed to be consumed by her own busyness lately.

"What am I going to do with myself?" she questioned, gathering her breakfast dishes.

She cleaned up the small mess that remained in the kitchen and popped all the dirty dishes into the dishwasher. There wasn't enough for a load, however, so Jana left them for later and decided to wash some of the windows. It was something she could do slowly and without too much difficulty.

The cool November air felt refreshing as Jana opened the front door and stepped out onto the porch. It revived her, but the feeling quickly faded. She looked around her, noting the dull colors of winter. She wished it would snow—at least then the ground would be covered in white. As it was now, everything appeared dead . . . just as Jana felt inside.

Jana began washing the outside of the living room window, contemplating Kerry and Rob. The thought of them together— of them planning to leave, of Rob being killed—was never far from Jana's reflections.

I don't know what to do anymore. Taffy says I must deal with this, but I don't know how. I don't know how to make it right. Instead I just ponder the same things over and over and get nowhere. What do I do with these thoughts, these memories? How do I actually "deal" with my life?

"Good morning."

Jana turned to find Taffy's pastor, Kevin Clifford, had ridden over on a bicycle. It seemed like the kind of thing he'd do, Jana thought. He dismounted and set the kickstand. "Is Taffy home this morning?"

"No, I'm sorry, you just missed her. She was going to have devotions with Stanley next door, then take a long walk. You might still catch her."

Kevin nodded. "I'll check there, and if that fails, I'll ride the path they always take."

"You're familiar with where my great-aunt walks?" It seemed odd to Jana.

"Well, this is a pretty small town. There aren't that many options," he said with a grin.

She thought him a pleasant enough man, but she would not allow a friendship with Kevin Clifford. She couldn't get past the fact that he was a pastor, especially when she was still struggling with her understanding of God.

She dunked her sponge in the soapy water. "I suppose you're right. I hadn't really thought about it."

"So how are you doing?" He climbed up the steps and stood on the porch just a few feet away.

Jana felt a surge of apprehension. "I'm fine."

"Care to talk with me for a few?"

"I really should wash the windows," she said, hoping the excuse would send him on his way.

"I could help you. I'm pretty good at washing windows. The church has twenty-four of them. You tend to get good at things like that when so much repetition is involved. You might even say I'm the window-washing king of Lomara."

She couldn't help but smile. "No. I don't need help, but thanks for the offer. Coming from a king, that means a lot." He chuckled, but then an awkward silence fell between them. Jana looked at the dripping sponge. The chill of the November air, combined with the dampness of the sponge, made her hands feel nearly numb from cold. She supposed this wasn't the best job for the day, but Taffy had been talking about doing it all week, and Jana had wanted to surprise her.

"You know, I'm not going to hit you over the head with a Bible," Kevin finally said.

Jana dropped the sponge in the bucket. "Maybe you should." Her comment surprised her. Was she challenging him to get spiritual with her—to help her understand where God was in all of this?

"I think you'd feel better if you could let go some of your frustration and ask the questions that are bugging you."

She looked at him oddly. "What questions?"

He shrugged and leaned back against the porch post. "Well, for starters, where was God in all of this? Why didn't He keep bad things from happening?"

"So where was He? Why didn't He?" she countered in a rather sarcastic tone.

Kevin gave her a hint of a smile. "Do you really want to talk about this or are you just humoring me?"

Jana appreciated his candor and his concern. "Come on inside. I have some coffee on, and I'd like to warm up."

He nodded and opened the door for her. "After you."

Jana left him in the living room, then went to pour them both a cup. "Do you take cream or sugar?" she called from the kitchen. She poured cream into her own cup and awaited his answer.

"One spoonful of sugar. Thanks."

She brought the mugs with her and handed him one. "I'm not sure where to begin," she said, sitting down. "I wasn't expecting this, but I guess if I'm honest, I'll admit that I need it."

He took a sip and nodded. "We all need to talk to someone

from time to time. Taffy's been concerned about you. She never speaks of the details, of course. She's very protective of you and your situation."

"My situation," Jana said with a laugh. "That's what it is all right. It's a situation, and I don't know how to make it go away."

"What exactly are you wishing would go away?"

Jana thought about that for a moment. "I don't know. I guess the memories—the pain. I feel like I'm grieving for two different things. My marriage and my husband. Does that make any sense?"

"Sure. You lost him when he left you. That was bad enough, but before you could deal with that, he's murdered."

She shook her head. "None of it makes sense to me. I feel guilty for feeling a loss—for calling myself a widow. But I feel just as guilty for not realizing my husband was unhappy enough to leave me. It's confusing at best."

"Life usually has those moments, but you can't let Satan blind you to the truth. God hasn't abandoned you. He said in the Word that He'd never leave you nor forsake you. Satan wants to convince you that God's a liar—because Satan is a liar."

Jana considered the words carefully. "When I accepted Christ as my Savior, I did so because Rob convinced me that Jesus would be the answer to all my problems. But now . . ." She couldn't figure out how she wanted to say what was in her heart. She was desperately afraid that the answer would condemn her in some way.

"But now Rob is gone, and you're not sure who Jesus is without Rob to base it on?"

"Well, sort of." She suddenly nodded. "Yes. I guess that's a part of it." And as strange as it sounded, Jana realized from her talk with Taffy that she was very much confused. Rob had always been the one to correct her by pointing out something in the

Bible. Rob had been the one to suggest areas of growth by using verses to back up his thinking. Jana had seldom gone to the Bible on her own until the previous Christmas. After that she felt like she was coming to see a lot of things more clearly. She'd felt confident that Rob would be proud of her—but instead, he'd seemed troubled.

"Jana, when you accepted Christ as your Savior, did you understand that Jesus died for you? That if you had been the only person in the world who needed a Savior, that He would have still gone to the cross?"

"Yes, I think so." She felt uncertain. "I know Rob told me that, but I'm not sure I understood it or even really heard it—at least not at first. Does that sound strange?" She didn't wait for an answer. "I guess I made Rob my savior instead of Jesus." The realization hit her hard.

"It happens, Jana. You can't beat yourself up over it. There are some people who need to be a savior to other people. They want people to rely on them, to hold them up as important and special. I don't know if that's what Rob did, but it's easy to see why you'd be confused about things now."

"It makes me angry," she said, putting her coffee aside. "He knew what he was doing. I'm sure of that. Rob liked power. He hated playing assistant to anyone. Now I can see that in his own manipulative way, he made me reliant upon him for my relationship with God." She thought for a moment. "The woman he ran off with told me that Rob started acting unhappy around last Christmas. Well, that's when I felt like I was finally starting to understand God for myself. . . . Now I don't know what to think or believe."

"It doesn't have to be that way. Jana, God didn't change. You can come to Him in confidence. Let me share a couple of verses with you to prove my point." He reached into his pocket and pulled out a thin but well-worn Bible. "In First Timothy two, verses five and six, it says, 'For there is one God and one mediator between God and men, the man Christ Jesus, who gave himself as a ransom for all men.'" He stopped and looked up at her. "Rob wasn't your savior, nor was he the way to God. Jesus alone is your salvation."

She nodded. "I believe that. I saw that for myself. I guess now I just don't know where to go from there—what to do with that belief."

"You put your trust in Jesus," Kevin said softly. "Not in Rob or a marriage that fell apart. Jesus is there for you, Jana. You just need to reach out to Him—in prayer and by reading His Word."

"But I don't know what to pray," she admitted sadly. "I feel so overwhelmed. I don't know where to start."

"Start with giving your feelings, your thoughts, your heartaches to Him. Let Him know how bad you feel—because, Jana, He already knows. He knows how angry you've been. He's heard your questions and your fears. All of those feelings are deceptive. We can't trust them, but we can trust Him."

"So you're saying take a step of faith?"

"Yes. Take a step in faith that God really is who He says He is—not who Rob says or who I say. But go back to the Word and learn who He is for yourself. Rekindle what you were coming to understand and the relationship you were finding for yourself."

Jana thought about Kevin's words long after he'd gone. It sounded too simple. Too easy. Shouldn't it be harder than that? Her life felt so complicated. How was it that something so important could be as easy as letting go—giving over to God?

"And it still doesn't answer all my questions," she said as she dusted the living room knickknacks. The old rage edged to the surface and threatened to swallow the calming effect of Kevin's discussion.

"Why don't I understand?" She looked upward, as though she might see God there looking back.

"I don't know why this had to happen to me. I don't know what I'm supposed to tell my child. I don't know how I'm supposed to live."

The more she focused on herself and the circumstances at hand, the angrier she felt. "It's not fair. It's not fair!" Tears came to her eyes. "I want to believe you care, God. But I don't know how to let go. I have a baby now. A child who will want answers, just as I've wanted answers all of my life. I have no answers to give!"

And then it dawned on her that maybe her mother had no answers either.

"I can't go on like this. It seems one minute I come close to glimpsing the truth and the next it's far beyond me." She began dusting again, only this time her strokes held more vigor. Tears blinded her eyes, and without meaning to, she knocked off one of Taffy's vases. It shattered around her feet.

She sank to her knees, sobbing uncontrollably. *I can't bear any more. I can't go on like this. God, help me.* She buried her face in her hands. *How can I raise a child by myself? How can I make a family for this baby when I don't even know what family is really about?*

She felt someone pull her into an embrace. Her surprise couldn't have been greater, for there on the floor, mindless of the broken vase, was Eleanor Templeton, cradling her daughter in a way such as she had never done. Jana was uncertain at first as to how to take it. She stiffened against her mother's touch.

"I'm not very good at this, I know," her mother whispered, "but I've come to realize something. While there are things worse than death, burdens are better carried when you have someone to share the load. You and I are so much alike. We try to carry it all ourselves, and then we get mad when we stumble and fall and break our backs against the weight of our problems."

Jana relaxed against her mother, anguish pouring from her heart. "I just feel like it will never be good again," she said through the tears. "I'll never be happy. Nothing will ever be right."

"I know," her mother said, stroking her hair. "I know exactly what you mean."

They stayed like that for what seemed an eternity. Jana didn't feel she had the strength to say anything more, and Eleanor seemed content to just hold her. The unbearable pain started to ease. Jana knew that somehow her mother had absorbed a portion of her child's pain.

"I've made a big mess," Jana said, being the one to pull away. "In so many ways."

"We all have," Eleanor admitted, "but now we are working to put it in order."

Jana nodded, then got to her knees. "I'd better get this cleaned up before Taffy comes home. This vase must have been an antique, and I feel awful for having destroyed it."

"You're in good company, child," Taffy said from the doorway. She came into the room with a smile on her face. "The president of the United States once came to my home in Washington, D.C., and broke the mate to that vase."

"But I have to confess," Jana said, wiping her tears, "this happened in anger. This was my fault, pure and simple."

"Just as it was the president's fault," Taffy replied lightly. "There's something about those vases that seems to bring out the worst in folks."

Jana began to grin, and even Eleanor couldn't keep from

smiling. "We are quite a trio," Jana commented, reaching out for pieces of the broken china.

"Yes," Taffy said knowingly. "We are a three-stranded cord. And Ecclesiastes says, 'A cord of three strands is not quickly broken.' We will find strength together."

Eleanor picked up the remaining pieces and got to her feet. Jana wondered if her mother would reinstate the wall that had kept them both at arm's length at the mention of those verses. Instead she said, "I've always avoided that passage of Ecclesiastes."

Taffy didn't react in surprise, but Jana couldn't help but stare at her mother oddly. Taffy only smiled and asked, "And why is that, dear?"

"Because it speaks against everything I believed," Eleanor said frankly. "Two are better than one because they have a good return for their work. If one falls down, his friend can help him up. But pity the man who falls and has no one to help him up!" She looked at Jana and extended her hand. "It's hard to see how wrong I've been."

Jana nearly started crying all over again, but instead, she fought back her tears and let her mother help her to her feet. She didn't fully understand what had happened, but for once Jana realized she didn't need to. From the look on her mother's face and the tears streaming down Taffy's cheeks, Jana knew that something good had taken place. It didn't matter if she understood the details. It was only important that she put aside the past and start again.

Twenty-eight

"I JUST DON'T THINK it's wise," Eleanor told Taffy as the old woman bustled around the room.

"It's a church retreat. How risqué can that be? I'll only be gone two days and will be in the company of the other church women the entire time. And we're only going up to the Big Mountain Retreat Center. It's not like I'm going to outer Mongolia by myself." Taffy paused and grinned mischievously. "Although remind me to tell you about the time I was abandoned in Hong Kong and ended up on the wrong water taxi."

"But what if you get sick? You aren't young anymore."

Jana saw her great-aunt's expression sober. She felt sorry for the way her mother babied Taffy—almost as if the woman had no ability to reason for herself.

"Eleanor, I know I'm not young, but neither am I feeble in body or mind. I wish you would stop telling me how old I am. I don't feel old."

Eleanor seemed taken aback. She sat down as if the wind had gone out of her sails. "I'm sorry. I never thought of it that way. I just worry about you."

"Well, stop. The Bible says we can't add a single day to our lives by doing that. In fact, I think it's sinful. Worry is like saying God can't."

Jana refused to get in the middle of this conversation. She liked the little changes she'd seen in her mother—in herself. To

266

jump in now, siding with Taffy as Jana felt confident she would do, would only make her mother feel that they were ganging up on her.

"Besides," Taffy said, pulling on her hiking shoes, "my money is paid and Stanley will be here any minute. He's going to drive me up to the retreat center. We're all supposed to meet there in time for lunch." She pulled on the laces and sent Jana a wink. "And they've asked me to be in charge of games this year. Oh, I have some doozies."

Jana laughed and Eleanor rolled her eyes. "I can only imagine," Jana's mother said.

"You both should have signed up to come with me. You could have kept an eye on me while having a great deal of fun." Taffy finished with the laces just as a knock sounded at the door. "That will be Stanley."

"You know, Aunt Taffy, you ought to marry that man," Jana teased. "He sure has it bad for you."

Taffy laughed. "Oh, goodness, why ruin a perfectly good friendship? I would wear that man out with my activities. You know, I read in one of my magazines the other day that most marriages fall apart because the couples weren't friends first. Isn't that interesting?"

"Rob and I were friends first and it didn't seem to help us. We had a lot of good times just talking and interacting at various functions," Jana said, shaking her head. "At least I thought we had good times. I guess it was all a lie."

"Why? Just because Rob left? Does that invalidate your feelings?" Eleanor asked.

Her mother's question surprised Jana. "I guess not, but it certainly invalidates what I thought were Rob's feelings."

"Now, child, you don't know that," Taffy corrected. "You can't know that. So instead of presuming the worst, I would advise you to think the best. Believe in your heart that Rob was truly happy then—that he loved you and cared about you—that your friendship was real. Maybe that changed later, but there's no reason to believe that the good experiences you had together were anything but the real deal. And if nothing else, *your* feelings were sincere."

The knock sounded again and Taffy went to answer it. "Sorry, Stan," she said, opening the door. "I was waxing eloquent."

He laughed. "You're always waxing something. You ready?"

"Absolutely. There's my bag. Why don't you take it out for me, and I'll be right there."

He tipped his hat at Jana and Eleanor, then picked up the small piece of luggage. "You ladies stay out of trouble now."

"With me gone, things are bound to run smoothly," Taffy teased. "After all, I'm the one who usually stirs things up."

Stanley nodded as he headed out the door. "I'm sure that's true."

Taffy took her coat from the closet. "I didn't mean to preach, Jana. I hope you didn't take it that way. I just get disheartened when people throw the baby out with the bathwater. A relationship goes sour in some area, so somehow that negates all the good things about that relationship. It doesn't add up for me. I hope you'll think about what I've said." She looked at Eleanor and added, "You too."

Surprised by her great-aunt's comment to her mother, Jana walked with her to the door. "You know that's a good way to stir up problems," she said under her breath as she kissed Taffy on the cheek. She hoped her mother hadn't heard.

Taffy only smiled and patted Jana's arm. "You can't be afraid of conflict and confrontation, Jana. That's what's happened with your mom." She glanced over Jana's shoulder to where Eleanor remained seated. "You two have a great time. I'll be back Sunday after the church service." She took up a large brown felt hat and, with a flamboyant air, positioned it jauntily to one side of her head. "I'm off!"

Jana closed the door, then rubbed the small of her back and stretched. She felt so tired these days. The baby was beginning to drop a bit and it wore Jana out. She crossed the room and plopped down in a chair in front of the fireplace. The gas fire put off a nice amount of heat, and Jana basked in the warmth.

"I'm going to start lunch," her mother said, interrupting the silence. "How does potato soup sound?"

"Perfect. I like soups in the winter," Jana admitted. "They fill you and warm you up at the same time." Jana yawned and closed her eyes. She thought about going upstairs for a short nap but instead decided to doze in the chair. She realized as she faded off that a few short months ago she would have felt anxious—even nervous—about being left alone with Eleanor. But now, even though things weren't perfect, they were peaceful. Jana relished that. She needed peace in her life. She needed to feel safe and content.

"Jana?"

She heard her name being called but couldn't figure out where the sound was coming from. Struggling to wake up, Jana realized her mother was standing over her with a tray.

"Are you ready for lunch?"

"You just went in there to make the soup," Jana said, yawning.

Eleanor handed her the tray. "That was well over an hour ago."

"Really?" Jana tried to balance the tray while scooting up in the overstuffed chair. "I guess I fell asleep."

"Looks that way."

Her mother pulled out a wooden TV tray and positioned it

in front of the chair. Jana put the smaller tray atop it and breathed deeply of the soup's aroma. "Oh, this smells so good."

"I've always liked this recipe," Eleanor said, now setting up her own tray. "I thought it might be nice to sit right here and eat in front of the fire."

"It's perfect. I really like the way this house is set up. I like the fireplace and the size of the rooms. I love the high ceilings. It gives it such an open feeling."

Eleanor nodded. "It's so unlike the house we had in New York."

Jana turned up her nose at the memory. "I think that place was at least two hundred years old."

"Maybe older."

Jana laughed and cautiously sampled the soup. "This is good. I'd like to learn how to make it."

"It's simple. I'll show you next time."

They sat in amiable silence, eating and contemplating the fire. From time to time one of them made a comment, but it seemed just as well that they enjoyed the quiet. Jana watched her mother from the corner of her eye. The woman was truly beautiful. Jana had never given it much thought, but her mother had aged gracefully. Her blond hair was dyed, so there was no sign of gray, and while there were some wrinkles in her face, they only served to give her character, not the suggestion that she was nearly fifty.

"Did you get the business put on the market?" Jana asked. She knew that after much contemplation, her mother had decided to get out of the bookstore business.

"I have the lawyer taking care of it. He'll handle the sale of my house as well," Eleanor replied. She pushed the tray aside and went to Jana. "Are you done?"

She nodded. "But you don't have to wait on me. I can get it myself."

"Nonsense. I'm already here." Her mother picked up the tray and took it to the kitchen.

Jana wondered if she'd come back and talk some more. She wanted to broach the subject of her own father and wondered if her mother would be receptive. She supposed all she could do was ask. Then if her mother got upset, she could be gracious and back down.

Following her mother into the kitchen, Jana found Eleanor rinsing off the dishes. "Mom, I don't want to ruin the peace between us, but I need to ask you something."

"So ask." Eleanor put the bowls in the dishwasher and turned to meet her daughter's question.

"Will you ever be willing to talk to me about my father?"

Eleanor blew out a long breath. "I've never talked to anyone about your father. I've never spoken of him—named him—to anyone."

"But why? Surely people knew him since you were married." Eleanor looked away and twisted her hands together. The action sent a realization through Jana. "You weren't married, were you?"

"No. I was never married, Jana." She looked at her daughter hesitantly.

"Is that why you've never wanted to talk about it?"

"I didn't want to talk about it because I was convinced that if I didn't speak about the past, it couldn't hurt me."

"But the man has been dead for years," Jana said, working hard to keep her voice even. "Surely he can't hurt you now."

Eleanor shook her head. "You just don't know how this truly could hurt you—hurt others."

"I suppose not," Jana said, realizing she probably would never get the answer to her questions. She was ready to walk away when her mother continued.

"I know I told you a bit about the commune—about my life there. But I didn't tell you everything. I never told you why I had to leave."

"You said your mother died."

"Sit down, Jana." Her mother motioned her to one of the kitchen chairs. "My mother died because she shot up an overdose of heroin."

"Oh," Jana murmured. She didn't know what else to say.

"I blamed myself for a long, long time. I truly believed that I was responsible for killing her."

"But why? The society you lived in promoted that kind of thing—drug use and whatnot."

"Yes," Eleanor said, coming to the table to join Jana, "but something in particular happened that caused my mother to take that final hit. Something that she couldn't live with."

"What? What happened to make her do that?"

"She saw my father sexually abusing me."

Twenty-nine

ELEANOR'S LIFE had taken her from the commune to a foster family whose values were as rigid in structure as her parents' had been loose. She didn't understand much of anything, nor did she care to. The officials who talked to her asked her over and over if she knew where her father was, while in turn she wondered about her brothers.

"Don't you worry about those boys," a social worker told her in a haughty, clipped tone. "We've got them in a safe place. What I need to know is what your father did to you."

But Eleanor didn't want to talk about her father. She was still in a state of confusion and grief. Her mother was dead and her father . . . well . . . he had been her best friend, and now that was gone.

For Eleanor the days were a blur of religiosity and condemnation. Her foster parents, two rather overweight, obnoxious people who had no children of their own, were convinced she was demon-possessed and prayed for her at all hours of the day and night. At one point they brought in a gathering of church people to pray over Eleanor. It was a bizarre ritual in which they made her drink a foul-smelling concoction, then pushed her from person to person until everyone had a chance to take hold of her and pray aloud.

Before the last person could even conclude his prayers, Eleanor became violently ill, vomiting all over the floor. The people gathered said it was a good sign that the demon had left her. It made no sense to her whatsoever.

Neither did her foster parents' actions the following day. Eleanor was awakened at four in the morning and forced to take a cold shower. The woman who'd become her foster mother then gave Eleanor a sacklike dress to wear.

Eleanor allowed the woman to take hold of her and half drag her from the bathroom to the large front room, where she'd been the night before.

"Get on your knees," the woman commanded.

Eleanor, weary from the lack of sleep and chilled from her freezing shower, did as she was told. What else could she do? The woman's beefy hand was already pushing her to the ground.

"Now you stay there and pray. You need to fast and repent of your sins. How evil for a child to entice a father to sin. You are a wicked girl, Eleanor Templeton. A wicked girl. The devil has chosen you as his handmaiden, but we won't allow for it here. We serve the Lord."

Eleanor looked at the woman in wide-eyed fear. The woman's shoulder-length curls seemed to bounce in emphasis as she spoke, and her double chin bobbed up and down. Eleanor might have laughed at the sight had the situation been different.

"Why aren't you praying?" the woman questioned.

Eleanor looked around the room hesitantly. "I don't know how."

The woman gave a gasp and a scream. She ran from the room and it was only a few moments before she returned with her husband. The man pulled on a robe as he entered the room.

"What do you mean you don't know how to pray? Were your people complete heathens?"

"I don't know."

The man glowered. "This is impossible. She's still full of sin

274

and deceit. We'll have to pray over her again tonight. She probably has more than one demon."

The woman nodded in an exasperated way. "The devil won't let her pray."

The last thing Eleanor wanted to endure was another round of vomiting and people touching her. She got to her feet. "I'm not going to let you do those horrible things to me again."

The woman looked flabbergasted. "It's the demon. He's speaking through her."

"I'll call the preacher," the man said.

Eleanor ran to the room they'd given her, not caring that she'd nearly knocked the woman over as she raced past her. She closed and locked the bedroom door, then immediately searched for her own clothes. Finding them rolled up in the trash can, Eleanor quickly pulled them on and went to the window. The lock easily slid back, and while the man and woman pounded on the bedroom door, demanding she allow them entry, fourteen-year-old Eleanor slipped out the window.

She didn't know where she could run. She didn't know what city she was in or the people. Still, she had to escape. These people were more frightening than just about anything she'd ever encountered.

She'd only managed to get about a mile away before a police cruiser pulled up alongside her. The officer got out of his car and called to her. "Are you Eleanor Templeton?" She froze in place. She looked at the man apprehensively and said nothing.

"Come on, get in the car, Eleanor. I need to take you back to your foster home."

She found her tongue. "I won't go. Those people are weird. They're doing weird things to me."

He frowned and exhaled a deep breath. "The only choices I have are to take you there or juvenile hall."

Eleanor had no idea what juvenile hall was, but neither did she care. "I won't go back to that place. I'll just keep running."

"Okay. Your choice. I'll take you to juvie."

Eleanor had no idea what awaited her at juvenile hall. She rode in the back of the police car in silence, wishing that she could have been the one to die instead of her mother. She kept thinking about how her parents had taught her that the world was a bad place—filled with bad, unhappy people. They may have lied about a lot of other things, she thought, but they didn't lie about that. People out here weren't happy at all.

The girls' detention center was nothing more than a jail, Eleanor soon learned. The crazy part was, she felt safer here than at her foster home. A woman dressed in a brown uniform came to take charge of her. When her records came through and they realized who, she was, Eleanor found them to be almost hostile in their regard.

"You need a physical," the woman said, looking at the chart. "You were supposed to have had one yesterday."

Eleanor had no idea what she was talking about. Why did she need a physical? Why did she need anything from these people? It was like the world had gone suddenly crazy.

"Since you're sexually active, you'll have to have a gynecological exam," the woman said, writing on the chart as she examined the papers.

Eleanor wanted to protest that she wasn't sexually active anymore, but she figured the woman wouldn't care. So instead of saying anything, she sat and studied the tiles on the ceiling.

"Have you ever been pregnant?" the woman asked.

Eleanor looked up in disbelief. "No."

"Is it possible you're pregnant now?"

Eleanor shook her head. "I don't know."

The woman nodded and went back to the paper. "Did you have multiple sexual partners?"

"No," Eleanor said in frustration.

Why all this focus on sex and pregnancies? Why didn't someone tell her the things she needed to know, like where her brothers were and where her father was? She wondered about her mother's body and whether there would be a funeral.

"So your father was your only sexual partner?"

Eleanor hated the reminder of what had passed between her and her father. "Yes."

"How often did he rape you?" the woman asked flatly. She looked to Eleanor as if demanding an answer.

Eleanor didn't know what to say. She knew what rape was. Sapphira had once told her about someone being raped. But that wasn't what had happened between Eleanor and her father.

"Look, Eleanor, you won't be in trouble. Just tell us what happened so that we can help you. Your father, as soon as he's found, is going to jail for a long time, but we need this information to keep him there."

"I don't want him to go to jail," she said in frustration. "He didn't rape me. He loved me."

"Grown men—fathers—do not show love in that way, Eleanor. You may have been taught that there was nothing wrong with what took place, but this was a hideous thing. You were a victim, and you need counseling and help or you'll never be a productive human being." She went back to her clipboard. "We'll have to make sure you aren't pregnant. If you are . . . well . . . there are ways to take care of it. We can't openly talk about that kind of thing. . . . It's not really legal . . . but there are ways."

Eleanor had no idea what the woman was talking about. The rest of the day gave her no more understanding, however. It turned into one nightmarish situation after another. Without being given the chance to protest, Eleanor found herself whisked away to an examination room, where she was told to strip and prepare for her exam. The experience was more frightening and painful than anything she had ever had to endure. She wept silently as they continued what they called their "exam," then without consoling her or offering her an explanation, told her to get dressed and be ready when the nurse came to draw her blood.

Eleanor felt violated and exploited, and she longed to fight them all, but she was far too defeated. Things only went from bad to worse as she was put into the company of other inmates. The girls there were not kind or understanding. They wanted to know what crimes Eleanor had committed to land herself in the detention center, and when she refused to tell them, they beat her up.

That night as she lay in her bunk, she wondered how life had ever gotten this crazy. She wanted to make it all go away—to wake up and realize it had all been a bad dream. But for two weeks, this was the only world she knew. Invasive . . . condemning . . . deadly.

On the day the guard came to take her to the office for release, Eleanor felt no excitement, no hope. They were no doubt sending her to another foster home; they'd already told her this would be the procedure. Eleanor tried to figure out a means of escape as she sat outside the administrator's office. Maybe she should go along with their plan, then sneak out of the foster home in the middle of the night when no one would see her. That would give her a good head start, and this time she'd know better than to just walk along the street.

"Eleanor Templeton," the secretary announced, "you're to go inside now."

Eleanor stood up and entered the office. There were three

people staring at her—smiling. Even the administrator was smiling. It gave Eleanor the creeps.

"Have a seat, Eleanor. I have someone I want you to meet."

She plopped down on the red leather wing-backed chair and said nothing. The woman sat to her right and the man sat on the opposite side of the woman. Eleanor knew they were watching her, but she refused to even look at them.

The administrator took his seat behind the desk and shuffled through a stack of papers. Clearing his throat, he picked up her file. "Eleanor, this is your aunt and uncle."

She looked at the man oddly. "I didn't know I had an aunt and uncle."

"I'm your mother's sister," the woman explained. "My name is Taffy, and this is Cal, my husband."

Eleanor crossed her arms and pressed her body against the back of the chair. "So what?"

"The court is appointing them as your guardians. You will live with them from now on. If you run away or cause them any problems, you'll be brought back here."

She wondered about the couple. The woman looked nothing like her mother. Were they really related to her?

"I don't even know these people. How do you know they aren't lying?" Eleanor protested. "Besides, what about my brothers? No one has told me anything about my brothers. And what about my dad? What about my mom? Did they have a funeral?"

Taffy knelt down beside Eleanor's chair. "We had a small funeral, and once you leave here with us, we'll take you to where we buried her."

Eleanor stiffened as the woman reached out to pat her arm. "What about my brothers?"

The administrator shook his head. "That isn't information I can give out."

"We will look for them, just as we have looked for you," Taffy declared. "We really do want to help you. Please give us a chance."

Eleanor found no condemnation in Taffy. Not then, and not five weeks later when the woman realized how hopelessly inept Eleanor was at social and living skills.

Living with Taffy and Cal was something of a dream after Eleanor's other experiences. Her aunt and uncle were rich for one thing, and Eleanor didn't want for anything—except understanding of where the rest of her family had gone.

The house, a palatial mansion in upstate New York, was something Eleanor couldn't have even imagined. She wished she could share it with Sapphira. The bedroom Taffy gave her was bigger than most of the houses Eleanor had grown up in, and the furnishings were tasteful and expensive. Including the fine china cup Eleanor had just broken.

"I'm sorry," she said, bending down to pick up the pieces.

"A lady must never bend over like that," Taffy instructed. "Crouch down, bending your knees. Keep your legs together and then pick up the pieces. Like this." Taffy showed Eleanor by example. "You're wearing a skirt, and when you bend over like that people can see . . . well . . . all the way to China," she said with a laugh. She smiled at Eleanor as she attempted to squat. "There, that's better."

They cleaned up the mess without a single word of condemnation from her aunt. Eleanor didn't quite know how to take it. "I'm sorry about the cup," she finally said.

"Nonsense. It's just a thing—meant to be used. You didn't mean to break it; it was an accident." They both took their seats, but Eleanor felt awkward and all thumbs as Taffy poured her a second cup of tea. "Let's try again."

"Why is this important?" Eleanor asked.

"Because you'll be invited to parties and teas. You need to learn some social skills in order to keep from breaking other people's china. Besides, we want to put you into a very nice school, and unfortunately there are many rules and structured routines that need to be followed."

"I don't want to go to school," Eleanor said, shaking her head. "They'll just be mean to me."

"Not for the prices we'll pay," Taffy said, laughing. "Actually it's a very nice school with very well-behaved young ladies. But you have very little composure. You simply weren't taught, and I'd rather work with you prior to sending you there. That way they won't laugh at you, because you'll perform just as well as they do."

But it wasn't quite that simple. In fact, it was nearly a year and a half before Taffy felt Eleanor could handle such an adventure. In the meantime, a private tutor was hired to help Eleanor learn the things that would be expected of her in a structured schoolroom.

Eleanor learned fast, faster than anyone expected. She had a great love—a passion actually—for numbers and reading. She flew through her studies and impressed everyone with the way she managed to catch up to her age group. By the time she was sixteen, Eleanor was enrolled at a posh day and boarding school, feeling confident of being able to hold her own with any of the prim young women who had been born to a life of privilege. But something else happened to Eleanor along the way. In order to survive, she was determined to never care about anyone again. She even guarded her heart against the vivacious Taffy.

That was probably the hardest part. Taffy had done nothing but love her and give to her. Taffy gave her time, her money, her love. Eleanor could find no fault with the woman, but neither could she yield her heart to Taffy. There was too much danger in loving other people. Hadn't she already realized that?

Eleanor graduated shortly before her nineteenth birthday, and the feeling was unlike anything she'd ever experienced. She had accomplished something for which people praised her. Her teachers and the principal commended her performance as near genius. As she presented the valedictorian speech to her small graduating class, Eleanor knew she had accomplished something no one had ever believed her capable of doing. Well, no one but Taffy. Taffy had made it clear that Eleanor could be whatever she wanted to be, and Eleanor had come to believe it.

"We've bought you a new car for graduation," Taffy announced. "But that isn't all."

Eleanor looked at Taffy and then Cal. Both had been so good to her. She had never known life could be like this. So calm, so ordered . . . so peaceful. Here at last was the place where she could feel content. Gone were the memories of her father's sinful wrongs against her and her mother's suicide. Gone was even the worry about what had happened to the brothers no one seemed able to track down. None of it mattered anymore, because Eleanor simply would not allow it to matter.

"We're going to Europe," Taffy announced. "Just you and me. We're going to do the grand tour."

"Europe—really?" Eleanor asked.

Taffy laughed. "Yes. Our bags are already packed; what little we're taking, that is. We'll shop and buy all new clothes in Paris and London. We'll have the most marvelous time—you'll see."

It was all so unreal to Eleanor. She thought briefly of her life in the commune and shook her head. Her father had been wrong. The world wasn't a horrible place with unhappy people. Sure, some people chose to be unhappy, but then there were people like Taffy and Cal who had a great zest for life. Eleanor had never seen her aunt so much as shed a tear or use drugs to escape the pains of her life. And why should she? There were no pains in Taffy's life—at least none that Eleanor could see.

Eleanor smiled and took the keys Taffy handed her. "Well, before we go, I want to try out my car."

Taffy laughed and motioned to the door. "But of course. The plane doesn't leave for six hours."

Eleanor paused by the back door and looked over her shoulder. "Thank you. Thank you both."

Thirty

ELEANOR LOOKED AT JANA. "It was a strange time in my life; things were so perfect and good. Dealing with my past and the guilt was hard, but I kept stuffing it down, refusing to let it harm me. Instead, I focused on other things. Europe was unlike anything I could have imagined. Taffy knew so many people—dignitaries and even royalty. We stayed in wonderful homes, palaces, and rambling estates. I went horseback riding, skiing, boating, shopping. Nothing was denied us."

"It sounds incredible," Jana admitted.

"It was. It was like being reborn. I had been so unaware of what the world offered. Even the wonder of sleeping in a real bed and having clean sheets. I'll never forget how incredible that felt. I experienced movies and television, parties and great wealth. I learned about politics and the games people played in those arenas. It was quite an education."

"What happened after your trip to Europe?"

Eleanor could see that her daughter was completely drawn into the story, and to Eleanor's surprise, she found that it was somewhat freeing to share it. Still, there was an awful detail yet to be told: the terrible truth about Jana's birth.

"I went to college," Eleanor said absentmindedly. *Should I tell her everything? Will she be able to deal with the truth—especially now, in her condition?* "I went to Harvard. Taffy got us a small apartment in Boston. She was gone a lot with Cal, of course, but when she was there we had a great deal of fun. I worked in a small bookstore, mainly to escape having to be a part of the social scene. I found that I was tired of parties and men trying to entice me into a relationship. I wasn't ready to be anyone's girlfriend."

"I never knew you went to Harvard," Jana said, shaking her head. "I thought you went to college when I was young."

"I picked up some classes, but I already had two years at Harvard."

"What made you quit?"

Eleanor drew a deep breath and shook her head. "I was doing well in my classes, but I became more and more aware of the type of classes I was good at: science. My professors and adviser began to recommend a premed path. When I realized I was taking after my father . . . well . . . it freaked me out."

"I can understand that," Jana said softly. "What did you do?"

"I started losing interest in my studies. I skipped class—a lot." Eleanor remembered it all as if it were yesterday. "I started failing and told Taffy I just couldn't deal with the stress. I even went to a psychologist for counseling. He told me it was some kind of neurosis and gave me something to calm my nerves. I guess now they'd call it posttraumatic stress syndrome." She shrugged, realizing the diagnosis wasn't important. "They determined that I was severely depressed and needed a change of scenery and lifestyle. Taffy decided I should put my education on hold and we would travel. We went all over the U.S. and Europe. I enjoyed the escape."

"But you didn't deal with the problem," Jana interjected, "and that had to make it worse in some ways."

Eleanor looked at her daughter, and as she recognized the compassion in her expression, she felt a deep sorrow for the lost years between them. Regret was a companion Eleanor had never allowed, but now it seemed she couldn't avoid it.

"It did make it worse—at times," she finally admitted. "But I tried to keep from thinking about my problems, and Taffy was a good one to keep me from focusing too long on sorrow."

"Yes, she's very good at that."

Eleanor thought carefully of how she might share the details of her life in those days before she found herself pregnant with Jana. She knew the truth would hurt—maybe forever change the life they had together.

"Taffy and I rented a flat in London. Uncle Cal was appointed as assistant to the U.S. ambassador, and he and Taffy would spend a good deal of their time there. Taffy thought it wonderful fun for us to find the perfect place and decorate it together. I must say it was a nice diversion. I have very pleasant memories of our time together. London was a fascinating town."

"I'd like to go there someday," Jana said wistfully.

Eleanor stared at her oddly for a moment. It had never even entered her mind that Jana might enjoy such a thing. "We'll have to do it, then. Maybe next summer when the baby is old enough to endure a trip like that."

Jana smiled. "Do you really suppose we could?"

"I don't know why not. I'll have the business sale finalized by then, and we'll have plenty of money. I'd imagine even Taffy would want to go."

"I couldn't picture us making the trip without her."

"Neither could I." She let her mind drift back to those weeks in London. "Taffy made London seem almost like a fairy tale."

———

There was something about London that spoke to Eleanor. Maybe it was the ancientness of the city—maybe it was the regal sense of royalty and pomp. Whatever it was, Eleanor found that London held a sort of balm that she had not expected.

They managed to find a lovely Georgian apartment with a large number of suites and sitting rooms. Taffy was pleased.

"We'll be able to entertain here in grand order," she told her niece.

"I think it's beautiful," Eleanor replied, studying the architectural design of the room. Someone had gone to a great deal of trouble to create an artistic trim in white marble. Grand columns looked like they were built right out of the wall, stretching up on either side of the fireplace and ending in a detailed pilaster that blended right into the room's crown molding. The details gave the high ceilings a character all their own.

Taffy fingered the draperies. "I think these will do. They aren't all that old."

Eleanor glanced at the heavy gold damask. "I think they make the room look regal."

Their days in London were spent adding their own personality to the new home, as well as keeping up with the right parties and people. Eleanor was fascinated by all that took place. She spent her days shopping on Oxford and Regent streets, and occasionally when Taffy was buying for Cal, they would go to Saville Row. Fortnum and Mason was Taffy's favorite place for specialty foods, and she and Eleanor shopped there religiously before each special tea or party.

Eleanor loved the ambiance of London and occasionally made her own way, walking in solemn study of various churches and palace homes. Her favorite was Westminster Abbey, where she imagined the history of England playing out. Nothing was as charming or wondrous as her time in London.

Neither was it as painful and detrimental.

Eleanor gradually became aware of problems between her aunt and uncle. Taffy was unhappy with Cal for several reasons. His mood had changed. He was drinking more and indulging in gambling, which constantly worried Taffy. His philandering was also more evident. More than once Taffy caught him in the arms of the maid or housekeeper. She also began to hear stories from their friends, and the details were quite troubling.

After several weeks in their new home, Eleanor began to hear arguments between her aunt and uncle. She'd never experienced this before and it concerned her greatly. She tried to talk to Taffy about it, but the woman wouldn't see her burdened with such misery.

"I've known what kind of man I married since the day we said 'I do.' But I had hoped he might change," Taffy told her seriously. "Remember this before you marry, Eleanor. Don't go into a relationship believing you can make a man any different than he is."

"I don't plan to marry," Eleanor said, realizing she meant it. She hadn't given such matters much conscious thought, but now it seemed logical. "But neither," she added, "do I intend to live with any man." She shook her head, remembering how hopeless she had felt the day her mother had admitted to merely living all those years with Eleanor's father.

"I suppose the thing for us to do is put our hearts back on the proper path," Taffy told her. "I've long been remiss in seeking God."

"Seeking Him for what?" Eleanor asked. She still had horrible memories of that foster home where God had been sorely misused.

"Let's have some tea—maybe go to Harrods afterward," Taffy suggested. "I'll tell you all about it over something wickedly delicious."

When they were settled in a small shop with tea and scones, complete with clotted cream and strawberry jam, Taffy continued. "Eleanor, I've given this a lot of thought. I was raised to believe in God, you know. I came from a family where God was a fierce judge of all we did or did not do. But over the years, I've come to understand that God was something more. God truly cares about us and our hearts."

"How can you say that? You've seen the way people misuse religion and God. You know what those people did to me in the foster home."

"Yes, but that isn't what I'm talking about. I've been reading some books—books that make me feel much different about God. I'm hoping you might read them too. I think if we can find a small church—not a great cathedral, but rather an intimate gathering of people who believe as we believe—then we might benefit greatly and find our souls assuaged."

"But what do we believe?" Eleanor asked, putting her china cup down. "I've only seen the confusion and penalties of believing in God. I don't understand Him, nor do I think I want to."

"But you would give it a chance for me—wouldn't you?"

———

Eleanor pulled herself out of the memory and looked at her daughter. "I gave her a chance because you know how persuasive Taffy can be. But what amazed me more was she was right. I found myself overcome with a peace that I couldn't begin to explain as I turned to God and accepted Jesus as my Savior."

"I didn't know you were saved, Mom."

Eleanor let out a sigh. "Something happened. Something that caused me to walk away from God."

Jana seemed to instantly understand. "My father."

Eleanor realized the time had come to explain the truth. "Yes." She halted, not sure that she could or should continue.

"Please, Mom. I need to know." Jana's pleading was Eleanor's undoing.

"I told you that Taffy was growing very unhappy with Cal. He was constantly chasing one skirt and then another. And he wasn't doing much to hide that fact. We were constantly caught up in the social life that was demanded of us as political figures, but Taffy wanted only to get away, so we began to plan a trip back to the U.S. We purchased our tickets and scheduled the flight for two weeks later.

"Taffy told Cal we were going and told him why. She said he needed time to rethink his priorities and decide for himself if he wanted to make their marriage work. This really surprised me," Eleanor admitted. "I hadn't expected such a thing from Taffy. I'd only seen her happy and confident, but then I realized she was just very good at keeping things under control."

"How did you find out she'd told Uncle Cal all of this?" Jana wondered aloud.

"I overheard them one evening. I couldn't sleep, so I'd come down the back stairs for something to eat. I was in the kitchen trying to figure out where the cook had put the leftover roast when I heard something upstairs. I lost interest in my snack because I could have sworn it was Taffy screaming. Not in surprise, you understand, but rather in her demands.

"I went up one flight and they were in the hallway having it out. Taffy told Cal he'd embarrassed her for the last time."

"What did Uncle Cal do?"

"I was afraid that he would hit her or yell back, but he didn't," Eleanor said, shaking her head. "Instead, he was speaking softly and sweetly. Cajoling her with his words—acknowledging that he didn't deserve such a good woman. It made me sick. Here she was pouring out her heart, and he was playing her for a fool. I knew it as clearly as I knew anything, and I wasn't about to let it go unchallenged. But then, to my surprise, Taffy yielded. She calmed down and allowed him to embrace her and continue to apologize. I went upstairs angry. I was determined that I would never allow a man to do such a thing to me. I was further determined to have it out with Cal the next day."

"And did you?"

Eleanor looked at her hands. It was an old habit whenever she wanted to avoid the moment. "I tried to catch him before he went to work, but he left too early. Then I thought I might go by his office, but when I showed up, I found out he'd taken the afternoon off. That really made me angry because I was certain he was out seeing some other woman.

"I went back home, and when Taffy told me she had a horrible migraine and was going to bed, I thought it good timing. Cal would come home from his affair and I would take him to task." She stopped for a moment and forced herself to look at Jana. "But he didn't come home until late. And when he came home, he was very, very drunk."

"What did you do?"

"Well, I knew there would be no reasoning with him at that point. He was staggering all over the house, so I helped him to his room. Unfortunately, he thought I was Michelle, one of the maids he'd been fooling around with." She stopped there, afraid to relive the moment. In her mind she could still hear his slurred speech in her ears . . . feel his heavy breathing against her face.

"I tried to fight him off," Eleanor murmured. Her words were stuck in her throat. "I tried." She looked at Jana.

"Uncle Cal raped you?" she asked in disbelief.

Eleanor could see the understanding was beginning to dawn. "Yes," she whispered.

Thirty-one

"ARE YOU TRYING to tell me," Jana asked in horror, "that I'm the daughter of Calvin Anderson?"

"You certainly are," Taffy said from the doorway.

Neither Jana nor her mother had heard Taffy return. Jana looked at her great-aunt, then quickly turned her stunned face to her mother. Eleanor buried her face in her hands. She was clearly mortified by the situation.

"I've waited for years for this truth to finally be discussed," Taffy said, stepping into the kitchen.

Jana shook her head. "I thought you were at a retreat."

Taffy laughed, as though they were discussing nothing more important than the weather. "I had the wrong weekend. Guess that's what I get for trusting myself with the details."

"I didn't hear you come in," Jana said.

The old woman took charge of the situation. "Well, it's a good thing. This is a conversation that has been long overdue. Now, both of you come out here into the living room. This may take some time, and I want to be comfortable."

Jana looked to her mother. It was clear that Eleanor just wished they would all disappear. But Taffy was right. This conversation was long overdue. Jana got to her feet and went around to her mother's side. "Come on, Mom. Let's go talk this out."

Eleanor got to her feet, shaking her head. "I didn't know she knew. I didn't think anyone knew."

Jana helped guide her mother to a comfortable overstuffed chair. She waited until Eleanor was settled, almost afraid that her mother might break completely apart. She seemed so fragile. Finally Jana took her own seat on the couch and looked to her great-aunt for answers. Taffy stood for several moments before pulling up an oak rocker and sitting directly in front of both women.

Eleanor finally looked up, and Jana saw there were tears in her eyes. "How long have you known?"

"Practically since it happened," Taffy admitted. "At least I surmised it to be the truth. Cal was impossible to live with after that day, and you were determined to get back to America and have little or nothing to do with anyone. I knew something terrible had happened, but I thought perhaps it was nothing more than you had walked in on Cal with one of the maids."

"So after you were raped," Jana said, turning to her mother, "you didn't tell anyone?"

"I couldn't," she said in a hoarse whisper. "I couldn't hurt Taffy that way. I couldn't bear the guilt I felt, and I couldn't risk having her or anyone else blame me as people had blamed me for enticing my father."

"You did nothing wrong," Jana declared. "Not in being molested and not in being raped. It wasn't your fault."

"Maybe not, but there are things you don't understand," Eleanor said, refusing to look her daughter in the eye. "Things I can't talk about—things that are just too ugly."

Taffy shook her head. "Sometimes the details aren't important to share, but sometimes they are. You have no reason to fear condemnation in this group."

"Cal didn't seem to even recognize me," Eleanor said, her voice still low. "He thought I was there for his pleasure. The entire matter so shocked and sickened me that after my initial attempt to fight him off, I just let him have his way. I didn't want to scream or cry out because the last thing I wanted to do was attract attention. I didn't want you to know." She looked up and finally met Taffy's gaze. "I let him do what he wanted."

"Child, you have no blame in that situation. None whatsoever. Cal told me all about the matter prior to his death."

"He did?" Eleanor was clearly surprised.

"Yes, but let me back up." Taffy drew a deep breath and her expression took on a look that suggested she was trying to gather her thoughts. After a moment she spoke. "I remember when we flew home and left Cal in London. I had already given him an ultimatum and threatened to separate permanently if he didn't stop fooling around. He promised he would, but in the days just prior to our flight, he began drinking so heavily that I knew something was bothering him. Like I said, I saw your moodiness as well and figured you'd had some sort of shared encounter. At that point I had no reason to suspect the truth, however.

"Once we were home for a time and you started having morning sickness, I began to rework my thoughts. When you found out for certain you were pregnant, I knew you had to have conceived in London."

"Despite the fact that I told you it was one of my American friends," Eleanor stated matter-of-factly.

"Yes, well, I knew you weren't close enough to anyone. You were seldom gone from home—especially during that time. I began to put it all together and realized that Cal had probably fathered the child. What worried me every bit as much as the thought of a one-time rape was the idea of Cal molesting you over and over as your father had done."

"No, it was just once," Eleanor said, seeming to relax a bit. "But it was nothing like what my father had done. Cal was violent. It was like he was taking all his anger out on me. It was painful and hideous." She looked away. "I can't believe I'm even telling you this."

"I'm glad you finally are," Taffy replied. "It needed to come out a long time ago. It was one of the reasons I kept trying to make contact with you and get you to come home . . . back to me. I felt I owed you a home and security, but more than that I loved you and wanted to take care of you in your time of need. Then when Jana was born, I wanted to give you both a home that would allow you all the comforts you deserved. I had already separated from Cal and planned to keep it that way, but then he grew ill and I focused my attention on him and lost track of you. By the time Cal died, I began to wonder if you weren't better off without me in your life."

Jana listened in silence, watching the matter play out like an afternoon soap opera. Everything she had ever longed to know was suddenly being set out on the table like evidence in a courtroom drama. Cal Anderson was her father. She was the product of a rape—a violent act of aggression. No wonder her mother couldn't bear to have her near. It all made so much sense now. Jana was a painful reminder of that hideous act.

"I don't understand," Jana finally said. "Did Mom just leave? But how could she resettle without money?"

Taffy turned her attention to Jana. "Your mother left my care when she was about four months along. I came home one day and she was gone."

"I'd made arrangements to live on my own," Eleanor murmured.

"Yes, through Cal," Taffy added.

Eleanor's head snapped up. "You knew?"

Taffy smiled compassionately. "I didn't for a time, but I ran across some papers later—probably close to the time you gave birth. I saw that Cal had given you about half a million dollars.

We never discussed finances. Cal wanted me to just spend as I pleased. He never told me where our money came from or went. But one day I saw the returned check, and that was the final proof I needed."

"I sort of blackmailed him," Eleanor admitted. "I'm ashamed of it now, but at that time I didn't know what else to do. When I was certain that I was pregnant, I went to him one evening when you were gone and told him the truth."

"I can imagine that didn't go over well," Jana said, shaking her head. She was beginning to feel worse than ever before. She knew it wasn't her fault that her mother had been raped, but now she understood why her mother had never wanted to discuss Jana's father. Now Jana felt guilty for having pushed her mother over and over for answers.

"Actually Cal was quite gracious about the entire matter," Eleanor said.

"He was that way," Taffy threw in. "He was always trying to right his wrongs by throwing money at it or by pouring on the charm."

"I told him that if he didn't help me, I would tell Taffy everything. I think he knew that Taffy would side with me, and he couldn't bear to lose her." Eleanor looked at Taffy. "He loved you, despite the things he did."

"I know he needed me," Taffy said, "but he didn't love me in the right way. His was a selfish, needy love that was all about Calvin Anderson and nothing about me or anyone else."

"I suppose I see that now," Eleanor said. "Anyway, I told him that I needed to be set up with a home and income. I knew the book business from having worked at the bookstore in Boston, so I wanted my own bookstore. Cal asked around and found a small shop for sale—complete with inventory. It was about a hundred miles from where you lived and seemed perfect."

"But by then, abortions were legal," Jana suddenly said aloud. "Why didn't you abort me—like you suggested I do with this baby?"

Eleanor met her daughter's eyes. "I was wrong to ever suggest that. I was speaking out of anger and pain . . . please forgive me."

Jana was taken aback. "Of course," she murmured.

"I never really considered an abortion. I did, however, pray for a son. I didn't want a girl because I knew that would only mean that she might have to bear all the misery I had known. I told Cal he would never be a part of my baby's life because he was without scruples and values. I couldn't risk letting him see you or be a father to you for fear that he might do the same things to you that my father did to me."

It was all making sense now. Jana realized that her mother had taken what she thought was her only option. She had guarded her heart against further hurt and buried the past as far away as possible. Unfortunately, it had cost her the ability to have a real relationship with her child.

The baby moved within Jana, as if affirming her new understanding. "And Cal never wanted to know me or deal with me because that would mean risking Taffy learning the truth."

"At first he tried to talk me into letting them adopt you. He said it wouldn't be that unusual for a young woman in trouble to let her relatives take her child," Eleanor told them. "I knew Taffy would love you, but I couldn't bring myself to risk letting you be vulnerable. I knew if you remained with me, I could keep you shielded from men and the world. I just didn't give thought to the fact that I was also denying you love and the security of family. Once I did realize that, it was too late."

"It's never too late—not with God," Taffy stated.

"I keep thinking of how I asked you about whether you'd ever had to forgive someone for something really painful." Jana looked to Taffy and saw the old woman's contented smile. "All the time you knew I was the child of your husband's betrayal, and yet you welcomed me here. You've shown me nothing but love."

"But neither of you ever deserved anything less," Taffy replied. "I only wanted you to see that—to know it for yourself. It was never an issue of placing blame or condemnation. That isn't what the Lord would have us do. You were both victims of someone else's sin, however, and there are always consequences to sin. Like a ripple effect in the water. Sin ripples out to touch the people around the one committing the wrong. I knew I couldn't protect you from the hurts you'd suffered, but I could help to bear the misery with you.

"When Eleanor came to live with us, I wanted very much to help her heal from the past. Remember when I used to try to get you to talk to me about what had happened?" She looked to Eleanor and waited for an answer.

"But it was so . . . well . . . embarrassing. I felt so awful—so guilty. I had been completely duped by the only person I felt truly deserved my love and trust." Eleanor paused and straightened, lifting her chin in that same defensive way Jana had seen in the past. "You can't understand this because I don't understand it myself—but my father made me feel special. I didn't dread the things he did to me. I . . . I . . ." She fell silent.

Jana realized what she'd been about to say, however, and put voice to that thought. "You enjoyed it, and now you feel guilty."

Eleanor looked at her daughter in what looked like relief. "Yes." She bowed her head. "God forgive me."

"But that—even that—wasn't your fault," Taffy insisted. "Our bodies are made to respond to certain stimulation. You might not believe this, but your guilt is a common problem with victims of molestation. I read it in one of my magazines. People blame themselves, thinking that if they'd done something different—if they'd told someone, if they'd not dressed a certain way—then they wouldn't have been molested. It's all hogwash."

"But you can't understand," Jana's mother continued. "My father's actions made me feel special—truly loved. He made it all seem reasonable."

"But you were brought up in a society that was open to everything," Jana countered. "How could that be the fault of a young girl? You were told it was right—good. You lived in such a secluded manner that you had no reason to think otherwise."

Eleanor shook her head. "I've tried to comfort myself with that over the years, but the guilt remains."

Guilt. Jana finally understood another piece of the puzzle that was her mother. "You aren't a bad person, Mom. You aren't a perverted person."

"But I feel like one. How could I have enjoyed myself? How could I have ever thought it was right?" Eleanor seemed to plead with them for answers.

"But you'd never been taught anything different, Mom. You were told it was right. You were raised in an environment that suggested it should be acceptable. You weren't given any reason to think it wrong."

Taffy nodded. "Exactly. How can children know what's right and wrong except that their parents teach them? You were isolated from the rest of the world. You had no reason to think it was a lie."

Eleanor began to weep. "I've always felt like I should have known better. Like I should have known better than to wait up for Cal—that I could have done something more to fight him off."

"Life is full of 'should haves,'" Taffy said. "I've borne my own guilt. Guilt that if I'd been wiser I would have been able to protect you from Cal. Guilt that I didn't get you more counseling—

more help. Guilt is crippling, and we must fight against it."

"But how?" Eleanor asked. "How do I just set aside a lifetime of guilt?"

"Exactly. How do I put aside my guilt?" Jana threw in. "Guilt that I should have seen my marriage falling apart—that I should have known about the affair. Guilt that I caused my husband's death because of my flippant remarks." She'd never verbalized that before. She did bear a tremendous amount of guilt over Rob's death.

"You certainly aren't to blame for that man's death," Eleanor said defensively. "You merely spoke the truth and that Broadbent man acted on what he perceived to be the right answer."

"Don't you see?" Taffy said. "It's the devil's way of trying to ensnare us. He wants us caught up in false guilt and grief. The devil wants us to buy into the lies he spins around us. 'If only I'd done this differently.' 'I should have done that.' It's like an avalanche that just keeps coming—lie upon lie. When all the time we could simply take it to the Master—give it over to Him."

"You sound so sure of that being the answer," Eleanor said, wiping at her tears.

"I wish it were that easy," Jana had to admit.

Taffy laughed. "You have both commented from time to time about wondering how I could have such a happy and positive disposition. You presumed it meant that I'd never borne pain, guilt, and suffering in my life, but both of you now know that I have endured great sadness and loss." She sobered with this. "I'm here as living proof to tell you that God is bigger than our pain and sorrows. He's bigger than our guilt. He is able to take anything we give Him and turn it around for good."

"Even husbands who commit adultery?" Jana questioned. "I don't see how anything good can possibly come of that."

"It brought you here, didn't it?"

"But only because of the betrayal and pain. Oh, and my empty bank account. How is that for good?"

"You and your mother have been able to work through the past. You've been able to lay the truth out for each other to see—to judge, if you will. You have bared your souls and have realized that you still have value in the eyes of those who love you. And in spite of everything—the guilt, the pain, the longing—God has brought the three of us together in order to heal. He has given us a new hope in Him . . . if we will take it."

"I'd like to take it," Jana said, knowing for the first time in a long time that she'd found a truth that she could grasp. "I'd like to be like you, Taffy. I so admire you. Opening your home to me—knowing who I was and not being afraid that I would remind you of all the bad things in your life."

"Jana, God calls us to forget that which is behind. There's a good reason for that. He knows the destruction of the past in our present lives. He wants us to know forgiveness and to be set free from the bondage that past sins can create. Sometimes, like now, the truth of the past needs to come out, but once it does, we needn't let it continue to take us captive. Instead, we now take the past captive."

"It sounds too simple," Eleanor said softly. She had composed herself and was no longer crying. "I can't believe it to be that simple, because I fought for years to bury the past and have nothing more to do with it."

"But there's a difference between taking the past captive and merely hiding away from it. If you have a criminal and you put him behind bars for the rest of his life, he can't hurt you anymore. It doesn't mean he ceases to exist, but the threat is no longer what it was. However, if you leave him free and merely avoid running into him, you know that the threat is always there. He might show up at the most inconvenient moment."

Realization dawned on Jana. She could finally understand what Taffy meant by dealing with the past instead of just shoving it aside. Her breathing quickened and the baby moved wildly within. It was finally clear. She could be free. She could give it all to God and really be free.

Thirty-Two

ELEANOR FELT as though a heavy weight had lifted from her shoulders. Confession was indeed good for the soul, but now that she'd confessed, it was like having a painful, raw sore to deal with. She worried that her impromptu declarations could be used against her at a later time—thrown back in her face to prove her the disgusting, wretched creature that she truly was.

Taffy seemed to sense her dilemma. "Eleanor, do you remember when we decided to seek out God in London?"

Eleanor immediately thought back to those days. "Yes . . . I remember how loving the people were. I remember thinking that if this was how it was to be a part of God's family—and not like what those foster parents had been—then I wanted to have it."

"And what happened?" Jana asked.

"Cal's attack happened. I figured why bother with all the rules and regulations of God's law if even when you were following them bad things still happened to you." She'd never talked about this with anyone, but that was the crux of the matter in plain English. God should have kept her safe, and when He didn't, He failed to be worthy in Eleanor's eyes.

"That's how I felt about Rob's adultery," Jana said. "I was doing what I was supposed to do. I was on the mission field, for pity's sake. I was there serving God, loving the chance to share the Gospel message with people who'd never had a chance to hear it, and I came home to my life falling apart."

Taffy said nothing, seeming only to take it all in. Eleanor couldn't help but wonder what she thought. Taffy always appeared to have the answers—she was always so confident of God's power.

"I just don't understand," Jana said, shaking her head. "I've tried to figure it out, but it doesn't make sense. God could have interceded and kept my life intact. He could have prevented the affair. He could have prevented the murder."

"He could have prevented the molestation . . . the rape," Eleanor added quietly. She looked to Taffy, not knowing how to pick up the shattered pieces of her life. "Why didn't He? Wasn't He powerful enough? Didn't He care?"

"Oh, darlings, you are asking the age-old question of why bad things happen to good people. Goodness, but folks have been tossing that one back and forth throughout the ages. Why didn't God keep Adam and Eve from sinning and nip all of that nonsense once and for all?"

"I've wondered that too," Jana said. "I mean, God is all powerful, so why didn't He just keep Satan out of the mix altogether?"

"Because He wanted us to choose," Taffy said softly. Her tone was almost bittersweet as she continued. "He didn't want to be a heavenly puppet master. He wanted to interact with His creation. He wanted to be a Father to His children, and He wanted His children to willingly love Him and obey."

Eleanor studied her aunt for a moment and considered her words. Taffy had never offered her anything but love and acceptance. She had never imposed her will on Eleanor—she had never demanded love in return. Taffy had tried to keep Eleanor safe from harm. It wasn't Eleanor's fault that Cal had raped her—it was Eleanor's fault for being in the wrong place at the wrong time.

My fault. The guilt again washed over Eleanor. *It was all my fault. If I had done things differently* . . . But even as she thought this, a spark seemed to ignite somewhere deep inside. *But I was trying to do something good. I was trying to help Taffy.* She shook her head. It was too confusing to sort through forty-some years of chaos. As she had always done in the past, Eleanor began to systematically sweep all the pieces under the rug of her subconscious mind.

Stop! a voice inside cried out against her. *Don't just push it all aside!* Eleanor thought maybe she was losing her mind. She looked at Taffy as if to ascertain the truth of the situation, but her aunt said nothing.

She looked to Jana . . . Jana, the daughter she had so wronged. How could she have been so cruel—so neglecting? Eleanor looked away quickly. The very sight of Jana was as painful as it was good. She loved her daughter. She had always loved her. Eleanor remembered the first moment Jana was placed in her arms. There in the privacy of her hospital room, Eleanor had cuddled her infant child to her breast and had known what it felt like to truly love another human being. And she had thrown it all away—terrified of the cost that would have to be paid if she gave her heart.

"I wish I could understand it all." Jana's words pulled her mother back to the present.

"So do I," Eleanor said. "I wish I could explain my part, but the words never seem to come. How can you possibly understand my decisions and choices when I don't understand them myself?"

"But I think I understand us better than I did," Jana told her. "I can see now why you wouldn't want me around. I couldn't help but remind you of a horrible experience. I can't even bear to think what it must have been like for you. You must have dreaded my very presence."

"No! That's not true. I dreaded the lies between us. I dreaded realizing the pain I had caused you. You have to know this, Jana: I have always loved you, but that love was overshadowed by my fears for you—my fears *of* you. I pray you won't do the same thing to your child.

"I know I've ruined a chance to have a good life with you," Eleanor continued. "I know that so many painful things have forever damaged the relationship we might have had. I truly wanted the best for you, however. I wanted to protect you and keep you safe from all the bad things that had happened to me. But I failed, and again, it's the guilt that I cannot bear." She felt the tears come. "I wanted to save you, Jana, and instead I managed to plunge you right into the heart of betrayal."

"You didn't cause my marriage to fall apart," Jana protested. "That was something I did to myself—something I did or didn't do."

"No," Taffy said, shaking her head. "You're both missing the important point here."

They turned and looked at Taffy. Eleanor had no idea what she might offer to make sense out of this mess. Still, Taffy always managed to speak with wisdom, so Eleanor was ready to listen. "Go on." She wiped at her tears and waited for the answer.

"Girls, life is difficult and full of hardships. Jesus even said in the book of John that 'In this world you will have trouble. But take heart! I have overcome the world.'"

"But He's God. Of course He's overcome the world," Eleanor said, feeling a bit angry. "How hard can it be for God to overcome?"

"But, Eleanor, if we are in Him—if we've given our hearts to Him and are trusting Jesus for direction in our life—we've overcome too. Because of His victory, we also have victory. What you two need to see is that sin has made our world imperfect. We will have trouble. That's a fact. That's life.

"We will also make mistakes," Taffy continued. "Hideous mistakes. Mistakes that sometimes are completely irreversible and others that can be mended. We are fallible. We are imperfect. But we needn't stop there." She looked at Jana. "Your marriage is over. Your husband is dead. You are about to bear a child."

"Yes and all alone, just like me," Eleanor murmured.

"But she needn't be all alone," Taffy countered. "Jana has a choice to make. She can choose to accept our help and love or reject it. She doesn't have to walk this part of her life alone, because we love her and are willing to be there for her. However, if Jana decides to reject our love, how can we force it upon her? How can we protect her if she refuses to be protected?"

"And how can God protect us if we refuse His protection?" Jana asked. "Is that it? If it is, I'm back to being completely confused. I don't understand any of this. I was doing exactly what I was supposed to do. God didn't protect me, Aunt Taffy. He let me get hurt. He let this horrible thing happen, just like He let Mom be molested and raped."

"And does that mean that God stood by and did nothing? Does it mean He was too busy to be bothered?" Taffy asked.

Eleanor and Jana exchanged a glance. The uncertainty was clear in the eyes of her daughter, just as Eleanor was certain it was evident in her own look.

Jana shrugged. "I don't know. I guess if I did, I wouldn't still be feeling alienated from Him."

"And I would have never walked away," Eleanor said. "If I had answers to these questions—answers that made sense—I would be a much happier woman."

Taffy chuckled. "I used to believe the same thing. Sometimes understanding the reason behind something does help a bit, but it still doesn't change what's happened."

"But if I could have understood why my father did what he did or why Cal raped me," Eleanor interjected, "I might have gotten over it—I might have been free of the past."

"Okay. Cal told me he was horribly drunk. He barely remembered the rape, but in his mind it wasn't rape at all, it was a game he always played with the maid." Taffy's piercing gaze drove home her next point. "So there. You have the answer of why; you can now understand that Cal never intended to rape you. He thought he was playing a game in his drunken state of mind. Does that make it better? Are you free?"

Eleanor let the words sink in. They offered no comfort or liberty. "No. Knowing the reason behind the rape doesn't change the fact that it happened." She shook her head. "I thought it would help."

"Look, sometimes we don't get the answers, but God urges us to trust Him, to walk on in faith. Can you do that? Can both of you put aside the unanswered questions and trust that God is bigger than anything you can ask Him? That He's more powerful than problems that seemingly have no solution?"

"That's asking a lot," Eleanor said. "At least in my book."

"But what's the alternative?" Taffy asked. "To live in misery and defeat, continuing to be alienated from God? Do you want that void in your life forever? You've both asked me at times how I can be so happy. Eleanor, you know you've commented on it constantly since coming here."

"It's true, I suppose. I figured if you knew the truth of my past, you'd never be as happy as you seemed to be. But now that I know you've always had the truth, it takes me by surprise. It's impossible to get my mind around the kind of peace you have in your heart."

Taffy was silent a moment before responding. "You know, as

Cal lay dying, he told me he envied my ability to bounce back from adversity. He confessed a lifetime of infidelity and corruption and begged me to tell him that he could have that same kind of peace. He wanted very much to die knowing that God could wipe the slate clean and welcome him home.

"I told Cal that God was able to forgive him his sins. I told him that I was able to forgive him as well. He was more surprised by the latter than the first."

"So if Rob asked God's forgiveness as he was dying, then just like that"—Jana snapped her fingers—"he gets a clean slate, a ticket to heaven."

Eleanor frowned. "And my father and Cal get the same thing?"

"Do you begrudge them forgiveness?"

"I find it hard to see justice in a molested child having to share all of eternity with her molester."

Taffy's expression softened. "My darling, we are all sinners. You. Me. Jana. Rob. Allan. Cal. We all choose our sins, and to God, they are all ugly. Sin is sin. Now granted, some sins cause greater consequences. They ripple farther and touch more lives. If you get caught up in neighborhood gossip and tell lies about Stanley, for instance, you will hurt several people—but mostly you will hurt yourself and Stanley. The consequences are there, although they pale in comparison to those of your father's actions against you." Taffy eased back against her chair and closed her eyes. "You see, I had to come to an understanding myself that my sins were just as bad in the eyes of God as Cal's infidelity."

Her confession shocked Eleanor. "But you couldn't possibly have ever done anything as bad as what Cal did."

"Couldn't I? You don't know that. My sins separated me from God in the same way his did. We are fallible and we will sin. But Jesus made a sacrifice so that all of those sins could be covered.

It starts in seeking forgiveness—in repentance."

"But my father never repented," Eleanor pressed. "Cal may have told you how sorry he was for what he'd done, but I'm convinced my father never saw anything wrong in what he did. Why should I forgive a man who's never even acknowledged the wrong he's done?"

"Forgiveness is as much for the one doing the forgiving as for the one who is forgiven. It's a freeing and liberating act that takes off the shackles and enables you to walk unfettered. When I forgave Cal his adulterous affairs—his rape of you, Eleanor—I was at peace . . . I was free from the past. Of course, it has been my choice to leave those things in the past. Just as it's your choice to leave your miseries there as well."

Eleanor wanted to believe her aunt, but it was so hard to accept that sin was sin in the eyes of God. That child molesters could be forgiven as easily as liars and adulterers. She understood that some sin had worse repercussions, but still it seemed unfair that God didn't have some kind of grading system when it came to sin.

The doorbell rang, startling the three women. They all jumped in unison, then laughed nervously at their reaction.

"I guess we've been a little intense," Jana said, struggling to rise.

"I can answer it," Eleanor said, beating Jana to her feet. "You just rest." She crossed the room before Jana could protest.

Eleanor opened the door to find Stanley on the other side. To her surprise, she smiled and felt no anger at his intrusion. Could it be her heart was already changing? Had the liberty that had come in her confession already started to soften her heart?

"Hello, Stanley. Won't you come in?"

He frowned and leaned against the doorframe. "I need some help. I think I'm having a heart attack."

"Jana, call 9-1-1," she called as she took hold of him. "Stanley thinks he's having a heart attack."

She heard action in the background as she helped Stanley into the house. "Come sit down." Taffy was already on her feet as they entered the living room.

"Stanley, what in the world have you done to yourself now?" Taffy asked, trying to sound lighthearted.

"Don't know. I started having chest pains after we got back. Thought it would pass." His face was so pale that Eleanor worried he'd waited too long to get help.

"That was an hour ago," Taffy said, noting the time. "Goodness, but you don't have a lick of sense."

"An ambulance is on its way," Jana told them, coming back to join them in the living room. "Can you breathe okay, Stanley?"

"Feels tight, but otherwise I'm all right. Figured maybe I should get help."

"Well, that's an understatement," Taffy said, coming to his side. She patted his arm. "You're in good hands now. We'll keep you under control until the EMTs get here."

It was only a matter of minutes before they heard sirens, signaling the arrival of the ambulance. Jana went out to the porch to wave the EMTs down.

"Do you suppose they'll be able to take care of me here at the clinic?" Stanley questioned.

"Could be," Taffy replied.

Eleanor doubted that this would be the case but said nothing. After all, it was worrisome enough to have the old man sitting there clutching his chest. No need to further escalate his concern.

Jana led the EMTs into the house. The first man nodded at Taffy and then knelt beside Stanley. "What have you been up to, Stanley?" He began to examine the older man.

"I wasn't doing much, Bart. I took Taffy to her retreat, but then we found out it wasn't scheduled until next weekend."

Bart nodded. "My Mary is planning to attend as well." He glanced up to his partner. "Hey, Mike, can you get his BP?"

"Sure thing." The man began the procedure to take Stanley's blood pressure while Bart proceeded to listen to Stanley's heart.

Eleanor noted Taffy's worried expression. She went to her aunt and put her arm around Taffy's shoulder. "I'm sure he'll be fine."

"He's reckless," Taffy told her. "It's a wonder he hasn't caused himself a full-blown stroke the way he works."

"I wasn't doing anything," Stanley protested. "Just driving around with you."

"Well now, Stanley," Bart said, laughing, "with a pretty lady like Miz Anderson, it's understandable. You probably got your heart racing with her at your side."

They all laughed at this, and even Eleanor joined them. She knew Stanley was completely besotted with Taffy. Why the two didn't get married was beyond her. Of course, she'd certainly never encouraged such a thing. In fact, if anything, she'd been discouraging the relationship in any capacity.

I've been so cruel, she thought. _I've never been very nice to this old man, and yet he's done nothing but offer kindness. I've sinned against him in my ugliness toward him. I know I've hurt him many times in the way I've treated him._ Guilt again emerged from the recesses of Eleanor's mind. She frowned. Could she really take it captive? Could she, of her own will, face that guilt and render it powerless by refusing to give it control?

By now the EMTs had hooked Stanley up to some machine and were monitoring his heart. "Stanley, I don't think this is a heart attack. Everything looks good," Bart announced. "But we're going to get you on over to the clinic. I've already notified the doc. Mike, why don't you go ahead and get the stretcher."

"I'm not going to the clinic on any stretcher," Stanley declared. "Especially if my heart is okay. I'll drive myself over."

"Oh no you won't. You aren't driving anywhere." Taffy waggled her finger at him. "You are going to behave."

"Not if it means going on a stretcher. Stretchers are for dead people."

Taffy gasped. "Stanley Jacobs!"

"Well, they are. And last time I checked, I wasn't dead."

"I could take him," Eleanor offered. "Would that be okay?" She looked to the men for an answer.

"You could follow us over. It's just four blocks, and I don't want to agitate Stanley further."

Eleanor looked at the old man. "Would that work, Stanley? Would you ride with me to the clinic?"

"Of course he will," Taffy answered for him. "He may be the most stubborn man in the world, but if he ever wants another of my apple cobblers, he'll do as he's told."

Stanley grinned. "Now I'm motivated." He started to get up, pulling the wires of the machine with him. "I'll expect that cobbler when I get back from the clinic."

"Hold on, Stanley. Let me get you disconnected before you destroy my equipment."

"You do what you're told," Taffy commanded, "and I'll fix you a cobbler this evening. For now I'm coming to the clinic and making sure you behave."

Within a matter of minutes, Bart and Mike had Stanley in the car. Taffy was in the back seat, and to Eleanor's surprise, so was Jana. Eleanor got in and snapped her seat belt on. "How are you feeling, Stanley?"

He glanced over and gave her a thumbs-up. "I'm getting a cobbler, aren't I?" He grinned and shook his head. "You're all being so good to me."

313

"Well, it's not like we had a choice," Taffy teased. "You come busting into my house complaining of a heart attack."

He smiled over his shoulder. "Guess I know how to get your attention."

Eleanor pulled out of the drive and followed the rescue team as Taffy replied, "Guess you do."

It was about four hours later that the doctor decided it was most likely the two corned beef sandwiches and healthy helping of cucumber and onion salad that Stanley had had for lunch that were causing his pain. With Stanley feeling considerably better, he offered Taffy a sheepish grin as he walked out of the exam room on his own steam.

"I should just forget about the cobbler," Taffy said, hands on hips. "Goodness, but you gave us all a fright."

"That's an understatement," Eleanor said, realizing she cared more about Stanley than she'd known. How was it that she had allowed herself to care?

She looked across the waiting room at Jana, who was chatting with one of the nurses, and then at Taffy, whose face fairly beamed relief. All of her life she had tried her best not to care about either of them, but what a fool she'd been. They were all very important to her—even Stanley. The realization was more startling than Eleanor could have imagined.

I really don't know myself at all. She sighed and thought again of the guilt in her life. There were choices to be made . . . a divided path that called for her to go one way or the other.

It's time, she thought. *Time to get to know myself, and maybe time to reacquaint myself with God as well.*

"Are you ready?" Taffy asked.

Eleanor smiled at the irony. The question seemed to reflect her thoughts. "Yes," she said softly. "I believe I am."

Thirty-three

JANA SAT IN the comfort of her room, rocking slowly back and forth. Thanksgiving was only days away, and Taffy was quite excited to have an excuse for a gathering. So far the only one coming besides Jana and her mother, however, was Stanley. Still, this seemed to be more than enough for Taffy.

Jana gently rubbed her abdomen, nearly overwhelmed by the love she already knew for her unborn child. The connection she felt with her child left Jana somewhat confused by the past, however. How could her mother have loved her as much as she'd said, then pushed aside that love out of fear?

"God, how do I keep it from happening to us?" She looked to her growing stomach. "I don't want to hurt you. I love you so much—I feel so compelled to mother you. But I have to admit, I'm afraid."

A Bible verse she'd memorized while she was in Africa came to mind. "'Do not fear,'" she whispered, "'for I am with you; do not be dismayed, for I am your God. I will strengthen you and help you; I will uphold you with my righteous right hand.'" They had sung it to music over and over. The precious words of Isaiah 41:10 came back to Jana in a flood of emotion.

God wasn't promising a perfect life in that verse, but He was promising companionship, strength, and help. "I want to believe that," she said, glancing upward. "I don't want to be afraid. If I'm afraid, I'll do the same things to this baby that my mother did to me. I know I'm not strong; she wasn't either. Even though I've always considered my mother a rock of strength, I realize now how broken she's always been. Why couldn't I have seen that sooner?"

Jana got up and walked to the window. Outside, the world had turned brown and dingy. Snow was promised for the holiday weekend, and heavy lead gray clouds covered the sky like a blanket.

"I wish I could have understood her pain," Jana continued in prayer. "I wish I could have been more sensitive to her needs." She rubbed her lower back and tried to stretch. The weight of the baby created a pull that left Jana constantly massaging her muscles.

With only a few weeks remaining until her due date, the doctor had told her she should be ready to go, and her mother was already suggesting the three of them take up residence in Missoula. Apparently, her mother had found some hotel that allowed for long stays at reasonable rates. The doctor didn't think it was necessary to actually move up, but it made Taffy and Eleanor feel better, so Jana had agreed. They would head up shortly after Thanksgiving as long as the roads were clear and the weather wasn't threatening a blizzard.

Jana had never anticipated anything as much as she had the birth of her child. She sighed with regret that Rob couldn't have been there too. Regret that he couldn't have been the man she'd made him out to be in her mind, her dreams.

"I thought I knew who he was and who I was when I was with him," she said, turning from the window. She walked to the nursery area of her room and fingered the bedding in the crib. "I thought he was my prince charming. I thought I could trust him with my heart." Tears came to her eyes. "I thought I could trust him with your heart too," she added as she once again gave her belly a loving touch.

"God, this seems so unfair. I'm so confused by what happened. I know Rob's gone, but I keep wishing there were a way for us to work things out. I want to be at peace, yet there isn't a real peace in any of this. I can't offer Rob forgiveness; he's not even here."

But you could offer Kerry forgiveness, a voice spoke deep in her soul.

Jana had thought off and on about Kerry since the woman had shown up on her doorstep. She remembered Kerry's tearful pleadings for forgiveness. Jana hugged her arms to her body. Could she give Kerry what she wanted? Could she forgive her?

Jana retook her seat in the rocker and considered the possibility. She drew a deep breath and blew it out. "God, I've been so wrong. I've been as stubborn about my hurts as my mother was about hers, and in the process, I've pushed you away because you represented Rob and all the things that had hurt me so deeply. I want to forgive Kerry and Rob—I do. But I don't know how. How do I let go of this?"

Taffy's words came back to mind. *"My sins separated me from God in the same way his did. We are fallible and we will sin. But Jesus made a sacrifice so that all of those sins could be covered. It starts in seeking forgiveness—in repentance."*

Jana nodded. The truth that her great-aunt had revealed was only now starting to sink in. "I need to repent of my anger and bitterness. I need to be forgiven too."

———

Eleanor studied a book of recipes, looking for just the right choices for Thanksgiving dinner. Taffy had already decided she would make two pumpkin pies from scratch. It was her grandmother's recipe, she'd told Eleanor almost conspiratorially.

Eleanor had been awash in thoughts of family ever since. Even now she found it almost impossible to concentrate. She hadn't allowed herself to think of her family since the time when she first came to live with Taffy. The pain of losing everyone had been nearly too much for a fourteen-year-old to take. But she had conquered it by refusing to even think about them.

But things had changed—everything had changed. Eleanor felt as though she were breaking free of a lifelong cocoon. But what did she do now that she'd emerged?

She looked at the open book and saw that the page listed recipes for glazed carrots. Her brothers had loved carrots. They grew well in the garden, and her mother was always frustrated to find that the boys had gotten into the vegetables and taken samples before she was ready to pick them.

Eleanor smiled at the memory of her brothers. Where were they now? What had happened to them? Should she try to find them or let well enough alone? After all, if they were still alive, they were no doubt caught up in their own families and problems. Why add to that worry? And if they were dead . . . Well, she didn't even like to think about that.

"Mom?"

Eleanor looked up to find Jana staring at her rather quizzically. "I guess I was daydreaming."

"You looked very . . . well . . . I don't know. Different," Jana confessed. "You looked intent on whatever your daydream was."

"I was actually thinking about my brothers."

"I'd nearly forgotten—do you know where they are?"

"No. After our mother died, the police took us away. I kept asking about them, but no one would tell me anything. Taffy and Cal even looked, and you would have thought with their powerful friends and money they could have found them, but something always went wrong. I finally stopped asking, and I think when Taffy and Cal realized I've given up, they gave up as well."

"What were their names?" Jana asked, taking a seat across from her mother.

"Allan Junior was the oldest. He was six years younger than me. Then Thomas was two years younger than Allan. Deliverance was a year younger than Thomas, and Spirit a year younger than Deliverance."

"Deliverance? Spirit? What crazy names," Jana said, laughing.

"Well, you have to remember my parents were hippies. Those were perfectly good names for hippie children. We had more than our share of Moonbeams, Sunshines, Stars, and of course tons of flower children. We had a Daisy, Lilac, Heather, Wisteria—it was crazy."

Jana grinned. "Well, we won't have any of that with this baby."

"Have you picked a name?"

She shook her head. "Not completely. I have some names I'm partial to, but I'm still not sure."

"It might be wise to wait until the baby comes and then decide. Maybe once you see him or her, it will come easily."

"I think you might be right." Jana fell silent, then brought the conversation back to the family. "Isn't it weird to know that there is an entire family out there somewhere . . . who knows you exist but doesn't know where you are?"

"It is strange, but you have to remember that until now I've kept those kinds of thoughts out of my head. I've refused to think about them." Eleanor ran her hand through her short blond hair and gave her head a little shake. "I don't know that thinking about them now is any wiser. I mean, we couldn't find them back then; why suppose we could find them now?"

"Because we have so much more in the way of technology and information. You have the Internet and computer databases. I'm thinking that if you really wanted to find them now, you probably could."

Eleanor considered that for a moment. Perhaps there was a way—but did she want to find them?

"I don't know if it would be wise, though," she finally said. She met Jana's eyes. "They might be happier not being found. After all, they could have looked for me as well."

"Maybe they did. You have to remember, back then the records were sealed and difficult to get into. The government thought they were giving the ultimate protection—not keeping families divided."

"I suppose you're right." The idea was something to consider, but Eleanor couldn't process it all right now. It had also occurred to her that if she found her brothers, she might find her father as well. Perhaps that was the real reason she'd avoided even thinking about where the boys had gone . . . because maybe, just maybe, they had left with her father and had been with him all along.

"So are you going to look for them?" Jana's question pulled Eleanor back into the present.

"I don't know. It's something to think about."

Thankfully, Jana let the topic drop. Instead, she got up from the table and went to the cupboard for a glass. "I've been thinking about something and wanted to talk to you about it."

Eleanor waited until Jana had poured herself some milk and returned to the table before asking, "What is it?"

"I've set my heart right with God," Jana began. "I've asked Him to forgive my anger and bitterness—my doubt. But in doing that, I've been thinking a lot about Kerry Broadbent."

"But why?"

"She asked for my forgiveness, and I refused her." Jana took a long drink and studied the glass for a moment. "That was wrong of me, but I'm not sure how to make it right, except . . . well . . . to call her up—maybe see her."

"Are you sure you want to take that route? You might be opening a very painful can of worms."

"But how can I deny her forgiveness when she humbled herself and came here to ask for it? I feel bad for the way I treated her, but at the same time, I know that I wasn't ready back then to absolve the woman who'd stolen my husband."

"But you feel you can do that now?"

Jana surprised Eleanor by nodding. "Yes, I do. I wouldn't have thought so a few days ago, but I've been praying and reading my Bible, and I know it's time. I just wondered if you would be upset or offended by this, because . . . well . . . I think I'd like to invite her to Thanksgiving dinner."

Eleanor was taken aback by this announcement, but she saw the need in her daughter's eyes. The process of working through her own spiritual crisis was something Eleanor still had not accomplished; however, she knew that Jana needed and desired her approval in this. Could she give it—and mean it?

"What do you think, Mom? Is that too off the wall?"

Eleanor gave her a smile and swallowed down all her protests. Was this what it was like to take thoughts captive? "No. Not at all. I think it's very gracious—a definite act of kindness."

Jana seemed to relax. "Thanks, Mom. I guess I'll go give her a call."

———

Jana's hands trembled as she reached for the receiver. She didn't know if Kerry had gone back to the home she'd shared with Jason, but that was the number Jana planned to try since she had it memorized from their years at the church.

As the phone began to ring on the other end, Jana's heartbeat crescendoed.

"Hello."

The sound of Kerry's voice left Jana momentarily speechless.

"Hello? Is someone there?" Kerry questioned.

"Yes," Jana finally managed. "It's Jana."

It was Kerry's turn to fall silent. For several moments neither one said anything, but finally Jana worked up the courage to continue. "I think we need to talk."

"Yes, I agree."

"I've been doing a lot of soul searching. It hasn't been easy, but I want to see you and talk about everything."

"Has the baby come yet?"

"No. I'm due in a couple weeks."

"Well, in that case you shouldn't be traveling. Why don't I come there—maybe next week after the holidays?"

"I was kind of hoping you might join us for Thanksgiving. Unless, of course, you have other plans."

Kerry said nothing, and for a while Jana feared she'd lost the connection. "Are you there?"

"I'm here," Kerry said, her voice breaking into a sob. "I'm sorry. I'm just . . . well, it's just . . . I was going to be alone on Thanksgiving."

"Well, now you don't have to be. We'd like you to join us if you'd feel comfortable doing so."

"Jana, I'm really touched." Kerry then added, "What time would you like me there?"

"We'll eat at two. Come anytime you like."

"I'll be there," Kerry promised. "I wouldn't miss it for the world."

Jana hung up the phone, pleased she'd done something positive—for her own sake, as well as Kerry's. It was the right thing to do, and somehow, Jana knew that it would make all the difference.

Thirty-four

JANA AWOKE TO the tantalizing aromas of pumpkin and turkey. She also came to the realization that this would be her first real celebration with family. In the past, she and Rob had celebrated Thanksgiving with some members of the church congregation, but they'd never had their own dinner. And growing up, she and her mother had never celebrated the day. In fact, little attention had been given to Christmas and birthdays. Jana remembered how envious she was of her friends, listening to stories at the boarding school about all the wonderful things the other girls had done on their breaks. When Jana had no stories to share, they made fun of her. After a time, Jana started making up things that she'd always dreamed of.

"My mom and I flew to California," she told them one year. "It was so nice and warm." She was nearly caught in the lie by another girl who demanded to know what part of California, as she had spent time there too and it had been cold.

From that time on, Jana spent her school breaks researching her story, ready to give the most intimate details of her excursions. She was convinced her friends never knew the truth.

Jana sighed at the memory. How lonely and inadequate she'd felt back then. There was nothing significant or important about Jana Templeton. She wondered how much better off Jana McGuire would be.

She remembered that Kerry would arrive today and hastened

to get dressed. Kerry had called the night before to say she'd be staying overnight in Missoula. She'd hoped to come prior to dinner so that she and Jana would have plenty of time to talk. Then if Jana changed her mind about having Kerry stay for dinner, Kerry assured her she would leave.

But Jana had made up her mind. She didn't like the idea of Kerry being alone on Thanksgiving. Worse still, she didn't want to be the cause of sending the poor woman back out onto the road with more snow in the forecast. Then, too, Jana couldn't help but remember Kerry was dealing with a loss as well, for Jason had been sentenced to life in prison.

Jana dressed in a soft knit maternity top and ecru wool slacks. The mauve color of the sweater was good for her complexion and the style was quite flattering. At least as flattering as it could be in her condition. Jana studied her profile in the mirror. It was clear the baby had dropped. Not only by sight, but by feel.

"It won't be long now, little one," she said, splaying her fingers across her abdomen. "Soon I'll hold you in my arms." The thought gave her great joy and filled an aching, empty spot in her heart.

"Rob used to be in that spot," she told her reflection. "My love for him made my life seem worthwhile." But now she would fill that place with her love for this baby and, of course, her love for God. It wasn't that she thought it would be easy, but Jana had already experienced a freedom in turning her bitterness over to God in exchange for His abundant peace.

Jana struggled into her shoes and socks, then slowly made her way downstairs. She could feel the chilled air of the upstairs gradually warm as she descended. "It smells so good in here," she announced, entering the kitchen.

Taffy, bedecked in a fire-engine-red broomstick skirt and black turtleneck, looked up with a grin. Long red birds of some type dangled from her ears, and a necklace of black and red beads was draped around her neck. "Good morning, my darling!" She pulled on an apron and came to where Jana stood. "You look wonderful! Happy Thanksgiving."

"And the same to you. I love your earrings."

"I bought them in Italy." She leaned in conspiratorially. "I paid way too much, however. I saw the exact same pair in a catalog the other day and they were much less expensive."

"Yes, but yours were purchased in Italy," Jana countered. "And that makes them special for so many other reasons."

Taffy straightened and raised her brow. "You know, you're absolutely right. I won't regret them."

"Won't regret what?" Eleanor questioned as she came in through the back door.

"My earrings," Taffy said, then hurried on. "I have the pies already cooling and thought I'd help you mix the stuffing."

"Did you sleep all right?" Eleanor asked Jana.

She shrugged with a grin. "As well as anyone in my condition ever sleeps."

"Well, you look lovely. I think those colors are good for you. You should wear them more often."

There was a time when Jana would have stiffened at the comment; she would have been convinced that this was her mother's way of giving off-handed criticism. But now Jana wanted to believe the best. "Maybe I can find something like it after the baby is born."

"We will definitely need to take you shopping after the baby's born," Taffy declared. "You'll need some good winter clothes. We get much colder here than you did in Spokane."

"Or New York," Eleanor added.

"We'll have to see," Jana said, pulling out a chair. She was so weary of carrying this load. "I have to be careful with my money—especially the insurance money." Rob's insurance had finally paid out, and Jana was determined to save a good portion for the baby's education.

"Pshaw!" Taffy exclaimed. "I keep telling you I'm a rich old woman who loves to spend her money on people she cares about."

"I'm fairly well off myself," Eleanor announced, to Jana's surprise. "I've invested wisely over the years, and with the sale of the bookstore, I'm very comfortably set."

"But I'm not, and I don't want to be a burden to either of you," Jana replied, her tone quite serious. "I love you both and would hate it if money ever came between us."

"Then don't let it," Taffy said. "I hate it when people talk finances and money before a cup of good coffee." She poured one and brought it to Jana. "It's decaf and the cream is right there in front of you."

Jana poured herself some cream, a warm rush of emotions nearly bringing her to tears. Taffy was so good to her, and now it seemed her mother's heart was changing as well. It was such a wonderful blessing.

The doorbell sounded and Jana struggled to her feet, convinced it was Kerry. "Let me answer it."

But opening the door revealed the pastor instead of Kerry. "Hello, Pastor Clifford."

"I wish you'd call me Kevin." He grinned and extended a foil-wrapped package. "I come bearing gifts."

"By all means, Kevin, come in then," Jana said with a laugh. "We always allow gift-bearing visitors."

He wiped his shoes on the rug and slipped them off as was the habit of most people who came to call.

"They're in the kitchen working their talents to perfection."

"Smells like it."

"Can I take your coat?"

"No, I can't stay long. Say, how are you feeling?"

She ran her hand over her abdomen. "Fat." She laughed in spite of herself. "But otherwise okay. I'll be glad when this baby is born." She realized without warning that she no longer felt the fear and alienation toward Kevin that she'd known before. It was a relief to be able to offer the man a more companionable attitude.

"My sister says the same thing. She thinks the end will never come."

"I know exactly how she feels. Sometimes I think I'll be like this forever." She motioned to the dining room. "Come on. Taffy will berate me if I don't get you in there for a cup of coffee."

"Coffee sounds good—especially with chocolate chip pumpkin bread," he said, again holding up his gift.

"Did your wife make that?"

He laughed. "I'm not married." He looked at her oddly. "What made you think I was married?"

"I'm not sure. I guess you mentioned your family once."

"I meant my mom and dad and brother and sister. My sister's staying with my folks now that her husband's guard unit is busy overseas. Anyway, my mom made up a bunch of this bread to give to my congregation. I do well to make a decent cup of coffee and keep the microwave from exploding. I stay away from really dangerous ventures like mixing ingredients."

Jana laughed as well. "Sounds like you need a keeper."

His grin broadened. "Are you offering?" He instantly reddened at the comment, realizing how out of line he'd been. "Just kidding."

Jana sobered. Her anger at God had been rectified, but the thought of another husband was far from her mind. "It's okay," she finally said. "I'm not thinking in that direction right now, but maybe someday I will."

He nodded, his expression completely serious. "Maybe when that day comes, you'll let me know."

Jana was surprised by his comment but managed to hide it. After all, Kevin had to know that any interest he held for her would have to be extended to her unborn child. "Maybe I will."

"Kevin! What brings you here on the holiday? Did your mom kick you out?" Taffy asked with a wink. "Need a place to eat?"

"Not at all. I came with this," he said patting the loaf of pumpkin bread.

"I'll bet I know exactly what that is. Come on into the kitchen. We're working on the dinner, but we can surely take time out for your mother's incredible chocolate chip pumpkin bread."

Taffy went to the cupboard and pulled out a mug. "You like it with one sugar, right?"

Kevin nodded and took a seat next to Jana at the table. "Hello, Mrs. Templeton," he said as Eleanor came to the table with small plates and a knife.

"Hello."

Jana could hear the reservation in her mother's tone but was surprised when she willingly sat down beside Jana. "Will you be staying with us for dinner today?" Eleanor asked.

"No, my mom would be pretty disappointed if I didn't eat with them." He glanced at his watch. "Yikes, I need to make this a short visit. We're eating at noon, and I still have five loaves to deliver."

Taffy put the cup in front of him. "Well, drink up."

Eleanor opened the foiled package and began slicing the bread. "I think you'll like this, Jana. I had some last year."

"She makes it every year," Kevin said, throwing Jana a smile.

"Stick around long enough and you'll see."

"We intend to have her here for ages and ages," Taffy interjected. "We're much too excited about having a baby in the house to let her go and move off."

"See, they only want me for the baby," Jana said, laughing. But then she caught her mother's look. Perhaps she had hurt Eleanor's feelings. "No, I take that back," she added quickly. "They've definitely made me feel that I'm welcome here for myself."

"That's for certain," Taffy said, taking the plate Eleanor offered.

"Indeed," her mother said and passed another plate to Kevin.

"Do we need butter?" Taffy asked.

"I don't," Jana said. "This looks plenty rich without any trimming."

"I've probably already had two loaves," Kevin chimed in, "and all without butter. The holidays are hard on pastors, you know. We get all sorts of food gifts, when what I really need is a gym membership."

They all laughed, though Jana could see the man didn't have an ounce of fat on him. She remembered seeing him bicycling all over town and wondered for a moment what it might be like to share a ride with him. But even as the thought came, she knew it was too soon. There would be time for such things later—when the time was right and her heart was whole again.

"Are you even listening?" Taffy asked.

Jana felt her face flush as they all looked at her with questioning faces. "I'm sorry, I guess I was lost in my thoughts. What did you say?"

"Kevin invited us to a potluck dinner after church on Sunday," Taffy reiterated.

Jana looked to her mother. "I think that sounds very nice."

"What should we bring?" her mother asked, surprising them all.

Jana smiled. It was in that moment that she knew deep in her heart that everything would be all right. It might take years to work through all the kinks, but a healing, an honest healing, had begun in their household—in their hearts.

———————

Kerry arrived not long after Kevin had gone. Jana greeted her at the door, feeling uncertain as to how she should approach the things she wanted to discuss.

"We're going to stay holed up in the kitchen," Taffy announced. "There is all sorts of work to be done if we're to eat at two."

"Do you need help?" Jana asked.

"Yes, I would love to lend a hand," Kerry said.

"Nonsense. It's my kitchen, and I barely tolerate Eleanor," Taffy said, giving her niece a sly grin. "You girls enjoy yourselves in the privacy of the living room. I've already got the fire going."

Jana was grateful for the opportunity for privacy. Even her mother seemed to have no problem with the arrangement. "Let us know if you need anything," Eleanor called as she followed Taffy into the kitchen.

"I know this is probably uncomfortable for you," Jana started as they moved into the living room. "It is for me." She could feel all of her old defenses coming into place. *This is the woman who stole your husband and ruined your marriage,* a voice seemed to whisper in her ear.

"Yes," Kerry agreed. "But it's also necessary. I'm not sorry to be here."

Jana took a seat in front of the fire. Kerry did likewise, admiring the holiday decorations.

Jana couldn't help but follow Kerry's focus as she commented on the gourds and small pumpkins along the mantel. "Taffy always goes all out. She loves festivities and celebrations."

"She seems very nice."

Jana fell silent. For all of her planning, she wasn't really sure what she wanted to ask or say. Before praying it through, Jana's desire had been to hurtle accusations and caustic remarks . . . to hurt Kerry and crush her spirit, leaving her as empty as Jana had felt. But not now. Now Jana wanted to be made whole, and she knew that wasn't going to come by tearing someone else apart. "Look, I'm not sure what we should talk about. I'm not sure what would be beneficial and what would be harmful."

"I know. I just want to tell you whatever you want to know," Kerry said. "I know the truth is important."

Jana frowned. "Why did he do this to me? Why did he stop loving me?" As she asked the questions of her husband's mistress, Jana felt overwhelmed with emotions. Anger resurfaced, as did the pain.

"Jana, if you're thinking this happened because you did something wrong, then stop. Rob and I are to blame—not you."

"I know, but I guess I keep trying to find that place where I failed Rob so much that he was driven into your arms."

"But that's not how it was," Kerry said, edging up on her seat. "I tried to tell you before that it developed because neither of us had any accountability. We were left alone to deal with my problems, and that turned into *our* problem. If there had been someone else there at the church or if Rob would have sent me to someone else for counsel, it never would have happened. Still, I'm not trying to pin this on someone else. We're to blame for not heeding the warning signs. You didn't do anything wrong, Jana."

Jana wanted to believe that—needed to believe it. "Were you

happy together?" She wasn't sure why she asked the question. She knew that if Kerry said they were, she'd be devastated.

"We were like survivors of a shipwreck," Kerry said, staring into the fire. "We weren't happy, we were just trying to get by. I was miserable from the start, trying to live with my guilt. I even told Rob we needed to call it off and go home to beg forgiveness."

"And what did he say?"

"That it was too late. That he'd already quit the church, served you with divorce papers, sold your jewelry. He felt there was no way you would take him back."

"I don't know that I would have taken him back."

"It would have been hard, I know. But I knew it was the only way to make things right. The last day we were together, I got up and made breakfast and told Rob that I was going home."

Jana studied Kerry for a moment. The woman seemed sincere enough, and she supposed there was no reason to lie about the matter. "What did he say?"

"He said he had no home except the one we'd made there in Seattle. He told me to reconsider. I asked him if he still loved you, and he countered by asking whether or not I still loved Jason. He knew I didn't." She toyed with the fabric on the arm of the chair. "He never answered me about you."

"He couldn't have loved me," Jana said without the pain she expected. "Not with the things he did to me, the way he treated me. I think I'm beginning to realize that Rob loved only one person and that was himself. I fit into the picture as long as I helped Rob to feel that love. But do you know what I think happened?" The realization was just dawning on Jana.

Kerry shook her head.

"I think Rob realized I was growing stronger in the Lord. I

think that intimidated him because he knew he was just faking it."

"You're probably right. I mean, he certainly wanted no part of God in Seattle."

Jana knew it was the missing piece. She had begun to make her relationship with God her own, and Rob could see it was only a matter of time before she realized what a liar he was. The problem, however, was that Jana hadn't come far enough in her spiritual walk to realize there was a definite separation between God and Rob. When Rob left, Jana was convinced in her soul that God had left too.

"What happened with Jason . . . when he came that day?" Jana finally asked.

Kerry drew a deep breath. "He had somehow found out where we were living. He was good at things like that, but I never figured he'd come looking for me. I had just come home from work and was about to open the door to our place when Jason came out of nowhere. He said he needed to talk to both of us. He seemed calm enough, and I thought fine, this is as good a time as any to seek forgiveness and go home."

"So what happened to throw things out of control?"

"I don't think Jason ever meant to stay in control. It's his nature to think things out and carry through with a methodical plan. His was no crime of passion, but rather a well-thought-out resolution. I think he'd come there with the sole purpose of killing all of us."

"All of you?" Jana could hardly believe it. "Why would he kill you? He loved you—that much I know. His every word was about you."

Kerry began to cry. "I know. I didn't deserve him or his love. I knew he loved me, but he didn't show his love in the way I thought it should be. He wasn't exciting or fun—he was just reliable, logical old Jason. Everything he did was thought out and meticulous. Even coming to Seattle to settle old scores."

"So he came to the house and then what?" Jana asked when the silence grew long.

"Rob was there with a guy named Don. We'd met him at a local restaurant. The guy was trying to get Rob a job in construction. Anyway, Rob was upset to see Jason—told him to get out or he'd call the cops. Jason didn't take kindly to Rob's anger. He pulled a gun out of his jacket pocket—one of his handguns. He told Rob to sit down and shut up, and that's exactly what Rob did."

"What about Don and you?" Jana forced herself to ask.

"Jason didn't seem to even see us. He started in on how Rob was the worst kind of man—leaving a woman who was expecting his child." Kerry looked at Jana. "I thought he was lying. I thought he was just saying that to hurt us or that you had lied to him in the hopes that it would get back to Rob. Anyway, I went to Jason and tried to convince him to leave. He wouldn't hear anything I said, and when I looked into his eyes, I could see the life had gone out of him. He was a complete stranger to me. That's when I got scared."

"What did you do?"

"I told Jason I was going to call the police. He said to go ahead, that by the time they got there it would be too late. Nothing has ever scared me as much as that simple statement." Kerry pushed back her long dark hair. "I figured he meant to kill us all."

Jana couldn't fathom the fear they had all faced. "I don't understand why he felt he had to do that. I feel guilty for my flippant remark about being better off with Rob dead, but I had no idea it would send Jason over the edge."

"I don't think it did. I think it was just Jason's way of putting things right," Kerry reasoned. "When Jason realized you had nothing and that if Rob died you'd at least have insurance money, I think he figured it was the logical answer to everything. Warped perspective, I guess, but that's the way Jason would have reasoned it out."

"So . . . well . . . how did it happen?" Jana forced the question. She needed to know the truth.

"Rob told Jason he was sorry. He even brought up the fact that I'd told Rob that morning that we needed to go home. Jason was kind of taken aback by this for a minute, and I thought maybe he'd rethink things. I told him it was true, and poor Don just sat there in stunned silence.

"Jason finally said it didn't matter—that he didn't think Rob would really go back and make things right. Rob swore he would, but Jason said it was too late. Then he shot Rob twice. Once in the head and once in the chest."

"Did he . . . oh . . ." Jana felt sickened by the news. She began to cry.

"He died instantly. He didn't suffer, except in waiting," Kerry said, tears streaming.

"I'm glad," Jana said, wiping her face with the back of her hand. "I don't know why it had to be this way, but I'm glad he didn't suffer."

"Afterward, Jason just stood there. I waited for him to turn the gun on us, but when he just kept standing there, staring at Rob, I figured it was over. I walked right up to him and took the gun away while Don called the police. I knew there was nothing I could do for Rob or Jason, but I kept praying I might somehow be able to make things up to you."

"There's nothing to make up, Kerry. Certainly nothing that any human being could change." She toyed with her hands for a moment, then looked back to Kerry. "I didn't think I could ever say these words, but I forgive you."

Kerry's hand went to her throat. "Oh, Jana . . . oh . . ." The words caught in her throat as she fought back new tears. For several moments she couldn't speak. The silence fell like a buffering blanket between them. Finally she lifted her tear-stained face. "Oh, thank you. You don't know what this means to me."

Jana thought back over the last few weeks. "I think I do," she said, knowing that the change in her heart had opened her eyes to the truth. Forgiveness was necessary for healing, even when forgiveness wasn't deserved. After all, who could honestly say that they deserved to be forgiven?

Thirty-five

"OH, BUT THAT WASN'T the best part," Taffy said. "We had flown to Washington at the invitation of President Johnson and his wife. As I told you," she said, leaning in, "Cal was gifted at riding the fence, and Democrats and Republicans alike simply loved him. Well, we were there in the White House no more than ten minutes when LBJ strode across the room and came up to Cal with a look of complete disgust.

"He said, 'I understand you're friends with that Kansas bunch.'" Taffy straightened with a knowing look. "He was talking about the Eisenhowers, Governor Avery, and the senators—all Republicans, don't you know. Cal, of course, was not put off. 'Why, yes, I am,' he told the president. LBJ nodded and replied, 'Funny bunch, those Kansans—they all seem to lean away from my issues.' Well, my Cal didn't miss a beat. 'That,' he replied, 'is because of all the hot air that's blown up from Texas—keeps 'em listing to one side.' Well, LBJ, not to be outdone, snaps back, 'Well, son, see if you can't get them turned around to list my way.'" Taffy and Stanley laughed, and Eleanor and Jana couldn't help but join in.

"Well, that was a marvelous dinner, ladies," Stanley declared, patting his stomach. "I'd say it's just about the best I've ever had."

Kerry agreed. "It was wonderful, and as much as I hate to say it, I'd better head back home. The snow has managed to hold off so far, but who knows for how long."

"That's true," Taffy said with an authoritative tone to her voice. "It would probably be wise to start out while there is still light."

"Do you plan to try to make it all the way back?" Jana asked.

"No, I'll probably stay again in Missoula, or if I feel there's no risk, I'll head on to Kellogg. It's the passes I worry about. Even if there isn't snow down here, there might be trouble up there."

"Good point. You should probably call to see if the interstate is open all the way," Eleanor suggested as she began clearing away the dishes.

"Let me help you, Mom," Jana offered.

There was something in Jana's mannerisms that instantly took Eleanor back in time. She remembered her mother, pregnant and working around the table. It was the first time Eleanor had allowed herself to realize that Jana looked very much like Melody. How had she not seen this before? *Maybe I have,* she realized, *and just didn't let myself acknowledge it.* Then again, maybe it was one more reason she had pushed Jana away, even as an adult.

Eleanor reached out and touched Jana's hand. "No, I think you should just go and see Kerry out, then rest." She was surprised when Jana agreed.

"I think you're right. I'm so tired."

"Well, it's no wonder," Stanley chimed in. "You're carrying around a whole 'nuther person. When's that little guy gonna make an appearance?"

"Now, Stanley, we don't know if it's a guy or not," Taffy chided. "And the baby will be born when he or she is good and ready. She's not due until the nineteenth of December."

"Oh, well then we'll have us a Christmas present early, eh?" he teased.

"Something like that," Jana said, patting her stomach. She followed Kerry out with a yawn.

Eleanor admired her daughter's strength. She knew it hadn't been easy to invite Kerry here. It couldn't have been a simple matter to sit down to dinner together either, yet Jana had handled herself with a graciousness that Eleanor couldn't begin to understand. This was the woman who had stolen her daughter's husband—had been there at his death. How could Jana calmly share a meal and company with her? All through the dinner, Eleanor had found herself taking up offense for her daughter, while Jana had seemed completely at peace with the matter. It amazed Eleanor.

Taffy and Stanley lent a hand in cleaning up, much to Eleanor's relief. She was more tired than she wanted to let on. Together they cleared the dirty dishes, and Taffy loaded the washer with Stanley ever at her side, helping. Eleanor meanwhile worked on the turkey, picking the carcass clean and packing the meat in sealed containers before placing it in the fridge. Before she knew it, everything was done.

"I'm gonna walk around the block with Stanley," Taffy announced. She waved off any protests Eleanor might offer. "I know it's cold. We'll bundle up."

"And if all else fails," Stanley said with a wicked wink, "we'll share body heat for warmth."

Taffy elbowed him and rolled her eyes. "I'll bring you an extra coat if you're worried." Stanley laughed and followed her out of the kitchen, singing a song Eleanor didn't recognize.

With Jana resting and Taffy and Stanley gone, Eleanor felt as if she had the house to herself. She found the silence to be a welcome relief. She went upstairs to her room and changed her clothes, slipping on comfortable old wool slacks and a white oxford-style shirt. Over this she pulled on a pumpkin-colored sweater and relished the warmth against the chill of her room.

Looking at a stack of papers she'd hoped to sort, Eleanor shook her head and went to her much-loved overstuffed chair. She sank into the cushioned softness and propped her feet up on the ottoman. Some days were meant for relaxation—although Eleanor had never quite mastered the art of being at rest.

She gazed around the room and remembered a time when she'd been a teenager and they'd come to this house for vacation. Back then there had been more land and, of course, horses. Eleanor had thought it a magical place to live. Perhaps that was why when Taffy suggested she come live here, Eleanor had jumped at the chance. She told herself it was because Taffy was old and needed her, but in her heart, Eleanor knew this house had been one of the best things in her memories. She had been a happy child here—but even better, she had felt safe.

That need for safety had haunted Eleanor all of her life. She'd never felt protected in the commune, especially after the police had started raiding there. Having later read much on the disturbing sixties and the hippie movement, Eleanor could easily see why her father and mother's way of life had been a threat to civil peace. Her family's way was not one of order and happiness, as they had suggested, but rather one of chaos and misery. Without drugs and alcohol, they would have been hard pressed to even endure the life they'd chosen.

Eleanor again realized how much Jana favored her mother. Eleanor used to refuse to even consider memories of her mother, for ultimately, remembering her suicide was just too painful. But now Eleanor opened her mind to such thoughts, letting them tiptoe in like shy children. She remembered her mother's bright smile and carefree spirit. Eleanor remembered working with her in the garden—learning and listening to the advice her mother offered. Other memories reminded Eleanor of times her mother had played with her children—laughing and singing.

"She loved us," Eleanor murmured. "I know she loved us. Even if she did become a mother much too early. Even if she did take her own life." For the first time, Eleanor wished she had a picture or some piece of memorabilia from the past.

She had been so convinced of the pain such things might cause, however, that she'd kept nothing from her time in the commune. In fact, she'd kept nothing from her past with Taffy and Cal or even with Jana. Oh, there were a few pictures taken when Jana was little, but Eleanor had been so intent on forgetting that she'd put away the good with the bad. She'd carried nothing forward except the heavy weights of guilt and regret.

"I've been such a fool." She looked upward. "I thought I was free of the past. I thought I'd done a wonderful job of removing it from my mind and heart. I kept nothing, thinking it would keep me from the misery and hurt, and instead it bound me more severely than I could have imagined."

Memories of her father came unbidden. Eleanor winced and closed her eyes tight, but the image wouldn't leave her. "I trusted you. I loved you—so very much. Why did you have to ruin that?" She felt the tears slip down her cheeks.

"God, I don't know if even you can help me. I want you to. I want to believe I'm worth the effort, but I honestly don't know if you've given up on me or not. If you haven't—if you think you can do anything with me—I'm ready to throw in the towel. I'm giving it over to you because I've already made such a mess of things." Her impromptu confession surprised Eleanor. But there was something else. Fear. She felt an overwhelming sense of fear. Over the last few weeks she'd struggled with that unspoken emotion. Fear had caused her to have several panic attacks, and fear had kept her from breaking free once and for all from the pain of the past.

She opened her eyes and realized she was tightly gripping the arms of the chair. Her knuckles were white and her fingers ached. "I'm afraid," she whispered. "Afraid the bad thoughts will never go away. Afraid the guilt will always haunt me. Afraid of how to live in the future without the past dictating my steps. I'm afraid I'll completely mess things up with Jana in the future—just as I did in the past. God, I don't know what to do."

A light knock sounded on her door. Eleanor tried to pull herself together before answering, "Come in."

Taffy peeked into the room. She started to speak, then noted Eleanor's condition. She immediately came to Eleanor's side. "I felt the need to find you—to make sure you were all right."

"I'm not all right, but I'm trying to be. I just don't know how."

Taffy sat down on the ottoman. "That's okay," she said with great love in her voice. "I know who does."

"I so enjoyed the potluck yesterday. My, but that was fun," Taffy exclaimed.

"Yes, it was," Jana agreed. "Those women can really cook. I enjoyed church as well. I thought Kevin was very capable in his preaching—so personable too. Rob was never that open and friendly in his teaching." Miserable in her discomfort, she tried to find a comfortable sitting position. She moved first one way and then another. "Oh, no matter what I do, it hurts. First I couldn't sleep, and now I can't even sit."

Eleanor raised a brow. "What do you mean it hurts?"

"You know. My back. I had such pain there all night, I couldn't even sleep."

Eleanor was worried, but Taffy seemed unconcerned. Eleanor came to Jana and knelt down. "When did it start?"

"My back? It's been hurting me for weeks, but never like this. This comes and goes in a pretty consistent manner. Sometimes it lasts longer than other times."

"Jana, I think you may be in labor," Eleanor said, looking to Taffy. "We need to call her doctor. If she's been in labor all night, she could very well be close to delivering that baby."

Jana struggled to the edge of her seat. "But I'm not having contractions."

"Those are contractions. At least that's my guess. I had back labor with you, and that's exactly how it was. Are you feeling any pressure?"

Jana's panic was evident in her expression. "Of course, but I've been feeling increasing pressure since the baby started dropping. What do we do?"

"We'll call the doctor first and see what he says."

They tried three times to reach the doctor and finally got through to his answering service. The doctor was tied up with some emergency. Eleanor then called 9-1-1 and wasn't at all encouraged to hear a recording stating that there was a multi-car accident on the interstate, and the emergency team and all available medical personnel had responded. That was the trouble with living in such a small town.

Eleanor tried to figure out what to do next. They didn't have a lot of options. She left a message that her daughter was in labor and they needed someone as soon as possible. She had barely hung up the phone before deciding she'd have to drive Jana to Missoula herself.

"I think we should get your bag and head to Missoula. The ambulance is tied up, and we probably can't afford to wait."

"I'm not sure that's wise," Taffy said, shaking her head. "What if the baby comes when you're halfway there?"

Eleanor knew she had nothing to offer Jana. None of them was trained in childbirth.

That's when it hit her. In a rush of waves that threatened to drown her where she stood, Eleanor realized she had been trained quite thoroughly in childbirth. Her father had given her a great deal of instruction in such matters, and she had assisted him numerous times. She fought against the idea. She wanted nothing of her father—no part of him. But she needed his training and wisdom now more than ever. She had no choice. It wasn't much, but it was all they had.

"I know what to do," Eleanor said, looking first to Jana and then to Taffy. "My father taught me."

"Then it would be best to stay here," Taffy said with authority. "We can set her up here and watch her. That way if she has to deliver, we won't be on the road, and if the ambulance is freed up and can get here, then we'll have that extra help."

Jana looked at her oddly. "I think that's . . ." She doubled over, her words lost in a cry of pain.

"I suppose you're right," Eleanor said to her aunt. "It would be good at least to check and see how far along she is."

"I trust you." Jana's upper lip was dotted with perspiration. "What do we do?"

Eleanor and Taffy made Jana comfortable in her bed. "I'll need a few things," Eleanor told Taffy. Eleanor verbally listed everything she could think of.

"You know, I have some magazines that talk about childbirth," Taffy offered. "I found the articles quite insightful. They're written for nurses."

Eleanor shook her head and laughed. "You get a nurses' magazine?"

"Well, why not? You never know when you'll need to know something. Like now."

345

"Get them," Eleanor said. "I'm going to examine Jana and see where she's at."

Eleanor helped Jana onto her back. "This won't be very comfortable. I need to see how far dilated you are. That will give us an idea of how much time we have."

It was impossible not to gasp in surprise, however, as Eleanor realized the baby's head was already crowning. She instantly realized her expression must have told it all.

"Something's wrong, isn't it?" Jana questioned.

"No, not really. It's just that . . . well . . . Jana, do you feel a need to push—to bear down?"

"I don't think so."

"Well, you'd know it if you did. When did your water break?"

"Water break? I don't know. I had to go to the bathroom earlier—it was kind of different. I didn't think about it." Jana sounded more frantic by the minute.

Eleanor knew she needed to keep calm herself or she'd never be able to calm her daughter. "Well, I think the baby is very close to being born. I can't believe you haven't felt worse than you have, but my own mother didn't realize she was in labor with Deliverance or Spirit, so I guess it happens." She smiled and shrugged, trying to act nonchalant about the whole thing.

Eleanor forced her mind to go back in time—to sit at her father's side and recall the things he'd told her. She remembered something about the cord and making sure the baby didn't strangle coming out. It was all about the control of the mother pushing and the doctor being astute enough to recognize any signs of trouble. Eleanor wasn't convinced she'd be that capable. After all, today's doctors had all sorts of equipment and means to recognize problems before they happened.

Oh, God, she prayed, *I need your help. Please don't let my lack of knowledge cause any harm to my grandchild.*

"Here's the magazines and towels," Taffy announced as she came in. "I did have a thought, however. What if I call the hospital in Missoula and have them send a helicopter?"

"You can try, but this baby is coming quickly. Besides, they'll probably be airlifting the accident victims," Eleanor said. She took the magazines from Taffy and thumbed through them. There wasn't time, however.

Jana cried out in pain. "I think something's happening. I feel . . . oooh." She grabbed her stomach. "I just don't feel right."

Eleanor tossed the magazines aside. "Taffy, did you get the other things I asked for?"

The older woman began pulling things from the pockets of her apron. "Here's the sewing scissors. They're newly sharpened—just had it done last week."

"I have rubbing alcohol in the bathroom. Take the basin and pour the alcohol over the scissors and sterilize them as best we can."

Eleanor did her best to explain to Jana what was about to take place. "I know you're afraid," she said softly, "but I feel confident we can do this."

Jana seemed to calm. "I've never known you not to accomplish what you put your mind to." Her face contorted. "Oh, I have to push. You're right." She moaned and gasped for breath. "There's no disguising this."

Eleanor smiled. "Well, let's get on with it then."

Taffy returned and began to pray for them as Eleanor laid out towels. As Taffy concluded, Eleanor suddenly thought about the growing chill in the room. "Taffy, do we still have that nice electric space heater?"

"Yes. It's in the hall closet. I was thinking about getting it out last night."

"Get it and put it in here—close to the crib. Once the baby

comes, we need to make sure he or she stays warm enough—until the rescue team can get here or until we can get her to the hospital. Maybe even get some of those receiving blankets warmed up for me. I don't think we have much time."

Taffy flew into action like a woman sixty years her junior.

"Well, let's do this," Eleanor said to Jana. "Let's get my grandbaby born."

———

Jana sighed in relief to be done with the pain. Drenched in sweat and tears, Jana offered God a silent prayer of thanks for seeing them through the birth. She still couldn't believe it was over.

"Here's your daughter," Eleanor said, bringing the baby to Jana.

Taking the bundle in hand, Jana pulled the squalling baby girl close. "She's beautiful." The baby's ruddy complexion seemed even redder against the pale blond hair that crowned her head.

"Another generation of women for our family," Taffy announced. "I think that very fitting."

Jana saw the tears streaming down her mother's cheeks. "Thank you, Mom. Thank you for what you've done for me—for her."

Taffy put her arm around Eleanor. "What a blessed day this is. Eleanor, you did a wonderful job. You brought a new life to us, safe and sound."

Eleanor shook her head. "No, God brought new life here today—to all of us."

Jana met her mother's eyes. "Yes," she whispered. "To all of us."

Thirty-six

ELEANOR WATCHED AS the pastor held her granddaughter up before the congregation. "We're here today to dedicate Meira McGuire to the Lord." He handed the baby back to Jana and picked up his Bible. "Meira means light in Hebrew, and Jana has decided it a very fitting name for her baby. Meira has brought a new light into the lives of her mother, grandmother, and great-great-aunt. May the light that she reveals be that of the saving grace of Jesus Christ, and may that light always guide her in times of darkness."

Eleanor heard the words and took them to heart. For the first time in so very long, she had hope again. Hope that God really could take charge of her problems and bring her through without destruction. For once, the true peace of Christ had given Eleanor the ability to look forward to the days to come instead of dreading them.

"I want to share the words of a song." With a grin, he added, "I won't sing them, however, as most of you have heard my voice and know I'm not gifted in that area." There were chuckles throughout the congregation as he continued. "As we dedicate Meira, I believe this a very appropriate choice."

Eleanor watched Jana cuddle the baby to her breast. Meira seemed interested only in sleeping, but the way Jana constantly watched her child—touched the tiny infant—made Eleanor smile.

"Lord, bless this little child, you love her too;
Given, yet here we stand, to give her back to you,
    to give her back to you.
Lord, bless this little child, guard her we pray;
Safe only in your hands, secure while in your way,
    secure while in your way.
Lord, bless this little child, cause now to bud deep
    in her tiny heart
A longing for her God, a longing for her God."

Kevin looked out upon the congregation. "The life of a child is an awesome responsibility. One that will require the strength and love of many, but particularly of her mother and father. Meira's father died last summer, and that leaves Jana with a bigger job—a job to bring Meira up in the ways of the Lord, to teach her the Word and what God desires for her life. To turn from wrong . . . to forgive . . . to love."

Eleanor couldn't help but take the words to heart. How very different things might have been if she'd turned to God for help when she found herself pregnant with Jana. How different her life might have been if she'd learned to forgive her father. The thought sparked something deep in her heart. Could she forgive him? Forgive him for the irresponsible life he'd lived and thrust upon his children? Forgive him for stealing her innocence? There had been a time when she'd loved him more than anyone on earth. Now, thirty-some years later, could she somehow forgive him the wrong he'd done her—the wrong that had set her on such a bitter path?

Could she forgive her mother for not protecting her? For choosing to take her own life rather than deal with the situation and care for her children?

Could she also forgive Cal for his drunken rape—forgive him

for the complete destruction of her ability to trust?

In forgiving, she remembered Taffy saying, *will come true free-dom.* Tears came to her eyes. She so wanted to be free.

"Who brings this baby to be dedicated to the Lord?" the pastor asked.

Jana stepped to the center and stood directly in front of Kevin. "I do," she said softly.

Eleanor and Taffy joined hands and stood directly behind Jana. "I do," Eleanor said clearly.

"I do," Taffy's more lyrical voice called out.

Jana turned and met Eleanor's tear-streaked face. They said nothing, but the look that passed between them crossed years and years of distance and barriers. It was then Eleanor knew for certain that everything would be different.

"Ladies, would you please turn and face the congregation," Kevin said in a barely audible voice.

They turned in unison to face the group of a hundred or so people. "And who will stand with these women—who will support them in godly love and guidance as they raise this child?"

Eleanor was amazed at the compassion she felt flow through the room. The congregation rose to their feet. "We will," they called together.

Jana heard the voices cry out in unison—offering their love, their support. She couldn't contain the tears that spilled down her face and dripped against her daughter's cheek. The moment was bittersweet; Rob should have been a part of this celebration, but he was dead. *There are worse things than death,* Jana thought, *but those things will not steal my joy and destroy my child's life. Not if I can help it.* And obviously not if the people around her had any say.

Such a wonderful feeling of love was being shared in this

room. Love that surrounded them and wrapped them in a warmth of protection and promise. Jana had never experienced anything like it before, although her own congregation in Spokane had tried hard to offer it.

By watching Kevin's example, Jana knew that Rob had been wrong. There was nothing positive about keeping people at arm's length. God intended for His children to help one another, to bear one another's burdens.

The pastor offered a prayer of consecration and blessing for Meira, and Jana could only rejoice in the moment. *Things will be different,* she promised her sleeping child. She would never leave Meira to fend for herself—she would always make sure she had the love and hope she needed for the future. And when the time came, and Meira wanted to know about her father, Jana knew God would teach her the right words to say.

"Amen," Kevin said, and Jana couldn't help but turn to meet his smiling face.

Who knows? she thought. *Maybe there will even be a chance for us. A chance to be a real family.* But even as she thought it, Jana shook her head slightly and looked to her mother and Taffy. Their loving smiles reassured her.

We are *a real family,* she thought. *And we will be there for one another.*

No matter what the future brings.

No matter what the past has been.